THE M
FROM NOWHERE

BY

VICTOR BRIDGES

MILLS & BOON, LIMITED
49 RUPERT STREET
LONDON, W.

TO

MY MOTHER

THIS BOOK IS DEDICATED

Published 1913
Copyright, 1913, in the United States of America by Victor Bridges

THE MAN FROM NOWHERE

WHEN you are really hungry, and have precisely one and sixpence to spend upon your dinner, the problem is one which requires a certain amount of consideration. I hesitated for some time between Parelli's and the Carci. At Parelli's they give you four quite decent courses for a shilling, which leaves sixpence over for a drink and a tip for the waiter. On the other hand, the tablecloths are generally dirty, and the atmosphere of the place about as poisonous as that of a Chinese joss-house.

In this respect the Carci is altogether its superior; but as a set-off, you don't get anything like as good a shilling's worth in the way of food. And food being my chief consideration at the moment, I finally decided on Parelli's.

As I pushed open the door, the first person I caught sight of was Billy Logan. For a moment I thought I must be mistaken, but a second glance showed me the long red scar running down from the corner of the eye, which Billy had brought away with him as his sole memento of an unsuccessful insurrection in Chile.

He was busy eating, and I walked quietly up to his table without his seeing me.

I

" Hullo, Billy!" I said. "What on earth are you doing in this peaceful spot?"

He looked up with a start. "Why, it's Jack Burton!" he cried. "Great Scott! man, I thought you were dead."

I pulled out a chair and seated myself opposite to him. "Sorry to disappoint you, Bill," I observed, "but I'm not fit to die just yet."

"It was that ass, Goldley," explained Billy, reaching across and gripping my hand, as though to make sure that I was really flesh and blood. "He told me you'd been knocked on the head at some God-forsaken place in Bolivia."

"Yes," I said dryly. "I believe there was a report to that effect. It suited me not to contradict it."

Billy grinned. "Well, I was a bit doubtful about it at the time. I couldn't see you getting wiped out by a dago."

"I precious nearly was, all the same," I said. "Here, waiter, table d'hôte, and a bottle of lager."

"You're dining with me," interrupted Billy.

"In that case," I said, "I'll have a bottle of burgundy instead of the lager."

"Bring two," called out Billy. "And now let's hear all about it," he added, as the waiter slid rapidly away. "Last time I saw you was at that little dust-up we had in Buenos Ayres. D'you remember?"

"I do, Billy," I said. "It was on account of that I went for a health trip to Bolivia."

Billy chuckled. "I gather you didn't exactly find it."

I lit a cigarette, pending the arrival of the *hors d'œuvre*. "I found something better than health, Billy," I said. "I found gold."

"Lord!" said Billy. "Where?"

" I don't think it's got a name," I replied. " Anyhow, I didn't wait to find out. I was on my own, and the whole country was stiff with Indians. Look here." I pulled up my sleeve and showed him the traces of a very handsome pucker left by a well-directed arrow. " That's one of their visiting-cards," I added.

Billy looked at it with the eye of a connoisseur. " You're lucky it wasn't poisoned," he remarked. " What about the gold ? "

" I can find the place again all right," I said, " but I want money. It's not a one-man job. That's why I came to London."

" Got it ? "

I shook my head. " On the contrary, I've spent what I had. They're a shy lot here, Billy—and I wasn't going to give the show away absolutely. I shall have to try New York."

" You're about right," answered Billy. " Unless you roll up in a frock-coat with introductions, the average Britisher's got no manner of use for you. You'll do better in the States. When are you going ? "

" As soon as I can get a ship," I replied. " I've hung on here till I've got just enough left to square my bill. To-morrow I shall go down to the docks and sign on in the first boat that will take me."

" I wish I was coming with you," said Billy wistfully.

" Why not ? " I suggested.

He shook his head. " I'm putting in for a job," he explained : " some prospecting business in Mexico that Maxwells' are running. They've kept me hanging about for six weeks, so I may as well see it out now."

" Well, give me an address of some kind," I said. " In case my business comes off and yours doesn't, I'd like to have you with me."

Billy pulled out a pencil and a bit of paper and scribbled down a few words. "This is where I'm staying," he said: "34 Vauxhall Road. I'll tell 'em where to forward letters when I leave."

I put the paper in my pocket, and turned my attention to the sardines and potato salad which the waiter had just dumped down in front of me. Billy's two bottles of wine, which arrived immediately afterwards, soon put us into a cheerfully reminiscent mood, and throughout dinner we yarned away about old friends and old days in the Argentine, where five years before we had first run across each other.

I suggested winding up the evening at a music-hall; but Billy, unfortunately, had some appointment connected with his job, which prevented him from coming. However, he not only paid for dinner, but insisted on lending me a couple of sovereigns, which, to tell the truth, I was very glad to accept. But for this, by the time I had paid my bill the next morning, I should have been practically penniless.

I said good-bye to him regretfully at the bottom of Gerrard Street, and then, walking across Leicester Square, made my way slowly down to the Embankment. I was lodging in Chelsea, and I thought I might just as well stroll home as waste threepence on a bus.

It was a fine, soft summer evening, with a faint breeze stirring the trees, and now and then lifting a scrap of paper from the roadway and dropping it again languidly after it had tumbled it a few yards. There were not many people on the Embankment; those that were there consisting chiefly of engaged couples, with here and there a tattered piece of human wreckage apparently on the look-out for a comfortable open-air lodging for the coming night.

I sauntered slowly on, clinking Billy's two sovereigns in my pocket, and pondering idly over my own affairs. I had left Bolivia four months before in high spirits, thinking that for the first time in my life I had a chance of making some money. That I had found gold in richly paying quantities I had no shadow of doubt, and I felt confident that in London I should be able to raise sufficient capital to get together a proper expedition for penetrating the interior. I knew enough of the Bolivian authorities to be sure that, as far as State permission went, a generous measure of bribery was the only thing necessary.

Seven or eight weeks in England had been enough to dash all my high hopes. I suppose English business men are naturally cautious—requiring to know a great deal about a stranger's record before they care to accept his statement. Now my record, though highly interesting to myself, had been of a little too chequered a nature to inspire confidence in the breast of a capitalist whose ideas of life are bounded by Lombard Street and, shall we say, Maidenhead. At all events, I had failed dismally in my purpose, and, as I had told Billy, had reached the end of my resources without getting any further in my quest than when I had started.

I was not sorry to feel that it was all over. My restless life had ill fitted me for the humdrum respectabilities of London, and I was beginning to regard the streets, the people, and indeed everything about me, with an intense and ever-growing distaste. It is true that New York would be as bad or even worse, but I had no real intention of wasting much time in that shrieking inferno. To start with, my funds would not allow it; and, in any case, I was beginning to get a bit tired of this dreary chase after wealth. If I could find

a sympathetic capitalist in a few days, well and good—
otherwise, I had quite made up my mind not to worry
any more about the matter.   Let the gold stop where
it was until some traveller more suited to the job than
I stumbled across it.   Life, after all, is the first thing,
and I was not going to waste mine hanging round office
doors, and interviewing fat gentlemen in frock-coats,
when the whole world with all its fun and adventure lay
before me.

Stopping under a lamp, and leaning over the Embankment, I gazed at the lights of a small steamer, puffing
its way busily down the Thames.   A great desire to get
out of this choking atmosphere of so-called civilisation
suddenly gripped me with irresistible force.   I seemed
to taste the smack of the salt sea upon my lips, to smell
again the warm, sweet breath of the open pampas.   My
heart beat faster and stronger, and I found myself
muttering some lines of Kipling—the only poet I've ever
cared two straws about—

> "The days are sick and cold, and the skies are grey and old,
>   And the twice-breathed airs grow damp ;
> And I'd sell my tired soul for the bucking beam-sea roll
>   Of a south Bilbao tramp."

Yes, that was what I wanted : the sea, and the sun,
and the plains, and, above all, life—raw, naked life, with
its laughter and its fighting, far away from these stifling
streets where men's hearts grow smug and cold.   I
threw back my arms, and took in a deep breath.

" My God ! " I muttered, half aloud.   " I'm out of this
for good and all."

" I congratulate you," said a voice.

CHAPTER II

MY nerves are under pretty good control, but I must confess that I jumped a little at this unexpected interruption. Wheeling round, I found myself face to face with a tall, broad-shouldered man in evening dress, which was half concealed by a long fawn-coloured overcoat. For a moment his features seemed strangely familiar, and I stared at him, wondering where I had seen them last. Then suddenly the truth hit me fair and square.

"Good Lord!" I said, "are you a looking-glass?"

Except for his clothes, the man was the exact image of myself.

He smiled—a curious smile that ended with his lips, and had no effect at all on the cold, steady blue eyes that were taking in every detail of my appearance.

"A most remarkable likeness," he observed quietly. "I never thought I was so good-looking."

I bowed. "And I never realised how well-dressed I was," I returned, in the same half-mocking tone.

It was his turn to start, though the motion was almost imperceptible.

"Even our voices!" he muttered. "Who was the fool who said that miracles don't happen?"

I shook my head. "The likeness," I said, "appears to extend to our ignorance."

There was a short silence, during which we still looked

7

each other up and down with the same frank interest.
Then he put his hand in his pocket and pulled out a
slim, gold card-case.

"My name," he said, "is Stuart Northcote. You may
have heard of it." He held out a card.

I don't think I showed my surprise, though goodness
knows I felt it. Like most people in London, I had
certainly heard of Stuart Northcote. Indeed, I could
hardly have avoided doing so, considering that the
Society papers had been full of little else but his doings
and his wealth ever since he appeared mysteriously from
nowhere at the beginning of the season, and rented Lord
Lammersfield's house in Park Lane.

However, I accepted his card without comment, as
though a meeting with a millionaire double were an
everyday event in my existence.

"My own name," I said, "is John Burton. I am
afraid that a card-case is outside my present scheme
of things."

He bowed. "Well, Mr. Burton," he began deliberately,
"since chance has thrown us together in this fashion,
it seems a pity not to improve our acquaintance. If
you are in no hurry, perhaps"—he paused—"perhaps you
would give me the pleasure of your society at supper?"

I don't know what it was—something in his voice,
I think—but, anyhow, I had a curious instinct that he
was extremely anxious I should accept. I thought I
would test him.

"It's very kind of you," I said, with a smile, "but, as
a matter of fact, I have just finished dinner."

He waved aside the objection. "Well, well, a bottle
of wine, then. After all, one doesn't meet one's double
every day."

There was a four-wheeler trundling slowly up the

Embankment, and without waiting for any further reply from me, he raised his hand and beckoned to the driver.

As the man drew up, a tattered figure that had been lounging on one of the seats a little farther down shambled hastily forward as though to open the door. My eyes happened to be on Northcote at the moment, and I was amazed at the sudden change that came over him. He looked like a man in the presence of some imminent danger. Like a flash, his right hand travelled to his side pocket with a gesture that it was impossible to misunderstand.

"Stand back," he said harshly.

The loafer, astonished at his tone, stopped abruptly in the circle of white light cast by the electric lamp.

"Beg pardon, guv'nor," he whined; "on'y goin' to open the door for yer, guv'nor."

Northcote's cold blue eyes scrutinised him keenly for a moment. "That's all right, my man," he said, in a rather different voice. "Here you are!"

He flung a silver coin—a half-crown it looked like— on to the pavement, and with a gasp of amazement the man dived to pick it up. As he did so, Northcote, still watching him, stepped forward to the cab and flung open the door.

"You get in, Mr. Burton, will you?" he said; and then, as I climbed into the cab, he turned to the driver. "The Milan," he said curtly, and then, following me, slammed the door.

As we drove away, I saw the white face of the loafer, who had apparently recovered his coin, staring after us out of the lamplight.

Northcote must have guessed that I had noticed his agitation, for he laughed in a rather forced manner "I dislike those fellows," he said. "It's foolish, of course,—one ought to pity the poor devils,—but some-how or other I can't stand their coming anywhere near me."

His words were easy and natural enough, but they did not convince me in the least. I have seen too many men in danger of their lives to mistake the symptoms.

However, the matter being essentially his business and not mine, I refrained from offering any comments. Indeed, I thought it more tactful to change the conversation.

"I'm afraid I'm hardly dressed for the Milan," I said. "I don't know whether it matters."

He shrugged his shoulders. "We will have a private room in any case," he replied. "It is more comfortable."

He spoke as though the Milan were some sort of Soho pot-house!

I was just thinking what a pity it was I had wasted such an excellent appetite on Parelli's when the cab turned the corner into the Strand. Putting his head out of the window, Northcote gave some instructions to the driver, which I was unable to catch. Their nature, however, was obvious a moment later, for, turning to the right just before we reached the flaring courtyard of the famous restaurant, the man drew up at a small side entrance.

We got out, and Northcote, after paying the fare, led the way into the hall, where a bland and very respectful head waiter came forward to meet us.

"I want a private room, and a little light supper of some kind," said Northcote.

"Certainly, sir, certainly," replied the other. "Will you come this way, sir."

He guided us down a long, brilliantly lit corridor, stopping at the end door on the left, which he opened.

We found ourselves in a small but luxuriously furnished room, with a table already laid for supper, and delightfully decorated with flowers.

"This room was engaged to-night by one of the Russian nobility," explained our conductor suavely. "The order has just been cancelled by telephone, so, if it will suit you, sir——"

"It will do excellently," broke in Northcote.

Another waiter who had followed us into the apartment came forward, prepared to take our coats and hats. Northcote stopped him with a gesture.

"You can leave them here," he said. Then, turning to the head waiter, he added curtly, "I shall be obliged if you will attend to us yourself."

The man bowed, and, signalling to his assistant to withdraw, presented the menu which the latter had brought in.

Northcote glanced at it, and then handed it across to me. "Is there anything particular that you would like?" he asked carelessly. "I fancy the resources of the Milan are fairly comprehensive."

I shrugged my shoulders. "I shall be more or less of a spectator in any case," I said. "You had better settle the question."

Northcote looked at the card again, and then ordered a couple of dishes the names of which conveyed nothing to me. "And bring up a bottle of '98 Heidsieck," he added, "and some of that old liqueur brandy."

The man bowed, and after pulling out our chairs from the table, noiselessly left the room. I could not help wondering whether the extraordinary likeness between Northcote and myself had struck him; but if it had, he had betrayed no sign of having noticed it.

"I always think a really good head waiter," I observed, "is the most extraordinary work of art in the world."

"Yes," said Northcote, seating himself at the table, "and, in consequence, the most contemptible."

"That seems rather ungrateful," I remarked.

Northcote looked at me keenly. "Can you imagine any man who was not wholly contemptible deliberately moulding himself into a piece of servile machinery in order to get an easy living? I have infinitely more respect for a thief than a successful waiter."

I laughed. "I dare say you're right," I answered. "Anyway, I must admit that I would sooner be a thief if I had to choose."

"What are you?" asked Northcote abruptly.

The question took me by surprise, and for a moment I hesitated.

"I am not asking out of mere curiosity," he said.

"I didn't think you were," I returned pleasantly. "That was why I was doubtful about answering you."

He smiled, looking at me curiously, with the same disconcerting intentness.

"Let us be frank, then," he said suddenly. "It happens that you have the power to be of considerable service to me, Mr. Burton."

He paused.

"Indeed?" I said, lighting a cigarette.

"On the other hand," he went on, "there is certainly a chance that I might be of some use to you."

I thought of the reported extent of his income, and then of my beautiful Bolivian goldfield.

"It is quite possible," I admitted gravely.

He leaned forward with his hands on the table. I noticed that they were muscular and sunburned—the hands of a man who has done hard physical work.

"But I must know more about you," he said. "Who are you? Where do you come from? What do you want from life?"

As he asked the last question, the door of the room opened, and the waiter came in, carrying supper.

While the man was handing round the dishes and pouring out the wine—a delicious wine it was, too, by the way—Northcote talked away lightly and cleverly about several more or less topical subjects. I answered him occasionally, in the same careless strain; but my mind was almost wholly occupied with the mysterious suggestion that he had just let fall. I was wondering what on earth the service could be that I was capable of rendering him. That it had something to do with our amazing likeness to each other I felt convinced; but beyond that it was impossible to guess. The whole thing—our meeting on the Embankment, his invitation to supper, and the strange hint of an unknown purpose in his actions—had all been so sudden and bizarre that I felt as if I had been caught up into some modern version of the Arabian Nights.

Still, there could be no harm in making him more or less acquainted with my innocent past and my embarrassed present. I had nothing I wished to conceal, except the whereabouts of my goldfield; and it seemed quite on the cards that, in return for this unknown service that he wanted from me, I might be able to interest him in my scheme. In any case, curiosity alone would have made me go through with the matter now I had got so far. I instinctively felt that Mr. Northcote's proposals when they came would be of a decidedly interesting nature.

So, as soon as the waiter had withdrawn, I filled up my glass again, and looking across at my companion with a smile, began to satisfy his curiosity.

"There's not very much to tell you, after all," I said. "To start with, I'm thirty-four."

He gazed at me keenly. "You look five years older," he said.

"Yes," I retorted. "Perhaps, if you'd been knocking about South America for fifteen years, you'd show some fairly obvious signs of it."

A momentary flicker of surprise passed across his face. Then he laughed dryly.

"Oh!" he said. "What part of South America have you been in?"

"Most of it," I said, "but I know the Argentine best."

"What were you doing?" he asked.

"It would be shorter," I said, "to tell you what I wasn't. I've been a ranchman, a cattle-dealer, a store-keeper, a soldier, a prospector, and several other little things that happened to roll up. South America is a great place for teaching one to take a spacious view of the day's work."

"So I believe," he said. "And what brings you to England?"

"An incorrect idea of British enterprise," I answered. "My last achievement in South America was to strike gold—quite a lot of it, unless I'm pretty badly mistaken. I came over here to try and raise some capital."

"And you've failed?"

I laughed. "The British capitalist," I said, "is still as rich as he was when I landed."

He nodded his head. "What are your plans now?" he asked.

"I'm sailing for New York as soon as I can get a ship," I answered.

"Have you many friends in London?" he demanded.

"There's my landlady," I said. "She is friendly

enough as long as I pay her bill, but that's about the full extent of my social circle."

There was a short silence. Then Northcote got up from his chair and, walking across the room, locked the door. I watched him with interest.

He seated himself again at the table, and lit a cigarette.

"Mr. Burton," he said, "what value do you put upon your life? I mean, for what sum would you be prepared to run a very considerable risk of losing it?"

He asked the question in such a business-like and unemotional manner that I could not repress a smile.

"I don't know," I said. "If I thought it was really valuable, I should be strongly inclined to put it up to auction."

He leaned across the table and looked me full in the eyes.

"If you will do what I want," he said slowly, "I will give you ten thousand pounds."

CHAPTER III

I AM fairly used to surprises, but there was a magnificence about this unexpected offer that for a moment took away my breath. I leaned back and surveyed my double with genuine admiration.

"You certainly do business on a large scale, Mr. Northcote," I said. "Do you pay in cash?"

For an answer, he thrust his hand into an inside pocket and pulled out a leather case. This he opened, extracting four bank-notes, which he laid on the table.

"Here are two thousand pounds," he said quietly. "If you accept, I will give you a cheque for the remainder."

I looked at the notes with that respectful interest that one keeps for distinguished strangers. There was no doubt that they were genuine. Then, with some deliberation, I also lit a cigarette.

"It must be a very unpleasant job," I said regretfully.

For the first time since I had met him, my companion laughed. It was a grim, mirthless sort of laugh, however, not in the least suggestive of encouragement.

"Yes," he said dryly: "if I threw it open to competition, I fancy that the entries would be small." Then he paused. "Before I go any further," he added, "will you give me your word of honour to keep what I am going to say entirely private, whether you decline or accept?"

"Certainly," I said, without hesitation.

"Very well." Again he stopped for a moment, apparently hesitating over a choice of words. "Within a few days," he said slowly, "unless I take certain steps, there is every likelihood of my being a dead man."

I thought of the little incident on the Embankment, and I felt that he was speaking the truth.

"To put it plainly," he said, "I must disappear. If I stay in London under my own name I shall certainly be killed. It may be a matter of days or weeks, or even months—that will depend on myself; but the end is sure and quite unavoidable."

I poured myself out a glass of brandy and held it up to the light. "The situation," I observed, "has at least the merit of being a simple one."

The same cold smile flickered across his lips. "It is not quite as simple as it seems. The gentlemen who are so anxious to accelerate my passage to heaven are doing me the honour of paying me a very close and intelligent attention. I might possibly be able to avoid them,—to-night, for instance, I believe I have done so,— but whether I could get out of the country alive is a very open question."

"Ah!" I muttered. Light was beginning to dawn on me.

He nodded, as though answering an unspoken question. "Yes," he said; "the thought struck me the moment I caught sight of you under the lamp. If I were a believer in the supernatural, I should say you had been sent by the Devil. I can't think of any other power that would be particularly anxious to assist me."

"Well," I said lightly, "if the Devil sent me, I am at least indebted to him for a good supper. What is it you want me to do?"

2

He paused again. Then, very slowly, he made his amazing suggestion—the words dropping from his lips with an almost fierce intensity.

"I want you to take my place in the world. I want you to change clothes with me to-night and go out of this restaurant as Stuart Northcote."

I took a deep breath and bent forward, gripping the table with my hands.

"Yes," I said, "and what then?"

"I want you to go back to my house in Park Lane, and for three weeks to live there as I should have done. If you are still alive at the end of that time, which is extremely improbable, you can do anything you please."

For one instant the thought struck me that the whole thing was a jest—the fruit of some ridiculous bet or the passing whim of a half-mad millionaire. But one glance at the hard blue eyes, which were still ruthlessly search-ing mine, swept the idea abruptly from my mind.

"But it's impossible," I broke out. "Even if you servants failed to see the difference, I should certainl' be found out directly I met any of your friends."

"How?" he asked. "They might think I had becom forgetful, eccentric, but what else could they imagine?'

"Oh, think of the hundred things I should be ignorai of: people's names, your appointments and busine affairs—even my way about the house. Why, I shou be bound to betray myself."

"I have thought of all that," he answered harsh' "If I couldn't provide against it, I should not ha made the proposal."

I looked at him curiously. "And what is there prevent me from taking your money and making attempt to keep my side of the bargain?"

"Nothing," he said, "except your word of honour."

There was a moment's silence. "Well," I said, with a short laugh, "the security seems rather inadequate, but if it satisfies you——" I shrugged my shoulders. "Now, let me see if I have got this interesting offer quite correct. In return for ten thousand pounds—two thousand in notes and the rest by cheque—I am to become Mr. Stuart Northcote for three weeks. It is highly probable that during that time I shall be assassinated. Failing this unfortunate interruption, I shall then be at liberty to resume my own character."

Northcote bowed, half mockingly as it seemed. "You have stated the idea admirably," he said.

I helped myself to a second glass of brandy, and sipped it with meditative enjoyment. The prospect of being a millionaire, if only for three weeks, distinctly appealed to me. Apart from that, there was something vastly attractive in the fantastic nature of the whole business. Only a few hours before, I had been grumbling to myself over the dullness and monotony of life, and here was Fate thrusting before me an almost incredible chance of adventure and excitement. I could feel my heart beating faster at the thought.

" If it is not too inquisitive a question," I said calmly, " I should rather like to know why your removal is a matter of such urgent importance to someone ? "

Northcote's eyes narrowed, and his lips set in a singularly unpleasant smile. " It is a private affair," he answered coldly, " and I'm afraid it must remain so. I can assure you, however, that in taking my place you will not be in danger except of assassination. I have committed no crime "—he laughed—" at least, no crime in the excellent eyes of the English law."

" That is comforting," I observed, "but, all the same, I should be more inclined to accept if I knew who it was that was so anxious to stick a knife into you."

"Unfortunately," he answered, "I don't know myself. If I did"—his face hardened for a moment into a cruel mask. "Well, I think you have a proverb about two being able to play at the same game. I can only tell you that the danger is real and imminent. I have good reason for believing that my own servants are honest, but beyond that I would trust no one."

"It seems to me," I said sadly, "that I shall have to stay indoors."

Northcote thrust his hand into his pocket, and pulled out a small red leather notebook.

"After the first ten days," he said, "you can please yourself. To start with, you would have to carry out certain engagements I have made, which you will find in this book."

"And you imagine I could do that successfully?"

Northcote nodded. "You have excellent nerves and plenty of common sense. Provided you give your word of honour to carry the part through to the best of your ability, I am perfectly ready to trust you. If you fail"—he shrugged his shoulders—"at least I shall have had my start."

A sudden mischievous joy in the promised excitement of the situation came flooding through my heart. With an almost involuntary gesture I thrust my arm across the table.

"Very well," I said. "I promise you I'll do my best."

He gripped my hand, and for a moment we sat there on either side of the table without speaking a word.

Northcote was the first to break the silence.

"I envy you your nerve, Mr. Burton," he said coldly.

"It's not as good as it was," I replied, with regret.

Northcote tore a slip of paper out of his pocket-book, and, laying it on the table, began to draw a plan in pencil. I pulled my chair round so that I could see what he was doing.

"I'm making you a rough sketch of the inside of the house," he said. "This is the ground floor, and here's the dining-room and the billiard-room. Your study and bedroom are on the first floor, exactly above. They open into each other—like this." He outlined the various rooms neatly and skilfully, writing their names in the centre of each square.

"That's plain enough," I said, taking the paper. "What about the servants?"

"There are only three of them—two women, and Milford, the butler. I have got rid of all the others during the last two weeks. These three have all been with me since I took the house, and I think you may trust them. Milford you certainly can. I've treated the man well, and he's by way of being rather grateful."

"Well," I said, "if *he* swallows me as Stuart Northcote, I expect I shall pull through."

"Yes," returned Northcote. "The only other person you need worry about is my cousin—Maurice Furnivall." He paused. "I believe I have promised to go down and stay with him for several days in Suffolk. If you can get out of it without difficulty, perhaps you had better. In any case, be very careful not to make a slip of any sort when you see him."

"What kind of man is he?" I asked.

Northcote frowned. "I am not sure. He is the only relation I have in the world, and to a certain extent I have trusted him. I sometimes think I have been foolish. If I knew for certain——" His brow darkened still more, and his hands clenched until the skin stood out white upon his knuckles.

"There is a suggestion of thoroughness about your methods, Northcote," I observed, "that rather appeals to me."

"If I had stuck at trifles," said Northcote grimly, "I shouldn't be here now." He pulled out a cheque-book, and, taking up his pen again, filled in a cheque for eight thousand pounds.

"Here's the money," he said. "There are a few hundred pounds in my account besides this, and if you like I'll sign a couple of cheques that you can fill in for current expenses. By the way, it may be necessary for you to imitate my signature—do you think you can do it?"

"My experience as a forger is limited," I said, "but I dare say I can manage it with a little practice. What are you going to do about money yourself?"

He laughed. "My arrangements have been made for some time. I have only been waiting the chance of putting them into practice."

There came a sudden knock at the door.

Northcote thrust his cheque-book back into his pocket, and then, getting up and crossing the room, turned back the key.

The head waiter entered, and stood apologetically by the threshold.

"I came to see whether you would require anything else, sir."

"I think not," said Northcote coldly. "You had better let me have the bill, though. I suppose there is no objection to our using this room for a little longer? We are discussing some business matters."

The waiter bowed. "Oh, certainly not, sir. Half-past

twelve is the hour we have to close; but even then, if
you cared to engage a bedroom——"

"That will be ample time," said Northcote.

He produced a five-pound note, which he handed to
the waiter, waving away the latter's offer of change.

With a gratified murmur of thanks, the man withdrew, leaving us alone.

Northcote locked the door behind him, and returned
to the table.

"I am ready," he said curtly.

In a moment I had slipped off my coat and laid it on
the chair.

Our complete transformation must have taken us
about a quarter of an hour. With the exception of his
patent leather shoes, which for absolute comfort were
certainly half a size too small, Northcote's clothes
fitted me with extraordinary accuracy. I put them on
with a certain deliberation, enjoying the sensation of
finding myself in really well-cut garments—an experience to which I had been a stranger for a good many
years. When I had finished, I examined myself in the
glass with no little satisfaction. As far as looks went,
the deception was perfect.

Northcote, who had meanwhile arrayed himself in my
own discarded blue suit, presented just as remarkable
a change. He seemed to be the exact image of the
reflection I was accustomed to see each morning in my
lodging-house mirror.

Stepping to the table, I filled up the two liqueur
glasses with a last taste of the Milan's excellent
brandy.

"Here's to our lost selves!" I said.

Northcote drank the toast, and setting down the
glass, handed me his cheque-book and latch-key, which

he had laid on the table in front of him. I put them away in my pockets with the notes.

Voltaire's last words came suddenly into my mind. "And now for the great adventure," I quoted gaily.

"We had better not go out together," said Northcote. Then he paused. "Good-bye," he added. "I don't suppose we shall meet again, unless there is really such a place as hell."

"I shall at least have a good chance of finding out first," I retorted.

I picked up the long fawn-coloured overcoat which lay on the sofa, and walking across the room, turned the key. Northcote stood where he was, his arms folded, watching me with his strange, mirthless smile.

"Good-bye," I said, "and good luck." And then, going out, I closed the door behind me.

Walking along the corridor of the hotel, I reached the side entrance by which we had come in. A man in livery, who was on duty, at once stepped forward.

"Taxi, sir?" he inquired.

"Yes," I said; "I'll have a taxi."

I felt quite cool, though my heart was beating a little faster than usual. This sort of thing was certainly more entertaining than hunting reluctant capitalists, or even hanging round the docks trying to fix a free passage to the States.

When the cab rolled up, I handed a shilling to the obliging gentleman in livery, and gave the driver Northcote's address in Park Lane. Then I stepped inside, and with a pleasant feeling of exhilaration settled myself back on the comfortably cushioned seat.

I had done it now—there could be no doubt about that! Unless I broke my word to Northcote, I was in for about as exciting a time as the most enterprising spirit could wish for. Apart from the cheerful prospect of finding a knife between my ribs at any hour of the day or night, I was faced with the truly colossal task of keeping up another man's identity for three weeks!

I began to wonder again whether it was not probable that Northcote was a lunatic, or that he was playing some stupendous practical joke at my expense. I ran over in my mind the whole of our interview, from the moment when he had waylaid me. There was certainly no sign of madness about him, apart from his amazing proposals; and if the whole thing were a jest, well, it promised to be a pretty expensive one for its author. Besides that, I felt sure that the man was in danger of his life, or at all events believed himself to be so. There was no acting about the sudden flash with which his hand had travelled to his pocket in that second on the Embankment.

Pulling out the paper which he had given me, I lit a wax match and began to study his plan of the house. It seemed simple enough. I only had to walk upstairs, and my bedroom was facing me on the other side of the landing, the windows apparently looking out into the Park. That knowledge, at all events, promised to be sufficient for the night. I could reserve anything in the nature of further exploration until the next morning.

By this time we had reached Hyde Park Corner, and, crossing the road, the driver turned to the right up Park Lane. Beyond knowing the number, I had not the remotest notion where Northcote lived, and I had something of a shock when we stopped quite suddenly outside an imposing-looking mansion only about a hundred yards above Apsley House.

"Good Lord!" I muttered. "I hope there's no mistake."

At all events, the number was on the gate-post right enough, and the driver seemed quite confident that he had reached his correct destination. So, pulling myself together, I stepped on to the pavement and handed the man half a crown.

He touched his cap respectfully, and putting in his clutch, glided away slowly in the direction of Oxford Street.

For perhaps thirty seconds I hesitated; then, mounting the broad stone steps, I thrust my latch-key into the door. It opened easily enough, and with a deep breath I stepped in over the threshold.

I found myself in a large circular hall, surrounded by several stone pillars and lit by an electric chandelier. A plentiful supply of palm trees in pots, and some beautiful hanging baskets of hothouse flowers, lent the place an air of luxury and comfort, which was increased by the deep easy-chairs of red leather scattered about in various corners. So far, I had certainly no fault to find with my new home.

I had just closed the front door, and was advancing across the thick, noiseless Turkey carpet, when there was a sound of discreet footsteps, and a man suddenly appeared from a curtained aperture at the back of the hall. He was a quiet, pleasant-looking fellow of about forty-five, with an alert, clean-shaven face, and hair just beginning to turn grey. His clothes were the conventional costume of an English butler.

"This," I said to myself, "must be Milford."

I took off my hat, so that the light fell full on my face.

"Any letters, Milford?" I asked easily.

I was watching him as I spoke, looking out keenly for the slightest start of surprise or hint that he had noticed something unusual in my appearance. But nothing could have been more natural than the manner in which he came forward and relieved me of my coat and hat.

"There were some letters by the last post, sir," he said. "I have placed them in the study."

"Thanks," I said, and turned towards the stairs.

"Shall I bring you up the brandy and soda now, sir?" he asked.

I had not the least desire for any more brandy, having already treated myself with unusual generosity in this respect at the Milan. Still, as a final drink seemed to be a nightly custom of Northcote's, I thought I had better follow his usual routine.

"Yes," I said, "you can bring it up."

I mounted the wide staircase, which was carpeted in the same luxurious manner as the hall, and, crossing the landing at the top, opened the door of the room which Northcote had marked as my study. The electric switch was just inside, and I turned it on, flooding the whole apartment with a soft, rich light thrown from an unseen arrangement of lamps somewhere behind the cornice.

It was a big and magnificently furnished room. Whatever faults Northcote may have had, the neglect of his own comfort was apparently not one of them. From the carved oak book-shelves and the huge easy-chairs down to the two or three little reading-lamps placed about on various tables, there seemed to be everything that luxury could demand or ingenuity contrive. I stood with my back to the open red-tiled hearth, gazing over it all with distinct approval.

There was a knock at the door, and Milford came in, carrying a tray, which contained a decanter, a syphon, and a glass. He placed these on a small table by the fireplace, and then withdrew as noiselessly as he had entered.

On the farther side of the room stood a handsome oak desk, at which Northcote was evidently accustomed to conduct his business and correspondence. I walked over to it, and seated myself in the chair.

So far, everything had gone surprisingly well. A kind of wild hilarity at the novelty of my amazing position was running through my veins. I felt inclined to burst out laughing, or to get up and waltz round the room.

The thought of Milford's emotions, however, if he should come in unexpectedly, prevented me from putting my feelings into action. I pulled out Northcote's pocket-book, and, opening it at the page where he had jotted down his immediate engagements, began to glance through them. As I did so, my left hand, in a curious, unconscious way, was playing with the framework of a small silver mirror which stood on one side of the desk.

It was the tiniest sound behind me that attracted my attention—a sound so soft that, if my hearing had not been particularly acute, I should certainly have failed to notice it. Without moving, I glanced sideways in the mirror.

A long curtain, which apparently concealed a recess at the side of the fireplace, was being gently moved aside. With every muscle tense, I watched the process, my heart beating steadily in swift, insistent strokes.

Then suddenly, to my amazement, a girl stepped out noiselessly into the room. Her face was deadly pale, and half hidden by the drooping hat that she was wearing; but even in the mirror I could see that she was astonishingly pretty.

For a moment she paused, then very cautiously she pulled out a small pistol of some kind from under the long cloak that she was wearing, and pointed it slowly and carefully at the back of my head.

CHAPTER IV

I MUST have fallen forward at the very moment she fired. There was no report, only the jar of a powerful air-spring, but the bullet crashed into the woodwork of the desk just exactly in a line with where my head had been a second before.

It was a pretty piece of dodging, but I was not ambitious for an encore. I was across that room and had my fair visitor by the wrist in considerably less time than it takes to read these words.

She made no attempt at resistance. Her failure seemed to have robbed her of any power of motion. She dropped the pistol as soon as I touched her, and stood facing me with wide-open, horror-stricken eyes.

With my disengaged hand I picked up the weapon. It was an air pistol of a rather formidable kind, quite capable of killing a man at twenty yards. I put it in my pocket, and, releasing my grip on her wrist, stepped back a couple of paces.

"Won't you sit down?" I said pleasantly.

My invitation had an unexpected result. With a low moan she put up her hands in front of her face, and then, before I could catch her, swayed forwards and sank slowly to the floor.

"This," I said to myself, "is the mischief."

However, I couldn't very well leave her lying there,

so, stooping down and raising her in my arms, I carried her to the sofa.

So far, things had travelled with such cheerful rapidity that I had had no time for reflection. But at this point it suddenly struck me that it would be as well to lock the door, in case Milford, or any other member of the household, had heard the crash of the bullet. So, crossing the room, I turned the key in the lock, and then came back to where my unconventional visitor was lying.

My first impression of her in the mirror had scarcely done her justice. There is a distinct gap between prettiness and beauty, and the girl who lay on the sofa was as lovely as a Greek statue. Indeed, but for the slightly parted lips and the long dark eyelashes, she might really have been chiselled out of marble. Her face was quite white, and only the faintest stirring of her breast gave any impression of life.

My acquaintance with the world has been fairly varied, but this was a situation right out of my previous line. Indeed, the problem of how to act for the best when shut up alone at midnight with a young lady who has just attempted to assassinate you is one of sufficient delicacy to baffle the most experienced. I decided that the first step was to bring her back to consciousness.

Putting some brandy into a glass, I carefully lifted her up and poured a few drops between her tightly-shut teeth. The strong spirit had an almost immediate effect. A faint tinge of colour stole into her face, and with a deep sigh she opened her eyes.

When she saw that I was holding her, she shuddered violently, and shrank back against the arm of the couch. It was not exactly complimentary, but I decided to overlook it.

"I hope you're feeling better?" I said, with an encouraging smile.

Her answer was a glance of such intense hatred and contempt that I instinctively got up from the sofa.

"Well," she said, "why don't you ring the bell, and hand me over to the police?"

She spoke in low, passionate tones and with a very slight foreign accent, but her voice was delicious. It was one of those deep, sorrowful contraltos that seem pathetic with all the woe of the world.

I looked back steadily into her indignant eyes.

"I object to the police on principle," I said. "Besides, I really don't see what they have to do with the matter. You have only smashed a desk, after all."

Before she could make any reply there came a sudden sound of footsteps on the landing outside, followed a moment later by a discreet knock at the door.

"Who's that?" I called out.

The somewhat apologetic voice of Milford answered me through the panels. "It's only me, sir. I fancied I heard something drop in your room, and came to see if I could be of any assistance."

For a second I hesitated, and then, walking to the door, I opened it just wide enough to prevent him from seeing in.

"It's nothing, thanks, Milford," I said. "I was cleaning an air pistol, and the thing went off and smashed the woodwork of the desk. We'll have a look at it in the morning. By the way, did anyone call for me while I was out?"

He shook his head. "No, sir."

"Well, I may run out and post a letter before I turn in," I added; "so, if you hear anyone walking about, don't imagine it's a burglar. Good-night."

" Good-night, sir."

I closed the door, and listened to the footsteps of my faithful retainer dying away in the distance. Then I fastened the lock, and came back to my visitor.

"Perhaps it would be as well," I said, "if you gave me back my latch-key before you forget."

She had risen to her feet and stood facing me like some beautiful animal at bay. Her cloak had fallen back, betraying the graciously moulded lines of her figure, shown off to perfection by the closely-fitting black dress that she was wearing underneath.

From her belt hung a small leather bag, of the kind that one sees in Bond Street shop windows. She opened this, and without speaking took out a key, and threw it down on the sofa.

"Thank you," I said. "And now, if you won't think me inquisitive, may I ask why you wanted to shoot me?"

She stared at me with a look in which loathing and surprise were very prettily mingled.

"Why do you pretend you don't know?" she asked contemptuously.

I shook my head. "On my honour," I said, "I haven't the remotest idea."

Her lip curled delightfully, and she drew herself up to her full height. "I am Mercia Solano," she said.

I bowed. "It's a charming name," I observed, "but, under the circumstances, Mercia seems a little out of place."

"Ah, you can jest!" she cried bitterly. "You were well named the Satyr of Culebra."

"Really!" I said. "You embarrass me. I had no idea people were so complimentary. But what have I done to deserve all these little attentions?"

3

"What have you done!" Her hands clenched, and her breast rose and fell in superb indignation. "You ask me what you have done, when the grass is still brown above my father's body!"

Burying her face in her hands, she broke down and sobbed like a child.

I must admit that for a moment I felt an unspeakable brute. Under my breath I cursed Northcote heartily.

"You can believe me or not, as you choose," I said, "but I had no more to do with your father's death than you had."

She stopped crying, and taking away her hands gazed at me wildly.

"Oh, what are you saying?" she moaned. "What is the good of lying to me? Wasn't I by his side when they shot him down? Look here——" She tore back the sleeve of her dress, baring her arm almost to the shoulder, and showing an angry red scar that seamed its white beauty. "Here is the very mark of your bullets, and you dare to stand there and lie to my face! Oh! are you a man or a devil?"

She sank down on the sofa again, in a very abandonment of passion and grief.

I crushed back a sudden savage desire to take her in my arms and explain everything.

"Look at me," I said, with some sternness, and she raised her head. "Do I seem to you like a man who is lying?" I went on harshly. "I swear to you by my mother's name, by everything I hold sacred, that I was in no way to blame for your father's death. I can't tell you more at present, but before God I'm speaking the literal truth."

The savage earnestness in my voice seemed to have some effect. Into her eyes, which were fixed on mine, there crept a kind of reluctant doubt, and with a puzzled gesture she passed her hand across her forehead.

"I — I don't understand," she said faintly. "Guarez——" Then she stopped abruptly.

"Yes?" I said, with an encouraging air. It struck me that Guarez was possibly a gentleman whom it would be healthy to know a little about.

But an obstinate fit seemed suddenly to have come over her, for her lips closed and she got up from the sofa without finishing the sentence.

It was vastly annoying, for I appeared to have been on the very verge of finding out something about my unknown and apparently strenuous past. I couldn't question her further without breaking my promise to Northcote—indeed, my conscience pricked me with having already failed to live up to the strict interpretation of my pledge.

"Well," I said, with a shrug of my shoulders, "we will leave it at that. Please consider yourself at liberty to leave the house when you choose."

I put my hand in my pocket and felt the pistol. "By the way," I added, taking it out and holding it towards her, "since you've given me back my latch-key, the least I can do is to restore you your property."

She accepted it with an air of bewilderment.

"Of course you have some more cartridges," I went on, "but I will trust to your honour——"

"Honour!" she broke out. "You talk to me of honour! *You!*"

The inference was so obvious that I could hardly pretend to miss it.

"Why not?" I demanded. "I've already told you I am perfectly innocent of the crimes you credit me with."

I stooped forward and picked up the key from the

sofa. " Perhaps you can tell me," I added, " whether there are any more of these useful articles wandering about London. If so, I think I shall go to the expense of a new lock."

She shook her head, still staring at me in a kind of puzzled wonder.

" I do not know," she said. " It makes no difference. Whether you are innocent or guilty, there is no power that can save you."

This was distinctly cheerful !

" Perhaps you're right," I said. " But at all events I shall see what the ironmonger can do in the morning. He may at least delay matters."

Going to the door, I opened it cautiously, and listened for a moment to see if any of my household were afoot.

" The coast seems clear," I said. " I'll come down to the hall and let you out."

She made a motion as if to protest, and then changed her mind.

" Very well," she said wearily.

With an inward prayer that no inopportune domestic would put in an appearance on the scene, I led the way cautiously down the big staircase. It was a strange experience, but by this time I was becoming case-hardened to strange experiences. Anyway, we reached the hall without misadventure, and, pulling back the latch of the front door as quietly as possible, I opened it sufficiently wide to allow my visitor to pass through. As soon as she was outside, I followed her, closing the door behind me.

" I'll just stroll along with you until you pick up a cab," I said carelessly.

In the lamplight I saw a flash of terror leap into her eyes.

"No, no," she whispered. "You must go back at once. It is not safe."

"I quite agree with you," I said. "It's horribly unsafe for a girl to be walking about London alone at this time of night. That's exactly why I propose to find you a cab."

She hurriedly laid her hand on my arm. "I don't understand," she said pitifully. "It's all so different from what I expected, but oh! please—please——"

There was a rumble of wheels, and a dejected-looking hansom came slowly trundling past. I signalled to the driver, who at once pulled up.

"Well, here we are," I said cheerfully; "so that settles the matter."

With a little gasp of relief she dropped my arm, and glanced nervously up and down the roadway.

I stepped forward and stood by the wheel so as to protect her dress. She got in, thanking me in an almost inaudible whisper.

"Good-night," I said, holding out my hand. "I'll leave you to tell the driver where you want to go."

There was an instant's pause, and then with a hurried gesture she bent forward and laid her hand in mine.

"Good-night," she said softly.

I felt the faint pressure of her fingers—the same slender fingers that had so nearly cut short my promising career, and a curious thrill of satisfaction ran suddenly through my heart.

Releasing her hand, I stepped back on to the pavement. I saw the driver raise the flap and bend down to catch her directions. Then he wheeled his horse round, and the cab jogged away steadily in the direction of Oxford Street.

" And here," I said to myself, " endeth the first lesson."

As the words rose in my mind, something caught my attention on the farther side of the road. There was a clump of trees exactly opposite, just inside the railings of the Park, and in the thick shadow beneath them I could have sworn that I had detected a movement.

My nerves must have been pretty badly on edge, for I as nearly as possible jumped for the area. Fortunately, I pulled myself together just in time. Taking out a cigarette, I lit it with some deliberation, and then in a leisurely and dignified fashion mounted the steps, latch-key in hand, and let myself into the house. All the time I had a horrible presentiment that at the next second a bullet would crash into the small of my back ; but, like most presentiments, it failed to materialise. Still, it was with a feeling of considerable relief that I closed the door and shot home the bolts at the top and bottom.

When I reached my study, the first thing I did was to mix myself a pretty stiff brandy-and-soda. I wanted it badly.

" If I keep this job going for three weeks," I reflected, " I shall probably end up as a confirmed dipsomaniac."

By the time I had got well into a cigarette, however, my natural good spirits had begun to reassert themselves. After all, I was still alive, and, apparently, so far quite unsuspected, which was about as favourable a situation as I had any right to expect.

Northcote, however, had plainly been speaking in good faith when he described his offer as one for which the competition would be scant if the truth about it were known. Granted that my first evening's experiences were a fair sample of what I might expect, my chances of survival seemed quite unhealthily remote. If

Mercia had been a man, I reflected grimly, by this time I should most certainly have been a ghost.

Who was she, and what had her relations been with Northcote? That the ruffian was responsible for her father's death was fairly obvious, but as to the circumstances of the tragedy I was still utterly in the dark. They must have been pretty bad to drive a young girl to such a desperate step, unless in some way or other she was being made a cat's-paw of by others.

Anyhow, I made no attempt to disguise from myself the fact that I was extremely anxious to see her again. Her beautiful face lingered in my memory as clearly as though I were looking at a picture, and somehow or other I still seemed to feel the thrill that had gone through me when she laid her hand in mine.

I had got as far as this in my meditations when it suddenly struck me I was becoming maudlin. Also, there could be no doubt that I was as sleepy as an owl.

I got up with a laugh and a yawn, and, turning on the light at the door, went into my bedroom.

It was a large apartment, even bigger than the sitting-room, and the magnificent four-poster bed was in keeping with its spaciousness. I made a tour of inspection, satisfying myself that there were no more charming ladies or visitors of any kind lying in wait for me, and then, carefully locking both the door of the room and the door into the study, I proceeded to take off my clothes and array myself in Northcote's silk pyjamas, which the faithful Milford had put out for me.

My last act was the result of a sudden inspiration. Before getting into bed, I crossed to the window and looked out very cautiously through a crack in the

venetian blind. Just as I did so, the dark figure of a
man rose out of the shadow of the trees opposite and
walked away quickly down the roadway.

I got into bed and turned off the light.

"Now I wonder," I said to myself, "if that could have
been Señor Guarez."

Five minutes later I was sound asleep.

CHAPTER V

CONSIDERING the amount of brandy that I had consumed, I awoke next morning feeling remarkably well. The first thing that met my eyes was the canopy of the bed. I stared at it in a kind of vague surprise, wondering how on earth it had got there. Then, with a sudden shock, the events of the previous evening came racing back into my mind. I realised that I was in Northcote's bedroom, and that someone was knocking gently but persistently at the door.

Jumping out, I thrust my feet into a pair of slippers that lay on the white sheepskin rug, and, crossing the room, unlocked the door. I expected to find Milford, but in place of that obliging retainer I was confronted by a pleasant-looking girl, neatly dressed in a print costume and cap. She was carrying a tray with a pot of tea and some letters on it.

" Oh, come in," I said, seeing that she was hesitating. Then, kicking off my slippers, I clambered back into bed.

She came across and laid the tray down on the table beside me.

" I have brought you up your tea, sir," she said. " Mr. Milford is not at all well this morning."

" Oh ! " I replied. " I'm sorry for that. What's the matter with him ? He was all right last night."

She shook her head. "I don't know, sir; but he seems very poorly."

"Is he in pain?" I asked.

"Yes, sir. He seems to be suffering a great deal."

"Well, you'd better send for the doctor at once," I said, pouring myself out some tea.

This was distinctly awkward. I certainly didn't want to be deprived of the services of the one person Northcote had told me I could trust.

"Shall I send for Dr. Ritchie, sir?" asked the maid.

I nodded. "Ask him to come round as soon as he can. I'll look in and see Milford after breakfast."

The girl finished her various duties in the room, and then withdrew. When she had gone I sat up in bed and began to examine the small pile of letters which lay on the tray. Most of them were obviously bills and circulars, but one which bore a crest on the back of the envelope seemed of more importance. I tore it open.

"105 BELGRAVE SQUARE, S.W.

"MY DEAR NORTHCOTE,—I had an interview yesterday with Rosedale, and, as far as I can see, everything is plain sailing. Rosedale suggests the first week in October for launching the Company. There are one or two matters still I should like to discuss with you, but we shall have an opportunity on Wednesday night.

"By the way, I've taken your advice and bought the *Seagull*. Morton wanted a devilish stiff price for her, but he was ready to take something on account. He'll have to wait for the rest till the Company's out !—Yours sincerely,   SANGATTE."

When I came to the ill-written, sprawling signature,

I whistled gently to myself. Stranger as I was to England, I knew Lord Sangatte very well indeed by reputation. And a pretty unsavoury reputation it was, too.

I reached out for Northcote's notebook, which I had taken out of my pocket the night before, and turned up his engagements for Wednesday. There were two or three cryptic references to appointments in the morning and afternoon, and then, scribbled in at the end in pencil, " Sangatte's dance."

"I shall certainly be there," I said to myself complacently.

That Sangatte and Northcote were promoting a Company was an interesting bit of information. As a commercial undertaking it should be out of the common. If rumour was correct, Sangatte was about as ripe a scoundrel as the English Peerage could show ; while such knowledge of Northcote as I possessed scarcely led me to believe that over-scrupulousness was one of his besetting virtues. On the whole, Wednesday night promised to be quite entertaining.

I got up leisurely, feeling very well satisfied with myself. In the sunshine, which was streaming pleasantly in through the open window, my adventure wore a much more cheerful and convincing aspect than it had done on the previous night. All my nervousness seemed to have vanished—in place of it I only felt a mischievous and highly enjoyable curiosity as to what would happen next.

Routing out Northcote's plan of the house, I discovered that the bathroom was three doors down, on the right-hand side of the passage. A proper full-length bath was a luxury to which I had not been introduced since my arrival in England, so with pleasurable anticipation I draped myself in Northcote's dressing-gown and set off along the corridor.

I found the bath already filled with warm water, while shaving materials of every kind were laid out on the table at the end of the room. With delightful deliberation I dallied over my toilet, smoking a cigarette and enjoying myself to the very limit of my ability. Then, refreshed and contented, I sauntered back to my bedroom, looking forward to the entertaining occupation of inspecting Northcote's wardrobe.

It proved to be on the same spacious scale as the rest of his belongings. After careful consideration, I selected a well-cut blue serge suit and a pair of Dobbie's brown boots, polished to a harmonious but unobtrusive richness that bore testimony to Milford's professional abilities.

Thus equipped, I strolled leisurely downstairs to the dining-room.

Breakfast was laid for me at the end of the big table, a pleasing combination of gleaming silver, fresh-cut flowers, and spotless napery. After the crude service of my lodgings, the sight of these unwonted accessaries gave me a really enviable appetite.

I had just seated myself, when the girl who had called me came noiselessly into the room, carrying several dishes and a fragrant urn of coffee.

"Dr. Ritchie is coming round as soon as possible, sir," she said, putting down the tray and beginning to arrange its various contents in front of me.

"That's all right," I returned. "I'll look in and see Milford as soon as I've finished."

For an agreeable half-hour I lingered over a couple of kidneys, a delicious piece of omelette, some toast and marmalade, and a large slice of hot-house melon.

Then, with a faint sigh, I extracted a Cabana from a box on the sideboard and moved myself into one of the big easy-chairs in the window looking out over the Park.

A breakfast such as I had eaten is particularly conducive to meditation, and it was scarcely surprising that my thoughts turned at once to the spirited events of the previous evening. Through the curling smoke of my cigar the beautiful, sorrowful face of my amazing visitor seemed to rise up again before my eyes. I repeated her name to myself with a kind of luxurious enjoyment. "Mercia Solano." It fitted her admirably. A name of music and colour, shot through with a certain indefinite sadness.

Who could she be, and what red chapter in Northcote's past had led up to the events of last night? That he had not this girl only to fear was evident from her own words. Besides, I could not imagine Northcote running away from a woman, however foully he had wronged her.

I racked my memory for any clues which last evening's adventure might suggest. There was her reference to Guarez—whoever Guarez might be. I wondered again whether he was the gentleman who had been skulking under the trees opposite, and if so, why he had not taken such a favourable chance of putting a bullet into me. And what was that complimentary term she had called me? The Satyr of something or other—Culebra, if I remembered right.

Where the devil was Culebra? The name seemed to be familiar to me, but, think as I would, I was quite unable to place it. The only thing I felt certain about was that it was somewhere or other in South America.

I began to wonder if the key to the mystery lay

there.　The names Guarez and Solano certainly suggested that troubled continent, while the abrupt end of Mercia's father also seemed thoroughly in keeping with the same cheerful environment.　I decided that I would hunt up Culebra on the map without any waste of time.

I had reached this point in my meditations when there came a knock at the door, and my nice-looking parlour-maid again entered.

"I wonder, sir," she began apologetically, "whether you would care to see Mr. Milford now.　He seems a little better for the moment, so I thought, perhaps——"

"You were quite right," I interrupted, getting up from the chair and putting down my cigar.　"I'll come with you at once."

I felt rather ashamed of myself, but for the time poor Milford's sudden illness had gone clean out of my head.

I followed her through the door at the back of the hall, and then down a big, winding stone staircase that led to the basement.　Milford's room was in front, just under the dining-room.

When I entered I found him sitting propped up in bed.　He was breathing with evident difficulty, and his face, which was a nasty grey colour, was covered with small beads of perspiration.

"Hullo, Milford," I said, "what have you been doing to yourself?"

He gave me a wan smile.　"I don't know, sir," he answered feebly.　"I felt rather queer last night, sir, and when I woke up this morning I was like this."

I felt his pulse, which was about as faint and irregular as a pulse could very well be.

"Dr. Ritchie's coming round to see you in a minute," I said, with assumed cheerfulness.　"He'll tell us what's the matter. I don't suppose it's anything very serious. Do you think you ate something that upset you yesterday?"

He shook his head. "No, sir. I had my dinner here, and after that all I took was my usual glass of beer at the Granville, round the corner. I don't think it can be anything——" A sudden spasm of pain contracted his face, cutting short his words.

"Well, you must lie quite still," I said soothingly, "and not worry about anything. We can rub along all right; if necessary, I'll get someone else in to help. All you've got to think about is getting fit again."

He looked up, a flash of gratitude lighting his suffering face.

"Thank you, sir," he said faintly.

As he spoke, there came a sharp ring at the front-door bell.

"I expect this is Ritchie," I said. "Now we shall find out what the trouble is."

It was not the doctor, however, that the girl announced when she came into the room a minute later.

"If you please, sir," she said, "Mr. Furnivall has called. I have shown him into the dining-room."

For a moment I wondered who the deuce this new visitor might be; then I suddenly remembered that " Maurice Furnivall " was the name of Northcote's cousin, about whose good faith my double seemed to cherish certain dark suspicions.

"Very well," I said, "I'll come up. If Dr. Ritchie calls while Mr. Furnivall is here, ask him to look in before he goes."

I mounted the stairs again, feeling just a little apprehensive about the approaching interview. I was still too new to my position to have complete confidence in my likeness to Northcote, amazingly successful as it had been up to now; and, with the possible exception of Milford, Maurice Furnivall seemed the most likely person to detect any shade of difference. However, this feeling lent a spice to the situation, and when I entered the dining-room it was with a certain sense of amused elation.

I took an immediate dislike to Master Maurice the moment I set eyes on him. A tall, sleek, well-groomed young gentleman, with black hair carefully parted in the middle and plastered down on each side, he was lounging comfortably in the arm-chair which I had lately vacated.

"Hullo," he drawled, "you're uncommon early this morning. What's up?"

"Milford's seedy," I said a little curtly.

"What's the matter with the fellow?" he asked.

"I don't know," I said. "I've just sent for Ritchie."

He shrugged his shoulders. "Well, you're doing him in style. A Harley Street specialist for a butler sounds all right. I should have called in someone a bit cheaper."

"I've no doubt you would," I said.

Something in my tone must have warned him that I was not feeling particularly amiable, for a distinct change came over his manner.

"I was only joking," he said a little lamely. "I'm sorry the poor fellow's off colour. A beastly nuisance for you, too."

I felt a strong desire to kick him, but my promise to Northcote restrained me.

"Yes," I said, "it's rather a bother. Have a cigar?"

He helped himself from the box which I held out.

"Any news?" he inquired.

I don't know why—he said it quite naturally—but it suddenly flashed across my mind that under this apparently innocent question there lurked a considerable amount of meaning. Could it be possible, I reflected rapidly, that he knew something about Mercia's midnight visit? It seemed wildly unlikely, but I made up my mind to test him.

"Yes," I said coolly. "I had rather a curious experience last night."

I was watching him as I spoke, and I could have sworn I noticed a slight tightening of the muscles in his face.

"Really?" he drawled. "What was that?"

I laughed lightly. "On second thoughts," I said, "perhaps I ought to keep it to myself for the present."

If he was really disappointed, he concealed it admirably. "That's just like you," he said, with a yawn; "you're always so confoundedly mysterious. I suppose it's the result of living under a wrong name."

This was news indeed, but I flatter myself I received it with admirable composure.

"I expect it is," I answered, selecting another cigar in place of the one I had discarded.

There was a brief pause in the conversation.

"Well, what about coming down to Ashton?" said Maurice, crossing his legs and leaning back in his chair.

I remembered Northcote's advice that I should refuse, but some obstinate streak at the back of my nature suddenly asserted itself. I think perhaps it was a feeling that Northcote's suspicions concerning the sleek young man in front of me were based on very good grounds that really decided me. I don't like running away from danger.

4

"When do you expect me?" I inquired carelessly.

Something very like a momentary flash of triumph leaped into his eyes.

"How about Thursday?" he suggested. "There's a good train from Liverpool Street at two-thirty, and I'll meet you at Woodford."

"Thursday would do all right," I said.

"We shall have a pretty festive crowd," he went on, knocking some ash off his coat. "Sangatte and York have both promised to come, and I think George Vane will most likely turn up. And then, of course, there'll be the Baradells." He looked at me with a sort of sly half-grin as he mentioned the latter name. Evidently my acquaintance with the Baradells had some special significance.

"That sounds tolerable," I said.

"At all events," he finished, "we ought to have some decent shooting. Reece tells me that the partridges are good, and there are always plenty of duck about."

I nodded thoughtfully. It struck me that if there was going to be any shooting I should be devilish careful whom I stood next.

I had just arrived at this sound conclusion when, through the open window, I saw a beautifully appointed limousine car glide up to the door.

"Here's Ritchie," I said. "I'll just see what he's got to say."

Maurice made no attempt to rise. "Right you are," he answered languidly. "I'll wait and hear the verdict."

I again felt a rich desire to box his ears, but, consoling myself with the reflection that it was possibly only a pleasure delayed, I walked out of the room, closing the door behind me.

I met the doctor in the hall. A grey-haired, clean-

shaven man of about fifty, with a pompous but rather
kind face, he came forward at once and shook my hand.

"Good morning, Mr. Northcote," he said. "I'm sorry
to hear your butler's ill. A most excellent fellow, I
should think."

"Yes," I said; "Milford is by way of being rather a
treasure. Come along down and have a look at him,
doctor. I'm afraid he's really bad."

I led the way down the stone staircase, and we
entered the room together.

If anything, Milford looked worse than when I had
seen him before. There were mottled patches on his
grey face, and his lips were twisted with pain. When
he saw us, however, he made a faint effort to raise
himself in bed.

Ritchie stepped forward at once. "No, no," he said
kindly; "you must lie quite still."

Then, pulling up a chair, he began to ask a few curt
questions, at the same time making a brief examination
of his patient's eyes and pulse. His face was rather
grave.

"I am afraid you have eaten something that has
disagreed with you very badly," he said at last.

Milford lay back on the pillow, his lips twitching
faintly.

"Am I going to die, sir?" he whispered.

"Oh dear, no," said Ritchie, with an encouraging
smile. "We shall have you perfectly well in a week or
so. Just for the moment, however, you'll have to keep
very still and do exactly what you're told. I shall send
you round a nurse at once, and look you up again
myself this afternoon."

Milford made a feeble motion as if to protest against
this luxury.

"That's all right, Milford," I said. "You are to do just what the doctor tells you, and not bother your head about anything."

He thanked me with a faint smile, and after tucking him up in bed, we left the room.

As soon as we were in the passage, I turned to Ritchie.

"Well," I said, "what's the matter?"

There was a short silence.

"The matter," said Ritchie, very quietly, "is that the man has been poisoned."

CHAPTER VI

I DON'T know whether I started, but the word gave me an unpleasant jar.

" Poisoned ! " I repeated. " Do you mean poisoned purposely ? "

Ritchie frowned. " I can't say. It's a curious case, but there's no doubt that he's suffering from some form of poisoning. It might be one of half a dozen."

" What are we to do ? " I asked.

"At present," said Ritchie, "the only thing to do is to give him a strong emetic and keep him warm. I'll send you in a nurse straight away, from St. George's, with full instructions. I shall come round again myself later in the morning."

I tried not to show it, but I was feeling horribly upset and very angry. Could it be possible that by accident Milford had fallen a victim to some delicate attention aimed at myself? Or had the mere fact of his loyalty to me been regarded as a sufficient reason for putting him out of the way? Whichever was the case, I took a very hearty resolve that, given the opportunity, I would make someone pay pretty badly for this mistaken effort.

I conducted Ritchie upstairs, and for some minutes we stood in the hall, talking about the case. I could see that the good man was considerably worried over its unusual features. Doctors see some curious things in their daily rounds, but to find a Park Lane butler suffering from apparent symptoms of wilful poisoning is enough to disturb even their unrivalled equanimity.

He refrained from asking me point-blank whether I had any suspicions in the matter, but I felt that the question was on the tip of his tongue. I suppose he thought it best, under the circumstances, to wait for further developments.

"I shall be round again about midday," he said finally, collecting his hat and coat.

"Very well," I said. "I shall probably be here, but if not, I'll ring you up and get your report."

Then I showed him out.

After the door had closed, I stood still in the hall for a moment in some doubt. I was wondering whether it would be advisable to tell Maurice what I had learned or merely to let him know that Milford was seriously ill. My instinctive mistrust of the young gentleman eventually prevailed, and I decided that, for the present at all events, I would maintain a discreet silence. Under the circumstances, it could hardly be wondered at if I felt suspicious of everybody.

When I entered the dining-room, he greeted me with a languid "Well?"

"Unfortunately," I said, "that's just what it isn't. Milford's bad—damned bad."

"What's the trouble?" he asked.

I shook my head. "Ritchie doesn't know," I replied, with a coolness worthy of Ananias. "He thinks it will probably be a matter of some weeks, however. I'm getting a nurse in to look after things."

Maurice yawned. "What a poisonous nuisance," he observed.

The epithet was happily chosen, if the remark was a trifle callous.

"Yes," I replied carelessly. "I suppose I shall have to engage someone else."

I had seen enough of Northcote to realise that if I wanted to preserve my identity, or rather his, I must guard myself against the grosser forms of sentimentalism.

"I tell you what it is," said Maurice, "you'd better stroll round to Seagrave's with me now. I've got to go to Hanover Square anyway, and we can drop in and fix things straight away. They're sure to have plenty of decent men on their books."

The suggestion seemed a sensible one; and although I fully shared Northcote's lack of confidence in his cousin, I had no wish to quarrel with the latter for the present. That was a luxury which I must postpone until I was a little more certain of my ground.

"Very good," I said. "I'll be ready in a minute. I must just go upstairs and get some papers."

"Right you are," he drawled. "Don't be too long."

I mounted the stairs feeling in anything but an amiable temper. Open danger one can face with calmness, but this back-door assassination business was beginning to get on my nerves. I understood why Northcote had been driven to such a desperate step, and I cursed my folly in not having insisted on a fuller explanation from him before tackling the business. The fact probably was that he wanted me to be killed; thus ridding himself for ever of the danger that threatened him. For all I knew, he might even have lied to me in what he did say.

However, there was no getting out of it now. Apart from going back on my word (a useful habit that has never particularly appealed to me), I was determined to see the thing through for my own satisfaction. I object to being murdered, even in mistake for someone else,

and it was my ardent wish to bring that objection
home very forcibly to my unknown friends. Besides,
there was Mercia. What precisely she was doing in
that galley I couldn't say, but, like the hero in a play, I
felt certain that it was " no place for her." I pictured
her in an altogether different environment, a pleasant
phase of thought which restored me to a more harmonious frame of mind.

What I had really come upstairs for was Northcote's
pocket-book. I had promised him to keep any engagements he had made for the first few days, and I wanted to
see if I had a programme mapped out for that afternoon.
When I turned up the page, I found two entries: one
an appointment with his tailor in Sackville Street at
12.30, and the other a directors' meeting of the London
General Traffic Company at the Cannon Street Hotel
after lunch. Neither sounded particularly important,
but for lack of anything better to do I decided to attend
them both. I was becoming quite interested in Northcote's private affairs.

When I came downstairs I found Maurice waiting for
me in the hall. It struck me again that there was a
kind of suppressed satisfaction in his manner, but I put
it down as being very probably due to my imagination.
In my present state of mind, it was easy to discover
suspicious symptoms in everyone.

" By the way," he said carelessly, as the door closed
behind us, " do you want to get another man perman-
ently, or just to fill Milford's place while he's seedy ? "

" Oh, only for the time, of course," I said. " I couldn't
part with Milford."

He nodded. " That will be quite easy. Seagrave's
can always turn you in a temporary man. You'd better
leave it to them."

I was about to observe that such was my intention, when a passing motor suddenly drew up with a jerk alongside of us, and a good-looking, elderly man in a grey top-hat put his head out of the window.

"Hullo, Northcote," he said; "you're the very man I wanted to see."

This was flattering; but as I hadn't the remotest idea who he was, I felt slightly embarrassed.

Maurice, however, unintentionally solved my difficulty. "Good morning, Lord Lammersfield," he remarked. "I hope Lady Lammersfield is better?"

His lordship paid no great attention to Maurice's kind inquiry. He nodded coldly, and observed that her ladyship was "about the same." I took a fancy to him at once.

"I can see you any time you like," I said, truthfully enough.

"Are you going to Sangatte's to-morrow night?" he asked.

"Yes," I said.

"That will do," he answered. "I'll look out for you there. I only want to have a short chat."

With a careless wave of his hand, which was obviously not intended to include Maurice, he sat back in his seat, and the motor rolled on up Park Lane.

"Pleasant fellow, Lammersfield," I observed mischievously.

Maurice stared after the departing vehicle with anything but an amiable expression.

"They don't seem to find him particularly pleasant in the Cabinet," he retorted.

I was sufficiently ignorant of English politics for this to be news to me.

"Perhaps he is misunderstood," I suggested gently. "A great many of us are."

Maurice looked at me keenly. "You're in a devilish funny mood this morning," he said. "I'm sorry for the people you're going to do business with."

From what I had seen of Northcote, this argued a perspicacity with which I had hardly credited my adopted "cousin."

"One must be agreeable occasionally," I said, "if only for the sake of variety."

Maurice laughed shortly. "I expect you'll be agreeable enough to Lammersfield," he replied.

There was obviously some hidden meaning in his words, but it seemed a little too risky to angle for an explanation. So I contented myself with a noncommittal smile, storing away the remark in my memory for future reference.

We turned into Hanover Square, and crossed the roadway towards Regent Street. I had not the remotest notion where "Seagrave's" was, but Maurice pulled up at a small house just beyond the big flower shop, and I at once noticed the name on a brass plate :

MESSRS. SEAGRAVE AND CO.

REGISTRY OFFICE.

We opened the door and walked in. It was a superior sort of office, more like a private room, with arm-chairs scattered about, and a table containing the latest weekly papers.

A rather pompous, elderly, grey-bearded man in a frock-coat at once stepped forward.

"Good morning," I said, by way of opening the conversation.

He bowed deferentially. "Good morning, gentlemen."

"I looked in to see if you can let me have a butler for a few days," I said. "My own man is on the sick list."

He raised his hands. "Dear me, sir, I am sorry to hear that. Mr. Northcote of Park Lane, is it not, sir? I believe we had the pleasure of supplying you with several of your present staff."

This also was information to me, but I received it with calmness.

"Perhaps you can continue the good work, then?" I suggested.

"Certainly, sir, of course. If you will take a chair a minute, I will just consult our books. I have no doubt that we have someone who would fill the vacancy."

Maurice and I seated ourselves, while he bustled off to the other end of the room and began to turn over the pages of a big ledger. I picked up a copy of *Punch*, but I had scarcely glanced at the first picture when our grey-bearded friend came hurrying back with the light of discovery in his face.

"Why, of course, sir, I have got the very man you want, sir. Stupid of me not to have remembered it; but, as a matter of fact, he was only entered on our books yesterday afternoon."

"And who is this paragon?" inquired Maurice.

"His name is Francis, sir. He is Sir Henry Tregattock's late butler. A most excellent servant, I believe."

"Why has he left?" I asked.

Mr. Seagrave shrugged his shoulders. "I should say he had saved up some money, and was tired of regular service. He has only entered himself on our books for temporary engagements. He is a Frenchman by birth, but speaks English perfectly, and his reference from Sir Henry is unimpeachable—unimpeachable."

"Have you had it confirmed?" asked Maurice.

"I rang up Sir Henry himself just after the man had been in, and he described him as the best servant he had ever had. Indeed, he seemed quite distressed at parting with him."

"That seems satisfactory enough," said Maurice, turning to me. "What do you think?"

I nodded. Curiously enough, I had met Sir Henry Tregattock about ten years before, when he had been the English Minister in Bolivia, and I remembered him as a level-headed man of the world, who was not in the least likely to give an excellent character to a servant unless the latter thoroughly deserved it.

"Well," I said, "if he likes to come to me, I'll engage him for a fortnight, at thirty shillings a week."

Mr. Seagrave beamed and rubbed his hands. "Very good, Mr. Northcote. Your terms are most generous, and I am sure he will be delighted to accept. I will telegraph for him at once, and he shall be round this afternoon."

"The only thing is," said I, "that I shall probably be out."

Mr. Seagrave pondered. "Perhaps you had better give me one of your cards, sir, with just a line in pencil to say that it is all right. I will take the man round to your house myself."

This certainly seemed the best arrangement, so, getting out one of Northcote's cards, I scribbled a few words across it to the effect that the bearer was the genuine article, and handed it to Mr. Seagrave.

With renewed protestations of his gratitude for my

distinguished patronage, the latter bowed us out of his office.

"I've got to go to my tailor's now," I said to Maurice, when we found ourselves outside on the pavement.

"Right oh!" he drawled. "Don't forget it's the two-thirty on Thursday, if I don't see you before."

"I shan't forget," I said cheerfully. "I'm looking forward to coming down to you."

And with this truthful if somewhat misleading remark, I waved him farewell and walked off in the direction of Sackville Street.

My interview with the tailor passed off quite success-fully. It appeared that Northcote had only arranged to call in order to inspect some stuffs for a new shooting suit. I decided on a kind of buff-coloured Burberry, which struck me as likely to be useful if I survived the next three weeks, and then, just to encourage trade, gave the good man a further order for a pair of riding-breeches. After that I strolled over to Thierry's in Regent Street and bought myself a couple of pairs of boots; for, although I could wear them, Northcote's were just a shade too small to be comfortable.

After my strict economy of the last few months, the spending of money in this fashion seemed to me a most attractive pastime. I therefore continued it by purchasing one or two other odds and ends at the Stores in Lower Regent Street, including a really admirable sword-stick, for which I paid nearly five pounds. Under the circumstances, it appeared to me cheap at the price.

I was in some doubt what to do with Northcote's cheque for eight thousand. No other bank except his own was likely to cash it without inquiries, and although so far my extraordinary likeness to him had emerged triumphantly through all tests, I still felt a little shy of facing the penetrating eyes of a cashier.

At last, however, I decided to risk it. The bank was the Piccadilly branch of the City and Provincial, so, walking back, I pushed open the swinging door and marched in with all the calm assurance that I could assume.

There were several people at the long counter, but the moment I appeared an elderly cashier stepped forward, with that polite haste that bankers only assume for their more important customers.

"Good morning, Mr. Northcote," he said, with some deference.

"Good morning," I returned. Then I paused. "I want to cash a cheque for eight thousand," I added. "Will my account stand it?"

He smiled. "As far as I know, Mr. Northcote. If you will excuse me, I will just consult the ledger and see how your balance stands. Of course it will be perfectly all right about the cheque in any case, but should you be overdrawing to any extent, perhaps you would prefer to see the Manager."

He departed to the back, returning a minute later with the gratifying information that there was precisely nine thousand one hundred and forty-eight pounds four shillings and sixpence to my credit.

I handed him Northcote's cheque, and without further discussion he opened a drawer and began to count out a pile of bank-notes.

"I am giving it to you in five-hundreds, Mr. Northcote," he observed. "Will that be convenient?"

"Quite," I said affably. It struck me as a most happy adjective to apply to five-hundred-pound bank-notes.

As soon as I was outside again I took a deep breath. The sensation that one has the best part of ten thousand pounds in one's pocket is the most richly satisfying emotion I have ever experienced. A few days ago I had trod this very pavement with nothing but a fiver between me and bankruptcy, and now here I was a veritable, if somewhat precariously situated, Crœsus. I decided to celebrate my promotion by lunching at the Criterion.

CHAPTER VII

OVER an excellent grouse, followed by mushrooms on toast, and illuminated by a bottle of Chablis, I leisurely reviewed the situation. So far, about thirteen hours had elapsed since I had parted from Northcote at the Milan, and if they had contained one or two disconcerting experiences, I decided that I might certainly consider myself lucky to have emerged as successfully as I had. I was still alive; I had ten thousand pounds in my pocket; and so far I had apparently played my part without arousing the faintest suspicion.

There was a reverse side to this attractive picture, of course. In the first place, I now had ample evidence that Northcote's dread of assassination was neither a joke nor a delusion. My own animated interview with Mercia, and the present condition of the luckless Milford, made it very plain that during the next three weeks any Insurance Company which knew the facts of the case would politely but firmly decline to accept my life at less than a hundred per cent. Of Mercia herself I was no longer afraid, but the mysterious Guarez, and possibly other gentlemen with equally suggestive names, were apparently still hanging around, waiting to carry on the good work which she had so unsuccessfully attempted to inaugurate.

Then there was this visit to Maurice. Somehow or other, I felt very uneasy about my hospitable cousin.

64

Even if Northcote had not warned me against him, his personality would have been quite enough to put me on my guard. All the time I had been with him I had had a curious feeling that underneath his easy manner there lurked a bitter and dangerous hostility. Why he should dislike me, or rather Northcote, I had no idea, and I was equally ignorant as to whether there was any possibility of his being connected with my other unknown friends.

Under the circumstances, it seemed like asking for trouble to have accepted his invitation. I haven't got that sort of nature, however, that can sit down patiently under a mystery—especially when my life is at stake —and I was determined to get to the bottom of things as rapidly and effectually as I could. A week at Maurice's country retreat appeared to offer considerable possibilities in this line, and I was cheerfully prepared to accept any extra risk which might be involved in the process.

If I had only had some pal in whom I could place absolute trust, I think I should have felt perfectly contented. It was more the loneliness of my situation than the prospect of being murdered at a moment's notice that disturbed my natural equanimity.

I was just pondering over this problem when suddenly, like a flash of light, a brilliant idea leaped into my mind. I brought my hand down on the arm of my chair with a bang that made a respectable old gentleman at the next table nearly jump out of his skin.

Billy Logan !

Of course ! What a double-blanked idiot I had been. If he had not fixed up his business with Maxwells Billy was exactly the man for my purpose. True as

5

steel, tough as whipcord, and game for any conceivable mischief that the world could offer, he would be a fitting partner for the mad business to which I had pledged myself.

I hastily ran through my pockets for the address which he had given me. A horrible doubt seized me that I might perhaps have left it in my blue suit, but just as I was giving up hope, I found it securely tucked away in the flap of my pocket-book:

W. G. LOGAN,

34 VAUXHALL ROAD, S.W.

I looked at it affectionately. With Billy to back me up, I felt equal to tackling half a dozen Maurices, with a Guarez or two chucked in to keep them company.

It was true that by confiding in Billy I should, in word at least, be breaking my promise to Northcote, but this didn't weigh very heavily on my mind. All that eminent financier was really concerned about was my keeping up appearances before the world in general and his would-be assassins in particular. This I fully intended to do; and if he didn't like my bringing in Billy to assist me, he would most decidedly have to lump it.

I made up my mind that I would drive down to Vauxhall Road directly my meeting at the Cannon Street Hotel was over. Meantime, I would wire to Billy telling him to be there to meet me.

Thoroughly cheered up by this happy inspiration, I paid my bill and told the waiter to order me a taxi. I was just leaving the restaurant when it suddenly occurred to me that I ought to telephone to Ritchie and find out how the unfortunate Milford was getting on.

There was a box in the hall, so I entered it and hunted up the doctor's number.

"Is that you, Ritchie?" I asked, in response to a curt "Hullo!"

"Yes," came the answer. "Who's speaking?"

"I'm Northcote," I said. "I wanted to know how Milford is."

"Oh, I'm glad you rang up. I'm happy to say he's much better. We've managed to get rid of the poison."

"Is he out of danger?" I asked.

"Practically, I think. It's rather difficult to say for certain, because we don't know what the poison was until we've analysed it. However, he's sleeping now, and his pulse is regular if a bit weak. The only bad symptom is a curious sort of mental torpor he seems to be suffering from. It's probably the result of weakness, but we shall have to watch him carefully. I've told the nurse to ring up and let me know how he is when he wakes."

"Well, that seems fairly satisfying, on the whole," I said. "I've sent in a new man from Seagrave's to look after things, so Milford will be able to get away for a bit as soon as he's better."

"The best thing he could do," returned the doctor. "A couple of days at Brighton will pick him up better than any medicine. I'll let you know about the poison as soon as I've got the analyst's report."

"Yes, do," I said; and then, thinking that the conversation was taking a rather delicate turn, I added: "I must go now. I've got a meeting at the Cannon Street Hotel at three o'clock. See you to-morrow morning."

"Right you are. Good-bye."

"Good-bye," I echoed, and hung up the receiver.

The knowledge that Milford was out of danger was a

considerable relief. I liked the man, and shared
Northcote's opinion as to his trustworthiness; while,
apart from that, if he had died I should certainly have
been placed in a devilish awkward situation. A police
inquiry into the private doings of Mr. Stuart Northcote's
ménage was a form of excitement which I felt that I
could very well dispense with.

Getting into my taxi, I started off down Coventry
Street, stopping at the Post Office in Leicester Square
to send off my wire to Billy.

I arrived at the Cannon Street Hotel just as a quarter
past three was striking. I was a little late on purpose,
as befitted the dignity of a King of Finance. A waiter
who was standing in the hall evidently recognised me as
Northcote, for he bowed profusely, and without comment
conducted me upstairs to a large room where a number
of prosperous-looking gentlemen in frock-coats were
sitting round a long table.

They one and all greeted me with a respectful courtesy
that still further heightened my opinion of Northcote's
abilities.

"Good afternoon, gentlemen," I said, seating myself in
a vacant chair at the head of the table.

There was a chorus of "Good afternoon, Mr. Northcote," and then a solemn-looking old buffer at my right
hand took up a printed paper and began ingratiatingly
to explain to me how far the proceedings had gone.

I need hardly say that my ignorance of business is
about as profound as it could possibly be. Sitting there
with all these eminent exponents of the art regarding
me with evident respect and apprehension appealed so
forcibly to my sense of humour that it was all I could
do to stop myself from bursting into a shout of laughter.
However, with a great effort, I managed to retain a

befitting gravity, and listened with a sombre frown to my neighbour's exposition. Finally, I nodded my head as though satisfied, and the business of the meeting again proceeded on its normal course.

What that "normal course" precisely was I have neither the ability nor desire to describe. A great deal of it was necessarily double Dutch to me, but I played my part with an impressive air of understanding that seemed to go down most successfully with my colleagues. Of course I spoke as little as possible, and then only when I was appealed to on some point of dispute. On such occasions I gave my decision with curt firmness, and I found that it was almost invariably accepted without further comment. I began to think the profession of a Financial Magnate was one in which I was peculiarly adapted to shine.

It must have been getting on for half-past five when the proceedings at length terminated. As we left the room, a bald-headed little man who had been exceedingly talkative all through came up to me and inquired whether I would do him the honour of joining him in a glass of champagne. I replied graciously that I had no particular objection, and with evident pride he led the way downstairs to the saloon bar of the hotel.

"Your good health, Mr. Northcote," he said, looking at me respectfully over his bubbling glass.

"The same to you," I replied, not to be outdone in politeness.

"A most satisfactory meeting," he went on, setting down his glass; "most satisfactory! Pensford gave a little trouble about those Debentures, but you soon settled him."

"One has to put one's foot down sometimes," I observed firmly.

"Yes, yes. Quite so, Mr. Northcote; quite so!"
Then he paused. "I was wondering," he added, a little
nervously, "whether you could possibly give me a tip of
any kind about those new South American goldfields."

I suppose I looked at him rather sharply, for he at
once put up an apologetic hand.

"Please don't think me intrusive, Mr. Northcote," he
added hurriedly. "Your name has been mentioned
very freely in the City in connection with them; but if
you would rather not say anything at present, of course
I shall understand."

His words had naturally given me a bit of a start. I
had no idea that, with the exception of my own discoveries in Bolivia, anyone had so much as smelt a fresh
goldfield in South America. Could this, I wondered,
be the mysterious "Company" alluded to in Sangatte's
letter? I lit a cigarette to give myself time to think.

"At the present moment," I said gravely, "I am not
in a position to impart any information on the matter."
(God knows this was true enough!) "But," I added,
seeing his evident disappointment, "a little later on I
might perhaps be able to give you a useful hint or two."

His greedy and rather pasty face brightened at once.
"I should be extremely grateful if you could, Mr.
Northcote," he said, "extremely grateful."

"Oh, that's all right," I returned, finishing up the rest
of the champagne. "Now I'm afraid I must be off.
I've got an appointment at six."

He followed me to the door of the hotel, protesting
his appreciation of my kindness, and respectfully waved
a podgy hand as a convenient taxi bore me away down
Holborn. It must be a good long way from the Cannon
Street Hotel to Vauxhall Road, but my memories of
the meeting were sufficiently entertaining to prevent my

noticing it. Indeed, I was still smiling thoughtfully to myself over the bald-headed gentleman's anticipations when the driver pulled up with a jerk outside a row of depressed-looking three-storey houses, fronted in dirty stucco.

"'Ere you are, sir," he said, leaning back and opening the door. "Number 34."

I got out and told the man to wait. In case Billy was not at home, it would be just as well, I thought, to have a cab in readiness. For all I knew, I might have been followed; and if that were the case, from what I could see of my surroundings it was not at all the sort of neighbourhood for an unattended stroll.

Mounting a dilapidated flight of steps, I gave a pull at the bell, which tinkled vehemently down in the basement. It was answered after a long wait by a round-shouldered elderly woman, who put her head round the doorway and peered at me suspiciously.

"Is Mr. Logan in?" I asked.

She shook her head.

"When will he be back?" I asked.

She shook her head again. "I dunno," she observed.

I repressed a strong inclination to swear. "I am a friend of his," I explained patiently. "I sent him a telegram this afternoon to say I was coming. Didn't he get it?"

"No," she replied; "'e didn't get no telergram."

"But it must have come," I objected. "I sent it off."

"Oh, it come all right," she said. "The telergram come all right, sir. I put it in 'is lookin'-glass. Only 'e ain't bin back not since yesterday."

"That's a nuisance," I observed. "Can I come in and write him a letter?"

She blinked doubtfully. "I dunno as 'ow 'e'd like it."

"Oh, he'd like it right enough," I assured her. "I don't want to go into his room; I'll scribble it in the hall, if you'll let me have a sheet of paper and an envelope."

Something in my sporting offer seemed to reassure the old girl, for she cautiously pulled back the door just wide enough for me to come in.

"I shan't be long," I called out to the cabman, and then, crossing the threshold, entered the house.

The landlady opened the door on the left-hand side of the passage.

"I s'pose it's all right," she said grudgingly. "This 'ere's Mr. Logan's room."

I followed her into Billy's sanctum, which proved to be the ordinary cheaply-furnished front parlour of a London lodging-house.

"I'll get yer a bit o' paiper," she added, shuffling dismally across it to a small desk against the wall. "'E gen'rally keeps some in 'is blottin'-book."

I seated myself at the small table in the centre, which was covered with a hideous rep cloth, and patiently awaited her investigations. It pleased me to think that I could soon transfer Billy to more congenial surroundings.

After fumbling about for a minute she produced the required articles and laid them on the table in front of me.

"Jer want some ink?" she asked.

"No, thanks," I said. "I've got a pencil. That will do quite well."

I turned back the cloth, and began to write, while the good lady, breathing heavily, stood and watched me.

"DEAR BILLY,"—I began,—" I'm writing this in your room, as your landlady will no doubt tell you when you come home. I wired you this afternoon, saying I was going to look you up; but, thanks to your disgraceful habit of staying out all night, the wire is sitting up, unopened, in your looking-glass.

"If you haven't fixed your business with Maxwells, chuck it at once. I've got something for you much more in your line. I can't explain now, but there's plenty of money in it, and I want you bad, Billy, very bad.

"Come along and see me directly you get this. I'm staying at 46A Park Lane. It's in the telephone-book under the name of Stuart Northcote, so if you like you can ring me up first. If you do, ask for Mr. Northcote, *not for me*, and the same thing if you come to the house. Don't make any mistake about this. In case I'm out, the servants will have instructions to ask you to wait, but you're not to mention my name, under any circumstances. Just ask for Mr. Northcote.

"I suppose this sounds mysterious, but I'll explain as soon as I see you.

"Don't fail me, Billy. It's the real goods all round."

I signed this "Jack Burton," and then folded it up and put it in the envelope, which I carefully fastened. I was not in the least anxious for Billy's landlady to read it, so, in order to give the gum a chance to dry, I felt in my pocket and produced a handful of money, from which I slowly counted out five shillings. She watched me with absorbed interest.

"May I offer you this," I said, "for putting you to so much trouble?"

"It's a pleasure, sir," she murmured, eagerly accepting the coins. "Allus glad to oblige a gen'l'man."

"Then perhaps you wouldn't mind giving this to Mr. Logan as soon as he comes in," I added, putting the letter in the glass alongside the telegram.

" I'll be sure to call 'is notice to it, sir. You can count on that, sir. I'm only sorry as 'e was out, sir."

She opened the door for me with almost painful subservience, and stood on the steps blinking and bowing while I walked down and got into the cab.

" Where to, sir ? " inquired the driver.

I reflected rapidly. Knowing that Milford was better, I had no particular desire to go back to Park Lane, even if the new butler had arrived. The thought of a solitary dinner in that big dining-room distinctly failed to appeal to me.

" Oh, drive me to the Café Royal," I said.

The cooking at that delightful establishment is good enough by itself to induce a certain satisfaction with the world. Backed as it was, in the present case, by my feelings of joy in the prospect of Billy's company, it lifted me into a state of serene optimism such as I had not known since my first fortnight in England.

I dined deliberately, choosing my wines after consultation with the head waiter, and also accepting the latter's excellent advice in the matter of a cigar. Then for the best part of an hour I sat and smoked, gently contemplating my fellow-diners through the haze, and finally deciding that not even the lady with the emeralds, who was undoubtedly the prettiest woman in the room, could hold a candle to Mercia Solano.

Having arrived at this conclusion, I paid my bill and strolled out to walk back to Park Lane. I had not forgotten the possible dangers of solitary pedestrian exercise, but the evening was fine, I had my trusty sword-stick with me, and I felt that I would be damned if M. Guarez or any other infernal Dago should compel me to spend the remainder of my life in cabs.

Nevertheless, despite this defiant mood, I took

particular care to keep my eyes open. The old rhyme
"Thrice blest is he who hath his quarrel just, but ten
times he who gets his blow in fust," has always struck
me as a peculiarly sound piece of philosophy, and I
scanned each harmless passer-by who approached with
a wary eye for any symptom of trouble.

Unless anyone took a pot-shot at me from the Park
railings, I felt that I was fairly safe, and my sense of
security was increased by seeing a comfortable-looking
Bobby standing right under the big electric light just
opposite my home.

He saluted me as I came up.

"Good evening, Constable," I said.

"Good evenin', sir," he returned. "No more trouble
with any of them beggars, I hope?"

It was just on the tip of my tongue to ask, "What
beggars?" when I suddenly recollected myself.

"No, thanks," I said, wondering what on earth he
meant.

"Since you complained to me, sir, I've been keeping
a good look-out, and I reckon they've spotted it and
cleared off."

In a flash I realised that Northcote must have taken
these ingenious means of rendering any vigil on the
part of M. Guarez and his friends a somewhat trying
affair.

"I'm much obliged to you," I said. "I don't want to
complain officially, but you might keep your eyes open
a bit longer. It's a nuisance to have people hanging
round the house."

As I spoke, I handed him half a sovereign, which he
accepted without a quiver.

"Thank you very much, sir," he said. "I'll see you're
not bothered again, sir. Don't you worry about that."

Bidding him good-night, I mounted the steps of my house, and was just getting out my latch-key when a telegraph-boy suddenly rode up on a bicycle and jumped off in the gutter outside.

He came up the steps, pulling out a wire from his bag.

" Is that for me? " I asked.   " Mr. Stuart Northcote? "

" Yes, sir."

I took it from him, and, tearing open the envelope held up the message to the light of the street lamp.   It consisted of seven words:

"Get rid of your new butler immediately."

I stared at it for a moment, and then laughed.

" Thanks," I said; " there's no answer."

CHAPTER VIII

I RATHER like surprises; but, as my old friend Jack Costello used to say, "You can have too dam much of a good thing."

With the telegram in my hand I went inside the house, shutting the door behind me. The light was full on in the hall, and sitting on the edge of the table I again read through the curt message:

"Get rid of your new butler immediately."

It had been sent off from Charing Cross at 9.58, and the sender, whoever he might be, was evidently a person of direct and frugal mind. The whole wire came to exactly twelve words, while for crispness of style its phrasing certainly left little to be desired.

I stared at it with mingled feelings of doubt, annoyance, and amusement. If the warning was genuine, and my new butler was really lurking behind the coal-scuttle with a dagger in his coat-tail pocket, who the dickens had taken the trouble to put me on my guard? It must have been someone acquainted with my movements that morning; but, so far as I knew, Maurice was the only person who answered that description. I couldn't exactly see Maurice wading in with a kindly caution; and in any case, if he had wanted to give me the tip, why couldn't he have done so when he had been with me?

On the whole, I was more inclined to think that the

wire was an attempt at bluff. It might be that my prompt engagement of another trustworthy servant in place of Milford had interfered with my friends' plans, and that they were hoping to frighten me into clearing him out.

Anyhow, there was obviously only one course to pursue, and that was to interview the gentleman myself without delay, and see what I thought of him. So, crossing to the fireplace, I rang the bell, and took up a dignified but alert attitude on the hearth-rug.

As far as promptness was concerned, Francis left nothing to be desired. Thirty seconds could hardly have elapsed before he had entered the hall, and was standing before me with a deferential bow of greeting.

I looked at him keenly. He was a tall, slim fellow of about thirty-five, with thick black hair and a rather sallow face.

"Well, I see you've arrived all right, Francis," I observed.

He again inclined his head.

"Yes, sir. I came round with Mr. Seagrave about three o'clock. He gave the cook your card, sir."

"Have you seen Milford?" I asked.

"Yes, sir. I had a short conversation with him."

"How is he?"

"He seems a little better, sir. He was anxious to go through the work with me, but I thought it best not to allow him to talk too much. I think I can manage quite satisfactorily, with what the cook has told me."

I nodded. "Quite right," I said. "There is really nothing to discuss. I only want you to look after me and carry out the ordinary duties of a butler. I'll tell you anything you want to know, if you come and ask."

He bowed a third time. "Yes, sir—thank you, sir."

"Well, I'm going to bed now," I said. "I shan't want anything else, except some hot water. You can call me at the usual time—eight o'clock."

I handed him my hat and stick, and, taking some letters from the table, sauntered slowly up the big staircase, which led to the landing above. At the first bend I purposely dropped a letter, and then, as though suddenly discovering my loss, turned to pick it up. The strategy, though ingenious, seemed to be a trifle uncalled-for. Francis was at the other end of the hall, with his back towards me, apparently placing my stick in the hat-stand.

With memories of the previous evening in my mind, the first thing I did on reaching my sitting-room was to walk across to the recess and pull back the curtain that covered it. Of course I knew it would be empty, but at the back of my mind I somehow or other had a ridiculous hope that I should find Mercia standing there, pistol in hand, and that delicious half-sorrowful, half-scornful expression on her face. I believe I would willingly have risked ducking another bullet if by so doing I could have ensured her presence.

But the recess was void — quite undoubtedly and stupidly void; and with a feeling of disappointment I sat down in a chair and began to open Northcote's correspondence. It contained nothing of any particular importance to me, consisting for the most part of bills and circulars, with one or two business letters that I contented myself with just glancing through. I had had enough of business for one day.

As I was looking at the last of them, I heard Francis enter my bedroom. After moving about for several minutes, apparently putting things straight for the night, he tapped gently at the sitting-room door and then opened it.

"Your room is quite ready now, sir," he observed.

"Thank you, Francis," I said.   "Good-night."

"Good-night, sir."

He withdrew noiselessly and went out through the bedroom, shutting the door behind him.

I waited until he had had time to reach the basement, and then, getting up from my chair, I began to take one or two simple steps towards securing my position.   Although in my heart I believed the wire to be a false alarm, it seemed to me that there would be no harm in adopting a few obvious precautions.

So, after lighting a pipe, I proceeded to indulge in a thorough search both of the bedroom and the sitting-room.   Having satisfied myself that there were no strangers or bombs lurking about, I locked both doors and carefully inspected the fastenings of the windows. These were quite secure ; indeed, so far as I could see, there was no way, short of gunpowder or a false key, by which anyone could enter either room without my assistance.   To make matters doubly safe, however, I collected all the fire-irons from the two grates (reserving only a poker for personal use in case of necessity) and deposited them in two heaps—one in front of each door. I am a light sleeper, and I reckoned that anyone making a forcible entrance from outside would do so to a musical accompaniment that would at once disturb my slumbers. Then, with a mind relieved, I leisurely undressed myself and got into bed.

There was an electric lamp on the table beside me, but by way of a reserve light I stuffed a box of matches beneath my pillow.   My trusty poker I placed down the side of the bed under the top sheet, ready to my hand should I be unseasonably disturbed.

One last look round satisfied me that my preparations

were distinctly efficient. As I flicked off the light and lay back on my pillow, I felt a kind of half-hope that there might really be something genuine in the warning I had received. It seemed a pity to have taken so much trouble for nothing.

Going to sleep is always a more or less instantaneous business with me, and, as far as I know, this night was no exception to the rule. At all events, I have no recollection of anything between the time I was fingering the handle of my poker in a kind of dreamy satisfaction and the moment when I started up suddenly in bed with the faint chink of fire-irons still sounding in my ears.

I woke with all my faculties keenly on the alert. Everything round me was in utter darkness, and my hand went out instinctively and closed upon the electric switch. I must have stayed like that for several seconds. My heart was beating rapidly, but I don't think I felt the least afraid.

Then I heard the door close very gently, and someone take a step forward into the room. Without making a sound, I reached under the clothes with my disengaged hand and stealthily withdrew my trusty poker. Having secured this, I wriggled over into such a position that I should be facing the intruder, and then, without further hesitation, I pressed down the switch.

My intention was either to hurl the poker directly the light went up, or else to take a flying jump from the bed and land my visitor a good swipe over the head before he could defend himself. It all depended upon whether he was carrying a revolver.

Unfortunately, neither of these excellent designs materialised. The switch went down with a sharp snap, but instead of a blaze of light flooding the room, everything remained in darkness.

6

I can tell you I didn't stop to wonder what had happened. The danger of my position struck me with a bang, and in less time than it takes to say I had hurled myself sideways off the bed in the opposite direction from the door.

I was only just in time.

Almost before I reached the floor I heard the crash of an overturning table, and then something came down on the pillow with a wicked thud that made the whole bedstead tremble.

I fell heavily full-length on the carpet, but it is ex traordinary what activity danger will occasionally lend one. No cat could have recovered her feet more nimbly or leaped back into the darkness with such masterly swiftness. The wall of the room was only about a yard away, and I fetched up against it with a jar that nearly knocked the breath out of my body. There I stood panting and shaken, but with the poker still gripped affectionately in my right hand.

It was not exactly an inspiriting situation—especially to a man in pyjamas and bare feet. The only bright spot about it was that my visitor, having bungled his first shot, was no better off than I was. Indeed, if, as I imagined, he was none other than my new retainer, I held the trump card by being a good way the heftier of the two. I couldn't picture myself being slaughtered by Francis, even in the dark.

Crouching down against the wall, I peered out into the blackness in front of me and listened intently. Since his first magnificent slap at the bed, my visitor had apparently rested on his laurels. I could hear him breathing quickly, but beyond that there was not the faintest sound. Not knowing what had happened to me, he was evidently waiting for inspiration.

I did some rapid but necessary thinking. If I called out for help, it was just possible that I should be sealing my fate; for should he be armed with a revolver as well as his other weapon, he would doubtless blaze away in the direction of my voice. Apart from this, I felt a very strong desire to settle the matter without assistance from anyone.

My best plan seemed to be to get to close quarters, trusting to Providence and the poker that I should get my slam in first. With this object in view, I began to creep noiselessly along the wainscoting, keeping my back against the wall. At the third step I ran against a small picture, which swung sideways and fell from its nail with a nerve-shaking crash. In a second I had dropped to the floor, where I crouched breathlessly, waiting the expected shot.

None came, however: only a slight movement from the direction of the bed told me that my visitor was on the alert. I stayed as I was, straining my ears to catch the smallest sound; and then, very faint but just audible to my excellent sense of hearing, came the stealthy tread of an advancing footstep.

During the next moment my mind worked pretty quickly. It was either a case of waiting where I was, or else rushing forward and lashing out blindly into the dark. Which I should have done I can't say, for it was at that crucial instant that my hand happened to touch the corner of the picture which had just fallen from the wall.

Never until then had Art properly appealed to me. I clutched that blessed frame with the gratitude of a starving man who has suddenly stumbled upon food, and changing the poker over to my left hand, rose swiftly and joyously to my feet.

At the slight noise which I made, the footsteps stopped. I knew, however, that my visitor must be desperately near, and for a tense second we both stood in absolute silence, each of us holding his breath for fear of betraying himself to the other.

Then out of the blackness ahead of me came the faintest possible rustle. Like a flash I whipped back my right hand, and hurled the picture with all the force I could straight at the sound.

I rather think it must have landed on the bridge of my visitor's nose, since no other point of contact could have produced such a yelp of surprised agony as that which cleft the darkness. I did not wait to jeer, but, ducking down again, took a couple of hasty steps to the left in the direction of the door. He evidently heard me, for, rushing forward, he landed a vicious smack on the wall, just above my head, bringing down the plaster in a scattering shower. I retaliated with a furious swipe at the empty air that nearly put my shoulder out, and then, feeling that so far I had had all the best of the duel, I leapt back out of range.

How the contest would have ended Goodness knows, for at that moment it was cut short by an unexpected interruption. From the passage outside came the noise of hurrying footsteps; then the door of the room burst open, admitting a ray of light that seemed almost blinding after the total darkness. A figure appeared on the threshold—a tall figure in white, holding a candle in one hand and a stick of some sort in the other.

I blame myself pretty badly for what happened next. If I had only had the sense of a caterpillar, I should have dashed for the door, so cutting off all chance of my visitor's escape. As it was, I'm blessed if I didn't actually jump away in the opposite direction, I suppose

from some silly idea that I was going to be tackled by a
fresh enemy.

I realised my mistake at once, but it was too late.
There was a swift rush of feet, a wild scuffle on the
threshold, and then the candle went out and I heard
Milford's voice shouting for help.

With an oath I hurled myself forward, stumbling
blindly over the scattered fire-irons. There was still a
glimmer of light in the passage, and by its aid I could
see two figures locked in a furious struggle.

Just as I reached the door, one of them collapsed, and
the other, breaking free, leaped wildly for the head of
the banisters. I was after him at once, and we went
down that staircase in a way that would have put the
fear of God into a couple of chamois.

If the front door had been locked, I should have had
him. As it was, he just got it open in time, and taking
the steps with a flying jump, landed clear on the pavement outside. With a last effort, I hurled my poker at
him through the gate, only missing him by the merest
fraction. Then he was off, bolting down the street like
a rabbit, and vanishing round the corner before you
could count five.

CHAPTER IX

I WALKED out into the roadway and picked up my weapon. Except for a solitary cat, scratching herself under the opposite lamp, Park Lane was absolutely deserted. As I stood for a moment, staring up and down the long, brilliantly-lit thoroughfare, I heard a neighbouring clock strike three.

I am not a person who gives up very easily, especially when I'm annoyed, but, dressed as I was, any further pursuit was out of the question. To dash down Piccadilly at this hour of the night, clad only in pyjamas and a poker, was to court a publicity that I was only too anxious to avoid. So, after a slight shiver, for my bare feet were beginning to get unpleasantly cold, I retraced my steps into the house.

As I closed the door, I heard a kind of stifled sob from the back of the hall, and, looking up, I saw in the dim light two women crouching against the banisters. They were both in their night-dresses, and one of them, whom I recognised as the parlour-maid, had her hair streaming down over her shoulders. Very pretty hair it was, too.

"It's all right," I said comfortingly. "Nobody's hurt."

The elder of the two women—the cook, I suppose—burst into a torrent of hysterical relief.

"Oh, sir! Oh, Mr. Northcote! Oh dear, oh dear! We thought you were all killed!"

"Not a bit of it," I said. "Go and put something on and find out what's the matter with the electric light."

My brisk and cheerful manner had the desired effect. Both women stopped sobbing, and, letting go each other's hands, rose unsteadily to their feet. The parlour-maid even found time to blush.

There were two candles flickering away on the hall table, and taking one of them, I hastily mounted the stairs. As I came up, I heard the sound of voices, and, reaching the landing, I found the faithful Milford apparently engaged in a wrestling match with a woman dressed as a nurse. When he saw me, he gave a sort of gulp, and sat down abruptly on an oak chest behind him.

"Well, Milford," I said severely, "this is nice behaviour for an invalid!"

He caught at the wall to steady himself, and I saw that the front of his night-dress was stained with blood.

"Are you hurt?" I asked quickly.

He shook his head. "No, no, sir; I'm all right. It was the other man—he was bleeding in the face."

I turned to the nurse, who, I felt, deserved an explanation. "It was an attempt at robbery," I explained shamelessly. "I got a new man in yesterday, and he must have come with a forged character. Anyway, when I woke up, I found him in my room; so, naturally, I tackled him. I suppose you heard the noise downstairs?"

The nurse, who seemed to be a singularly self-possessed lady, nodded her head. "My patient did," she said, arranging a shawl that she was carrying round Milford's shoulders. "I tried to keep him in bed, but it was useless. He pushed me away and rushed upstairs just as he was. All I could do was to follow him and light the candles."

"You couldn't have done anything better," I observed. "But for them, God knows where we should have been. The blackguard had evidently been monkeying with the electric light."

"I was in the hall," she went on, "when you rushed past. After you'd gone, I hurried upstairs, and found my patient trying to follow you. I hope I did right in stopping him. You didn't seem to be in much need of help."

"Of course you were right," I said. Then, turning to Milford, I laid my hand on his shoulder. "You're a good friend, Milford," I added, "but you're a mighty bad patient. You must go back to bed at once."

He smiled faintly, but made no answer. Lifting him to his feet, and supporting him with my arm, I helped him slowly downstairs—the nurse following. Just as we reached the basement, the electric light went up, and the parlour-maid, this time with the addition of a dressing-gown, appeared in the passage. She still seemed a trifle embarrassed.

"We found out what was the matter with the light, sir," she said. "It had been turned off at the main switch."

"Well, that's all right," I said. "You and Cook go to bed now. There'll be no more trouble. It was only an attempt at burglary on the part of that new man I got in yesterday. He's cleared out, and we can't do anything more until the morning."

A few minutes later, having seen Milford safely tucked up and left the nurse in attendance, I made my way back to the hall, where I fastened the front door and put out both the candles and the electric light.

My visitor had left traces of blood all across the carpet, and I found spots of the same article decorating both the staircase and the landing above. It was evident that his study of art had been as intimate as it had been brief.

Somewhat cheered by this discovery, I entered my room, and, turning up the light, shut the door. The place was in a cheerful state of confusion, for, in addition to fire-irons, broken glass, and fragments of picture-frame, the overturned table and its contents were scattered generously round the room.

I tidied up things as well as I could, and then examined with some interest the marks left by the two unavailing swipes which my opponent had dealt at me in the duel. What his weapon was I could not say for certain, but from the traces which it had left behind, it appeared to have been something in the nature of an axe. My pillow was practically cut in half, while the dent which he had made in the wall left me with a certain sense of thankfulness that my head had not been in the spot where it landed.

After removing such portions of Park Lane as still adhered to my bare feet, I got into bed, turning my mangled pillow over on its other side. I left the electric light full on, for sleeping in the dark had, somehow or other, ceased to appeal to me. Then, with the agreeable feeling of a day well spent, I curled myself up under the clothes, and in five minutes I was fast asleep.

A little brisk exercise in the small hours of the night must, I think, be an excellent thing for the health. At all events, I woke up next morning feeling splendidly fit, and came down to breakfast with an even better appetite than on the previous day. My constitution requires an occasional stimulant, and with the job which I had undertaken there appeared to be little chance of its being denied this luxury.

I regret to say that the pretty parlour-maid seemed less fortunate. I was too sleepy to pay much attention to her when I was called, but later on, when she brought me in my eggs and bacon, I noticed that she had dark shadows under her eyes, and a general air of having spent a bad night.

"I am afraid you didn't sleep very well," I said.

She shook her head. "Neither me nor Cook closed our eyes the whole night, sir," she replied reproachfully.

"Oh, I'm sorry for that," I said. "You must go to bed early this evening, to make up for it. Have you heard how Milford is this morning?"

"The nurse seemed to think he was doing well, sir. I believe the doctor is coming round almost at once."

The words had scarcely left her lips when, through the window, I saw Ritchie's car roll up to the door, and Ritchie himself step out.

"There he is," I exclaimed, getting up from the table. "Ask him to come in here a moment, will you."

She went out, and I heard the front door open. A minute later, the doctor, carrying a glossy hat and dressed in an irreproachable grey frock-coat, entered the room.

"Good morning, Mr. Northcote," he said, extending a hand, which I shook heartily. "And how is the patient this morning?"

"Well, doctor," I said, "that's one reason why I wanted to see you. We had rather an exciting time last night."

He raised his eyebrows interrogatively, and without

further waste of time I trotted out the same old lie which had already done duty for the nurse.

"It was a burglary," I said, "or rather, an attempted burglary. I had engaged another man, called Francis, in place of Milford, and I woke up in the middle of the night and found him in my room, trying to break into my desk." (This last touch, I thought, was particularly happy!)

"Dear me! Dear me!" interjected the doctor, in a shocked voice.

"Of course I tackled him," I continued; "but he made such a noise that, unfortunately, he woke up Milford. In spite of his nurse, the plucky fellow insisted on coming upstairs; and just as he reached the landing, my man broke away and made a dash for the door. There was a scuffle in the passage, and Milford got bowled over."

"Bless my soul!" said the doctor. "Was he hurt?"

"No," said I; "that's the funny thing about it. Knowing how seedy he was, I expected to find him dead; but, on the contrary, he seemed to be none the worse for it."

Ritchie nodded his head. "It's quite possible," he said thoughtfully. "A shock of some kind may have been just what he needed. Still, it must have been touch-and-go. What happened to the man?"

"Unfortunately," I said, "he got away. It's an extraordinary case, because I engaged him through Seagrave's, and his references were all right, according to them. I'm going straight round there now."

"I should," said the doctor, "and, what's more, I should put the matter in the hands of the police right away."

"Quite so," I assented cordially, though it was the

very last thing I had any intention of doing; and with this extra fib I led the way down to the basement.

Far from being any the worse for his night's adventure, we found the gallant Milford sitting up in bed, shifting a large bowl of bread-and-milk with evident enjoyment.

"Hullo, Milford!" I said. "That looks hopeful."

The good fellow positively grinned. "I feel much better to-day, thank you, sir. I really think I can get up and do my work."

"I don't know about that," remarked the doctor, laughing, "but there's no doubt that fighting burglars agrees with you. Let's feel your pulse."

The nurse, who had taken the chance of removing the empty bowl, here observed that her patient had slept soundly ever since we had put him to bed.

"Oh, he's much better," said the doctor—"there can be no question about that. Indeed, I don't think it would do him any harm to get up. Of course he mustn't think of work for another day or two, but otherwise we can consider the cure complete. In future, I shall recommend one burglar to be taken nightly for any case that I feel doubtful about."

Chuckling heartily at his own jest, he accompanied me upstairs. "It really is a most remarkable recovery," he said. "The man is practically all right again—pulse a little weak, but otherwise nothing the matter with him. It just illustrates the value of a sudden mental shock in cases of collapse. By the way, I received the analyst's report this morning."

"Oh!" I observed. "What did he say?"

The doctor frowned. "Well, it's curious, but he admits that at present he's baffled. There are distinct traces of a vegetable poison of some kind, but it responds to none of the usual tests. However, he's going to make some further researches, so I suppose I shall hear from him again."

"You must let me know," I said brazenly, handing him his hat. "I mean to get to the bottom of this."

Promising he would, and congratulating me again on my frustration of the burglar, the worthy man went off. What his private opinion of my household must have been I hardly liked to contemplate; but since he showed no signs of communicating it to the police, I was well content to let matters rest as they were.

Before starting out to have a little chat with my friend Mr. Seagrave, I summoned the parlour-maid and gave her instructions that if Billy Logan rang up or called while I was out, she was to tell him that he would find me at home any time that afternoon. Then, equipping myself with my trusty sword-stick, I set forth for Hanover Square.

It was my intention, as you may imagine, to speak some very plain words to the portly gentleman who had sent "Francis" round on the previous day; but, as some forgotten philosopher once observed, "it takes two to make a quarrel." One can't be brutal to a worm, and Mr. Seagrave more nearly represented that creature than anybody I have ever met.

The moment I entered his office he fell upon me with apologies so abject that my pretty talent for remonstrance had no chance of asserting itself.

"You have received my note, Mr. Northcote. I can't tell you how distressed I am that such a thing should have occurred in this office. On behalf of the firm I tender you our deepest, our most sincere apologies. I only trust that there have been no regrettable consequences. What the scoundrel's object was, Heaven knows. I——"

"Look here, Mr. Seagrave," I interrupted, "what the dickens are you talking about? I've had no note from you yet."

He goggled at me, rubbing his hands together, and cringing like a frightened spaniel. I suppose he must have had some unpleasant experiences with my spirited double.

"You must just have missed it, Mr. Northcote," he said. "I sent it round by one of our young men a quarter of an hour ago. The fact is that we have heard from Sir Henry Tregattock this morning completely repudiating any knowledge of Francis. I had written to him overnight, asking him to confirm the character, and in reply he stated that he had no idea what I was alluding to. He had never had a servant of that name, and had not communicated with me in any shape or form. It's unparalleled, amazing, incredible, but there can be no doubt that someone else answered the telephone in Sir Henry's name. Still, if there have been no unfortunate developments——"

I laughed in rather a nasty fashion. "Unfortunate developments!" I repeated. "Are you aware, Mr. Seagrave, that the man you sent me yesterday not only attempted to rob the house in the night, but did his best to murder me?"

To say that Mr. Seagrave collapsed would be an altogether inadequate expression.

"Oh dear, oh dear!" he moaned. "This is terrible, sir, terrible! Such a thing has never occurred in the whole history of the firm. It will ruin us when it comes out—absolutely ruin us!"

His frank egotism rather pleased me.

"I don't suppose it would do you much good," I replied : "but is there any reason why it should come out?"

I saw a ray of hope leap into his distressed face.

"The fact is," I went on, "that I object to publicity in a case like this. In the first place, I'm much too busy to be bothered about it. The man's gone, and, as it happens, there's no harm done. I don't want a lot of infernal policemen tramping all over my house." (This was true enough.) "But you ought to be more careful," I added severely.

"We ought, sir; indeed we ought. I will never accept a telephone reference again. I should be more grateful than I can say if you can see your way to overlook the matter. The scoundrel must evidently have had an accomplice in Sir Henry's house."

"Well, you must square things with Sir Henry as best you can," I said. "All I want is not to be troubled any more in the matter."

I turned to leave the office, and he bowed me out, fervently protesting that my peace should not be disturbed, and that he would for ever consider himself my most humble debtor.

Quite pleased with the success of my interview, I made my way back to Park Lane, only stopping at a shop in Bond Street to purchase one of those linen belts which are made to wear next the skin. In view of my somewhat uncertain circumstances, it seemed to be tempting Providence to wander about London with ten thousand pounds in my pocket.

During my walk home, my adventure of the previous night served to occupy my thoughts in a not unpleasant fashion. It was agreeable to reflect that at least one of my unknown friends was bearing my handiwork in fairly legible type. Whether "Francis" was the mysterious Guarez, or another gentleman with similar aims, it was at least certain that for a few days I should be able to recognise him under any disguise. I registered a grim vow that no stranger with a dismantled bridge to his nose should have the opportunity of approaching within striking distance of me.

All the afternoon I waited in, in the hopes of hearing from Billy. By six o'clock, however, no message had arrived; and, feeling rather worried, I strolled downstairs to see how Milford was getting on. I found him fully dressed, sitting in an easy-chair in the pantry, and reading the *Daily Telegraph*. The nurse had gone.

He seemed quite touchingly pleased to see me, but it was all I could do to persuade him to retain his comfortable seat. He appeared to think a kitchen chair altogether beneath my dignity.

"What I can't make out, Milford," I said, "is how you managed to upset yourself."

He was silent a minute. "I can't help thinking, sir," he replied slowly, "that it must have been that glass o' beer I had at the Granville."

"But surely," I objected, "if the beer poisoned you, it would have poisoned everyone else."

"I don't think the beer would have poisoned me, sir, if it had been left alone," he said pointedly.

"What do you mean, Milford?" I asked.

He shifted a little uneasily in his chair. "Well, sir, it may be fancy, and you may think I'm speaking foolishly, but I can't help having an idea that the man I was speaking to may have put something in it when I wasn't looking."

"The man?" I said. "What man?"

"It was a chap in the bar, sir. A big, foreign-looking

fellow he was. He started talking to me when I came in, though, as far as I know, I'd never set eyes on him before. It's my belief that for some reason of his own he put something in my drink."

This theory of Milford's fitted in so exactly with my own suspicions that for a moment I felt as if I were partly guilty.

"Would you know him again?" I asked.

"Oh yes, sir. He was a big, black-haired fellow, with one shoulder a little higher than the other. I didn't fancy him when he came up and spoke to me."

I was just going to observe that the landlord of the premises might possibly be able to tell us something about the gentleman, when there came a tap at the door, and the parlour-maid entered.

"If you please, sir," she said, "Mr. Simpson is here."

It was an embarrassing moment, as of course I hadn't the faintest notion who Mr. Simpson might be; but once more Milford came to my rescue.

"I sent him a message to come round, sir. You said you might be motoring down to Woodford to-morrow if it was fine, so I told him he'd better look in and see whether you wanted the car."

This was news indeed. Up till that moment I had no idea that I belonged to the noble army of car owners.

"Quite right, Milford," I said, getting up. "I think I shall motor if it's anything like a decent day."

I went upstairs and found Mr. Simpson in the hall. He proved to be a small, dark, clean-shaven man dressed in the conventional garb of a chauffeur.

"Good evening, sir," he said, touching his forehead. "I just looked in about the car. Mr. Milford said you might be wanting it to-morrow to go down to Suffolk."

7

"Yes," I said, "I shall if it's fine."

I had quite decided by this time that I would motor down to Woodford instead of going by train.

"Will you be wanting me, sir?" asked Mr. Simpson.

I reflected rapidly. I am not much of a hand at steering a car, but still, I had tackled the task with average success on several occasions in Buenos Ayres. What was worrying me was the question of Billy. If he turned up in time, I intended taking him down to Woodford with me, and putting him up at the nearest inn; and there was just the chance that if Simpson came the latter might give the show away to one of Maurice's servants. On the whole, I decided to drive myself.

"No," I said, "I shan't want you, Simpson. Have the car round here at ten-thirty, and put some cans of petrol in. I shall only be away for two or three days."

He touched his forehead again respectfully, and withdrew.

My latest discovery had put me into a very cheerful frame of mind. With a car at my disposal I felt much better equipped for my visit to Woodford. I was a long way from trusting Master Maurice, and a motor is a devilish handy thing if you happen to want to leave a place without ceremony or delay.

The only fly in my ointment was the non-arrival of Billy. I was beginning to fear that he must have fixed up his job with Maxwells, and that I should have to get through as best I could without him. However, I have made it a rule in life never to hunt for trouble before it arrives, so, still hoping for the best, I went upstairs, and began in a leisurely manner to array myself for Lord Sangatte's party.

I had ordered a little dinner for eight o'clock, and while I was discussing the excellent sole and cutlets which the cook sent me up, I further impressed upon the parlour-maid that if Billy arrived during my absence he was to be detained at all costs.

"Tell him," I said, "that I shall be back before long, and that I can put him up for the night. I suppose there is a room ready?"

"Oh yes, sir," replied the parlour-maid; "it's only a question of airing the bed."

"Air it, then," said I; "and, whatever you do, don't let Mr. Logan go till I come back."

I waited on till half-past ten, amusing myself by smoking a couple of cigars, and routing out such of Northcote's clothes as seemed to me suitable for the country. Then, as there was still no sign of Billy, I put on my hat and coat, and, sallying forth from the front door, summoned a taxi, and ordered the man to drive me to Belgrave Square.

Sangatte's house proved to be a big, detached mansion, standing in its own grounds, and occupying the whole of one corner. It had a pillared entrance—a sort of Greek portico, from which a red awning stretched down to the main gate.

There were a number of carriages and motor broughams arriving and departing, with a policeman at the gate signalling to the next as soon as the one in front had deposited its cargo. Whatever his morals might be, Sangatte evidently entertained in style.

My modest taxi rolled up in its turn, and I got out, and mounted the carpeted steps that led into the house. To the left of the hall, which was full of immaculately dressed men and women, the latter blazing with diamonds and displaying a lavish amount of white arms and backs, stood a large anteroom, where a couple of liveried footmen were waiting to relieve us of our coats and hats.

Having got rid of these impediments, I returned to the hall, and slowly made my way towards the staircase, at the top of which Sangatte was presumably receiving his guests. Several people greeted me by name, and one or two beautiful ladies smiled at me across the hall in the most encouraging fashion. It struck me for the first time that Northcote might possibly have left me legacies of a more agreeable nature than those which I had at present encountered!

At last I reached the landing, where a solemn-looking butler who was posted there evidently recognised me.

"Mr. Stuart Northcote," he announced in a magnificent voice.

Lord Sangatte, who, with the assistance of an elderly, grey-haired lady, was welcoming each guest in turn, stepped forward on hearing my name. He was a tall, well-built man of about forty-five, with a heavy, clean-shaven face and hard blue eyes. I took a vigorous dislike to him immediately.

"I'm glad you've turned up, Northcote," he whispered, shaking my hand. "You got my note—eh? I want to have a chat with you as soon as I've got through with this tomfoolery."

"Right you are," I returned. "Where shall I find you?"

"Oh, come to my study," he said hurriedly. "I'll slip away about eleven, and you'll find me there." Then, raising his voice, he added: "I don't think you've ever met my aunt—let me introduce you. Aunt Susan, this is Mr. Northcote."

The smile which the elderly lady gave me could not have been described as ¡effusive even by an optimist, but such as it was I accepted it with a good grace. Indeed, knowing what I did of Northcote, I rather sympathised with the old girl. Sangatte evidently noticed her lack of enthusiasm, for an angry light danced in his eyes. However, he said nothing, and I passed on into the ballroom beyond, discreetly concealing the amusement that I felt.

To the strains of a band, which I could just hear above the loud hum of conversation, a crowded roomful of people were moving spasmodically about in what I believe is technically known as " a Boston." I stood for an instant in the doorway, momentarily dazzled by the blaze of light, the gleam of diamonds, and the wonderfully coloured frocks that kept on flashing past me with a provocative swirl of silken petticoats.

Suddenly I realised that there was someone behind me waiting to go in. I stepped aside, looking up as I did so, and my heart seemed to perform the absurd and inconvenient feat of jumping into my mouth. For, just in front of me, her hand resting lightly on the arm of an elderly man, whose features seemed curiously familiar was Mercia Solano.

CHAPTER X

I WAS so glad to see her that I as nearly as possible made an idiot of myself. Indeed, I was just on the point of stepping forward and recklessly claiming her acquaintance, when something in Mercia's face made me pause. She had gone very pale, and I could see that the hand which was resting on her companion's sleeve had unconsciously tightened. Her troubled eyes looked momentarily into mine with an expression partly of fear, partly, it seemed to me, of relief.

Then she moved on, and the next instant I heard someone behind me pronounce my name. I turned instinctively, and found myself face to face with Lord Lammersfield, the handsome, elderly, debonair states-man who had stopped me on the previous day in Park Lane. In evening dress, and wearing the ribbon of the Garter, he made a strikingly distinguished figure.

"Ah, Northcote," he said, with an easy wave of his hand, "I was just wondering whether you had arrived. It's a mere matter of chance, finding anyone in this human maelstrom."

With an effort I pulled myself together.

"Yes," I said lightly. "Sangatte ought to provide a crier and a bell. Not that the latter would be much use."

Lord Lammersfield smiled cynically. "The human voice," he remarked, "is a very curious thing. Singly, it can be charming ; collectively——" He shrugged his shoulders.

"Collectively," I finished, "it strikes me as the most unpleasant of all animal noises."

"An excellent description," said Lammersfield. "Suppose we exchange it for the smoking-room and a couple of Sangatte's cigarettes. I want to talk over one or two matters, if you can spare me ten minutes."

"Why, certainly," I replied ; and turning from the door of the ballroom, I accompanied Lammersfield across the crowded landing and down a long gallery hung with family portraits. The smoking-room was at the extreme end, and when we entered we found ourselves in solitary possession.

I naturally felt curious as to what the "one or two matters" might be which a Cabinet Minister was anxious to discuss. It was just possible, I reflected, that Northcote might have been mixing himself up with politics, and as I was vastly ignorant of such things myself, I was keenly on my guard lest I should betray the fact by some inept remark.

My mind was soon to be relieved on this point, but in a totally unexpected fashion. As a matter of fact, Lammersfield's opening words baffled me much more than any political observation could possibly have done.

"It's no good beating about the bush, Northcote," he said quietly. "I haven't got the money at present, and it is quite impossible for me to raise it."

If, in my surprise, I didn't blurt out, "What money?" it was more by the grace of Heaven than from any particular intelligence on my part.

"To put matters quite frankly," continued Lammersfield pleasantly, "I am in your hands. If you choose to press me, I shall have to sell up Cranleigh and retire from politics.   The British public will forgive anything on the part of its leaders except adultery or loss of money.   The latter, I believe, is regarded as the greater crime of the two, especially when, as in my case, it arises from a long period of unsuccessful racing.   Should you care to wait, I will pay you directly I have the opportunity.   On the other hand, if my present diabolic fortune pursues me much longer, there will probably be nothing left of Cranleigh for you to realise on."

By this time I had recovered myself sufficiently to grasp the situation.   It was plain that Northcote must have lent money to Lord Lammersfield—a large sum of money, from the way the latter was speaking—and that the nominal day of reckoning was at hand.   What Northcote's object had been I had no idea, but I realised with rapid satisfaction that it put me in the position of being able to do a good turn to a man who might prove extremely useful.   There is nothing more agreeable than being generous with other people's money, and I determined to make the most of my opportunity.

"There is an Indian proverb, Lord Lammersfield," I observed, "which says that 'Hurry is the Devil.'   In the present instance I am inclined to agree with it."

"It would certainly be the devil to me," admitted his lordship frankly.   "My five thousand a year from the Home Office is all that I have to live on at present.   If I can hold out till next year, things ought to right themselves a little.   There will be some insurance money coming in in the spring, and I have a couple of yearlings at Cranleigh, on which Morris is building very high hopes.   Still, we can hardly consider them a trust security!"

I laughed.   If only an average Liberal voter could have overheard his respected leader, what a study his

face would have been.   I began to wonder whether all
Cabinet Ministers were as delightfully human as Lord
Lammersfield.

"Well," I said, knocking the end off my cigarette,
"they are good enough for me.   I rather like a slightly
speculative investment."

If my companion failed to satisfy one or two of the
conventional ideas of a successful British statesman, he
was at least the master of his emotions.   He received
my words without the faintest change of expression.

"It might sound a little ironical to say that I am
deeply indebted to you, Northcote," he answered.   Then
he paused.   "To be quite candid," he added, "I never
expected that you would take this—how shall we put
it?—impersonal attitude.   Your last letter on the
subject——"

"Ah!" I interrupted quickly, inwardly anathematising
Northcote.   "We'll dismiss that last letter if you have
no objection.   I have changed my mind since then."

Lammersfield accepted this eminently true information with a courteous inclination of his head.

"As you please," he said.   "You leave me under an
immense obligation to you.   I can only add that if there
is any matter in which I can be of service to you, now
or at any time, you mustn't hesitate to mention it.   The
Home Secretaryship is a singularly distasteful office to
an intelligent man, but it has at least the merit of
putting one in a position to be occasionally useful to
one's friends."

I smiled.   His lordship's cynical outlook on human
nature and on the privileges of Cabinet rank amused
me intensely.   He was evidently prepared for some
request on my part in return for the favour I had
done him, and I wondered what Northcote would have

asked if he had been in my place. I had no doubt that my enterprising double must have had some purpose at the back of his mind when he originally advanced the money.

Throwing away my cigarette into the fire, I got up from my chair.

"Thanks very much," I said; "but at present I don't think there is anything I want to bother Whitehall about. I shall remember your offer, though. Perhaps some day I may get arrested for exceeding the speed limit."

Lord Lammersfield laughed dryly. "I shall hold myself in readiness for a summons to Holloway," he said, with a bow. "Meanwhile, suppose we return to the scene of festivity. In a weak moment I said I would introduce some protégée of my wife's to several of our leading statesmen; and although, personally, I don't admire the young lady's taste, after all, a promise is a promise."

As fate would have it, almost the first person I saw as we re-entered the ballroom was Mercia. She was standing against the wall, listening rather absently to a sombre-looking gentleman with long grey whiskers whom I recognised from his pictures as one of His Majesty's most incompetent judges. A sudden determination seized me, and I turned to Lammersfield.

"You know everybody," I said. "Who's that pretty girl over there with old Beauchamp?"

He looked across. "Ah yes! charming, isn't she? Beauchamp makes up in taste what he lacks in intelligence. She is a discovery of Lady Tregattock's, I believe—a Miss de Rosen. They are reported to have picked her up somewhere in South America. I will introduce you to her if you like."

With the memory of " Francis " still pleasantly fresh in my mind, this information about Lady Tregattock was, to say the least, a trifle startling. However, Lammersfield's keen eyes were on my face, and I managed to suppress any sign of surprise.

"Well, if it's not bothering you too much," I said carelessly.

"On the contrary," he returned, " I should consider it an amiable duty to rescue any attractive young woman from Beauchamp."

I followed him across the room to where the ill-assorted pair were standing.

"Miss de Rosen," he said, with a courteous bow, " may I have the pleasure of introducing a friend of mine—Mr. Stuart Northcote." Then, turning with a smile to the judge, he added lightly, "Ah, Beauchamp, you're the very man I want to see. Can you spare him a moment, Miss de Rosen? I'll leave Northcote to entertain you."

The thing was done so smoothly and with such delightful dexterity that, almost before I realised it, I was left alone with Mercia, and Lammersfield was strolling off, with his hand on the shoulder of an exceedingly annoyed-looking judge.

"If I am ever tried for my life," I said, with a smile, " I hope Beauchamp won't be on the Bench." Then, without waiting for a reply, I added abruptly, " I want to talk to you. Can we get out of this and find a couple of seats somewhere? "

She accepted my arm, and the mere touch of her hand upon my sleeve filled me with a ridiculous sense of happiness. We made our way through the crowded ballroom and down the broad staircase into the hall below, where desultory carriage-loads of late-comers

were still arriving. To the right of the hall was a
conservatory — a wonderful fairyland of azaleas and
other flowering shrubs; and in the far corner, under the
shelter of a couple of giant palms, I found two comfortable and fairly secluded chairs.

Mercia had seemed very charming to me the other
night, but here, in the softly shaded light which gleamed
upon her bare shoulders and just revealed that strange
look of sorrow and tragedy in her eyes, her beauty held
me in a kind of enchanted silence.

"I have been wondering if I should ever see you
again," I said at last, with a little sigh of satisfaction.

She looked up at me with a sudden flash of anger
that was amazingly becoming.

"Aren't you satisfied yet?" she said bitterly. "You
have made me hate and despise myself for the rest of
my life. Do you suppose that I can ever see you without remembering that I have betrayed my father?"

"If you mean that you would have pleased your
father by putting a bullet through my head," I returned,
" I think you are misjudging him."

She leant forward, her hand resting on the arm of
the chair and her dark eyes fixed almost piteously on
mine. "I wish I understood," she said. "Somehow, I
can't believe that you are lying to me, and yet——"

" And yet?" I echoed, as she paused.

She turned away with a little gesture of despair. " I
pray to God," she said wearily, "that after to-night we
shall never meet again."

" There is a good chance of your prayer being granted,"
I remarked—"at least, if one may judge by my experience yesterday."

She looked up quickly. "What do you mean?"

I shrugged my shoulders. "Only that a butler I

engaged in the morning made a highly creditable
attempt to murder me in the middle of the night."

I saw her face turn pale. "Oh!" she said, and she
laid her hand upon her breast. "Were you—were you
hurt?" she faltered.

"No," I said, "I wasn't hurt. I am afraid the butler
was, rather; but that was his fault. It's so difficult to
see what one's doing in the dark." Then I paused and
looked her full in the face. "The curious thing is," I
added, "that the man was sent to me with excellent
references from Sir Henry Tregattock."

She met my gaze without flinching, but the last vestige
of colour had left her cheeks.

"Sir Henry Tregattock?" she repeated in a kind of
mechanical way.

"That's right," I went on, assuming a cheerful, confidential tone. "I got the fellow through Seagrave's—
those people just off Hanover Square. There was no
mistake about it, because I'd been round there myself
in the morning, and Seagrave had assured me that not
only was the reference all that it ought to be, but that
he had rung up Tregattock, and had it confirmed over
the telephone."

She started very slightly, recovering herself at once.
"Yes," she said in a whisper.

I lay back in my chair, rather enjoying myself, though
I must confess I felt a bit of a brute. 'Now we come
to the interesting part of the story," I said. "This
morning I learned from Seagrave that not only was the
reference a forged one, but that somebody else had
actually answered the telephone in Tregattock's absence.
Sir Henry himself, apparently, knew nothing whatever
about the matter."

She was silent for a moment, her brows slightly

knitted and a puzzled expression in her eyes. "I don't understand," she said at last. "Why did you want a new butler? The other night — there was a man there——"

"Ah, yes," I interrupted; "the excellent Milford. But, you see, some of your friends had been kind enough to poison him."

"Poison him!" she echoed; and then, leaning forward, she stared at me in obviously genuine horror. "Do you mean that he is dead?"

"Oh dear, no," I said lightly. "We are rather a tough couple, Milford and I. Still, they did their best —and, after all, you can't throw stones, you know! You missed me shockingly at five yards."

I am afraid the last little pleasantry was rather wasted. Mercia had momentarily covered her face with her hands, and when she took them down I saw that her beautiful eyes were alight with anger and indignation.

"But this is dreadful!" she broke out. "I did not know—I—I had heard something, but indeed I did not know. It——" She checked herself abruptly.

"It was the genial M. Guarez, no doubt," I said. "Just the kind of thing I should expect from a man with a name like that. I really didn't imagine that you had anything to do with it."

"What time," she asked, speaking rather more calmly, "did these people ring up the telephone?"

I shook my head. "I don't know the exact hour, but I can find out. Anyhow, it was on Wednesday afternoon."

"Ah!" she said, with a quick little intake of her breath. Then she paused. "You know that I am living with the Tregattocks?" she added.

"Lammersfield has just told me," I answered. "But

it doesn't matter. I am going down to Woodford to-
morrow, to stay with Maurice Furnivall, so you are not
likely to have the distressing experience of coming
across me again—at all events for a few days."

She looked at me strangely. " You think you will be
safer there ? " she asked.

I laughed. " Well, things can't be much more strenuous than they are in town ; and, after all, Maurice is my
cousin, you know."

" Your cousin ! " she repeated, half incredulously ; and
then a sudden light of revelation dawned in her eyes.
With a quick gesture, she leaned forward and laid her
hand on my sleeve. " Don't go," she said hurriedly.
" I——"

At that moment there was a sound of footsteps in the
hall, and round the corner of the palm trees came the
ever-to-be-accursed figure of Mr. Justice Beauchamp.

"Ah, Miss de Rosen," he began, with the kind of
ponderous fatuity that passes for humour on the Bench,
" I find you, like the Arab maiden, beneath the palms."

Mercia, dear thing, smiled in her most charming
manner. "And for the same reason," she said lightly.
" The ballroom is unbearably hot."

" Without the other attractions of the desert," I added.
" There, at least, one's toes are not trodden on."

" Nevertheless," observed the judge, addressing Mercia
and ostentatiously disregarding me, " with your permission, I am going to take you away from your oasis. On
my way to rejoin you, I met Sir Henry. He is anxious
for a moment's conversation with you, and I promised
to bring you back with me."

He offered his arm, and, after hesitating for the fraction of a second, Mercia got up gracefully from her
chair and accepted it.

As she did so, she flashed one swift glance at me
"You must tell me the rest of your story later in the
evening, Mr. Northcote," she said.

I bowed, and then stood there for a moment, looking
after them, as the garrulous old gentleman, who obviously imagined that he had scored off me, conducted her
triumphantly out of the conservatory.

They had certainly left me something to think about.
That Mercia was living with the Tregattocks, under
another name, was in itself a startling bit of information ;
while, taken in conjunction with the forged testimonial
and its fraudulent confirmation, it began to throw light
on several previously rather dark corners.   And yet I
fully believed her denial of any complicity in the Milford
affair.   Of course she had tried to shoot me, but, somehow or other, that seemed a very different sort of thing.
Poisoning butlers was a branch of assassination with
which I could not associate Mercia at all.

. I began to wonder how she had got to know the
Tregattocks.   Lammersfield had said something about
their having picked her up in South America, and this
fitted in accurately enough with my suspicions of the
other evening,   Her own phrase, " the Satyr of Culebra,"
suddenly recurred to my mind, and I remembered that
I had never hunted up the place on the map, as I had
meant to.   Tregattock, I knew, had been Minister in
Bolivia for some years, so it was more than possible that
he too was mixed up in my unknown and apparently
very shady past.

Then there was Maurice, whom at present I was quite
unable to fit into the picture.   Mercia had, for some
reason or other, given me a pretty plain hint that that
amiable young gentleman was not to be trusted—and,
indeed, Northcote's words and my own instincts had

already led me to a similar conclusion. And yet, if he
was a cousin, and one whom Northcote had apparently
always treated well, why on earth should he be mixed
up with Mercia and those Dago friends of hers, who,
probably for excellent reasons of their own, were so
eager to finish my career? It was just possible that, as
my nearest relation, he might have an eye on my ill-
gotten gains; but one hesitated to accept quite such a
damning theory even about Maurice.

I was still puzzling my brains over all these infernal
complications when a quick step sounded on the tessel-
lated pavement, and, looking up, I saw Lord Sangatte
coming briskly towards me.

"Good!" he said. "I thought I might find you here.
Come along into the study."

To tell the truth, in the excitement of meeting Mercia,
I had forgotten all about the appointment he had made,
and his running across me in this opportune fashion was
just a stroke of luck. However, naturally enough, I
didn't inform his lordship of this fact, but accompanied
him across the conservatory towards a door on the
farther side, which he opened with a small Yale key. I
was certainly having a most entertaining evening.

Sangatte's "study" was just the sort of room I
should have expected. That is to say that, with the
exception of a large writing-desk, there were no indica-
tions that it had ever been the scene of that severe
mental energy suggested by its title. Its chief furniture
seemed to be a plentiful supply of easy-chairs, a large
tantalus spirit-stand, and a very professional-looking
card-table in the farther corner.

My noble host started the proceedings by carefully
locking the door. Then, observing that "a drink
wouldn't be a bad thing," he poured out a couple of

8

stiff brandies-and-sodas, and handed one of them to me.

"I wanted that," he said, setting down the empty glass. "I'm just about played out, Northcote, I can tell you. A week of this awful entertaining business would finish me. Have a smoke?"

He held out a cigar-box, and I helped myself to a very promising Laranaga.

"Yes," I said, "I can imagine a pleasanter way of spending the evening."

He laughed sourly. "Well, they're going to pay for it—that's one consolation."

Crossing the room to the desk, he opened a drawer, and took out several sheets of typewritten paper.

"Here it is," he said, handing them over to me. "Rosedale and I roughed it out after our last talk with you. I expect you'd like to take it home with you, but you might run through it first, and see if anything strikes you now. I shall be seeing Rosedale again to-morrow."

With a pleasing sense of anticipation, I accepted the papers, and settled myself down comfortably in one of the easy-chairs. One glance showed me that I held in my hand the rough draft of a prospectus, for across the top of the first page, in big capital letters, ran the following announcement:—

THE AMALGAMATED GOLDFIELDS
OF SOUTH AMERICA LTD.

CAPITAL £2,000,000.

CHAPTER XI

I LOOKED at it for a moment with a kind of dazzled admiration. Then, after taking a pull at my cigar to restore my composure, I read through the whole precious document from beginning to end.

It appeared to me to be one of the finest and boldest works of fiction that had ever fallen into my hands. Briefly speaking, it commended in glowing terms to the notice of the British Public a new and magnificent group of goldmines which it declared had just been discovered in the northern provinces of the Argentine. Being fairly well acquainted with the district myself, I felt almost certain that the statement was a colossal lie, but I must admit that the evidence produced was extraordinarily convincing. The Board of Directors consisted of Stuart Northcote, Esq., Lord Sangatte, Sir Matthew Rosedale, and Señor Bonito Morales, the ex-President of the Republic. The latter gentleman I knew to be one of the completest scoundrels that even South America has produced, a fact which confirmed my suspicions as to the fraudulent nature of the entire business.

While I was reading, Lord Sangatte paced up and down the room behind me, apparently trying to recover from the unwonted exertion of being civil to a large number of people in succession. As I laid down the paper he turned impatiently and inquired what I thought of it.

"It seems fairly convincing," I said coolly, "but we might improve it a little yet."

"Well, there will be the notices in the financial papers to go in," answered Sangatte. "Rosedale is seeing about that. He says he can do the whole thing for twenty thousand in shares."

It sounded a fairly cheap way of swindling two millions out of the pockets of the British Public, so I contented myself with an approving nod.

"And then there'll be Lammersfield," went on Sangatte. "If you can only work your business with him, the thing's as good as done. With an ex-Home Secretary on the Board, the shares will go like hot cakes. I know the idiots."

It only needed this illuminating observation to make the whole affair plain to me. I saw at once that North-cote must have advanced the money to Lord Lammers-field in order to compel that genial nobleman to fall in with his schemes. As Home Secretary, it would, of course, be impossible for the latter to accept a Director-ship of any kind, so Northcote's plan had evidently been to compel him to resign office by a judicious mixture of bullying and bribery. With Lammersfield's name on the Board, "The Amalgamated Goldfields of South America" would, as Sangatte observed, sell "like hot cakes." It was a pretty little scheme, worthy indeed of the high opinion I had already formed of my talented double.

"Lammersfield will be all right," I said, with a gentle irony that was wasted on my companion. "He is in my hands."

Sangatte grinned evilly. "I thought as much. I saw you talking to him to-night. You're a good man of business, Northcote; I will say that for you."

I accepted the compliment with a gracious smile, though I felt a severe temptation to show his lordship that as a man of action I was still more accomplished. Indeed, with the honourable exception of Maurice, I had never met anyone whom I felt a more ardent desire to kick.

Blissfully unaware of his peril, Lord Sangatte helped himself to a second drink.

"I think I told you in my note," he said, "that I'd fixed up about the *Seagull*. That old devil, Morton, wanted a thousand for her, but I beat him down to nine hundred in the end. She's a decent boat, for her size, but——"

His interesting discourse was suddenly cut short by a discreet knock. With an irritable exclamation, he crossed the room and flung open the door.

"Well, what is it?" he demanded.

The footman, who was standing on the mat, bowed apologetically. "I beg your pardon, my lord, but her ladyship has sent me to ask you if you could come upstairs."

I regret to say that Lord Sangatte swore. "Very well," he added; "tell her I'll be up in a minute." Then, shutting the door and turning to me, he observed graciously: "I suppose I must go back and make myself pleasant to all this scum. You take the prospectus and let me know what you want altered."

I put the papers in my pocket, and followed him out into the conservatory, where, before we had taken a couple of steps, we were pounced on by a stout and elderly lady who made up for her regrettable lack of costume by an almost painful display of jewels.

With a muttered excuse, Sangatte bolted, leaving me to face the fire.

I had not the remotest notion who my new friend might be, but, fortunately, my ignorance did not matter, for she started talking at once with a velocity and vehemence that gave me no chance of replying, even had I wished to. As far as I could gather, Northcote had accepted some invitation from her which he had failed to comply with, for she began rebuking me with an arch playfulness that I found very distressing.

"Of course I know what you great financiers are— the terrible demands you have on your time. We poor Society people have to catch you when we can. But, my dear Mr. Northcote, you can't think how disappointed poor Minnie was. The silly child has taken quite a fancy to you—ha, ha, ha! She was quite rude to poor dear Lord Clevedon, who has been really most attentive to her. But girls are all alike, aren't they? I always say that the thing we haven't got is just the thing we want. Terribly hot, isn't it? They seem to have asked everyone in London. I was just saying——"

To save my reason, I cut short the torrential outpour by asking the good lady whether I couldn't have the felicity of taking her in to supper. She jumped at my offer with avidity, and, still bubbling out an inexhaustible store of commonplace, accepted my escort upstairs to the big room where Sangatte's guests were restoring their spent energies.

On the way, through the interruption of a ferret-faced youth who waylaid us on the stairs, I discovered that my companion's name was Mrs. Garnett. Beyond arousing in me a certain vague sympathy for Mr. Garnett, this information was not of much use, for the only Garnett I had ever known was a gentleman whom I had seen shot in a saloon brawl in Villa Maria some years previously.

Under the circumstances, I refrained from inquiring whether he was any relation, contenting myself with looking after my companion's wants, and interjecting an occasional hearty " Yes " or " No " whenever there was a sufficient break in the monologue to warrant such an intrusion.

We must have been in the supper-room for a good half-hour altogether, during the course of which I consumed the best part of a bottle of champagne, and, as far as I remember, pledged myself definitely to come down to Staines on the following Saturday and relieve the vexation of the amorous Minnie. Of course I had no intention of doing anything of the kind, but even my natural affection for the truth had become temporarily paralysed, and I should have agreed to anything rather than attempt to argue.

On returning to the ballroom, Mrs. Garnett's attention was happily diverted by some rash stranger. I took the opportunity of escaping, but only to fall into the clutch of the aged Director of the London General Traffic Company, who had sat next me at our merry little meeting on the previous afternoon.

The old gentleman buttonholed me with such obvious gratification that, although I was very anxious to find Mercia and continue our conversation, I didn't like to hurt his feelings by being too curt with him. When eventually I got away, the ballroom was filling up again, but there was no sign of the one beautiful face for which my eyes were hungering. I tried both the landing and the two long corridors where people were sitting out, but I drew blank in each case. If Mercia was not at supper, it was evident that she must be in the conservatory, so down I went, praying devoutly that no more of Northcote's entertaining acquaintances would waylay me on the road.

To my surprise, I found the place quite empty. I suppose the combination of supper and a ballroom in which it was now possible to dance were attractive enough to keep people upstairs; anyhow, I took advantage of my solitude by seating myself in a retired corner, close to the door of Sangatte's study, and indulging in a surreptitious cigarette.

It was possible, I reflected, that Mercia might have gone home. I would have one more look round, and if this proved to be the case, I determined that I would follow her example. Somehow or other, I had a sort of presentiment that Billy was waiting for me in Park Lane, and the thought of the cheery grin with which he would receive my astounding confidence made me long to hurry up our meeting.

As for my—— What was that? From within Sangatte's room had come a sudden faint cry, followed almost immediately by the muffled crash of an overturning chair. I leaped to my feet, listening intently, and then again—Good Lord! it was Mercia's voice! In one stride I had crossed the intervening space and gripped the handle of the door. It was locked, but I was in no mood for ceremony. Stepping back, I gave it the full benefit of my fourteen stone, and with a crash of splintering wood it flew open before me.

Sangatte was standing in the centre of the room, his face flushed and angry. Mercia, panting, indignant, and pale, leaned against the mantelpiece. When his lordship saw who it was that had so rudely disturbed his privacy, his expression changed momentarily to one of utter bewilderment. Then, with a furious scowl, he advanced towards me.

"What do you think you're doing?" he demanded, in a hoarse whisper.

I took absolutely no notice of him.

"Miss de Rosen," I said, in my most cheerful manner, "I think this is the dance you were kind enough to promise me."

Mercia laughed softly.   "I think it must be," she said.

I stepped forward, and for the fraction of a second Sangatte barred my path.   Then his good angel must have whispered in his ear, for he moved suddenly aside, and, without so much as glancing at him, I advanced and offered my arm to Mercia.

"I am sorry I was a trifle late," I said calmly.

With a charming little smile, she put her hand upon my sleeve.   "You are always the soul of promptness, Mr. Northcote," she said.

If looks could kill, we should neither of us have reached the door; but Providence having fortunately arranged otherwise, Sangatte's murderous expression had no other effect beyond adding to my secret felicity. As we went out, I looked at him over my shoulder.

"I'll come back and have a chat with you, if you'll wait here, Sangatte," I said.

He made no answer, and I conducted Mercia into the conservatory, closing the somewhat unhappy-looking door behind me.

"Our acquaintance," I observed, "seems fated to be rather an exciting one."

"It seems fated," she returned, "that I should be under an obligation to you.   I suppose the gods are amusing themselves at our expense."

I laughed contentedly.   "I don't grudge them their fun," I said.   "I was beginning to think you had gone home, and that our interesting little conversation would have to remain unfinished."

She stopped for a moment, and looked quickly round, as if to make sure that there was no one within hearing.

"I meant what I said," she whispered hurriedly. "Don't go to Woodford. I—I can't explain to you; indeed I am wrong even in warning you; but make some excuse to-morrow—don't go."

"If we went upstairs and found a couple of chairs," I suggested, "perhaps——"

"No, no," she interrupted quickly. "I can't stay here any longer. Sir Henry is waiting to take me back; and, in any case, I could tell you nothing more."

We had reached the big hall, where several people were standing about, apparently preparing to leave. Amongst them I noticed the elderly white-haired man who had been Mercia's companion when she first entered the ballroom. I realised now that he must be Sir Henry Tregattock, which explained to me why his face had seemed familiar. He looked much older, however, than when I had met him in La Paz ten years before.

He saw us at once and came forward to meet us.

"Oh, there you are, Mercia," he said. "I was wondering what had happened to you. I don't want to hurry you, but——"

He stopped abruptly. His eyes were fixed on mine, and he had suddenly drawn himself up with a gesture in which amazement and hostility were very evenly blended.

Mercia had gone rather white. "You—you know Mr. Northcote," she faltered. "I will go and put on my things. I shan't be a minute."

She vanished from my side, leaving me in what appeared likely to be a somewhat embarrassing position. It seemed to me highly improbable that Sir Henry could possibly remember me from our five minutes' conversation in the dim past, and, in any case, if he did, there was no earthly reason why he should have bristled up in this alarming fashion. It struck me at once that he must be mistaking me for my double.

" I think Miss de Rosen is right, Mr. Northcote," he remarked, with icy politeness. " We have met before, but under rather different circumstances."

"Yes," I said boldly. " I had the pleasure of five minutes' conversation with you in La Paz ten years ago."

His eyebrows lifted the fraction of an inch. "Indeed ! " he remarked dryly. " But I was referring to a somewhat later date. Possibly your experiences in San Luca were not sufficiently pleasant to warrant your retaining any very clear recollection of them."

This was what Billy would have called " a jab in the plexus," but I received it without wincing.

" I have never been in San Luca in my life," I replied boldly.

Sir Henry Tregattock's real answer was written legibly in his eyes. What he actually said was almost as direct.

" I fear San Luca is not as fortunate as you make out."

It was the first time that I had ever been called a liar, at all events by a man, and for a second my temper almost got the better of me. I took a step forward, and then I recollected my promise to Northcote. With a big effort I crushed down my anger.

" It is at least plain that you have retired from diplomacy, Sir Henry," I said.

We were both so intent upon paying compliments that for a moment neither of us noticed that Mercia had returned. It must have been fairly evident to her that the situation was a trifle strained, and she had doubtless hurried over her preparations to prevent things from reaching any distressing crisis. In a white satin opera cloak, with a light Indian shawl thrown over her hair, she looked more beautiful than ever. Coming up to Sir Henry, she laid her hand lightly on his arm.

"Shall I ask them to call the carriage?" she said.

He turned at once, and with a bow to Mercia I stepped back into the conservatory and left them together.

My brisk little interview with Sir Henry had put me in rather an aggressive mood, and it occurred to me that the promotion of a clearer understanding with Lord Sangatte would be an agreeable way of spending the next few minutes. So, without wasting time, I crossed the conservatory and knocked at his door.

"Come in," he said.

He must have guessed who it was, for there was a distinct and regrettable lack of cordiality about the invitation. However, I accepted it for what it was worth, and, entering the room, closed the door behind me.

Sangatte was standing with his back to the fireplace, looking about as amiable as a tiger with a headache. I strolled up to him, and stationed myself in an equally impressive attitude against the end of the sofa.

"Look here, Northcote," he broke out, making an evident effort to keep his temper, "I'd like to know what on earth you think you're playing at."

"We are both looking for information," I returned

"I want to know what you mean by insulting Miss de Rosen."

He scowled at me for a moment, and then laughed— a singularly unpleasant, suggestive sort of laugh.

"Oh, that's how the land lies, is it!"   Then he paused.

My fingers itched to take him by the throat and bang his head against the wall, but, fortunately for us both perhaps, that cursed promise of mine to Northcote held me back.

"Well, I don't know what you think about it," he said surlily, "but it seems to me that you and I can't afford to quarrel about a woman just at present.   Women and business don't mix."

"I think they will in this case," I said, "unless you play the game a little straighter."

He favoured me with a glance which no one could have described as affectionate.

"You're taking a queer line, Northcote. I'm not a safe man to threaten, as you ought to know."

I laughed. "If it comes to that," I said, "you're not altogether ignorant about me."

It was a chance shot, for at present I was quite un-aware how much of my double's unsavoury career Sangatte was really acquainted with.   That his know-ledge was fairly extensive, however, was plain from his answer to my remark.

"I'll give you credit for being a pretty complete scoundrel, Northcote," he observed graciously, "but, all the same, I tell you plainly I'm not going to stand any interference in this business.   You play your hand, and I'll play mine."

"My only objection to that," I observed, "is that your hand seems to be such an excessively dirty one."

He flushed hotly. "It's a new thing to find you play-ing the moralist," he sneered. "What's the matter? Do you want to marry the girl?"

I kept my temper. "Suppose we leave Miss de Rosen's name out of it," I suggested. "We'll say that, until the Company's launched, it will be safer for you, and better for business generally, if you can manage to restrain your emotions within decent limits."

There must have been a dangerous note in my voice, for, angry as he was, I could see that my words had sobered him. He made one last effort at bluff, how-ever.

"If you think you can frighten me," he declared, "you've got your money on the wrong horse. This isn't South America, you know."

I smiled. "If it was, I shouldn't have troubled to warn you," I said pleasantly.

There was a short silence, Sangatte eyeing me mal-evolently and, I suppose, weighing up the situation. At last he shrugged his shoulders.

"Well, have it your own way," he snarled. "I'm not going to wreck the Company for the sake of any woman in the world."

"That's right," I said cheerfully. "I thought you'd take a reasonable view of the matter."

As I spoke, the big timepiece in the corner gave out a deep, solitary tang. It was one o'clock. I remembered that Billy might possibly be waiting for me.

"Well, as we've settled that little matter," I observed, getting up from the sofa, "I think I shall go home." Then I paused. "Good-night," I added. "I must thank you for a most delightful evening."

Lord Sangatte's expression was not lacking in elo-quence, but as he condescended to make no reply, I did not prolong the conversation. Leaving the room, I strolled across the hall to where I had left my coat and hat, and putting them on with the assistance of the powdered footman, I went down the steps and out into the Square.

The stimulating events of the evening were jostling each other so joyously in my mind that for the moment I had quite forgotten my ever-present danger. I walked briskly along, reflecting over the knowledge that I had acquired, and trying to straighten things out into their proper relation with each other.

I now had a pretty good idea of how I stood both with Lammersfield and Sangatte, while my acquaintance with Mercia seemed to be progressing on the most desirable lines. Whether in her heart she still believed me guilty of all the bloodthirsty crimes she had originally laid to my charge I could not quite make up my mind. If she did, it was all the more encouraging that she should have warned me against Maurice.

It suddenly struck me that I had never told her about the mysterious wire, which, without doubt, had been the means of saving my life. That the warning had been a genuine one was now fairly obvious. Could she have sent it herself? and if so, how did it fit in with her almost passionate disclaimer of any knowledge of the Milford affair?

I racked my brains vainly over the problem for several minutes, and then my thoughts flitted to Sir Henry Tregattock. Brief as my interview had been with him, it had left me with my first gleam of information as to Northcote's past. San Luca! So that was where the key to the mystery lay! And a devilish likely place too, I reflected, unless rumour had been more than usually misleading.

I began to regret that in my wanderings in South America I had never penetrated into the festive region in question. All I knew about it was that, after having been for two years in the grip of that infamous fili-buster, Ignace Prado, its worthy citizens had finally succeeded in blowing him and his palace sky-high, and in selecting another President more to their taste. Very likely Northcote had been mixed up with this ruffian, and if so, there was some excuse for M. Guarez and the other gentlemen who were so anxious to murder me.

The thought of being murdered suddenly brought me back to my immediate surroundings. I had left the house in such a whirl of various emotions that it had never occurred to me I was doing an exceedingly foolish thing in walking home alone at this hour of night.

Supposing I had been watched and followed! In-stinctively I turned round and looked sharply back down the long curve of lighted pavement. I was just in that short but rather desolate stretch behind St. George's Hospital — an ideal spot for anyone who wanted to stick a knife into a passing stranger without arousing public interest.

My inspection, however, proved reassuring. There was no sign of any impassioned Dago creeping stealthily in my tracks; indeed, the whole thoroughfare looked about as deserted and peaceful as a London street possibly could.

Stepping out into the roadway, and keeping a watchful eye each side of me, I quickly covered the remaining hundred yards that separated me from Hyde Park Corner. Here, as usual, despite the lateness of the hour, there was a certain amount of life and movement. A stolid-looking policeman was moving slowly down the Park railing, four or five belated taxis were standing in the gutter, while a cheerfully illuminated coffee-stall seemed to be doing a brisk business amongst the drivers and their touts.

With a comforting feeling of security I crossed the road, and set off up Park Lane. The full distance was only about one hundred yards, and I had covered perhaps three-quarters of this, and was just getting out my latch-key when, without the slightest warning, the thing happened.

From the dark shadow of a doorway a noiseless figure suddenly leaped out on me with the fierce swiftness of a panther. I saw the gleam of a knife, and at the same instant I lashed out with my fist—I think the quickest and most savage blow I have struck in my life.

9

CHAPTER XII

WE must have got home together. I felt a sharp pain in my shoulder, like the touch of a red-hot iron, and my assailant staggered back five yards and fetched up against the wall with a bang that echoed across the street. As he did so, there was a clatter of footsteps, and down the pavement came the figure of a man, sprinting towards us with silent but business-like rapidity.

The gentleman who had disturbed me did not wait for further developments. He must have been a tough soul, for, despite his collision ·with the wall, he set off like a hare, twisting away round the corner to the left, and disappearing from sight before the newcomer could reach us.

Directly the latter came under the full glare of the nearest electric lamp, I saw it was Billy. I gave a whoop of joy, which pulled him up short in his tempestuous career.

"Burton!" he cried. "Gad! I might have known it." Then he burst out laughing. "Where's the other chap?" he demanded. "Have you eaten him?"

"No, Billy," I said. "He's gone—vamoosed. He didn't like the look of you." Then a sharp pain flickered through my shoulder. "I believe he's punctured me, though," I added ruefully.

In a moment Billy was by my side. "Bad?" he demanded sharply. "Can you wait while I fetch him back?"

I laughed and shook my head. "I don't want him, Billy," I said; "thanks all the same. Give us an arm and let's get back to the house. It's all right—I'm not booked this journey."

"Not by a long way," cried Billy stoutly. "It would take a pickaxe to kill you. Come along, and we'll have a squint at it."

I could feel the blood running rather freely down my arm, so, without wasting any more time, I accepted the support he offered, and we toddled up the pavement as far as my gate. I was still holding the latch-key in my hand, but there was no need of it, for the front door was wide open.

"Hullo, Billy," I said; "have you been entertaining in my absence?"

"I'll tell you all about it in a minute," he replied. "Damages first, though. You may have got it worse than you think."

"It feels messy," I admitted. "Shut the door and let's go up to the study."

What Billy doesn't know about knife-wounds may be justly regarded as superfluous information. He quickly but carefully relieved me of my dress-clothes, and then, slitting up the rest with a pair of scissors, brought the injured portion of my anatomy to light. It consisted of an ugly-looking cut just on the outside of my arm, from which the blood was slowly welling in languid spurts. A brief examination, however, removed the frown from his brow.

"It's nothing," he said; "only a small vein. I'll dodge that up in no time."

"Don't speak in such a disappointed way, Billy," I retorted. " I'm quite satisfied."

He grinned, and, taking out his handkerchief, tied it tightly round my arm. Then, going into the bedroom, he emerged a moment later with a basin of warm water, a clean towel, and a bottle of listerine.

"You seem to know your way about," I observed.

" I ought to," he answered. " I've been waiting here for you the last three hours. Now look out for squalls —I may hurt you a bit."

Ten minutes later, bandaged up in the best professional style, I was lying peacefully on the sofa, while Billy mixed a couple of brandies-and-sodas to relieve our respective fatigue.

"You're in the chair," I said, accepting the drink which he handed across. " Get your yarn off first and then I'll talk."

Billy shrugged his shoulders. " My bit won't take long," he said. "I only got your note at nine o'clock to-night. Those Maxwell people sent for me to come up to Liverpool, and when I got there, they kept me hanging about for twenty-four hours, and then refused to give me the job."

" I hope you remonstrated," I said gently.

Billy smiled. " Old Maxwell knows my opinion of him—if that's any comfort. Anyhow, I got back to London feeling a bit sick and wishing I'd fixed up with you, and there was your blessed note sitting in the glass. I jumped into a cab and came round here at once. The girl who let me in said you were at some party or something, and that I was to wait and sleep here. Well, I waited till a quarter to twelve, and then I rang for her and asked her whether you were making a night of it. She said she didn't know, and she looked so infernally sleepy that I told her she'd better go to bed, and that I'd sit up for you. She hummed and hawed a bit, and said she had something important to tell you. 'Well, whatever it is,' I said, 'it will keep till the morning;' and finally she went off and left me here with the brandy. I stuck it till about one o'clock—then I got rather fed up and went down to the front door for a breath of air. I'd only been there about two minutes when I suddenly saw a kind of dog-fight going on, and, knowing your warlike nature, I guessed it was probably you. So I jogged along to see what was up, and—and here we are."

"And here we are, Billy," I echoed, "and here's your very good health."

We drank to each other in silence, and then Billy put down his glass.

"And now," he said, "perhaps you'll be kind enough to explain. Last time I saw you, you were broke to the wide, and just setting off to the States. Now I find you living in Park Lane like a giddy millionaire, and calling yourself Stuart Northcote. What's it mean, you old ruffian ?"

I finished my brandy-and-soda and settled myself comfortably back amongst the cushions. "I will tell you what it means," I said; "but you're not to interrupt me till I've done."

Then slowly, carefully, and, I think, without leaving out any important detail, I described to him everything which had taken place since we parted in Leicester Square. Billy sat and listened in silence, his head resting on his hand and his eyes fixed on mine. It was not until I had finished that he ventured on his one embracive criticism.

"Well, I'm hanged," he remarked.

He rose from his chair, and with his hands in his pockets paced two or three times up and down the room. Finally he broke into a long, low, delighted chuckle.

"Lord!" he said; "it's—it's colossal!"

"I thought you would be pleased," I replied contentedly.

"Pleased!" He stopped his perambulation. "It's the most gorgeous thing I've ever struck in my life. You were always a nailer at finding trouble, but this beats the band."

"And you'll come and see me through, Billy?"

He brought his fist down with a bang on the table. "I'm with you, my son," he said, "to your last half-penny."

There was a short pause, while Billy, overcome with the magnificence of his emotions, again attacked the brandy.

"Now let me see if I've got it right," he began, resuming his progress up and down the room. "You think that Maurice What's-his-name — this cousin of yours—is in with the gang that are trying to put you through it?"

"Well, it was by his advice I engaged Francis," I pointed out.

"And I'm to come down with you to-morrow and put up at the nearest pub—eh?"

"That's right," I said. "You see, I'm not much afraid of anything happening to me in the house. However much of a scoundrel Maurice may be, he's not the sort to run his neck into a noose if he can help it. My own idea is that some of these gentle Dagoes who have been making things so lively up here will probably follow me down and try to arrange a convenient accident.

Maurice was talking a lot about the excellence of the shooting."

" I see," said Billy thoughtfully. " And that's where I shall come in."

" Precisely. Between us we ought to be able to scent any trouble that's hanging around. I've got my mark pretty plainly on one of the beauties already."

" I wish we knew who you were," remarked Billy, after pondering over the situation for a moment. " It would simplify matters so—wouldn't it? It must be something to do with San Luca. Let's get out a map and have a squint at the hole."

" Yes, Billy," I said, " and hunt up a place called Culebra. I'm the ' Satyr of Culebra,' according to Mercia, and I should like to know exactly where my happy home is."

Billy searched through the bookshelves, and lugged out a big atlas and Gazetteer. " Here we are !" he said, turning up the index. " Culebra 10–35, 85–38. Great Scott ! It's in Costa Rica."

" That doesn't help us much," I observed.

" The funny thing is," said Billy, " that I'm sure I've heard the phrase somewhere — ' the Satyr of Culebra.' "

" Perhaps they breed them there," I suggested. " It sounds a likely place."

" And here's San Luca," he went on, turning back to a map of South America. " Let's see what they say about it. ' An inland republic, bordered by Brazil and the Argentine. Population, 300,000, including Indians —composed of a few negroes, and whites of Spanish and mixed descent.' "

" That's M. Guarez all right," I commented.

" ' President,' " he read out, " ' General Silveira de Selis, succeeded the late Ignace Prado, who had defeated and murdered the first President, Manuel Solano.' "

"What!" I almost shouted. "By Gad! that settles it! Mercia Solano must be his daughter, and there's no doubt that my bright double must have been one of Ignace's blackguards. No wonder the poor girl wanted to shove a bullet into me!"

Billy laughed. "It does look rather like it. All the same, she must be a pretty venomous damsel, I should think."

"She's a darling, Billy," I said firmly. "And I won't hear a word against her. I like a girl with plenty of spirit."

"You've got one," retorted Billy grimly. "You'll make a pretty pair between you." Then he got up and looked at his watch. "You ought to turn in now, Jack," he added, "if we're going to start at half-past ten. That jab of yours will be all right in the morning, but you've lost a bit of blood, and you'll want some sleep—tough as you are."

"You're right, Doctor," I said reluctantly, for, strenuous as my evening had been, I didn't feel in the least like bed. "We'll continue these interesting speculations tomorrow on our way down."

"By the way," said Billy, "what about my traps?"

"Oh, that's all right," I answered, getting up carefully from the sofa. "We'll stop the car somewhere and buy you a bag and a toothbrush. Money doesn't count these days."

"Good," said Billy. "I want a new outfit badly."

I showed him his room first, and then, coming into mine, he helped me to finish undressing without disturbing the bandage. Beyond locking both doors, I took no further precautions. I felt that even M. Guarez and his friends must have an occasional evening off, and that after my little dust-up outside I might reckon on a few peaceful hours.

My hope proved to be well founded. I slept right through the remainder of the night without interruption, and was only awakened next morning by the tapping of the pretty housemaid at my door.

As before, I jumped out of bed and let her in. I remembered, of course, what Billy had said on the previous evening about her having something important to tell me, but my first glimpse of her expression would have made this fact quite plain to me.

"Well," I said, bracing myself up, "what is it now?"

She put down the tea beside my bed. "If you please, sir," she said, "do you know what's happened to Mr. Milford?"

I stared at her in amazement. "Bless my soul!" I ejaculated, "you don't mean to say that he's in trouble again?"

"He went away last night, sir, soon after you left the house, and he's never come back."

I digested this startling information in silence.

"Went away!" I repeated at last. "How did he go away? He was much too seedy to walk, surely?"

She shook her head. "I don't know about that, sir. A boy brought a note for him, and he went away at once in a cab—a taxi-cab, sir."

I began to laugh. I really couldn't help it. "Well," I said, "Mr. Milford about takes the biscuit."

The pretty housemaid looked at me in a rather startled fashion. "Perhaps he's funny in his head, sir. Cook and me thought that perhaps he didn't rightly know what he was doing. He seemed very queer, sir."

I nodded. "I shouldn't wonder if you've hit it," I said.

As a matter of fact, her theory didn't strike me as being at all a probable one, but for the moment I could think of nothing else to say.

"You might ask Mr. Logan to come in," I added, as she prepared to withdraw. "We'll see about Milford as soon as I get up."

A moment later Billy came in, blinking, in his pyjamas.

"This is a nice game, Billy," I said. "We've lost Milford now." Then I proceeded to tell him what I had just learned.

The comic side seemed to strike him as forcibly as it did me. Anyhow, he sat down on the bed and grinned at me cheerfully.

"There's no monotony about this job," he observed; "that's one thing to be said in its favour. What on earth can have happened to the chap?"

I shook my head. "Goodness knows," I said, "unless he's been decoyed away and spifflicated by the gentle Guarez. I should hardly have thought he'd have been such an ass, though."

"I suppose he isn't one of the gang?" suggested Billy hopefully.

"No," I said. "I feel pretty sure Milford's straight. Why did they try to poison him, otherwise, and why should he have waltzed in and lent me a hand the other night? I'm rather worried about it, Billy."

"Yes," said Billy. "It's awkward. What are you going to do?"

"I don't know," I said, getting out of bed. "I can't put the police on. We must wait and see—that's all."

"And, meanwhile," observed Billy, "let's have a look at that arm of yours."

He took off the bandage, and inspected the fruits of my last night's adventure with an approving eye.

"First chop," he pronounced. "Healed up as clean as a whistle. That's the result of having led a decent and moral life. I think we'll keep the bandage on to-day, however, just to make certain."

"Well, you can put it on again after I've had my bath," I said. "By the way, can you drive a car?"

Billy nodded. "I've done a lot of it. Buenos Ayres reeks with 'em at present."

"You can drive me down to-day, then," I remarked. "I'm not a professor at the best of times, and with this arm on me I'd rather be excused."

"You leave it to me," said Billy confidently.

We each of us had a bath, after which Billy did up my arm, and I returned his kindness by lending him some shaving tackle. The cook's emotion at Milford's disappearance did not prevent her from sending up another excellent breakfast, to which we did ample justice, Billy being vastly impressed at the luxurious scale on which I lived.

It was then ten o'clock. The car was ordered for ten-thirty, so, lighting a pipe, I took advantage of the remaining time to go downstairs and interview what was left of my domestic staff. I was beginning to fear that, in view of their recent experiences, both the cook and the housemaid would be giving me notice, or clearing out while I was away, and this was a tragedy I was determined to prevent if possible.

I found them in the kitchen, and, knowing that a rapid attack is the best weapon of defence, I promptly opened fire.

"This is a dreadful nuisance about Milford," I said. "There's no doubt the poor fellow must have been queer in his head. I shall have inquiries made this morning, and I expect that we shall find him all

right, but, meanwhile, I'm wondering what to do for
the best. After our last experience, I don't want to
get in a new man without the most careful inquiry.
Do you two feel equal to looking after the house for
me until I come back? It's rather a large order, I
know, so I intend to give you double wages, if you
consider that arrangement satisfactory."

My sporting offer proved successful. Both women
at once expressed their readiness and ability to wrestle
with the problem, the cook going so far as to observe,
with respectful enthusiasm, that she would do more than
that to oblige a gentleman like myself.

They were obviously thirsting to discuss Milford's
disappearance, but, under cover of finishing my packing,
I escaped upstairs again to the hall. There I found
Billy admiring the marble pillars.

"This little hut must have cost a bit," he said
critically. "I wonder what Northcote's income is."

"Well, it's four hundred pounds a year less than it
was," I said, patting my belt with some satisfaction.
"Come along up and help me strap my bags."

We had just finished our preparations when I heard
the car roll up to the door, and looking out of the
window, I saw the faithful Simpson preparing to
dismount.

"He will bring them out, Billy," I said. "Don't you
worry."

Going downstairs, I gave instructions to this effect,
and while my belongings were being placed in the
car, routed out a couple of Northcote's best coats—
one for Billy and one for myself.

"How's the car going, Simpson?" I asked, as the
chauffeur, having secured my luggage, opened the door
with a respectful salute.

"Very sweetly, sir," was his comforting reply. "I ran through 'er last night, and I don't think you'll have no trouble. The petrol's in at the back, sir."

"Mr. Logan's steering her," I said. "I've hurt my arm."

Billy, who had climbed into the driving-seat, made a brief inspection of the levers, asked one or two questions, and then, starting on the switch and sliding in his clutch, set her moving gently down the street.

"Thank goodness we're off," I said, with a little sigh of relief. "I'm just about fed up with Park Lane, Billy."

He smiled, and, cutting neatly across the bows of an on-rushing motor-bus, swept us away down Knightsbridge before the indignant driver of the latter could recall a single adequate word.

"This is the wrong way, isn't it?" he inquired. "What's the programme?"

"I must send a wire to Maurice first," I said; "then we must pick up some traps for you. What about Harrod's?"

"Oh, Harrod's will do," said Billy. "I'm not proud."

He twisted the Napier off to the left down Brompton Road, and pulled up outside the big shop. As we entered through the swinging doors I handed him a bundle of notes.

"Get what you want, Billy," I said, "and shove it in the car. I'll send off the wire."

My message to Maurice, composed after some little deliberation, took the following shape:—

"Don't trouble to meet train. Am motoring down. Arrive dinner.—NORTHCOTE."

Having sent this off, I purchased a good map of Essex and Suffolk at a neighbouring counter, and then set off to find Billy.

I discovered him in the shirt department, laying in an impressive stock of under-clothes, which a sombre assistant was packing away into a large new Gladstone bag.

"Found what you wanted?" I inquired.

Billy nodded. "They're doing their best," he said kindly. "Not quite my usual style, but good enough for the country."

The assistant's face was a study, but we had no time to waste in appreciating it, for there were still various trifles needed, such as a sponge and a tooth-brush, to complete the bag. Having secured these, we returned to the car, and deposited the Gladstone with the rest of the luggage.

Climbing in, Billy took the wheel, and I spead out the map on my knee.

"Right away," I said. "Bank first; and then slap down through the East End."

And, with a triumphant toot, we slid oft upon our journey.

CHAPTER XIII

IT was just about half-past four when we entered the outskirts of Woodford. The car had gone well enough; indeed, except for a slight collision with a farm-cart in the neighbourhood of Chelmsford, our journey down had been a monotonous success. We pulled up at the Plough, an old-fashioned two-storey inn in the centre of the town, which boasted a red-and-white notice-board proclaiming its possession of a "Garage."

"This looks all right, Billy," I said. "If Maurice's place isn't too far away, you'd better put up here."

We ran the car into the yard, and then climbed out, leaving our luggage in the back, and made our way into the bar. There were two men sitting in the corner, talking to each other, and a middle-aged lady presiding over the drinks.

I took off my hat to her, and ordered a couple of whiskies.

"Do you happen to know," I asked, "where Ashton is—Mr. Maurice Furnivall's place?"

"Ashton!" she repeated. "Now, I've heard the name: it's quite close here somewhere. I expect the Coroner could tell you. Mr. Rowe, the gentleman wants to know where Ashton is."

One of the men in the corner looked up. "You've not far to go," he observed. "Straight on through the town and then down the hill to the left. Maybe a matter of a mile and a half. You'll find the drive gates on your right."

I thanked him and invited him to join us in a drink, an offer which he accepted with cheerful alacrity. For a coroner he seemed a very genial person.

"Can I have a bedroom here for a few days?" inquired Billy casually.

"Oh yes, I think so, sir," replied the lady behind the bar. "I'll just call Mr. Martin."

She went out, returning a minute later with the landlord, a side-whiskered gentleman in shirt-sleeves.

Billy repeated his request, and, informing us that there was plenty of room in the house, our host conducted us out of the bar, and up a winding staircase to the landing above.

"This is a nice bright room," he said, opening the door on the left. "Looks out on the main street, too—kind of cheerful-like."

"That's good," said Billy. "There may be a dog-fight, or a runaway horse, or something—one never knows. I'll take it, anyhow."

"Can we have some tea?" I asked.

The smiling landlord nodded his head. "Certainly, sir; I'll have it sent into the dining-room. This way, sir."

We retraced our steps downstairs, and entered a long room hung round with pictures of deceased race-horses, intersected by portraits of the Royal Family. In a few minutes, a Suffolk damsel of buxom proportions brought in tea, a full-dress affair consisting of jam, watercress, bread-and-butter, and two kinds of cake.

Dealing gently with this tribute to our physique, Billy and I discussed our plan of campaign, and fixed up the best arrangements we could. I agreed to slip out from

Ashton next morning before breakfast and meet him in the main road to Woodford. In the meanwhile, he was to pick up all the information possible about Maurice and his belongings, making special but judicious inquiries as to whether a gentleman with a broken nose, or another sportsman with one shoulder higher than the other, had been seen decorating the neighbourhood.

"I'll leave the car with you, Billy," I said, "and take a cab on to Maurice's. Then, in case we want it in a hurry, we can be sure of getting it."

"But won't they want to know what you've done with it?" he objected.

"I shall tell them the truth," I said, "or very nearly. I shall say the engine wanted looking to, and I left it in the garage here."

Billy looked at me admiringly. "Jack," he said, "a good parson was lost in you."

We ordered a cab, in which I placed my belongings, and then, giving Billy a few more bank-notes in case of emergency, and instructing him not to make love to the buxom housemaid, I clambered in and set out on my journey to Maurice's.

Ashton proved to be a good-sized, half-timbered house, standing back in its own grounds some way from the road. As my cab rumbled up the drive, I caught sight of two men sitting on a seat in the garden, and, drawing nearer, I saw that one of them was Maurice. They both rose as soon as we pulled up at the front door, and came across to meet me.

"Hullo," said Maurice. "I thought you were going to motor down?"

I shook hands with him, and also with his companion, a stout, florid man who looked like a retired bookmaker, but who obviously appeared to know me.

10

"So I did," I answered, "but I left the car in Woodford. The engine was working all wrong, somehow."

"That's the worst of motors," observed the fat man, "always goin' dicky—what?"

"Brought your chauffeur?" inquired Maurice, as a footman came out and gathered up my belongings.

I shook my head. "No," I said, "I didn't think he was necessary this time." Which, you will observe, was strictly true.

It may have been my imagination, but I fancied I saw a slight gleam of satisfaction pass across my "cousin's" face. "Well, come along into the garden," he said, "unless you'd like tea, or anything. Baradell's gone to town for the night, and York and Lady Baradell are out; but Aunt Mary's about somewhere. Do you know where she is, Vane?"

The fat man pulled his moustache. "Waterin' the roses," he observed laconically. "Miss York's with her."

Our discussion was cut short by the sudden appearance of the two ladies in question, who emerged from behind a shrubbery and advanced across the lawn to meet us. "Aunt Mary" was a middle-aged, quiet-looking woman with grey hair—her companion a tall, handsome girl of about twenty-eight, in a smart tailor-made costume.

I had an awkward moment, wondering if I was supposed to know them both, but the way in which they greeted me removed all doubt on this point.

"I'm so glad you were able to come down," said Aunt Mary, without any obvious enthusiasm, however. "It's not often you can tear yourself away from London."

"It's not often I get such charming invitations," I replied, shaking hands with her.

She looked at me in a rather surprised way, and it suddenly struck me that I was being a little too pleasant for the real Northcote. Whether "Aunt Mary" was any relation or not I had no idea, but she probably knew my double fairly well, and in that case was doubtless familiar with his character. As writers say, it behoved me to be careful!

Miss York showed more inclination to be friendly. "I hear you've brought your motor, Mr. Northcote," she said. " I hope it's big enough to take us all."

I laughed. "I've brought it as far as Woodford," I said, "and then it struck. However, it will be all right again in a couple of days, I think."

"Beastly fraud, isn't he, Miss York?" observed Sir George Vane, with quite unconscious humour.

"Well, it doesn't matter," put in Maurice languidly. "You couldn't use it if it was here. We're going to shoot to-morrow, the next day is the Cuthberts' garden-party, and the day after that, this cricket-match business that Bertie's got up."

"Oh, cricket!" said Miss York contemptuously. "Bertie's mad about cricket. Do you play, Mr. Northcote?"

"Not often," I replied gravely, and I heard Maurice laugh to himself.

There was a sound of footsteps in the drive, and we all looked up.

"Here are Bertie and Lady Baradell," said Miss York. " I wonder where they've been?"

I suddenly recollected the significant grin with which Maurice had mentioned the Baradells' name, when he had called on me in Park Lane, and with some natural interest I scanned the approaching figures. "Bertie," who, I gathered, was Miss York's brother, was a typical army man of about thirty, but his companion—well, Lady Baradell certainly could not be dismissed with any such cursory notice.

Tall and graceful, she moved towards us with that sort of almost insolent satisfaction which some beautiful women habitually suggest. Beautiful she certainly was, but compared with Mercia (I instinctively compared every-one with Mercia now) it was the beauty of fire against sunshine. Fire indeed seemed a very fitting simile for Lady Baradell. It glimmered in her wonderful bronze hair, and smouldered dangerously in the deep brown eyes with their curious golden-tinted irises. Her dress, a daring affair of almost flame-coloured material, com-pleted the illusion.

"And so the great man has taken pity on us," she said in her slow, musical voice. "Was London so terribly hot as all that, Mr. Northcote?"

"I seem to have a very undeserved reputation," I protested. "No one enjoys the beautiful things of life more than I do."

Lady Baradell raised her eyebrows and looked round with a smile.

"Saul among the prophets!" she said. "Maurice, what has happened to him?"

I waited for Maurice's answer with a little malicious amusement.

"I don't know," he drawled. "I asked him myself, the other day, and he said that one must be agreeable occasionally, if only for the sake of variety."

There was a general laugh, cut short by the distant sound of a gong.

"Time to dress," observed Aunt Mary. "Dear me! how quickly the evenings go!"

We all moved back towards the house, Maurice

thrusting his arm through mine and remarking in an
affable fashion that he would take me up and show me
my room.

This he did, bringing me to a large, cheerful apartment looking out over the garden.

" You'll be all right here, I think," he said. " No one
to disturb you, except the Baradells—they're across the
passage. Sure you've got everything you want? "

" Yes, thanks," I said.

" Dinner eight o'clock," he added, and, going out,
closed the door.

I dressed myself in leisurely fashion, taking, as I did
so, a kind of mental stock of my experiences since my
arrival. So far, things appeared to be progressing quite
satisfactorily. It was true I had been a trifle too genial
for the part of Northcote, but of my identity no one in
the house, even including Maurice, appeared to have the
faintest suspicion.

About my fellow-guests I had not yet quite made up
my mind. Vane and York seemed harmless enough in
their respective ways, and I could hardly believe that
they were concerned in the plot against me—if such a
thing existed. Lady Baradell was a more complicated
issue. Light and chaffing as her remarks had been,
some subtle instinct warned me that our relations were
on a more intimate footing than would have appeared
from her greeting. Whether she knew anything about
Northcote's history or not I was, of course, unaware, but
I felt sure that some kind of understanding existed
between them.

As I tied my tie in the glass, I examined myself
critically by the light of two candles. The likeness was
certainly astounding. If I had not known that I was
in reality Jack Burton of Buenos Ayres and God knows

where else, I would have sworn that the face which looked back at me was that of the man from whom I had parted in the Milan Restaurant three strenuous days before.

When I got down to the dining-room, I found the whole party assembled, with the exception of Lady Baradell. She swept in a moment later, looking superb in a low black evening dress, and wearing a magnificent collar of emeralds, which were just the right stones to go with her wonderful copper-coloured hair.

I was detailed to take in "Aunt Mary," not, I think, wholly to the latter's satisfaction. Lady Baradell, with Sir George Vane as a partner, sat on the other side of me.

I forget what we talked about during dinner—most of it the usual stock of trivialities, I fancy, enlivened by some very ancient anecdotes from Sir George, who seemed to possess a magnificent wardrobe of "humour's cast-off clothes." I remember getting so bored with the third of his long-winded efforts that I was seized with a mischievous determination to tell, in an amended form, the interesting tale of my experiences with "Francis." It struck me that if Maurice had been responsible for planting that gentleman in the house, a naïve narration of the consequences might convince him that my suspicions with regard to his kindly self were still unaroused. He must know by now how the attempt had ended, and silence in the matter on my part might well seem suspicious.

"By the way, Maurice," I said across the table, "I've never told you about that butler of mine that Seagrave sent me."

If the fellow was really guilty, his nerve was magnificent.

" No, you haven't," he said coldly. " How did he turn out ? "

I smiled. " A little abruptly," I answered, " and in the middle of the night." Then, seeing that I had secured the attention of the table, I proceeded to sketch my adventure much as I had painted it for the benefit of Mr. Seagrave. I left out, however, all references to Sir Henry Tregattock.

There was a chorus of surprised comment as I concluded. Lady Baradell looked at me with a curious light in her eyes.

" What a ruffian ! " she exclaimed. " I hope you hurt him."

" I fancy his nose must be still a little sore," I observed contentedly.

" But it's dreadful to think of a man like that being at large," said Miss York, with a little shudder. " Didn't you go to the police ? "

I shook my head. " I really couldn't be bothered. I told Seagrave, and left it in his hands."

Maurice leant back in his chair and laughed. " I'm frightfully sorry for putting you on to such a rotter," he remarked frankly. " I always thought Seagrave's were absolutely trustworthy. It's lucky you can look after yourself so well."

" Oh, it wasn't your fault, Maurice," I said generously.

" I should describe it rather as Francis's misfortune," put in Lady Baradell.

" Well, we'll leave you to discuss it over your port," said Aunt Mary, rising from her chair. " You'll find us in the billiard-room, Maurice, when you've done."

As soon as we were alone, Maurice pulled his chair up alongside of mine. " Are you game for some shooting to-morrow, Stuart ? " he asked, " I thought if it was fine we might go out after duck. Reece says they're coming in now in good quantities."

"Yes," I said quietly. "I'm quite ready for any amount of shooting."

"That's good," said Maurice heartily. "With four guns, we ought to get some fine sport."

I was inclined to agree with him, but any observation that I might have made to this effect was cut short by Sir George Vane, who promptly took the opening afforded by the mention of ducks to plunge into another ancient and, this time, rather obscene tale. We listened courteously until the ordeal was over, and then Maurice suggested a move into the billiard-room. Here we found Miss York practising strokes with some skill, while Aunt Mary and Lady Baradell looked on.

"I've got to go out a minute and interview the keeper," said Maurice. "Suppose you four have a game of snooker till I come back. I shan't be very long, and Vane will score for you."

The suggestion filled me with a momentary uneasiness. As it happens, I am rather above the average as a snooker-player, three years' constant practice in Buenos Ayres with some of the most accomplished sharpers in the world having left a decidedly beneficial effect on my game. On the other hand, I had no idea how Northcote played, or whether he played at all.

Captain York relieved my embarrassment.

"If I remember rightly, Northcote," he said, "you're a bit of a dab at this business. I think I'd better play with my sister."

"That's very polite to me," protested Lady Baradell, laughing.

"Don't you worry, Lady Baradell," put in Maurice;

"you'll beat them easily. Stuart never loses at anything."

Guessing that in the back of Maurice's mind this last remark referred to my dealings with Francis, I smiled inwardly to myself.

"I'll try and do my best," I said, "but that's rather a large compliment to live up to."

Maurice went out, and, placing the balls, we settled down to the game. Thanks to a really ingenious display of strategy on my part, it provided us with a thrilling contest. I played just well enough to keep our side ahead, without arousing any suspicions that I was not doing my best. York and his sister were both good, steady second-raters, while my partner's contributions consisted of occasional and very dazzling flukes.

It was after one of these that York observed, laughing, "If I didn't know Sir Charles, I should say that you were very unlucky in love."

As he spoke, I was just chalking Lady Baradell's cue, and for the fraction of a second her hand touched mine.

"I don't think I am," she said, with a curious smile.

It might have been a coincidence, but somehow or other the incident left me feeling a little uncomfortable. My peace of mind was not restored by observing that on several occasions afterwards, when the others were not looking, Lady Baradell favoured me with a smile which nothing but the most mule-headed modesty could describe as lacking in kindness. It seemed as though I had stumbled all unwittingly into another and exceedingly embarrassing complication.

However, I played on philosophically until the game ended, at which point in the proceedings Maurice returned. We then abandoned snooker for a five-

handed game of pool, during which Sir George Vane
and Aunt Mary solaced themselves with picquet.

At half-past ten some drinks arrived on a tray, and
after we had dealt with them, Aunt Mary hazarded the
opinion that bed seemed to her a sound proposition.

"And so say all of us," chimed in Miss York, politely
suppressing an incipient yawn. "I can hardly keep my
eyes open. We'll leave you men to ruin yourselves
over bridge, or whatever horrible vices you indulge in
after we've gone."

"My vice," retorted her brother, "will take the short
form of one modest little cigarette. Lady Baradell
walked me off my legs this afternoon."

There was a general laugh, during which Maurice
stepped forward to the table to light the candles, which
had been brought in with the drinks.

"Good-night," said Lady Baradell, shaking hands
with York and Sir George. "I believe I am the only
one who isn't tired, after all." She came across to me.
"Good-night, Mr. Northcote;" then, so softly that
they only reached my ears, she added the two words,
"*au revoir.*"

It was a situation which most men would have
received with enthusiasm, but personally I derived no
joy at all from it. However, I returned the little
private pressure of her hand, and said, "Good-night,
Lady Baradell," in my most amiable manner. Under
the circumstances, I could scarcely do anything else !

I don't think I played a very prominent part in the
half-hour's conversation that followed. The other men,
if I remember rightly, were discussing the prospects of
various horses in the October handicaps. Apart from
the fact that I know nothing, and care less, about
English racing, my thoughts were busy on a sporting

topic of an altogether more delicate nature. It may perhaps seem a little strange that I should have allowed such an affair to embarrass me (Billy would have shrieked with mirth at the very idea), but, since I had met Mercia, my previous views on certain matters had undergone a change, and, as far as I could see, the result promised to be awkward !

Maurice, who had glanced at me rather curiously once or twice, eventually asked me whether I was feeling sleepy.

" I'm about ready for bed," I admitted. " I was up till some unholy hour last night at Sangatte's."

" I'm with you," joined in York. "We'll let Vane and Furnivall settle the Cambridgeshire between them."

We took our candles, and, bidding the others good-night, left the billiard-room. I parted from York at the top of the staircase, and, passing Lady Baradell's room, turned into my own, and shut the door behind me.

It was a warm moonlight night, and I opened my window wide and leaned out for some time before beginning to undress. I still felt worried and a little apprehensive. The proverbial statement about "a woman scorned" appeared to me a very mild way of expressing what Lady Baradell's emotions would probably be under a similar provocation. I hoped some instinct would tell Mercia what I was risking on her account.

At last, however, the beauty of the garden, bathed as it was in great spaces of silver and shadow, gradually began to soothe my mind into a state of sleepy tranquillity. Finally, with a little yawn, I dismissed Lady Baradell and all the other complications that

surrounded me to their proper place, and, drawing
down the blind, undressed and got into bed.

I think it must have been the light that kept me
awake, for I generally go to sleep at once. As it was,
I lay for some time in a kind of drowsy semi-
consciousness that was just stealing into slumber, when
a faint sound suddenly brought me up alert and open-
eyed. In a moment I had jumped out of bed.

The door of my room opened quietly, and in the
pale gleam of the moonshine I saw Lady Baradell.
She was wearing a long blue silk dressing-gown, her
feet were bare, and her bronze hair floated down over
her shoulders. I must admit she looked wonderfully
attractive.

Closing the door noiselessly, she glided towards me,
a laughing gleam of triumph in her eyes.

"Ah, Stuart, Stuart!" she whispered, holding out
her hands.

I don't think I have ever felt quite such a fool in
my life.

CHAPTER XIV

I SUPPOSE it was inevitable that even my best efforts at being pleasant should have failed to convince Lady Baradell that my feelings towards her had not changed. People do not as a rule choose quite such unconventional hours for calling except with the expectation of a considerably more enthusiastic welcome than I was prepared to offer.

I saw suspicion and anger gathering slowly in her face, and finally she stepped back and clenched her hands.

"Why are you trying to deceive me?" she broke out passionately. "There is someone else. Tell me the truth, Stuart, at once."

The truth being exactly what I didn't want to tell her, I remained in a state of embarrassed silence.

"Oh, there's no need for you to speak," she added bitterly; "I know you too well." Then rage, murderous, ungovernable rage, flamed suddenly into her eyes. "You fool! Do you think I am the sort of woman to be picked up and thrown aside at a man's whim? Did you imagine for one single moment that you could deceive me?"

"No," I admitted sadly, "I didn't."

She laughed—an unpleasant, mirthless laugh, and, throwing back her hair, stared me full in the face, looking like some splendid tigress.

"I love you, Stuart," she said steadily; "I love you

as I don't think many women have loved men; but
I will see you dead before I let any other woman
have you."

Then, without another word, she turned and left
the room.

I stood for a moment where I was, gazing at the
door. I felt rather like a man who had unwittingly
touched off a dynamite cartridge. Whatever might be
the precise value of Lady Baradell's last threat, I knew
that I had managed to make an enemy more dangerous than any Northcote had already bequeathed me.
With a heartfelt deliberation I cursed my double and
all his works.

Somewhat relieved by this outbreak, I again retired
to bed. As a sleeping draught, however, I found that
Lady Baradell was a distinct failure. For a couple
of hours at least I must have tossed about restlessly,
turning over in my mind every aspect of this new
development which threatened to complicate still further
my already harassed path. Indeed, it was only sheer
physical fatigue that at last closed my eyes in a
welcome unconsciousness.

. Sleep, however brief, always has the excellent effect
of restoring me to my natural cheerfulness. I woke
up next morning as buoyant as though no midnight
reception had interfered with my customary eight hours.
The morning sun was blazing into my room through
the open window, and a discreet-looking man-servant
was laying out my bath.

"Would you like it hot or cold, sir?" he inquired.

"Cold, this weather, I think," said I. "What time
is breakfast?"

"Nine o'clock, sir. It's just gone a quarter to eight
now."

"Good," I observed approvingly. This gave me plenty of time to make my toilet like a gentleman and get out and see Billy in the roadway, before joining the rest of the party over their eggs and bacon.

It was exactly half-past, by the clock on the mantelpiece, as I left my room. I went downstairs quietly and quickly, for I had no wish to run into Maurice or anyone else, and made my way across the garden and out through a small side gate into the main road. The birds were singing gaily in the hedges, and out of a blue sky the sun shone down with the most comforting warmth. As the Yankees say, I "felt good"—distinctly good.

Billy was sitting on a bank just round the first corner, smoking his pipe. He waved me a cheerful greeting.

"They've not scragged you in the night, then," he said with satisfaction.

"On the contrary, Billy," I said, "I have met with nothing but affection and kindness." I seated myself beside him and sniffed critically. "I don't think much of your 'baccy," I added.

"It's the Plough's best," retorted Billy. "You're getting swelled head." Then he slapped me on the shoulder. "Jack," he said, "I've found my job in life —I can give Sherlock Holmes two stone and put him out in the first round."

Billy was not given to boasting, so I looked at him with interest.

"Proceed, William," I said encouragingly.

He stuffed the 'baccy down with his thumb and chuckled to himself. "Last night," he began, "I did a bit of scouting. I thought it would be just as well to sniff around and see how the land lay, so, as soon as I'd had some grub, I tootled along here as far as the lodge

I hung about outside for a bit, taking my bearings, and
then, as there wasn't anybody about, I dropped in over
the hedge and tracked up through the shrubbery till I
got to the house. I'd been there about ten minutes,
squatting down under a bush, when who should come
up the drive but your old dot-and-carry-one friend!"

"Who?" I inquired.

"Why, the chap who doctored your butler's drink.
At least, it was exactly like your description of him. A
big, ugly, lopsided beggar he was, with one shoulder
about an inch higher than the other."

"Go on, Billy," I said. "This is getting exciting."

"Well, he crawled up in a hang-dog sort of way, and
sat down on the balustrade just in front of where I was
hiding. I thought he was expecting somebody, and
sure enough, he hadn't been there many minutes when
out came a fellow in evening-dress—your cousin, I should
reckon, by the cut of his jib."

"Maurice did take a little air after dinner," I observed.
"He said he wanted to see the keeper."

"Did he?" drawled Billy. "Well, he saw him all
right. They stood there jawing for the best part of
twenty minutes, and all about you, my son."

"Was it interesting?" I asked.

"What I heard was, but I only got on to about every
tenth word. They were doing the whispering act most
of the time. Seemed to me they were fixing up something for to-day—something about you and the sea
wall, as far as I could get it."

I nodded. "There's going to be an accident at our
shooting party this afternoon, unless I'm much mistaken," I said.

"Looks like it," answered Billy grimly. "They
seemed cursedly pleased with themselves, anyhow.

The only other thing I heard was about your girl with the pistol—what's her name?—Mercia."

"Mercia!" I echoed. "What were they saying about her?"

Billy grinned in a very aggravating manner. "I like to see you getting interested, Jack," he said. Then, removing his pipe, he knocked out the ashes against the bank.

"Billy," I said, "you're playing with death. Get on."

"I only heard her name," he chuckled. "The lopsided gentleman trotted it out and repeated it about four times. I think he was annoyed with her over something, from the way he was speaking. Your cousin seemed to be rubbing it in."

A sudden uneasiness about Mercia's safety flashed through my mind. I had excellent proof that we were dealing with a pretty reckless gang, and if it was known that she had warned me against coming to Ashton she might well be in as grave danger as myself.

Billy evidently read my thoughts. "I think she's all right at present," he said, "for the simple reason that the whole gang seem to be hot on your track. I've not told you the best part yet, Jack. I've actually had the luck to run 'em to earth."

He sat back and looked at me proudly.

"By Jove, Billy!" I cried. "You're a wonder! How did you do it?"

"Well, after the little confab was over, and your cousin had cleared off into the house, I gave old Dot-and-carry-one time to get back into the road, and then I followed him. I had to give him a couple of hundred yards or so, or he might have tumbled to it. He went straight back to Woodford, and, as luck would have it, I was just in time to see him turn into a pub.—not the Plough ;

11

another one this side of it. I followed him in, and found
him shifting raw brandy. He's a Dago right enough—
these's no question about it."

"Did you speak to him?" I asked.

Billy shook his head. "I thought it best to lie low.
The landlord, who was a talkative sort of ass, seemed
to know him, so I waited a bit, and, after our pal had
cleared off, I asked who he was. 'Oh,' said the landlord, 'that's an Eyetalian gentleman, Moosyer Baretti.
He's just taken the Hollies, Colonel Paton's house,
for some months. Moved in yesterday, I believe. Nice,
pleasant-spoken gent he is, too.'"

"There's room for all opinions," I said, with a laugh.
"Milford didn't fancy him at all."

"The landlord thought no end of him," said Billy.
"In fact, he got quite confidential. His brother, it
seems, was gardener at the Hollies, so of course he
knew all about it. There's Dot-and-carry-one, and a
lady he calls his wife, and another chap who arrived
to-day. I asked whether he had a broken nose, and he
said no; so it can't be Francis."

"I expect it's the gentleman I owe this stiff shoulder
to," I said. "Nice little family party, anyway. Where
is the Hollies?"

Billy jerked his head up the road. "Quite close," he
said, "just outside Woodford. A small white house on
the left. I mean to inspect it to-night." Then he
paused. "Jack," he said, "I'm not quite happy about
this shooting business."

"Neither am I," I answered truthfully.

"Why do you go? Can't you make some excuse?"

I shrugged my shoulders. "What's the use? It only
means they'll try some other way. At least I know
what to expect this afternoon."

"Yes, there's that," said Billy. "Look here, I've got an idea. Suppose I get hold of a boat and cruise around outside the sea wall while you're shooting? I might be of use some way or another—one never knows."

"Right you are, Billy," I said. "There's nothing like having command of the sea." Then I looked at my watch. "I ought to be trotting back," I added; "it's just on nine. I'll let you know about meeting you to-morrow, if we don't run across each other this afternoon. We're due down on the marsh about half-past five, I think."

"Well, be careful, old son," said Billy, gripping my hand. "By the way, have you heard anything about Milford?"

I shook my head. "I left my address with the cook and told her to write if he turned up; but there was nothing from her this morning. It beats me altogether. I could understand their trying to shift him in order to plant 'Francis' on me; but after that little business failed, what on earth could their game be?"

"Lord knows," said Billy. "But they've got him, evidently. Perhaps he was more in with Northcote than we think. Anyhow, it's no use worrying. Keep your eyes skinned this afternoon, and give me a hail if there's any trouble."

He went off up the road, and, after waiting for a minute until he had rounded the corner, I set off back to the house.

As I came across the garden, I saw Maurice and York standing outside, on the terrace.

"Hullo!" cried the latter, "you've beaten us all. I thought I was down first."

"It was too fine to lie in bed," I explained. "I've been inspecting the country."

If Maurice had any suspicions, he kept them to himself. "I should never have accused you of laziness,"
he answered. "Come along in and let's have some
breakfast. The gong's just gone."

We entered the dining-room, where Aunt Mary was
occupying herself with making the tea, and had scarcely
settled into our places when we were joined by Miss
York and Lady Baradell, who came in together.

If I had not genuinely admired the latter before, I
should certainly have done so now. Far from there
being any trace of embarrassment in her manner, she
appeared to be the most cheerful and unconcerned
person in the entire party.

"Dear me! How terribly energetic everyone is!"
she said, looking quizzically round the room. "Even
Mr. Northcote down! I thought he always breakfasted
in bed."

York laughed. "Down!" he echoed. "Why, he's
been out catching butterflies."

"The early bird," I said, "is improving in his taste."

"Well, what are we all going to do this morning?"
inquired Aunt Mary briskly. "I suppose you won't be
shooting till this afternoon, will you, Maurice?"

The latter shook his head. "We might pick up a
few rabbits if anyone wants to," he answered; "but it's
no good trying for duck till later. What do you think,
Stuart?"

"The duck will do for me all right," I said. I didn't
see any reason for running myself into unnecessary danger.

"Let's have some tennis this morning," said Miss
York. "We haven't tried the lawn yet. You play,
don't you, Mr. Northcote?"

Having never touched a tennis racquet in my life, I
was reluctantly driven to lie.

"I think I'll look on and applaud," I said. "The car back-fired the other day, and my wrist's still reminding me of it."

There was a general murmur of sympathy, which Maurice capped by inquiring, I thought a little anxiously, whether I was sure I felt up to shooting.

"Oh yes," I said; "I can still hold a gun straight."

After some discussion, it was agreed that Miss York and Maurice should take on her brother and Vane. Vane, it appeared, was the duffer of the party, while York, having played for the army, was evidently a cut above the others.

The tennis lawn lay at the side of the house, and after breakfast was over, and we had had a look at the morning papers, we took out some chairs and placed them in the shadiest spots we could find which commanded a view of the court. I was just settling myself down when I saw Aunt Mary coming towards me.

So far I had had very little conversation with my hostess, her manner at our first meeting, though courteous enough superficially, having plainly showed me that I was by no means a welcome guest from her point of view. Since then, however, she had perceptibly thawed, and on the present occasion she came up to me with a smile on her kindly, rather worried, face.

"I want to have a little talk with you, Stuart," she said as I pulled round a chair for her.

"By all means," I answered, wondering what she might be leading up to. "We've hardly had the chance of a chat since I came."

She looked at me thoughtfully. "You seem to me to have changed a great deal lately."

This was in the nature of a frontal attack, but I met it calmly. "Yes," I said, "I have changed."

"And for the better," she added. "Stuart, when you first came back from South America, I disliked you intensely."

I bowed. "You were quite justified in doing so," I said.

"I don't know what your life out there had been," she went on, "so it's not fair that I should judge you, but all my instincts seemed to tell me that you were bad—bad through and through. I dreaded your influence over Maurice."

She paused. The idea of anyone demoralising Maurice, if my judgment of that young man was anything like correct, struck me as bordering on the humorous. However, Aunt Mary's penetration into Northcote's character was sufficiently startling to prevent my smiling.

"It will be Maurice's own fault," I said bluntly, "if he comes to any harm through me."

She laid her hand on my arm. "I believe you, Stuart," she said. "Since you have been down here this time, I seem, somehow, to have reversed all my previous opinions of you. It's curious, because, as a rule, my first impressions never alter."

"I am glad to provide the exception," I said. "And I'm glad, too, that Maurice has someone who takes an interest in him."

"Ah!" she said; "it's about Maurice that I want to speak to you." Then she hesitated a moment. "I am afraid Maurice is getting into bad hands," she went on. "There is something on his mind—something that has changed him terribly the last few months. It may be his money affairs—I know he has been betting very heavily on horses—but I can't help thinking that there's some other trouble as well."

I thought that I had a pretty shrewd notion what the other trouble was.

"There is no one I can speak to about it except you, Stuart," she added unhappily. "You at least are our nearest relative, and you have seen a great deal of life. You know the temptations that a young man like Maurice may get into. I want you, if you will, to try and help him. With all his faults, he is dear Alice's boy. If it is only a matter of money, we might be able to put things right between us, perhaps; only I don't like to question him myself. He would take it so much better from you."

I felt intensely sorry for the poor lady. Maurice was evidently very dear to her; and although I believed firmly that the young blackguard was scheming to murder me, I had no wish to bring any more lines of sorrow into her careworn face.

"I give you my word," I said simply, "that I'll do anything I can to keep Maurice out of trouble."

She gave me a faint but very genuine smile of gratitude. "Thank you, Stuart," she said. "I am sorry I misjudged you so." Then she got up from her chair, just as the tennis party came, laughing and talking, out of the billiard-room door which led into the garden. "I must go and look after my house," she added: "I haven't even ordered the dinner yet. By the way, if you're duck-shooting, I suppose you will all be late. I must ask Maurice."

The latter, looking very cool and supercilious, in white flannels, was just advancing across the lawn. Aunt Mary went up to him, and after a moment's conversation continued her way to the house.

Miss York waved her racquet at me. "We shall expect lots of applause, Mr. Northcote," she said gaily.

"You needn't bother to clap if your wrist's bad, but you must cheer like anything."

"The tennis-court shall echo with it," I returned encouragingly.

Miss York laughed. "That's right," she said. "Here's Lady Baradell coming to help you."

Even if I had wished to retreat, it would have been too late. Graceful and beautifully dressed as ever, Lady Baradell was coming across the garden towards the spot where I was sitting.

"You have made yourself comfortable, I see," she said, smiling.

"Oh, trust Northcote for that," put in Vane, with a chuckle, as he hung up a wonderfully coloured blazer in the tree behind.

"You've got the best of it, anyway," added Maurice languidly. "I think we are all mad to play tennis in this sun."

"Well, let's hope there will be some method in your madness," replied Lady Baradell. "As spectators, we shall be very critical."

She sank down into the chair which Aunt Mary had lately vacated, fanning herself slowly with a big palm-leaf which she was carrying in her hand.

"Stuart," she said, when the others had taken their places in the court, "I wonder what you think of me?"

"At the present moment," I said, "I think that you are the most beautiful woman in Suffolk."

She laughed, looking up at me sideways out of her curious golden eyes. "I think I was a little hysterical last night," she said softly. "But you were rather cruel, Stuart, you know. There are several ways of breaking bad news. Who is she?"

I hesitated a moment. "I wonder if you would believe me," I said, "if I told you the truth."

"Game—love!" There came a triumphant cry from Miss York, as Vane with misdirected energy sent a ball soaring into the kitchen garden.

"Game—love," repeated Lady Baradell, staring out over the lawn with half-shut eyes. "Ah, yes, Stuart, I shall believe you."

I leaned forward and looked at her steadily. "In a month's time," I said, "you will forgive me everything for the sake of last night."

There was a short silence. Then she answered in a low voice: "There can be no question of forgiveness between you and me."

Even as she spoke, I saw the door of the billiard-room open, and Aunt Mary, accompanied by a tall, grave-looking man in dark clothes, came out on to the lawn.

Lady Baradell laughed gently. "My husband," she said, "has all the virtues—even punctuality."

CHAPTER XV

"I've ordered dinner for half-past eight," said Aunt Mary, "so don't be later than eight if you can help it. We shall all be famished by then."

"We shall be back before that," returned Maurice. "The flight's about half-past six, and it's only half an hour's walk from the marsh."

We were standing in the drive with our guns—he and I and York and Vane. A slack afternoon, succeeded by an early tea, had followed the tennis, and now we were just setting out upon our duck-shooting expedition. Baradell had declined to make one of the party, presumably preferring the society of his wife.

"We'll make a round through the fields first," said Maurice. "It's no use getting to the water before six, and we may pick up a few pheasants and hares if the light's good enough."

I did not wait for instructions, but slipped into a place between York and Vane. I thought it very unlikely that Maurice would himself attempt anything in the gun-accident line, but even so, there was no point in running unnecessary risks. You never know what sudden happy inspiration may illuminate the mind of an embarrassed heir.

Off we went, the dogs ranging round us, and a couple of nondescript gentlemen in corduroy trousers bringing up the rear. It relieved my mind to perceive that neither of them had guns.

This sort of shooting was, of course, quite new to me, but I have too often been dependent upon my gun for my supper to be likely to miss anything in the nature of a confiding English bird. Indeed, when York sang out his congratulations to me for toppling over a fast-flying pheasant, I began to think that perhaps it would be more judicious if I restrained my abilities. Except for his money-getting and love-making talents, I was so confoundedly in the dark as to what Northcote could do.

About half-past five we arrived at the bank of a long salt-water creek. It was perhaps a quarter of a mile wide, and protected from the sea by a strip of land running parallel with the coast. A desolate sort of spot, very like bits of the Argentine seaboard, without so much as a cottage or a hut to break the loneliness of the surrounding marsh. The only object in sight was an old punt, moored to a stake under the bank.

"We must split up now," said Maurice, turning to the rest of us. "There are four or five places where you can get a good shot at the duck as they come over, and this is one of them. What do you say, Stuart? Would you like to stay here?"

He asked the question with such frank carelessness that for a moment I wondered whether it was really possible that he was planning my extinction. Anyhow, I had no intention of refusing. I wanted to see what was going to happen.

"I'll stay where I am, certainly," I said. "What's the programme?"

He pointed to a small, sandy spit covered with reeds, half-way across the creek.

"You must punt over to that," he said, "and tie up the boat this side. About half-past six the duck will come right over you, and if you're well hidden you ought to get in a couple of good shots at least."

I nodded approvingly. "Where will you be?" I asked.

He jerked his head towards the right. "Oh, we shall be down the coast. Do you think you know your way to the house?"

"I guess I can find it," I said, smiling. The idea of being "bushed" on three miles of Sussex mud-flats struck me as a rather entertaining one.

"Well, then," said Maurice, "perhaps you won't mind finding your own road back when the flight's over. It will save us coming round this way again. Don't bother about the duck. If you leave them in the punt, I'll tell one of the men to come back and bring them up to the house."

"We'll send him along with a trolly—what?" put in the humorous Vane.

They tramped off, leaving me alone in my glory. For some few minutes I sat on the bank, watching them walking away down the creek, and wondering what pleasant surprise Maurice's arrangements might fore-shadow. That there was mischief of some sort on foot I felt certain, but it was difficult to guess exactly what shape it would assume. Standing up, I cast a wary eye over my surroundings. As far as I could see, with the exception of the little island to which Maurice had directed my attention, and the long strip of land opposite, there was no cover anywhere sufficiently big to conceal a rabbit. Of Billy I could see nothing: if he was hanging about in a boat, it must be round the bend of the coast away to the left, where the sea wall jutted out into the saltings.

Untying the punt, I stepped in and pushed off towards

the island. It struck me that if the danger lurked there, it would be just as well to land before the rest of the party were out of hearing. Unless York and Vane were in the plot, which seemed highly improbable, my safety would be pretty well assured so long as they were within reasonable distance.

A few strokes of the paddle brought me to my destination. The island, though thickly covered, was sufficiently small for me to see that I had it entirely to myself. I tied the punt to a snag on the landward side, and after one last look round settled myself down to wait for the duck, or whatever else might turn up.

I had been there for perhaps ten minutes, when from the strip of land on the farther side of the creek came the weird, melancholy cry of a curlew. I took my gun and started to rise cautiously to my feet. As I did so, a sudden inspiration—a veritable flash from the gods—leaped into my mind. I sank down again and, taking off the slouch hat I was wearing, placed it on the barrels of my gun. Then, very slowly and cautiously, I raised it above the reeds.

Bang!

Off spun the hat, with a bullet-hole clean through the middle, and a violent tingling jar in my arm told me that part of the barrel had apparently gone with it. I dropped the gun, and without a moment's hesitation jumped high into the air, crashing down full-length amongst the reeds.

It was a trick highly popular with the ingenious Indians of Bolivia, who by this means tempt their guileless and well-pleased opponent to come within reach of the knife which they invariably carry. Something of the same purpose was at the back of my mind, and it was with a grim smile of satisfaction that I discovered that

one of my gun barrels was still undamaged. Lying
there, hidden by the thick vegetation, I quickly extracted
the cartridge from the other. Then, stealthily as a puma,
I wriggled my way forward until I reached the edge of
the island. Parting the rushes, I peered cautiously
through.

From the strip of land away to my left a small boat
was just putting out into the creek. It contained two
men, and even at that distance I could see that one of
them was without doubt the "Eyetalian" aristocrat
whom Billy had stalked on the previous evening. The
other, who carried a rifle in his hand, I put down as my
Park Lane friend.

For a lop-sided sculler, the big chap certainly made
his boat travel. It fairly bounded towards me across
the creek, the passenger crouching in the bows, his gun
ready for immediate action. Like Robert Bruce's friend,
they were evidently coming to "mak' siccar."

With a gentle smile I cuddled myself back under
cover, pushing forward my gun so that only the extreme
point of the barrel protruded through the reeds. There
was no mercy in my heart, though, as a matter of fact,
I felt little personal resentment against either of my
approaching visitors. It was Northcote, not me, that
they were really trying to shoot, and their reasons were
probably very commendable. Nevertheless, it was my
intention to plug them both as accurately as possible
so soon as they came within effective range of my
twelve-bore. If there was any subsequent trouble, I
had a bullet-hole through my hat to give evidence in
my favour; and after all, when certain death is in one
side of the balance, it's not much good bothering about
the other.

Nearer and nearer they came the man in the bows

peering forward and searching the island with a keen gaze. I placed another cartridge ready beside me, and then, levelling my gun straight at his chest, put my finger on the trigger. It was at that moment that the boat stopped.

For one second I thought my trick had been discovered, and I as nearly as possible loosed off without waiting for any further developments. Then, just as I was hesitating, there came the unmistakable crack of a Mauser pistol, and I saw a big splinter fly up off the side of the boat. With an oath the big fellow swung round and sculled off furiously down the creek, while his companion, raising his rifle, blazed back in the direction from whence the bullet had come.

I can tell you I didn't waste any time. Wriggling back out of my ambush, I crawled swiftly through the rushes to the farther side of the island, and there, as I expected, I saw the faithful William. He had shipped his oars and, kneeling in his boat, was just taking a careful aim after the retreating pleasure-party.

"Chuck it, Billy!" I sang out.

Down went the pistol, and in another moment, with a triumphant shout, he was pulling in towards the island.

"Damn it, Jack!" he said, as the boat ran up the bank and he leaped on shore. "I thought they'd downed you that time. Look at the blighters!"

He pointed down the creek, where our late assailants were travelling away from us with a vigour which would have done credit to a championship pair at Henley. Then, sitting on the bank, he burst into a roar of laughter.

"Oh, great!" he gasped, when he had sufficiently recovered. "Jack, my son, you're all right when it comes to gunning. You had me on as clean as a whistle. I'd have sworn they'd got you."

"If you hadn't come cruising around in that fashion, Billy," I said, "I should have got them. You've saved me from the horrid sin of shedding blood."

"I could have pipped them all right myself," he protested. "That Dago with the gun had lost his nerve. How did it all come about?"

As briefly as possible I put him in possession of the facts. "It was a plant," I finished: "there's no doubt about it now. I should have been found shot, if I'd ever been found at all. Guarez and his pal would have cleared out, and Maurice, with a beautiful fat alibi to keep him out of trouble, would have stepped into the family property. It's a wicked world, William."

"You're right," said Billy, shaking his head; "but fortunately it makes a bloomer sometimes. I saw the whole thing. I'd tied my boat to the sea wall round the point there, and crawled up on to the top. I watched you punt over to the island, and I was just coming along to keep you company when that misbegotten skunk let drive. I thought you were a goner, Jack! You did that stunt so devilish well it took me in completely."

"I hope you felt sorry," I said.

"Sorry!" laughed Billy. "I was in a black rage, I can tell you. If you hadn't popped up like a Jack-in-the-box, I'd have filled those two Dagoes fuller of lead than a racing yacht."

"I'm glad you didn't, Billy," I answered. "I'm looking forward to doing something in that line myself." Then I looked at my watch. "It's half-past six," I added. "That's the time the duck were due to arrive. I'm afraid we've frightened them!"

"I reckon we have," said Billy. "If I was a duck, I should steer clear of this place for a fortnight. You'd better come round with me to the point, and then we'll cut across land to Woodford and have a drink. You can be back at the house by eight."

"Good!" I said. "If I'm a bit late, it will keep Master Maurice guessing. He isn't likely to have seen his pals, so it will be a pleasant little surprise for him when I roll up safe and sound."

Leaving the punt where it was (I was not in the mood to save Maurice's keepers any superfluous trouble), we pushed off in Billy's boat, and sculled rapidly up the creek. There was no sign anywhere of our late friends, but a faint sound of shots down the coast told us that the rest of my party were apparently busy with the duck.

"I wonder if Maurice is shooting straight," I said, with a chuckle. "He must have heard our little fusillade, and I suppose he thinks the whole thing over by now. Rather trying for the nerves, coming into a fortune all of a sudden!"

"It will be a lot more trying coming out of it," retorted Billy. "I'd give a fiver to see his face when you walk in."

We left the boat at a small landing-stage the other side of the point, and making our way across the fields, came into Woodford over the railway line. I spent about half an hour with Billy at the Plough, drank a couple of sherries and bitters, and talked over our future campaign.

"There's nothing like leading trumps," I said. "I shall tell them straight out when I get back that some-one tried to shoot me. I want to hear Maurice's ex-planation."

Billy nodded. "That's the right game," he answered.

"If you lie low, he'll know that you suspect him. Play the hand for all it's worth, and see what happens."

"I mean to," I said briskly. "I shall even go so far as to tell him that I have a witness in the shape of a kind tourist staying at the Plough, who happened to be out shooting. Perhaps he'll come and see you, Billy!"

"I hope so," said Billy; "I know so few English gentlemen!" Then he chuckled in characteristic fashion. "Meanwhile," he added, "I'm going to do a bit more scouting. I don't know whether your pals will clear out after this little 'fox pass,' but I mean to have a squint round the Hollies to-night and see what's going on. I don't approve of 'Eyetalian' noblemen waltzing around with rifles. They want watching."

"And washing too," I said, "from the glimpse I had of them." Then I got up. "I must be off now," I added, "or I shall be late for the resurrection."

Billy came with me as far as the door. "Shall I meet you somewhere to-morrow?" he asked, "or can you manage to look in here?"

I reflected a moment. "I'll come round in the afternoon," I said. "I'll tell them I want to see how the repairs to the car are getting on."

Feeling pleasantly elated at the thought of the surprise in store for Maurice, I struck out along the road to Ashton at my most brisk pace. I had covered about three-quarters of the distance, and was just turning the corner where I had met Billy before breakfast, when I noticed ahead of me a small boy with a rather dirty face lounging against the bank. As I came up, he straightened himself, looked at me keenly, and stepped out into the road.

"Beg pardon, sir," he said, "but are you Mr. Northcote?"

"That's right, my son," I replied.

Putting his hand in his pocket, he produced a well-thumbed envelope. "Lady asked me to give you this, sir."

I took the letter and opened it. By the rapidly fading light I could just see to read the contents—

"If you put any value on your life, you will leave Ashton immediately. Guarez and the others have followed you down, and your cousin is in league with them. It is my fault, so I take this last chance of warning you. I can do no more. If you are indeed wrongly accused, I pray God that you will escape while there is yet time. Destroy this letter.   M. S."

"Where did you get this?" I asked.

He hesitated. "Lady told me not to tell."

I put my hand in my pocket and pulled out five shillings. "Look here, my son," I said, "I'll give you that if you'll answer my question."

He shook his head sturdily. "I promised the lady, guv'nor."

I put back the money, feeling rather ashamed. "Tommy," I said, "you're a good boy. How did you know I was Mr. Northcote?"

"Lady described yer, guv'nor. Said yer was a big gent with a brown face."

"Did she!" said I, laughing. Then I paused a moment, thinking rapidly. "Will you take a note back for me?" I asked. "The lady didn't say you weren't to do that, did she?"

He shook his head.

"Very well," I said; "you do it, and I'll give you ten shillings."

The magnitude of the sum fairly staggered him.

"'Arf a quid!" he gasped.

"The terms are synonymous, Tommy," I said, producing the coin. "Here you are."

He clutched it tightly in his little brown paw, and while he was recovering from the shock I tore out a page from my pocket-book and wrote my message—

"Will you meet me to-morrow at three o'clock at the Plough at Woodford, or else leave a note for me there, saying where I can see you?

"STUART NORTHCOTE."

This I folded up and handed to the boy. "There you are," I said. "Give that to the lady as soon as you can."

His sudden access of fortune seemed to have paralysed his tongue, for he contented himself with another nod, and then darted off up the road as fast as his legs would carry him.

I waited until he was out of sight, and then I lifted up Mercia's melodramatic little warning and kissed it. If it had come a trifle late, it was none the less welcome— and as for its wording, well, it was good enough for me. My heart was filled with a kind of wild triumph, for surely the fact of her trying to save me was sufficient proof that she had believed my word in the face of all evidence to the contrary.

If I could only see her to-morrow, I would leave her in no doubt as to my feelings. I longed to clear up the whole infernal mystery, but my oath to Northcote rose like a wall between me and my desire. In love as I was, I couldn't bring myself to betray his secret until the accursed three weeks had run their span.

Tearing up the note into tiny fragments, I scattered them judiciously to the breezes, and, continuing my way, turned in at the side gate. It was now quite dusk, and even if anyone had been watching, I doubt if they would have seen me approaching across the lawn.

As it was, I got right up to the terrace without being spotted. The French window, which led into the smoking-room, was open, and, keeping away from the light which streamed out in a great golden beam, I advanced cautiously until I was within a couple of paces.

Then I heard Maurice's voice. " It's a most extraordinary thing," he was saying. "The punt was tied up to the island, according to George, and yet there wasn't a sign of him anywhere."

I smiled softly.

" I hope to God he hasn't fallen into the creek," said York's voice anxiously. "We'd better all turn out, hadn't we, and have a good hunt, before we tell the women ? "

"That will be best," said Maurice. " I really am uncommonly anxious about him."

I stepped in quietly over the threshold. "In that case, Maurice," I said, "let me hasten to relieve your feelings."

CHAPTER XVI

I DON'T think I shall ever forget Maurice's face! His cheeks went the colour of grey ash, and for several seconds he stared at me with a sort of incredusoul horror. If I had any remaining doubt as to his guilt, it was certainly settled in that dramatic interval.

At last, with a great effort, he recovered himself sufficiently to give a sickly laugh.

"By Jove, you gave us a start, Stuart!" he said. "We were just wondering whether you'd fallen into the creek."

"No," I replied cheerfully, "it was only my hat that went in." And taking off the article in question, I held it up to the light so that they could all see the bullet-hole.

"Great Scott!" cried York, "what's the meaning of that?" He seized the hat, and began examining the damage with vast interest, Sir George peering over his shoulder.

"It means," I retorted, "at least twenty-five shillings. That's one of Lincoln & Bennett's best." Then, with a kindly eye on Maurice, I proceeded to relate my spirited and entertaining experiences.

When I had finished there was a short silence. It was broken by Sir George, who, with his usual intelligence, went straight to the heart of the matter.

"B—b—but that was murder," he stammered, "cold-blooded murder!"

"I should describe it rather as hat slaughter," I said coolly, "but the intention seems to have been pretty obvious."

Maurice, whose face had not regained its colour, broke in with an oath. "It's those infernal marshmen!" he cried. "I've had trouble with them before, but never anything of this kind."

"What do you mean?" asked York, looking up from the hat.

"Why, there's a gang of scoundrels round the coast who make their living shooting duck. I was cautioned about them when I took the place. They think they own the marsh, and that no one else has a right to shoot there. I've heard lots of stories about their blackguardly tricks, but of course I never imagined for a moment they'd go as far as this." He turned to me. "My dear chap," he added, "I can't tell you how sorry I am."

I thought I could tell him very accurately, but I contented myself with shaking the hand that he thrust impulsively out.

"Don't worry about it, Maurice," I said. "These little accidents will happen."

"You take it uncommonly coolly, Northcote," broke in Sir George. "If it had happened to me, I'd have had the whole damned countryside arrested by now— by Gad, I would!"

"I shall put it in the hands of the police at once," said Maurice. "Do you think you could recognise the two men?"

I should love to have said yes, just for the pleasure of watching his face; but I thought it might be a bit awkward to make such a statement in view of a subsequent visit from the police.

" I couldn't swear to them," I said, " but I dare say the obliging stranger at the Plough could. He got a better sight of them than I did."

This, without committing Billy, would, I thought, at least give Maurice an unpleasant quarter of an hour.

" Well, it's disgraceful ! " burst out Vane ; " that's what it is—disgraceful ! It's all this confounded Government —setting class against class—that leads to this kind of thing. If I had my way, I'd shoot them down—every man Jack of them."

I was a little in the dark as to who Sir George's imaginary victims might be, but, in any case, the sentiment struck me as being a fairly sound one.

" Perhaps we'd better not say anything further about it to-night," I suggested. " I don't want the loss of a hat to disturb the whole house."

There was a look of relief on Maurice's face. " You're right, Stuart," he said. " It would only upset the women. We'll go over to Woodford first thing in the morning and see the Inspector. I'll have these brutes run to earth : you may be sure of that."

With this comforting assurance, we separated to dress for dinner.

The latter meal, and indeed all the rest of the evening, passed off cheerfully enough. Lady Baradell and Miss York both seemed to be in excellent spirits, chaffing us unmercifully over the very minute bag of duck (one and a half couple) which we had managed to bring back from our expedition. I could not help wondering what they would have said if they had known as much about the sporting possibilities of the Suffolk coast as I did.

I went to bed early, and just for a change passed a quite uneventful night. I had become so used to entertaining beautiful ladies or grappling with would-be assassins that for a time I felt positively neglected. However, if the night was dull, the next day promised to be exciting enough, so I consoled myself with this reflection and went peacefully off to sleep.

The topic of our visit to the police was broached tactfully at breakfast next morning by Maurice.

"I am afraid Stuart and I will have to run over to Woodford on business," he announced.

There was an immediate chorus of protest from the ladies. "Oh, but we've promised to give them their revenge at tennis," said Miss York.

"I didn't know there was any business at Woodford," remarked Lady Baradell. "I thought the entire population spent their time talking politics at the street corners."

"Oh, it's only a little matter," said Maurice. "It won't take us long. We'll drive over in the trap, and I'll be back here by eleven."

"Well, if you must go," put in Aunt Mary, "you might tell Cooper to send some marmalade. You remember, Stuart; Maurice is sure to forget."

I pledged my word that the marmalade should be faithfully dispatched; and with these two somewhat incongruous errands before us, we set forth after breakfast in a dogcart. Maurice, who was handling the reins, seemed to be a little depressed.

"I hope the police will be able to find the scoundrels without making too much fuss about it," he said, flicking the steed viciously with his whip. "One doesn't want the papers to get hold of a thing like this."

I quite believed that nothing would annoy him more. "We must hope for the best," I said cheerfully. "I don't mind a little trouble, if I can help you clear the neighbourhood of a gang like that."

I have no doubt that he was grateful for this magnanimous sentiment, but he didn't trouble to express it in words. We tooled on down the road in silence, and passing through the outskirts of Woodford, drew up at the police station, where a polite gentleman in corduroy trousers shambled forward from a side-walk and took the horse's head. On the steps stood a depressed-looking constable, who touched his helmet when he recognised Maurice.

"Is the Inspector in?" asked the latter.

The constable at once brisked up. "Yes, sir; just come along 'arf a minute ago. D'ye want to see him, sir?"

Maurice nodded, and clambering out of the trap, we followed Robert up the steps and into the office.

The Inspector, a large, solid-looking person, was seated at a desk laboriously writing. As we entered he laid down his pen with a sigh and wiped his fingers on his trousers.

"Good morning, Mr. Furnivall," he said. "What can I have the pleasure of doing for you this morning?" Then, seeing me, he added politely: "Good morning, sir."

"Good morning, Inspector," said Maurice. "We have come on rather a serious business."

The Inspector assumed what I can only imagine he meant for an official expression. Placing his hands on his knees and turning his toes in, he leaned forward and scowled at us.

"How's that, sir?" he inquired.

I felt a wild desire to retort, "Not a bit like it!" but fortunately Maurice took up the dialogue. In curt and apparently indignant phrases he described the gross outrage of the previous day, turning every now and then to me to confirm his statements.

Poaching and robbery," he finished, "I can put up with, but when it comes to a cold-blooded and deliberate attempt to murder one of my guests, I think it is time that the police interfered."

A more dumbfounded man than that poor police inspector I have seldom seen. He listened to the story with an amazement that bordered on the pathetic, and when Maurice had finished, produced a red cotton handkerchief and wiped his forehead.

"Lord bless us, Mr. Furnivall!" he observed. "Who'd have thought it?"

Then his professional instincts got the better of him. "I'll make a note or two of your statement while it's fresh in me mind," he added, pulling out a large notebook. "What time might the incident have occurred?"

"The incident," I replied, "occurred as nearly as possible at a quarter to six."

"Ah!" said he, jotting down the fact; "and maybe, sir, you'd be able to recognise the men?"

I shook my head. "I doubt it," I said. "It was getting a bit dusk, and I wasn't exactly in a position to stare at them. You'd better try the gentleman at the Plough who came to my rescue. He had a much better sight of them."

"Ah!" said the Inspector, "his name being——?"

"Oh, Loman," said I, "or something like that."

The Inspector wrote it down, and then shut his notebook with a determined air.

"I'll look into the matter at once, gentlemen," he said. "I don't want to make no promises, but I reckon that by to-morrow we ought to know something about it. They're a rough lot, them marshmen, but this'll be a lesson to 'em. I'll teach them they can't go shooting at gents promiscuous like—not while I'm Inspector."

This little personal touch rather appealed to me.

"Thank you," I said. "I'm sure the case couldn't be in more efficient hands. I'm going over to the Plough now, so I'll tell Mr. Loman, or whatever his name is, that you'd like to see him."

We went outside, where the gentleman in corduroy trousers was still affectionately clutching the horse's bridle under the critical eye of the constable.

"Are you coming with me?" I asked Maurice. "I should like to introduce you to my rescuer—he seems rather a decent sort of chap."

Maurice shook his head, I thought a trifle sullenly. "I must get back for the tennis," he said. "Ask your friend over to Ashton to-morrow—he might like to see the cricket."

Considering that he believed Billy to be responsible for spoiling his admirable arrangements, this seemed to me really handsome.

"Right you are," I said cheerfully. "I shall have a look at the car afterwards, so don't expect me till you see me. By the way, isn't there a tea-fight or something on this afternoon?"

Maurice nodded. "The Cuthberts are giving a garden-party, and I believe Aunt Mary said some of us might stroll over. But don't you bother about it, if you've made other arrangements." He brought out the latter remark with a kind of suggestive leer, that told me plainly he was thinking of Lady Baradell.

"Thanks," I said coolly. "You're an ideal host, Maurice." And leaving him to chew over this compliment at his leisure, I strolled across the street in the direction of the Plough.

I found Billy sitting alone in the bar parlour reading the morning paper, and taking an occasional pull at a large tankard of ale.

"I hope I'm not interrupting your breakfast, Billy," I said.

He jumped up smiling, and flung down the paper on the seat.

"I guessed you'd be over early," he said.

"Then you guessed more than I did," I retorted. "Why this confidence?"

He walked round behind the bar, and taking down an envelope which was sitting up among the bottles, tossed it across to me.

"Here's your love letter, my son," he said. "I told the barmaid you'd be in for it this morning."

I picked it up, remembering with a sudden thrill of pleasure my message to Mercia.

"When did this come, Billy?" I asked.

"A boy brought it last night about half-past nine. I happened to be in here, so I told them you were staying at Ashton, and would no doubt be calling round after breakfast. Not a bad shot—eh? Who is it? The lady with the gun?"

I tore open the envelope and quickly read the contents—

"I will be in the old windmill just beyond Barham Bridge at four o'clock."

There was no signature, but I didn't need one.

"Since you took up detective work, Billy," I said, "your powers of deduction are improving."

He chuckled, and coming back from behind the bar flung open the French window.

"Let's go out into the garden," he said. "I've tons

to tell you, and the barmaid will be back here in a minute."

We went down the steps which led to the square patch of lawn behind the house, and seated ourselves on an old wooden bench in the sunshine.

"Things are moving," I said, taking out a pipe and beginning to fill it with some care. "Maurice and I have just been interviewing the local inspector. The attempted murder of Mr. Stuart Northcote is now a problem for the police."

Billy whistled. "That's good," he observed. "Did Maurice give 'em any tips?"

"No," I returned; "they're looking to you for those. I've explained how an obliging tripper, residing at the Plough, sailed in and rescued me. You're quite a hero, Billy. The police want to see you as soon as possible, and Maurice has asked me to invite you over to Ashton to-morrow to watch the cricket match."

Billy slapped his knee. "That's good travelling," he observed, "precious good. But don't think you're the only one who's making history. I've got a little shock to spring on you that knocks spots off any of your news." He paused, and then tapped the note which I was still holding in my hand. "Do you know where your fair assassin's hanging out?"

I shook my head.

"Miss Mercia Solano," said Billy, leaning back and folding his arms, "is, at the present moment, the honoured guest of M. Baretti."

I jumped up off the bench. "Good Lord, Billy!" I said, "is that a fact?"

He nodded. "And what's more," he added, "I've seen her. Last night, after that note came, I slipped out and went up to the Hollies. First of all I had a good look at the place from the road. All the blinds were down and the shutters closed in front, so I made a bit of a circle and got in through the plantation at the back. There was a window open there on the second floor, with a light in the room. Well, to cut the yarn short, I climbed up one of the trees nearest the house and had a squint in."

"And you actually saw Mercia?" I demanded.

"I saw the whole charming bunch of 'em," said Billy. "There was Dot-and-carry-one; and the gentleman who put a bullet through your hat; and a frowsy-looking sort of female; and last, but not least, your own particular bit of trouble. At least, I suppose it was. A well-built sort of girl, with stunning eyes?"

I looked at him with pity. "You have your points, Billy," I said, "but don't try to describe a beautiful woman. What were they doing?"

"Jawing at her, as far as I could make out," he answered, with a grin. "Of course, I couldn't hear anything—I was too far away; but I could see them waggling their hands and shrugging their shoulders in the best Dago fashion. Looked to me as if they were trying to persuade her to do something she didn't want to—stick a knife into you, I expect."

"I shouldn't wonder," I said, "but I'll find out this afternoon. She's going to meet me at four o'clock."

Billy frowned. "Isn't that rather running your head into it unnecessarily?" he asked. "She's staying with them in the house, and, after all, you know precious little about her."

"That's just the reason why I want to find out some more," I retorted. Then, laying my hand on his shoulder, I added more seriously: "I've got to see her, Billy; I can't get on without her any longer."

He grunted. "Well, it's no good saying anything if you've made up your mind: I know that. All the same, I think you're an ass, my son. What are your plans?"

"Well," said I, "I thought I'd hang about here and look at the car and do a bit of shopping while you went across and interviewed the police. Then we might have some lunch, and after that I'll go off and meet Mercia."

"Where's the trysting tree?" inquired Billy.

I gave him the note.

He read it through, grunted again, and then handed it back to me. "You know your own business best," he said, "but, if you take my tip, you'll shove a gun of some sort in your pocket. Where is this blessed windmill?"

"I don't know," I said, "but I'll find out while you're making love to the Inspector."

"What am I to say to him?" demanded Billy.

"Oh, just tell him that you were out duck-shooting, and spotted two sportsmen blowing holes through my hat. If he asks you whether you could recognise them, you'd better say they were a couple of rough-looking blackguards something like police constables. We don't want him to get on to the Hollies yet awhile."

Billy laughed. "All right," he said, getting up; "I'll handle him with the gloves on. I may as well be off now. Don't get into any more mischief while I'm away."

We parted company outside the hotel, Billy going off to the police station, and I strolling up the street in search of Aunt Mary's marmalade. Having secured this, and given instructions that it was to be sent to Ashton at once, I proceeded to make a further inspection of the old town. My wanderings brought me eventually to the bar parlour of the Bull, the second principal hotel, which struck me as a very suitable place for making inquiries as to the whereabouts of Barham Bridge.

I was enlightened on this point by a genial, clean-shaven gentleman in sporting get-up, who was engaged in shifting a morning sherry-and-bitters.

" Barham Bridge!" he said.   " Oh yes; it's about two miles up the road to the left.   You can't mistake it, because there's an old ruined mill standing back in the field just beyond."

I thanked him, and we chatted away cheerfully for about a quarter of an hour, in the course of which I discovered that his name was Cumming, that he lived in the neighbourhood, was a keen yachtsman, and by profession a well-known writer of bloodthirsty adventure-stories for the popular weekly papers.   I only regretted that circumstances prevented me from being equally confidential.   But for my promise to Northcote, I felt that I could have given him a plot which would have made him my friend for life!

Returning to the Plough, I received the key of the garage and indulged in a brief inspection of the car. My knowledge of motors is decidedly limited, but as she started up all right, it seemed to me that there couldn't be much the matter with her.   So I contented myself with filling up the petrol tank and pumping in some oil.   It was while I was engaged in the latter operation that Billy reappeared.

" They told me you were out here," he said.   " Nothing the matter with the car, is there?"

" No," I said, "she's all right.   I was only filling her up, because I'm thinking of using her this afternoon. How did you get on with the Inspector?"

13

Billy smiled wickedly. "We've made great friends," he said. "I'm going down on the marsh with him this afternoon to help hunt out the criminals. He says it's a dangerous job."

"It will be a pretty thirsty one," I returned, "if you stick to it long enough. I'm afraid you've been stuffing the poor man up shamelessly, Billy."

"He didn't want it," chuckled Billy, thrusting his arm through mine. "I do, though. Come inside and have some grub. The chase starts at half-past two."

We entered the long dining-room, where an elderly waiter brought us an excellent lunch of cold partridge and Stilton cheese, which we assisted in its progress with a couple of bottles of Jacob's Pilsener. As Billy said, "You can't hunt murderers on air," a remark which I considered applied with equal force to the nice conduct of a somewhat complicated love scene.

"Besides, that's not all my day's work," he added. "When I get back, I'm going to pay another call at the Hollies. There's a drain pipe under that window which looks as if it would bear my weight all right."

"Look here, Billy," I protested, "it's my show, and you're doing all the dangerous part of it."

"That's a matter of opinion," he laughed. "Anyhow, I'm quite satisfied. If you'll tackle Miss Mercia Solano, I'll take on Humpty Dumpty and the others with the greatest pleasure."

He got up, glancing at his watch. "I must be off," he added. "I promised to call for Sherlock at a quarter-past, and one mustn't keep the Law waiting. I'll tell you all about it to-morrow. What time does the cricket match start?"

"Oh, Goodness knows," said I: "about eleven, I suppose."

"Well, I'll be around some time in the morning. So long, old son, and don't forget that all women are born liars."

"Except Mercia," I added.

CHAPTER XVII

I PULLED up the car just this side of Barham Bridge, and turned her on to the strip of level grass that ran parallel with the road. Mercia seemed to have chosen a pleasantly isolated meeting-place. Away to my right, on the top of a small hill, stood an old weather-beaten, half-ruined windmill; but with this exception, nothing broke the flat monotony of the far-stretching Suffolk pastures.

Opening the gate, I made my way up the rough track, which in more spacious days had apparently been the miller's roadway. It struck me that if Mercia was playing me false, I was offering a really beautiful target to anyone in the mill; but I don't think it can have been this reflection that was sending the blood dancing so cheerfully through my veins.

Anyhow, I strode on briskly till I reached the top, where I took a final glance back to see if I was still unobserved. Then, as I looked round again, I found Mercia. She was standing in the doorway of the mill, pale and beautiful as ever, and at the sight of her my heart gave a great jump that seemed almost like a shout of triumph. It was only with a big effort that I stopped myself from picking her up in my arms and kissing her.

"Ah, it's good to see you again," I said, holding out my hands.

She drew back with a quick, frightened gesture.

"You have not been followed?" she whispered.

I stepped inside. "No," I said; "I came in the car. It's down at the bottom of the hill."

She gave a little gasp of relief. "I was so afraid. I thought they suspected. It's madness our meeting like this."

"Then I. pray God I shall never be sane," I said, with a low, reckless laugh. "Oh, Mercia,—my sweet, white, wonderful Mercia,—do you think life has anything for me that I wouldn't throw away with both hands for the sake of seeing you!"

The passion in my voice brought a faint tinge of colour into her face. She leaned against the side of the mill and put up her hands with a little pleading gesture.

"Ah, don't, don't!" she whispered.

I shook my head, smiling down at her tenderly. "Anything else, Mercia mine," I said; "but you might as well tell the sun not to shine as tell me not to love you."

I tried to take her hand, but she wrenched herself free.

"You mustn't say these things to me," she cried, half sobbing. "Isn't it enough that I should have tried to save you? Are you quite merciless? Oh, go, while there's yet time. Go out of my life, and let me forget you."

"I won't," I said obstinately. "I love you with every beat of my heart, Mercia, and all the murdering half-castes in South America shan't come between us."

She looked at me piteously. "Do you know what you are saying? Don't you understand how impossible it is that the daughter of Manuel Solano can ever be anything to you?"

"No," I said stoutly, "I don't. I've already sworn

to you that I had no hand in your father's death, and you believe me—I know that you believe me."

She raised her eyes to mine. "Yes," she said, more calmly, "I do believe you. Should I be here if I didn't? I believe you against my own eyes, against the evidence of all San Luca, against reason itself. That is why I am trying to save you from the others."

A thrill of triumph shot through me at her words.

"Mercia," I whispered softly, "Mercia."

She lifted her hands again, as though to motion me back.

"But if you did not kill my father," she went on, "you know who did. Tell me the truth—ah, for God's sake, tell me the truth!"

The broken pleading of that piteous cry nearly shattered my resolve. But I had pledged my word to Northcote, and with a great effort I steeled myself to be true to it.

"I know nothing for certain," I said. "If the others believe me guilty, they are wrong. But why not leave them to take their own vengeance? They seem quite capable of it."

She drew herself up with a shudder. "It is too late now. There is only one escape from the League— death. When they came to me and told me that you were still alive, I joined them gladly, recklessly. I thought that, at least, I should be able to avenge my father. Then that night in Park Lane I learned, for the first time, that I was wrong. I deceived them, I lied to them. It would have been no good my telling them the truth: they would never have believed it. Even now, I think they suspect me."

Her half-incoherent sentences gave me my first glimpse of the real truth.

"Mercia," I said, "who do you think I am?"

She stared at me in bewilderment.

"You are Ignace Prado," she said slowly.

"Before God," I answered, "I am nothing of the kind."

There was a moment of strenuous silence. Then, with a wild, impulsive gesture, she laid her hand on my arm. "Who are you?" she whispered fearfully. "Speak, tell me! I feel as if I was going mad."

I caught her hands and drew her towards me. "Mercia, my heart," I said, holding her tightly in my arms and looking down into her dear, startled eyes, "you must give me your trust, as I have given you my love. We have got caught up, you and I, into a tangle of the Devil's own spinning, and God knows how it's all going to end. Listen. I swear by my love for you that I am not Ignace Prado, and that I know nothing of your father's death. More than that I can't tell you for the present, but you must believe me, Mercia—you *shall* believe me," I added, almost savagely, as she freed herself from my embrace and leaned back panting and pale against the wall.

"I feel that you are speaking the truth," she gasped, "but oh! you are in terrible danger. Guarez and the others will kill you, as surely as the sun rises, unless you leave here at once—unless you disappear altogether. They at least are convinced that you are Ignace; and your cousin, Maurice Furnivall—he is the man that has betrayed you—it was he who first told the League that you were in London."

"Yes," I said grimly, "I fancied I was indebted to Master Maurice for that kindness."

"And you will go, you will go immediately?"

"I shall go, Mercia," I said, "at precisely the same time that you do. If you imagine I am going to clear

out and leave you alone with that cheerful gang of
cut-throats, you're making a mistake."

"Oh, but you must," she said beseechingly. "I am
in no danger. Really, I am in no danger."

"I don't believe you," I said bluntly. "Does Sir
Henry Tregattock know where you are?"

She looked confused. "He—he thinks I am with
friends," she stammered. "I am going back there in
a day or so. I will go directly you have disappeared."

"You'll do nothing of the kind," I said. "If I go,
you'll come with me. I won't stir a step from Woodford
unless it's to take you back to London."

She gazed at me despairingly. "What's the use?"
she cried. "They will only kill us both."

"Will they?" I said. "At present, I think they've
got their hands full trying to kill me."

She shook her head. "The League never fails. It's
only a matter of time. Within a week, you will be
dead—you and your friend too. Oh, you don't know
what danger you are in. Listen. There were four others
besides Prado and Lopez whom the Council condemned,
and every one of them has been killed since. You
know what happened to Lopez."

"I don't," I said. "I know nothing about the infernal
business except that they've bungled me three times,
and that somehow or other they've managed to get
hold of the wretched Milford. I should stick it out
now in any case, if only for the sake of revenging him."

"Milford," she repeated, looking at me in horror.
"Is that the man they tried to poison?"

"Yes," I said. "He vanished two days ago, and
Heaven knows what's happened to him by now."

She drew a deep breath. "Ah," she whispered,
"that explains the disappearance of Da Costa. He

was watching the house, and he was to write to Guarez every day. We have heard nothing."

I gave an exclamation of surprise. "By Jove!" I cried, "perhaps Milford's——"

A sudden sound of voices outside pulled me up abruptly. Instinctively, I whipped my hand to my pocket, and for a moment we stood there in absolute silence. Then came the noise of footsteps, followed almost immediately by a remark in a man's voice, and the little trill of a woman's laugh. I recognised the latter at once, and in a flash I had made up my mind.

"Come, Mercia," I whispered quickly. "It's two of our own party from Ashton. We must see this through. Leave it to me to explain."

She made no answer, and we stepped out through the doorway into the sunshine.

About ten paces away, York and Lady Baradell were coming up the hill towards us. As we appeared in the opening they stopped, and for a moment all four of us stood looking at each other in a prettily embarrassed silence.

York was the first to speak. "Then it *was* you Northcote!" he observed. "Lady Baradell declared it must be your car."

"Lady Baradell was right," I returned cheerfully. "Let me introduce you all. Miss de Rosen, Lady Baradell, Captain York."

Lady Baradell, who had favoured Mercia with one swift, incisive scrutiny, smiled sweetly.

"We were walking over to the Cuthberts'," she remarked, "and we happened to see your car standing on the grass. I had no idea you were an antiquary, Mr. Northcote."

"No," I said coolly; "I have so many hidden talents."

York, who seemed to feel that the atmosphere was strained, made a tactful effort to clear it.

"Car all right?" he inquired sympathetically.

"I was just testing it," I said, "and, in the course of doing so, I as nearly as possible slaughtered Miss de Rosen."

Mercia smiled with delightful composure. "I have always told Mr. Northcote he drives much too fast. I thought I should be safe from him in the wilds of Suffolk, however."

"You're staying here?" put in Lady Baradell, in a smooth voice.

"Quite close by with some friends," answered Mercia carelessly, "and that reminds me I ought to be getting back, or they'll be wondering what's happened to me. Good-bye, Mr. Northcote; thank you so much for your ride. You must come over and see us before you go away. Good-bye."

She smiled graciously to the others, and turned as if to go.

"May I have the pleasure of seeing you back, Miss de Rosen?" I suggested. "I have been guilty of bringing you all this way out of your road."

"Oh no," she said, laughing. "I can take a short cut across the fields. I am quite used to walking about the country alone, really."

She gave me a little wave of her hand, and set off at a brisk pace across the hill. Her coolness left me flabbergasted.

Lady Baradell, who had been looking at me with a kind of malicious amusement, smiled mockingly.

"What a popular man you are, Mr. Northcote," she

observed. "You can't get away from your friends, even in Suffolk."

"No," I said. "The country seems to be sown with them. Next time I want a little seclusion, I shall stop in London."

"Pretty girl, that," said York, looking approvingly after Mercia's retreating figure.

I was not going to be drawn into any further confidence.

"Suppose I motor you on to the Cuthberts'?" I suggested. "I'll promise to drive carefully."

"That's a sound idea," answered York, with enthusiasm.

"Well, it must be very carefully," said Lady Baradell. "You fortunate men aren't bothered with clothes and hair. I don't want to arrive looking like a suffragette after a fight with a policeman."

It was so impossible to conceive Lady Baradell in such a condition that we both laughed.

"There is no danger," I said. "You saw how un-ruffled Miss de Rosen was."

"It was quite remarkable," admitted her ladyship sweetly.

Down the hill we went, and two minutes later, with York beside me and Lady Baradell ensconced in the back, I was carefully steering the car over Barham Bridge and along the winding Suffolk road, which twisted in and out between the lush meadows and small coppices.

York, of course, knew the way, and, following his directions, we soon came in sight of an old Jacobean mansion rather the worse for wear, standing back in pleasantly timbered grounds.

"How are you going to get back?" I asked.

"Furnivall and my sister are coming over in the carriage," said York, "and there'll be plenty of room for us."

"In that case," I said, "I think I'll desert you basely at the door."

"Oh, come along in," protested York. Then, turning to Lady Baradell, he added laughingly: "Tell him he's got to; he'll obey *you*."

She shook her head. "I am afraid I sympathise with him. I am sure he can find a much more pleasant way of spending his time than talking about turnips and the vicar."

York groaned. "Well, I call it uncommon mean of you, Northcote," he grumbled, as we turned in at the lodge. "You and Vane have both shied off."

"It's the privilege of age," I said, slowing up the car as we came round to the front door. "I'll meet you at dinner, and hear all about it."

Any remark York may have wished to make was cut short by the appearance of the butler.

Lady Baradell, looking extremely unlike a suffragette, stepped daintily out, and in another minute I was speeding away again down the drive on my way back to Woodford.

I was burning to tell Billy about my latest discoveries, but when I reached the Plough I discovered, as I had feared would be the case, that he had not yet returned from his man-hunting expedition on the marshes. I put the car away in the garage, and hung about for the best part of an hour and a half in the vain hope that he would turn up. Finally, I went into the lounge and wrote him a short note, which I gave to the barmaid. I told him that I had made some novel and highly interesting additions to our stock of knowledge, and begged him to turn up at Ashton next morning without fail. Then, feeling that I had already been long enough away to excite Maurice's suspicions, I set off on my way back to the house.

I reached Ashton, curiously enough, just at the same time as the carriage. As a matter of fact, it passed me in the drive, and when I got up to the front door, I found Maurice and the others standing round the porch.

"Well, I hope you are properly ashamed of yourself, Northcote," cried York, with a laugh. "Here we are, four hopeless wrecks, while you and Vane and Baradell have been selfishly enjoying yourselves."

"Was it as bad as that?" I asked sympathetically. "How is the vicar, and how are the turnips?"

"The vicar's all right," returned Miss York, with a wry face. "He was there at tea."

"Was that the vicar?" observed Lady Baradell dryly. "I thought it was one of the turnips."

There was a general laugh, which was interrupted by the appearance of Maurice's man, carrying a telegram on a silver tray.

"I beg your pardon, sir," he observed, "but this came this afternoon just after you had left. I thought it might be important."

Maurice took the wire, and as he began to open it we resumed our conversation, Miss York demanding a laughing explanation as to how I had been spending my afternoon.

In the middle of my answer, which I must admit was not of a wholly truthful nature, I happened to look up in Maurice's direction.

Over the top of the wire I got a glimpse of his eyes, staring at me with a kind of devilish mixture of hatred, triumph, and incredulity. It was only for an instant. As our glances met the expression vanished from his face as though it had been wiped off by a sponge, and with a short laugh he crushed the wire in his hand.

"Well, this is a pretty sort of nuisance," he remarked.

There was a chorus of, "What's the matter?"

"I am afraid I shall have to go up to London to-night. There's — there's some confounded trouble about a trusteeship or something—I don't quite understand from the wire; but they want me to come and talk it over as soon as possible."

Everybody, except myself, hastened to express their sympathy.

"Oh, it doesn't really matter," said Maurice. "I have no doubt I shall be able to get down again to-morrow, or at latest the day after. You mustn't think of breaking up the party—any of you. I dare say this silly business won't keep me more than a few hours, after all, and Aunt Mary will be only too delighted to look after you. Ah, here she is."

Aunt Mary, who had just joined us from the hall, was immediately acquainted with the news.

"Must you really go, Maurice dear?" she said. "What a horrid nuisance! I suppose you have to catch the nine-fifty from Woodford. Of course, I won't hear of anyone cutting short their visit. Stuart will play host for you while you are away, and we'll manage to amuse ourselves somehow."

"Yes," said Maurice, looking at me with a friendly smile. "You'll see to things, won't you, old chap? I'll just run in now and put my traps up. Dinner at the usual time, of course."

As he spoke, the dressing gong sounded, and we all trooped into the house.

I made my way up to my own room, where I lit a cigarette and sat down on the bed.

"Now what the dickens," said I to myself, "can have been in that wire?"

CHAPTER XVIII

IT was not York's fault that I took no part in the cricket match. His persistent and pathetic appeals to me at breakfast to fill the vacant place in his eleven were worthy of a more hopeful cause.

"Oh, leave Mr. Northcote alone, Bertie," broke in his sister at last. "You've got ten people already, and that's quite enough for the silly game."

"Ten!" retorted her brother. "What's the good of ten, and half of them village boys? Orbridge are a frightfully hot side."

"They'll be hotter still by the time the match is over," I said, looking out contentedly into the blazing sunshine. "It's no day for violent exercise. I'm going to sit in the shade and criticise."

"You'll get on very nicely, I'm sure, Captain York," put in Aunt Mary consolingly. "You always make such a lot of runs yourself."

"Besides," suggested Lady Baradell, with a characteristic smile, "think of the honour of winning against odds. If Mr. Northcote played, it would be a foregone conclusion."

"Well, it's just my luck," grumbled York dejectedly. "If I'd known Furnivall was going off to London like this, I'd never have got the match up. We shall have no one to bowl now, and we shall probably be fielding all day."

"A most healthy form of exercise," I observed. "Think of the appetite you'll have for dinner."

York, however, declined to be comforted, and it was in a very dispirited frame of mind that after breakfast he marshalled his team in the well-kept cricket field at the bottom of the garden. They consisted chiefly of local talent from Woodford, assisted by York himself and a sporting young doctor in the neighbourhood, who arrived on a motor bicycle. The Orbridge team drove over in a brake, reaching the ground about a quarter to eleven.

While the preparations were on foot, I strolled about with Miss York, keeping a watchful eye for Billy. I don't think I showed any outward symptoms of disturbance, but my interview with Mercia on the previous day had left me very uneasy in my mind, and I was naturally anxious to hear if Billy had made any further discoveries. Besides, I felt sure that in some way or other Maurice's hurried departure for London was connected with my humble affairs—a fact which by no means relieved my perplexity. Whom he could have heard from, unless it was the missing "Da Costa" (whom I imagined to be none other than my old friend "Francis"), I was quite unable to conceive.

Lady Baradell, Aunt Mary, and Sir George came out just before the match started. Baradell himself had been persuaded by the energetic York to don flannels, though, as he pathetically observed, he had not touched a cricket bat for a dozen years. The rest of us established ourselves in chairs under the shade of a couple of large elm trees, and resolutely prepared to take an interest in the proceedings.

Lady Baradell glanced across at her husband with an expression of amusement. "Charles looks charming," she observed to Miss York. " Your brother's clothes fit him to perfection. I hope he won't get too excited."

"You're not to laugh at him, my dear," said Aunt Mary. " I think it's simply splendid of him to play. I am sure he is setting an example to all of us—especially to you, Stuart."

"Charles," remarked Lady Baradell, "always sets an example. It's his profession."

Miss York laughed. " Do you set an example too, Mr. Northcote?" she inquired, turning to me.

" Only on the principle of the 'awful warning,' " I said; " but it's just as effective."

" Mr. Northcote," put in Lady Baradell softly, "is a law to himself. It is a very convenient arrangement if one has the strength of mind for it."

" Who's this coming?" interrupted Aunt Mary suddenly.

We all glanced up in the direction she was looking, and there, just clambering over the stile that led into the field, was a figure in grey flannels which I recognised at once as Billy.

I hastened to explain. " He's a man named Logan," I said, "who's staying at the Plough. We met him when we were out shooting, and Maurice asked me to invite him up to the cricket."

Aunt Mary, who was evidently the soul of hospitality, beamed good-naturedly. "Oh, how very nice!" she said. " Perhaps he'd play."

" I dare say he would, if you asked him," I replied mischievously, getting up from my chair.

Billy, who has never suffered from shyness, came straight across to where we were sitting, and took off his hat. In a few words I made the necessary introductions.

14

" I am so glad you were able to come, Mr. Logan,"
said Aunt Mary graciously. " Won't you take part in
the game for us? Captain York is one man short, and
I know he'd be delighted if you would help him."

I watched Billy's face with quiet enjoyment. " I am
afraid cricket is not much in my line," he replied
politely. " In fact, to tell the truth, I have never even
seen it since I was at school. But surely Mr. Northcote
is playing?"

" Mr. Northcote is doing nothing of the kind," I observed, with a threatening look at Billy. " He knows
his limitations."

" Uncommon modest chap, Northcote," put in Vane,
with a chuckle, " especially on a hot day."

Our conversation was interrupted at this period by
the appearance of the Orbridge eleven, who, having lost
the toss, streamed out on to the field, tossing the ball
to each other in the most approved fashion. York and
one of the villagers, heavily protected against casual
concussion, followed them to the wickets.

The match started, and for the next half-hour our
comments were chiefly confined to laudatory ejacula-
tions, such as " Good shot, sir," " Oh, pretty stroke."
Knowing nothing about the phraseology of the game,
I was careful to follow Vane's lead in this respect, a
piece of strategy which I noticed that Billy was also
adopting.

When York was eventually bowled for thirty-six, in
a well-intentioned but misdirected effort to hit the ball
into the neighbouring county of Norfolk, I thought
the time had arrived for a little private conversation
with William. I nudged him gently so as to give him
the tip, and then getting up from my chair, I suggested
ᵗhat we should stroll round to the pavilion and con-

gratulate the dismissed batsman upon his impressive performance.

"I'm glad you got a move on," said Billy, as soon as we were out of hearing. "I've some pretty interesting news for you, my son. And what's more, I'm dying for a smoke."

"Well, we'll just go and pat York on the back first," I said. "Lady Baradell's sure to be watching us."

Billy looked at me suspiciously. "Who is Lady Baradell?" he asked. "Seems to me you've been keeping her dark. Another of 'em—eh?"

"Lady Baradell," I answered cheerfully, "is a very charming woman, but she doesn't come into our particular trouble—at least, not officially."

"I see," said Billy.

We caught York at the entrance to the pavilion, flushed with his exertions and magnificent in a red and yellow blazer. I introduced Billy as the gentleman who had rescued me from the marshmen, and we chatted away for a few minutes about the attempted crime, and congratulated York upon his spirited innings.

"You're the hero of the hour," I said, waving my hand towards the small group under the elm trees; "go and receive your laurels."

He sauntered off, protesting with true English mock modesty that he had played "a rotten innings," and Billy and I made our way to a deserted bank on the farther side of the field.

"Not bad news, I hope, Billy?" said I, a little anxiously.

"It's not altogether serene," he answered, in a rather grave voice. "I'm afraid your girl's in a bit of a mess."

My heart seemed to tighten.

"Nothing serious yet," he added quickly; "but those beauties up at the Hollies have found out, somehow, that she met you yesterday, and, unless I'm badly mistaken, they've locked her up."

"How did you hear this?" I demanded.

"Through the window," said Billy. "If it had only been a little wider open I'd have heard a lot more, but fresh air's death to a Dago." He lit his pipe and puffed away energetically for a moment. "I climbed up the drain-pipe," he added. "It was as easy as falling off a tree."

"You're a brick, Billy," I said warmly. "What did they actually say?"

"Well, you know the way Dagoes jabber—half-Spanish, half-English, and going nineteen to the dozen all the time. As far as I could hear—I was hanging on by my eyelids all the time, you must remember—someone had sent a message telling them that you and Mercia had been spending the afternoon together. They were devilish sick about it, and seemed to be discussing what to do with her. The gentleman who plugged you was very vicious. If he'd been running the show, I wouldn't have given twopence for Mercia's chances; but fortunately old Dot-and-carry-one's the top dog there. He stuck it out that there must be no violence at present, and the others finally agreed with him."

"He's lucky," I said grimly.

Billy nodded. "Damned lucky," he repeated. "If they'd come to any other conclusion, I should have plugged the bunch of them through the window. I had my gun on me. As things turned out, I thought it best to postpone the picnic."

"It won't be for long," I said. "We must have Mercia out of that to-night, whatever happens."

"Yes," agreed Billy gently. "I think it's time we led trumps. What's your news?"

Without waste of words, I told him about my conversation with Mercia and the arrival of the mysterious wire for Maurice.

"By Jove!" he said, staring at me thoughtfully, "that does open up matters a bit. Fancy Northcote being that damned villain Prado! I always heard he was an Englishman, but I didn't believe it. No wonder you're unpopular, my lad."

"I'd like to know how he escaped," I said, "and what this infernal League is that's on his track."

Billy smiled. "A man like Prado," he answered ironically, "is likely to be out when people start blowing up his palace. I shouldn't wonder in the least if he did it himself, and used the chance to sneak out of the country. As for the League—well, you know as well as I do what these rotten little South American States are like. Prado probably belonged to some secret society that helped him murder Solano and bag the Presidency; and then, when he'd got the job, I've no doubt he rounded on them. They must have some pretty strong reasons for chasing him round the world like this."

"Well, strong reasons or not," I said, "I'm going to fetch Mercia out of that house to-night and take her up to London. I shan't rest till I know she's safe with the Tregattocks."

"I'm with you," said Billy simply. "How do we work it?"

I thought rapidly. "We'll take a tip from Maurice," I said. "You go back to Woodford, and send me a wire about five o'clock saying that I'm wanted in London immediately. That will give me an excuse for getting away. I'll tell them that I'm going to motor up, and then I'll drive over and meet you at the Plough."

Billy nodded. "Right you are," he said. "I'll see the car's ready." Then he chuckled. "We ought to have quite a cheery little evening," he added, rubbing his hands together.

"It's business, Billy," I said, "not pleasure. We don't want any fighting if we can get Mercia away without."

"There's a precious fat chance of that," observed Billy. "I can see old Dot-and-carry-one handing her over with his blessing—can't you?"

"He can take his choice," I answered.

There was a short silence. "And what's the next move when we get to London?" inquired Billy.

I shrugged my shoulders. "It's not much good making plans," I said. "Man proposes and Señor Guarez disposes. The only thing I've quite made up my mind about is that I'm not going to give the show away before the three weeks are out. They've got my back up, Billy, apart altogether from my having given my word to Northcote."

Billy nodded. "There's Milford, too."

"There *was*," I said. "And that's another good reason for hanging on. We'll clear that business up whatever happens." Then I paused. "I should like to put a spoke in Sangatte's wheel if I could," I added reflectively.

"Well, we shan't be dull," said Billy, smiling. "I think I'd better shift my quarters, and come and camp in Park Lane."

"Why, of course," I said. "You don't suppose I'm

going to let you out of my sight till it's all over?
I want you to be my best man."

"Anything to oblige," returned Billy. "Though I
guess I'm more likely to be chief mourner."

As he relieved himself of this encouraging statement,
I suddenly spotted Sir George and Miss York strolling
round the ground towards us.

"That's settled then, Billy," I said hurriedly. "You
get the car ready and send me the wire, and I'll meet
you at the Plough at about seven o'clock."

He nodded, and we both got up as the other two
approached.

"We've been sent to fetch you back," began Miss
York "Men are scarce in the grand stand, so you
mustn't be selfish."

"Doocid good innings of York's—what!" remarked
Sir George. "Very pretty shot that late cut of his."

"Charming," I said, with enthusiasm; while Billy,
evidently feeling that the ground was dangerous, contented himself with a reflective smile.

We all four sauntered back to the small group of
chairs under the elm trees, where York was explaining
to Aunt Mary and Lady Baradell some of the finer
beauties of the game.

"You'll stay to lunch, won't you, Mr. Logan?" said
the former. "We always prepare for an indefinite
number on cricket days."

"That sounds distinctly hopeful," I said, with a laugh,
as Billy signified his pleasure in accepting. "It's just
the sort of lunch that I shall be delighted to meet.
Nothing makes one more hungry than watching other
people exert themselves."

"What an excellent appetite you must enjoy, Mr.
Northcote," put in Miss Vane mischievously.

Lady Baradell laughed dryly. "An excellent appetite," she repeated, "but tempered by a stern sense
of self-control. That is why Mr. Northcote is so
successful."

At this point, a sudden roar of "How's that?" pro-
claimed the downfall of another wicket. "That's nine,"
observed York gloomily. "Nine for ninety-eight, and
only Sir Charles left."

"You might have expressed it a little more kindly,"
said Lady Baradell.

There was a general laugh, and while York was
endeavouring to explain his meaning, we saw Baradell
come out of the pavilion, looking mightily depressed.
He walked to the wicket, took guard, as I believe it's
called, and carefully marked the spot with one of the
bails. Then he faced the bowler, played forward with
belated dignity, and had his middle stump sent flying
out of the ground.

"There, but for the grace of God," I remarked, "goes
Mr. Stuart Northcote."

"Poor dear Sir Charles," murmured Aunt Mary,
getting up from her chair; "at least he tried."

"And that," said Billy, following her example, "is the
best of all epitaphs."

With the dismissal of the unfortunate Baronet, the
two teams adjourned for lunch.

Cricket lunches, I should imagine, are much alike
everywhere, so I will spare you any lengthy description
of the repast. I need only say that at Aunt Mary's
request, as the leading representative of the family, I
installed myself at the head of the table, an honour
which was considerably enriched in attraction by the
presence of Billy. Whenever I caught his eye in the intervals of carving cold lamb, I felt an almost irresistible

desire to burst into a shout of laughter. I could not help picturing the faces of the worthy company if I had only been able to get up and explain the true facts concerning my presence at the banquet.

Such an interlude being unfortunately out of the question, we finished our lunch, smoked our pipes, and after chatting amiably over the course of the match and other exciting topics, sauntered back to the cricket field.

Not being anxious to appear too intimate with Billy, I left him to amuse himself with Lady Baradell and the others, while I promenaded round the ground with Sir George. Billy, who always gets on with women, seemed perfectly contented : indeed, it was not until just on half-past three that he got up and made his excuse to Aunt Mary.

"You will come and see us again, won't you, Mr. Logan?" urged that hospitable lady. "My nephew will be back to-morrow, and I want you to meet him."

"I want to myself," said Billy heartily. "I've heard so much about him."

He shook hands all round, lingering a moment over the operation when it came to Lady Baradell, and then strode off, waving a cheerful farewell to York, who was perspiring freely in the outfield.

"A delightful man," observed Aunt Mary. "I wonder what he can be doing down in this part of the world."

"He thinks of buying a place," explained Miss York. "He says he's tired of wandering about, and wants to settle down."

I repressed a chuckle just in time.

"That would be very nice," said Aunt Mary complacently. "He is just the sort of man we want. I was telling him about the Primrose League, and he was most interested in it. He would be quite an acquisition to the neighbourhood—don't you think so, Lady Baradell?"

Lady Baradell smiled.

To me, the rest of the afternoon dragged in the most distressing fashion. Even if I had been able to take an interest in the cricket, I should still have been feverishly impatient for the evening. The thought of Mercia, helpless in the hands of that precious pack of scoundrels, filled me with a horrible restlessness that made the effort of sitting still and exchanging semi-humorous banalities about the match almost intolerable. I longed for Billy's wire, so that I might have an excuse for escaping into the house to put my things together.

As it was, I was compelled to sit matters out, until the game terminated in a glorious victory for the visitors by sixty-three runs. There were the usual congratulations and chaff,—poor Sir Charles Baradell coming in for a rather unfair share of the latter,—and then, after filling themselves up with tea to an alarming extent, the triumphant Orbridge warriors clambered into their brake and departed. It was while the rest of us were slowly making our way back up the garden that the telegram arrived.

I saw Maurice's butler advancing from the house bearing the inevitable silver tray, and all my muscles seemed instinctively to tighten. It's good to feel that the time for action is at hand, when you've been chafing your heart out all day.

I took the wire and opened it, with an apology to Aunt Mary.

"Must see you to-night. Important business in connection with the Company.   JACOBS."

I gave a nicely calculated laugh, just tinged with annoyance.

"It never rains but it pours," I said ruefully. "First Maurice is called off to town, and now I've got to go."

"What, to-night!" exclaimed Aunt Mary and Miss York simultaneously.

"I'm afraid so," I admitted; "it's a matter of business." And then I read out the wire aloud. I couldn't very well show it them, considering that the somewhat awkward statement, "sent off from Woodford 5.40," was decorating the left-hand corner.

"Oh dear, dear, I am sorry," cried Aunt Mary. "And there's no train till the nine-thirty, too."

"Oh, that doesn't matter," I said. "If you can give me a lift into Woodford, I'll motor up."

"But what about your dinner?"

"After that tea," I declared, laughing, "dinner is a minor consideration."

Aunt Mary looked genuinely distressed. "But, of course, you must have something to eat," she said. "I'll tell cook to put you up some sandwiches and a flask. They'll be ready by the time you've packed."

And without waiting to hear my protests, the dear, kind soul hurried off into the house.

I followed, courteously declining the butler's proffered assistance in packing, and going up to my room, proceeded to stuff my belongings into the handsome Gladstone bag and dressing-case which Northcote had bequeathed to me. I had just finished when I heard the trap roll up to the front door.

The whole party had assembled in the porch to see me off.

"You'll come back, Stuart, if you possibly can," said Aunt Mary.

I felt rather a scoundrel, though it really wasn't my fault. "Why, of course," I said cheerily. "Miss York has promised to teach me tennis. You don't think I am going to miss such a chance?"

"You might ring up Maurice at his rooms and come down with him to-morrow," she suggested.

I nodded. "That's a good idea," I said, "if he'll trust himself to the motor. Well, good-bye, everybody."

I shook hands with them all, except Lady Baradell, who was standing by the trap patting the horse's neck. As I stepped out and the butler put my bags in, she came up to me.

"Good-bye, Stuart," she said, in a low voice. "Will you do a little commission for me?"

"Certainly," I said.

With a quick movement, she handed me a scrap of folded paper. "You'll find it there," she whispered. Then, as she gave me her hand, she added aloud some laughing remark apparently for the benefit of the others.

Thrusting the paper into my pocket, I climbed up into the trap beside the coachman. A farewell wave, a chorus of good-byes, above which there came some vague words from Aunt Mary about "the sandwiches—under the seat," and I was spinning off down the drive through the long avenue of beech trees.

It was not until we were well out on the high road that I took out Lady Baradell's "commission." It consisted of a few words scribbled hastily on half a sheet of the Ashton notepaper—

"Maurice's message last night concerned you. I think you are in great danger, but I don't know what."

And there are some gentlemen who profess to understand women!

CHAPTER XIX

"A GOOD, heavy spanner," I said, "will be about my mark."

Billy rummaged in the tool-box, selected the article in question, and handed it over to me.

"If you get well home with that," he observed, "we shan't have much need of a gun."

I stored it away in my side pocket. "No guns, Billy," I said, "except as a last resort. This is going to be a case of 'all done by kindness.'"

Billy grinned, and walking round to the front of the car, proceeded to start her up.

The hands of the big clock in the stable-yard were just pointing to half-past seven. We had squared our account with the Plough, swallowed down a hasty meal, and strapped our belongings on the grid at the back. Everything, so to speak, was cleared for action, and as we slowly turned out of the yard into the street I could feel my heart beating a little quicker than usual with a pleasant sense of anticipation.

Beyond the fact that we meant to get Mercia out of the house, we had made no particular plans. Somehow or other, we should find a way of breaking in, and, as Billy said, once inside, it would take more than a couple of Dagoes to stop us.

We steered our way through the quiet old town, which looked singularly peaceful in the mellow light of the setting sun.   There was something delightfully incongruous between these pleasant, well-ordered streets and the wild enterprise on which we were embark- .ing.   I smiled to myself at the thought of what the emotions of some of the worthy passers-by would have been if they could have guessed our immediate purpose.

The Hollies lies a mile and a half outside Woodford, on the Orbridge road.   Billy, of course, thanks to his two previous expeditions, knew every inch of the land He halted the car under the shelter of a small plantation of pine trees, about a hundred yards from the house, and then as quietly as possible turned her round.

"She'll be all right here at the side," he said, in a low voice, "but we'd better leave the engine running.   Might be in a bit of a hurry when we pick her up."

I nodded my approval, and going round to the back of the car, took out a couple of pieces of stout cord with which we had thoughtfully provided ourselves.   Billy, meanwhile, having left everything ready for a flying start, proceeded to equip himself out of the tool-chest with a duplicate spanner to mine.

"We'll work round and up through the shrubbery," he whispered, weighing the implement in his hand. "That brings us out just opposite the back door."

"Right you are, Macduff," I said contentedly; "lead on."

It was already getting dusk, even in the open, and once under cover of the thick trees we practically said good-bye to daylight.   Both Billy and I, however, possess a good working knowledge of woodcraft, gained from bitter experience, and I don't think we made more noise than was absolutely necessary.   Anyhow, we finally arrived safe, if a trifle dishevelled, at the low railing which separated the back garden of the Hollies from the wood.

Here we paused, crouching down side by side, and surveying the back of the house with a kind of suppressed exhilaration.

Billy laid his hand on my sleeve. "Look here, Jack," he whispered, "I'll trail across first and see how the land lies. You stop here, and cover me with the gun. You're a better shot than I am."

It was just like Billy to bag the dangerous work with such an excuse, but this was no time for arguing.

"Go on, then," I said. "Give me a hoot when you want me to join you."

He wriggled off noiselessly through the undergrowth in the direction of a large fir tree, which cast a gloomy shadow straight across the lawn. For a moment I was just able to make him out, creeping silently down this sombre pathway.

I shifted my gaze to the house and, revolver in hand, watched keenly for any sign of life. There were four windows looking out at the back, two on the ground floor and two above. They were all in darkness and, so far as I could see, tightly closed.

I spotted Billy once more, just by the back door. Then he disappeared again, and for perhaps five minutes I waited in cold tension, my eyes fixed steadily on the house.

Suddenly, very faint, came the hoot of an owl.

I thrust the revolver into my hip pocket, and picking my way through the undergrowth, cautiously followed Billy's track across the lawn. I found him crouching down under the left-hand window, almost invisible against the thick creeper.

"I've got it," he whispered, putting his lips right up

against my ear. "There's a window open at the side—the pantry, I think. We can get in there."

He led the way round, stealthily as a panther, and I followed, clutching the spanner affectionately in my hand. The distance could not have been more than about twelve yards, but I have never reached a destination safely with greater thankfulness.

We found ourselves facing a small window about two feet from the ground. The top sash was a few inches open, and through the gap we could see a faint glimmer of light stealing in under the door opposite.

"I'd better go first," whispered Billy. "You're so devilish big, you'll probably stick."

I nodded, and with infinite care we lowered the sash, until every possible inch of space was available. Then, mounting on my back, Billy inserted his legs, and wriggled himself down bit by bit, until his feet touched the floor.

For a moment we paused, listening intently for any sounds in the passage. None came, and Billy, leaning forward through the window, again whispered in my ear.

"Head first, Jack. That's the only way for you."

I took his advice. I never thought I should get through, for my shoulders are at least a couple of inches broader than Billy's, and it had been a tight fit for him. A mighty squirm, combined with a sharp pull from inside at the critical moment, just did the trick, however, and there I was standing beside him in the darkness, sore but triumphant.

We waited a few seconds so that I could recover the breath which had been nearly squeezed out of my body. Then, treading as delicately as Agag, we advanced towards the door. Feeling about in the darkness, I discovered a latch, and the gentlest pressure showed me that the way was clear.

"Ready, Billy?" I whispered, drawing out my revolver.

"Right oh," came the swift response.

I swung the door open, and we stepped out swiftly into the passage.

We found ourselves in a long, low corridor lit by one gas jet, which was flickering away feebly over a baize door at the end. Except for the loud ticking of a clock in the room opposite, the place was as silent as a tomb.

Up the passage we crept, our ears strained for the first sound of danger. Billy made a mean effort to get to the baize door first, but I just managed to forestall him. Gripping the handle, I swung it open, at the same time raising my revolver ready to shoot if it were needed.

We were looking into the hall, a square, ill-furnished, dimly lit place, from which a staircase ran up to the floor above. There were a couple of doors opposite, both shut, and behind one of them we could hear the sound of voices.

Billy laid his hand on my arm, and for a moment we stood there motionless. Then came the unmistakable clatter of dice, followed a moment later by a burst of laughter and a peculiarly foul Spanish oath. In a second we had crossed the hall.

"*Madre de Dios!* I'm tired of this. You have the luck of Satan!"

There was the scrape of a chair as the speaker pushed back his seat.

Billy's hand was on the door-knob.

"Ready, Jack?" he whispered.

15

I nodded.

There was a crash, a gleam of light, and side by side we hurled ourselves into the room.

About what happened next I shall always be a bit confused. I recollect seeing a man in front of me—a big, dark fellow, his face wild with amazement and terror, his hand grabbing the back of the chair from which he had just started up. Then I suppose I must have flung my spanner, for his face seemed suddenly to double up, and he went backwards across the table with an ear-splitting shriek. As I leaped forward, I had a swift inspiring vision of Billy battering somebody's head against the wall, and the next thing I knew was that I was kneeling on the floor with a moaning, bloodstained object writhing feebly in my grip.

A few quick turns of the cord which I had whipped out of my pocket, and I rose to my feet again, panting and exultant.

Billy's voice, cheerful and cool as ever, rang out across the room.

"Well done, Jack! Now come and give us a hand with this lot."

He was in the farther corner, sitting comfortably astride of a furiously agitated mass of arms and legs, from which proceeded an unintelligible smother of Spanish and English blasphemy. He looked up smiling as I strode across.

"Get hold of that off leg, old son, will you?" he added. "Take care he doesn't bite: he's very peevish."

A brief scuffle, and our second captive was as trussed and helpless as the other.

Billy jumped up with a laugh. "Good work that," he said, "devilish good!" Then he walked across to where

I had left my prisoner. "I say," he added, "you've put it across old Dot-and-carry-one all right. Spoilt his beauty for keeps from the look of it."

I picked up my discarded spanner.

"I'll leave you here, Billy," I said. "I'm off to find Mercia."

He nodded. "Right you are. Don't forget there's a female Dago about somewhere. She might be nasty."

He leant down over the writhing figure on the floor, and without waiting any further, I hurried out into the hall.

For a second I hesitated, wondering whether to go upstairs or to search the back regions first. The latter seemed the most likely spot, so crossing the hall and pushing open the baize door, I entered the passage up which we had so lately crept.

The first door on the right, where we had heard the clock ticking, proved to be the kitchen. It was empty, except for a solitary cat that arched her back and spat at me from the window-sill.

I gave a hurried glance round, and then stepped back into the passage.

"Mercia!" I shouted. "Mercia!"

From the end of the corridor came a faint, stifled sound, like the cry of someone buried alive.

Two savage strides and I had reached the spot— a worm-eaten trap-door in the floor fastened down by a wooden bar. In my furious haste, I wrenched the thing off bodily, and then gripping the ring with both hands, tore away the flap.

A short flight of stone steps met my gaze. I cleared them with a reckless jump, and the next moment, in the close, warm darkness, Mercia was in my arms.

"Ah," she cried, "it's you, it's you!" and I could feel her dear hand moving up and down my sleeve with a sobbing, half-incredulous joy. Then, somehow, our lips met, and all the barriers between us went down like matchwood in that first passionate kiss. I drew her up into the passage, and gazed hungrily into her white face. She was trembling violently, and my own hands were shaking like leaves.

"They've not hurt you, Mercia?" I whispered. Then my eyes fell on her wrist, circled by four livid bruises "My God!" I cried savagely, "who did that?"

She hastily drew her sleeve over the marks.

"It's nothing, it's nothing," she sobbed. "Oh, I'm so glad you've come!"

I caught her arm, and gently turned back the covering so that I could see the bruises. They were the marks of a man's fingers,—there could be no question about that,—a vicious, brutal grip, which might easily have broken her wrist.

"Who was it, Mercia?" I repeated.

"It was Rojas," she added; "but it doesn't matter. He would have killed me last night if Guarez had not stopped him. Oh, let's get away before they know you're here."

"It's too late for that, Mercia," I said coolly. "They know I'm here all right. Billy's sitting over them with a spanner in the drawing-room."

She gazed at me half-sceptically, and then the old delicious smile broke through the mist of her eyes.

"They said last night that you were the Devil. I think I am beginning to believe them."

I laughed happily. "They'll be sure of it now," I said. "Where's the woman?"

"Juanita? She is in London. Guarez sent her up

this morning to find out about Da Costa. She is to come back by the last train."

"I am afraid we shall miss her, then," said I. "We must leave here in ten minutes. Can you be ready, Mercia?"

"Yes, yes; I am ready. I have only to put a few things in my bag. But how are we going? Where are you taking me?"

"The car is outside," I replied. "I'll explain everything when we've started. I've got a few words to say to Señor Rojas first."

"You are going to kill him?" she asked dispassionately.

I shook my head, smiling. "No, Mercia," I said. "Not at present. He makes life so interesting, I really couldn't spare him."

"It would be best," she said simply. "And Guarez as well."

There was a childish candour about her point of view that appealed to me immensely.

"Well, you're right, of course," I said; "but they are so absurdly sensitive on these points in England. If it was San Luca, one might be reasonable."

Taking her hand, I led her into the hall, and at the foot of the stairs I drew her into my arms, and kissed her again on the mouth and eyes and hair before I let her go.

I watched her as far as the first landing, and then, opening the door, came back into the sitting-room.

Billy had shifted the two prisoners into the centre of the floor, and was seated comfortably on the edge of the table smoking a pipe.

"It's all right," I said. "The woman's in London, and I've found Mercia. She'll be ready to come with us directly."

He nodded. " I heard you."

" How's Guarez ? " I asked, going across to my injured enemy.

" So that's Guarez, is it ? " said Billy, slipping off the table. " Oh, he's all right; you've only smashed his face a bit. There's no real damage done ; I've been having a squint at him."

It must be admitted that my late adversary was not a pretty sight. He lay on the floor saying nothing, but glaring savagely at us out of one eye. The other had temporarily struck work.

" He's had enough, anyway," I said ; " but I've got one or two words to say to the other gentleman. Let me introduce you. Señor Rojas of San Luca, Mr. William Logan of London. Billy, what do you think one ought to do to a man who crushes a girl's arm till it's nearly broken ? "

" Flog him," said Billy cheerfully.

A muffled imprecation—too poignant to repeat, I am afraid—broke from the prostrate Dago.

" Besides," added Billy, " it may teach him to use prettier language."

He bent down, and with a swift jerk hoisted the prisoner to his feet. I looked round the room. In the farther corner was a stout ash walking-stick, leaning invitingly against the wall.

Whatever natural taciturnity Señor Rojas may have possessed vanished abruptly when he saw me pick up this useful weapon. He burst into a hideous jargon of Spanish,—the dog-Spanish of the Argentine Hinterland, —whining and imploring that we should not put this indignity on him.

" Kill me, Prado," he shrieked. " Kill me. I do not fear death."

"Shut up," said Billy. "The Devil's much too good a chap to be landed with a skunk like you. Come over."

He hauled the squirming figure across the table, and held it there by the simple expedient of lying across its head.

I gave the stick a tentative swish through the air. "This, my friend," I said in Spanish, "will teach you not to bully women."

Whether my optimistic prophecy was fulfilled I cannot say, but certain it is that Señor Rojas was no hand at suppressing his emotions. He howled and screamed with a vigour that warmed my heart, and it was only when his voice finally cracked, and the entertainment became less inspiriting, that I threw down the stick.

Billy released him, and he slid down on to the floor, blubbering and sobbing like a naughty boy.

"Here endeth the second lesson," observed Billy irreverently. Then, turning over the lachrymose figure with his foot, he added in a kind voice: "Take my tip, sonny, and pad your trousers next time you come out Prado-shooting."

I laughed and threw the stick in the corner of the room. "We'll leave that as a keepsake," I said. "Come along, Billy. I expect Mercia's ready by now."

We went out into the hall, shutting the door behind us, and thus cutting off the somewhat incoherent curses of Señor Rojas. Mercia, carrying a bag in her hand, was just coming down the staircase. From the sparkle in her eyes, I gathered that some echoes of our revelry must have reached her ears.

"Mercia," I said, taking the bag, "this is Billy. We owe a lot to Billy."

She gave him her hand with that sweet grace that characterised every movement.

"How can I thank you?" she said softly.

Billy bent down and kissed the tips of her fingers. "I don't want any thanks," he answered, straightening himself and looking at her with his frank smile. "I love a row any time."

"Are you quite ready, Mercia?" I asked.

She nodded, and we went out, closing the front door behind us.

The car was standing where we had left it, its big head-lamps throwing two broad beams of golden light up the deserted road. As we reached it, Mercia, who was walking between us, suddenly swayed. I caught her in my arms, or I believe she would have fallen.

"I—I think I must be a little faint," she faltered. "I've not had anything to eat since last night."

I swore with some vigour. Then, picking her up tenderly, I carried her to the car and placed her in the back seat.

"We'll soon remedy that," I said. "I was an idiot not to have thought of it before."

I wrenched open my bag, and took out the sandwiches and whisky with which the ever-to-be-blessed Aunt Mary had so thoughtfully provided me. Mercia smiled gratefully; and the first sip of the spirit brought back a faint fleck of colour into her white face.

Billy was standing by, his brows drawn down in an angry frown.

"We let that cur off too easily," he growled. "Shall I go back and give him some more?"

"No, no," said Mercia. "I am much better. I am sure you have hurt him quite a lot. I heard him crying, and I was glad; but you mustn't hurt him any more. Take me away from this place—that's all I want."

"Just as you like," said Billy reluctantly. "I should love to have had a cut at him, though."

He took his seat at the wheel, while I climbed in beside Mercia and tucked her up comfortably with the rug. A minute later, we were spinning southwards through the cool night air along the road to Woodford —and London.

I shall never forget that drive. A strange, delightful sense of intimacy had sprung up between Mercia and myself, and I sat there holding her dear hand under the rug in a rich contentment that needed no words for its expression. Despite the dangers and perplexities that still surrounded us, there seemed no longer to be any cause for worry and doubt. The barriers were down— we knew that we loved each other, and in the light of that knowledge the world and its difficulties slipped temporarily into insignificance.

Indeed, it was only with a painful effort that I at last succeeded in wrenching myself back to the very necessary thought of our future proceedings.

"Mercia," I said, "when are the Tregattocks expecting you back? Soon?"

She nodded her head. "I told them I should be away for a few days. I did not know how long."

"Well, it seems to me," said I, "that the best thing we can do when we get to London is to drop you at an hotel. Then you can go back to them to-morrow, as if you'd just come from Woodford."

"And you?" she asked anxiously.

"I must go back to Park Lane. Whatever happens, I must stay there for another fortnight."

"But it is madness," she whispered fearfully; "more

than ever madness now. Do you think Rojas will forget——"

"No," I interrupted, smiling; "I'm quite sure he won't forget for a long time. All the same, I've no intention of running away. I shall have Billy with me, and we're a fairly useful combination." Then I looked straight into her eyes. "Mercia," I said, "why did you come to Woodford?"

"Guarez sent for me," she answered simply. "He said that you were to die the next day, and I thought that perhaps I might save you."

"But why did he want you?" I persisted.

"I think he guessed," she said slowly. "Da Costa saw us that night in Park Lane, and since then Guarez has suspected that you cared for me. He meant to use me—how do you say?—as a decoy. I was to bring you to the Hollies, and once there——" She shivered.

"Things didn't pan out quite as he intended," I finished, with a laugh. "How did he find out about our meeting?"

"Your cousin sent a message."

"Maurice?" I cried. "But he didn't know!" Then a sudden idea struck me. "By Jove," I said, "Lady Baradell must have told him."

Mercia looked at me calmly. "Lady Baradell?" she repeated, "the beautiful woman who loves you?"

I sat up with a jerk. "Who told you that?" I demanded.

She shrugged her shoulders. "No one told me. I was watching her eyes when she spoke with you."

"Were you!" I said, with some admiration. I was learning quite a lot about women these days. Then I paused. "I wish I knew why Maurice had bolted up to

London," I added regretfully. "I'm sure he's got some mischief up his sleeve."

"To London?" echoed Mercia. "Has your cousin gone to London?"

In a few words I acquainted her with the details of the telegram incident. "If it was about me," I finished, "I can't think who sent it, unless it was your missing Da Costa."

She shook her head. "It could not have been Da Costa. He would have let Guarez know first if there had been anything to tell. It is more like that it was Lord Sangatte."

"Sangatte!" I repeated in amazement. "What on earth has Sangatte got to do with this business?"

Mercia looked troubled. "I do not know, but I fear that your cousin must have told him something. They were speaking of him last night; they—they——" she faltered.

"Yes, Mercia?" I said.

I felt her clasp tighten. "I think that he would help them, if they should give me to him. I think that was why Guarez would not let Rojas kill me."

It took an instant for the blackguardly scheme to sink into my mind. Then, at a very opportune moment, Billy blew the horn, drowning the comment that forced itself from my lips.

"If that's the case," I said slowly, "I must have a little talk with Sangatte."

There was a short silence.

"Mercia," I went on, "why do you call yourself Miss de Rosen? I suppose Tregattock knows who you are. He evidently recognised me as Prado at the dance."

She shook her head. "No; he doesn't know that I am Mercia Solano. He was a friend of my father's when he was in San Luca, but I was only a little girl then. Later, when I was coming to England, some friends wrote to him about me, and Lady Tregattock invited me to stay."

"But why did you hide your real name?" I asked.

"I did not want my father's murderer to know that I was in England," answered Mercia. Then, with a kind of passionate break in her voice, she turned to me. "Oh, I have trusted you—I do trust you with all my heart! But tell me—ah, for pity's sake tell me!—who are you—you who are so like Prado that even Guarez has been deceived?"

I would have given much to be able to answer her questions, but like a black barrier my promise to Prado rose between us. I knew well that deeper even than her love for me was her passion for revenge on the man who had killed her father; and scoundrel as Prado might be, I had given him my word that for three weeks I would keep his secret.

"Just a few days longer, Mercia," I pleaded "God knows I would tell you everything now if I could, but I have given my word, and I can't break it."

She did not answer for a moment. Then slowly came the whispered words: "It shall be as you wish. I trust you always, because—because I love you."

A sudden furious blast from Billy, a violent swerve of the car that nearly took us into the hedge, and we were out on the road again with a pretty duet of abuse following us through the darkness.

Billy looked round with a smile. "Close shave that," he observed. "Fancy making love in the middle of the road!"

"Where are we?" I asked.

He pointed ahead to a clustered mass of lights that spread out long tentacles into the darkness.

"That's Romford, or ought to be. I shall have to slow up a bit now. We're getting into civilisation."

Through the apparently endless suburbs of London we slowly picked our way south-westwards. Billy steered with a cheerful confidence that was characteristic of him, never troubling to ask the way, but apparently contenting himself with an occasional glance at the stars to make sure that he was keeping in the right direction. As he observed to us over his shoulder, "You couldn't very well miss London, even if you tried."

The result was that we came in by a route which made up in length what it lacked in refinement. Interminable slums, lit by flaring public-houses just discharging their crowds into the street, rolled past us in monotonous succession. Twice we had to slow up to allow for the passage of two perspiring policemen and an obstructive prisoner, followed in either case by a vociferous, but judiciously unenterprising, crowd.

At last the houses began to give place to warehouses and factories, and in a few minutes we were threading the practically deserted thoroughfares of the City.

"We're all right now," observed Billy complacently. "Where do you want to go to?"

"Mercia is going to put up at an hotel for the night," I said. "We'll take her there, and then go on to Park Lane."

"What about the Inns of Court?" he suggested. "I stayed there for a fortnight last month, so I know the manager."

Mercia, who was looking very tired, nodded her head.

"That will do, Billy," I said. "Then you can go

in and see him and arrange about the room. Tell
him we've had a breakdown or something."

We passed the Mansion House and turned down
Cheapside, pulling up at the door of the hotel, where
Billy disentangled himself somewhat stiffly from the
wheel.

"I'll just run in and fix things up," he said. "I
shan't be a minute."

Mercia and I sat on in the car, in the broad lamp-
lit thoroughfare, which at this hour was practically
deserted. I took her hand and raised it gently to
my lips.

"Till to-morrow, dearest," I said. "I'll ring you
up first thing in the morning, before you go to the
Tregattocks'. Then we can arrange about meeting."

She drew the fingers of her other hand down my
sleeve. "And you will be very careful," she pleaded,
"for my sake?"

I smiled at her reassuringly. "Mercia mine," I
whispered, "I have something to live for now."

Billy came out of the hotel, accompanied by a pleasant-
looking, middle-aged man with a short grey beard.

"It's all right," he said. "M. Paulhan will see that
Miss de Rosen is quite comfortable."

The manager bowed. "I will be sure that Made-
moiselle has everything she wishes."

I opened the door and helped Mercia out, a porter
who appeared from the hotel possessing himself of
her bag. I insisted that she should go straight up to
bed, for she was obviously so tired that she could hardly
keep her eyes open. So we parted in the lounge,
Mercia going up in the lift, and Billy and I getting
back into the car.

"I expect we shall find the house all locked up," I

said. "I ought to have sent them a wire from Woodford to say we were coming."

"Well, it can't be helped," returned Billy. "We shall have to knock 'em up, that's all. Where do you keep the car?"

"Goodness knows," I laughed. "I never thought of asking Simpson."

Billy steered neatly round the corner of Park Lane. "It doesn't matter," he observed. "There's a big garage in Piccadilly. I'll shove her in there for the night after I've dropped you."

We slowed down and came to a stop outside the house. Through the glass above the door I saw that the hall was lit up.

"Someone's about, after all," I said.

"I expect they've got the policeman to supper," chuckled Billy. "Pleasant little surprise for 'em—eh? You go and knock, and I'll wait and see it's all right."

I walked up the steps, and thrust my key into the door. As I did so, it suddenly swung open, and I found myself face to face with a man who was standing just inside the threshold. Over his shoulder, I caught a momentary glimpse of the white, startled face of my pretty housemaid.

For a second I stared at the man without speaking. He was tall, broad-shouldered, and middle-aged, with a short, grizzled moustache and keen, watchful eyes.

"If you won't think me inquisitive," I remarked politely, "may I ask who you are?"

"I am Inspector Neil of Scotland Yard," he said slowly. "I believe that I am addressing Mr. John Burton."

It was a nasty shock, but I met it serenely.

"Well?" I returned.

Billy had jumped out of the car, and was coming up the steps.

The man raised his hand, and laid it quietly but firmly on my shoulder.

"Then, sir," he said, "it is my duty to arrest you."

There was a short pause.

I looked at him in frank amazement.

"Arrest me!" I repeated.   "What on earth for?"

The answer came with prompt and startling clearness—

"For the murder of Stuart Northcote."

CHAPTER XX

ONE seldom does the right thing in moments of great emergency. As an innocent man I suppose I ought to have started back and exclaimed, "Good heavens! What is the meaning of this outrage?" But, to tell the truth, I did nothing of the kind.

I stared blankly at my new friend for a moment, and then suddenly burst into a peal of laughter which I was quite unable to suppress. My mirth seemed to infect Billy, who sat down on the railings and chuckled like a fool.

The Inspector's face was a joy!

"I'm awfully sorry," I jerked out at last. "Suppose we go inside?"

Still keeping his hand on my shoulder, the Inspector stepped back, and Billy and I followed him into the hall—the former shutting the door behind us.

"Now," I said, "perhaps you'll be kind enough to explain."

As I spoke, there was a sound of heavy footsteps, and a police constable came tramping down the staircase.

The Inspector looked at me with a not unfriendly interest.

"There is not much to explain, sir. I have a warrant for your arrest for the murder of Mr. Stuart Northcote, and it is my duty to inform you that anything you say now will be used in evidence against you."

" But what makes you think Mr. Northcote is dead ? " I inquired.

" Because his body," returned the Inspector grimly, " is at present in the East Street mortuary."

I have had several fairly unpleasant shocks in the course of my life, but this one was something of a novelty. Even Billy, whose usual equanimity nothing but an earthquake can disturb, was surprised into a long low whistle of amazement.

So they had got him after all ! Despite his un- scrupulous cunning, despite the almost devilish ingenuity with which he had covered his tracks, Ignace Prado's long and black account was ended. I thought of Mercia, and I was glad.

" As a breaker of news, Inspector," I said, " you seem to me a little abrupt. When did this regrettable accident occur ? "

" It's not my place to answer any questions now, sir," replied the Inspector civilly. " The charge will be read over to you at the station ; and if you wish to employ counsel, we shall afford him the usual facilities."

I nodded. " You'll forgive me bothering you," I said, " but I've had so little experience of being arrested for murder. What happens next ? "

The Inspector's eyes twinkled. " I shall have to ask you to accompany me to Bow Street, where you will be detained until this charge is cleared up."

" May I come too ? " inquired Billy, coolly lighting a cigarette.

" This is Mr. Logan, Inspector," I said. " I don't know whether you're looking for him as well ? "

The Inspector shook his head. " I have no warrant

for your arrest, sir; but since you arrived with Mr. Burton, I shall have to keep you under observation till to-morrow."

"That'll be all right," returned Billy cheerfully. "I've only got to put the car in the garage; then I shall come back and go to bed. You'd better leave Robert with me. He can have a shake-down here, and we'll stroll round to Bow Street together in the morning."

I don't know how much experience of this kind of work Inspector Neil had enjoyed, but our method of accepting the situation evidently struck him as being both original and entertaining.

"Very well, sir," he said, with a broad smile. Then turning to the constable, he added: "Jackson, you are responsible for this gentleman till to-morrow morning. You will report to me at Bow Street by telephone if you have anything further to communicate."

The constable saluted.

"And ring up now for a taxi."

As the man stepped forward towards the telephone, my pretty housemaid, who all this time had been hovering in the background listening to our conversation, suddenly came forward. Her face was very pale, and she was clasping and unclasping her hands in a pitiable state of agitation.

"Oh, what does it mean, sir? They're never going to take you to prison, sir?"

She gasped out the words—her eyes fixed pleadingly on mine.

"It's quite all right," I said soothingly. "You stay on here and look after the house for me. I shall be back in a couple of days."

"Oh, sir," she sobbed, "I hope I haven't said anything I oughtn't to have! They've been asking us

questions—all sorts of questions, sir. Oh, I wouldn't
have said anything to hurt you, sir—not for the world, I
wouldn't!"

The poor girl's distress was so genuine that I must
admit I was rather touched. I laid my hand on her
shoulder.

"It's generally best to tell the truth," I said, "and
I'm sure you did that."

"Cheer up, Gwendoline," added Billy kindly. "We're
not in the soup this journey—you can take my word
for it."

There came the sharp *honk-honk* of a motor horn
from outside, followed by the noise of a taxi pulling up
at the door.

I turned to the Inspector.

"That sounds like our carriage," I observed. "Ought
I to be handcuffed or anything?"

He shook his head, smiling again. "I don't think
that will be necessary, sir."

"So long, Billy," I said. "See you in the morning.
"You'll look after Robert, won't you? The cook's
got the key of the cellar."

Billy nodded. "Good!" said he. "We'll do ourselves proud—eh, Constable?"

And in this altogether inappropriate fashion I went
down the steps to take my trial for murder.

There were not many remarks exchanged during our
drive to Bow Street. I saw it was no use questioning
the Inspector any further, and, as you may imagine, I
had quite enough to think about without wasting my
energies in making conversation. The whole thing had
happened so unexpectedly and so quickly that I was
only just beginning to grasp it as an accomplished fact.

There seemed to be little doubt that Prado must have

met his death at the hands of the missing Da Costa. That the rest of the gang were quite innocent in the matter I had fairly convincing evidence. Where and when the tragedy had been played out I was quite unable to guess, and it was equally puzzling to know how the police had discovered the secret of my identity. Maurice's hurried departure from Ashton was doubtless connected with this, and I could understand now why he had looked at me with that strange expression of half-incredulous triumph when he read the wire.

Despite the seriousness of the situation, I was not particularly upset. Indeed, my principal sensation, apart from an ardent desire to get to bed as soon as possible, was one of genuine relief to feel that the business was over and done with. Fond as I am of the strenuous life, I had had just about enough of Mr. Stuart Northcote. There was a strange pleasure in being Jack Burton again, even with a charge of murder hanging over my head.

My musings were cut short by the cab pulling up outside Bow Street. The Inspector got out first, and I followed, to the evident excitement of several midnight loafers, who peered at us from the safe distance of the opposite pavement.

We went straight up the steps and entered a long, brightly lit corridor. A policeman who was standing there favoured us with a keen glance of curiosity, and respectfully touched his helmet to my companion.

The latter opened a door on the right. "This way," he said.

It was an office, a big and very tidy room, with two roll-top desks, at one of which a grey-haired, soldierly-looking man in plain clothes was seated, writing. He looked up as we entered, and I saw him start slightly as his eyes fell on me.

"It's Mr. John Burton," said my captor, with a pardonable touch of pride in his voice. Then he turned to me. "This is Inspector Curtis. He will read you the charge."

Inspector Curtis had quickly conquered his momentary emotions. "Where was the arrest effected?" he demanded sharply, studying me with considerable interest.

"At Park Lane," returned the other. "I was making inquiries, when Mr. Burton arrived in a car with a companion. I have placed the latter under observation. No resistance was offered."

Inspector Curtis nodded, and rising to his feet crossed the room to a series of pigeon-holes, from one of which he took out an official-looking paper.

"I will read you the charge against you," he said.

I am afraid I cannot recall now the exact phraseology of this impressive document. Briefly speaking, it accused me of having wilfully done to death one Stuart Northcote on the night of the 17th of September at a place called Baxter's Rents in East Street, Stepney. I need hardly say that, sleepy as I was, I listened with the utmost attention while the good man read it out slowly in a serious voice.

"Thank you very much," I said, when he had finished. Then for the life of me I was unable to control a long and most inopportune yawn.

"I really must apologise," I said. "It was most interesting: but the truth is, I'm half asleep."

Both of them smiled.

"You can turn in at once, if you wish to," said Inspector Curtis, folding up the document. "You are also at liberty to communicate with your solicitor or to send any other message."

I shook my head. "A bed," I observed, "is all I

want at present. We'll do the communicating to-morrow morning."

"Come with me, then," remarked Inspector Neil, and turning round he conducted me out of the office and down the corridor to a small, plainly furnished bedroom, the window of which was heavily guarded with iron bars. There was a bed, however, and the sheets looked clean, and in my present state of sleepiness that was more than enough for me.

"You will be able to send round to-morrow for your own things," said the Inspector, "but I think you'll be comfortable enough for to-night."

"I'm sure I shall," I returned.

"There's one other thing, sir. I am afraid I shall have to run through your clothes before I leave you. We are compelled to search everyone under arrest by regulations."

"Right you are," I said. "I've really no intention of cutting my throat, but if it's the rule——"

I held up my hands, and with deft fingers he went swiftly through my pockets, taking out the contents.

"These will be entered and returned to you," he said. "Good-night."

"Good-night," I replied; and turning the key in the lock, the good fellow tramped away down the passage, leaving me to myself.

I am afraid I was much too tired to indulge in any of the proper emotions for a wrongly accused prisoner. Indeed, beyond reckoning out in a vague sort of way that the murder must have taken place on the night of Sangatte's party, I did not bother my head any further about the matter. Stripping off my clothes as quickly as possible, I scrambled into bed and flicked off the

switch which controlled an invisible electric light. Five
minutes later I was as sound asleep as I have ever been
in my life.

If the French gentleman who said that life was only
worth living for its new experiences was right in his
statement, I had no reason to complain when I woke up
next morning. It was certainly a novel sensation to
open one's eyes in a police station under a charge of
murder, and to find an affable-looking Inspector standing beside one's bed with a bag in his hand.

It was my captor of the previous day, and the bag
which he was holding was the one which I had brought
up with me from Woodford.

"Good morning," I said, smiling at him sleepily.

"I'm glad to see you slept all right," he returned.
"There are your things. I sent round to Park Lane
for them first thing this morning."

"That was uncommonly good of you, Inspector," I
replied gratefully. "Now I shall be able to do you
credit in the dock."

He grinned amiably. "We can give you a breakfast,
of course, and if there's anything special you want, you
can send out for it."

I shook my head. "I'll leave it to you," I said. "It's
not often one gets a chance of sampling His Majesty's
hospitality."

"Very good." He paused a moment. "You will be
taken before the magistrate at eleven o'clock. Any
letters you wish to write will be attended to at once,
provided they are in order. I will let you have some
paper and envelopes with your breakfast."

I nodded.

"And if you would like a shave," he continued, "I'll
send round for a barber."

"It seems to me," I said, "that, next to the Savoy, Bow Street is about the best hotel in London."

The Inspector smiled again. "We try to make prisoners on remand as comfortable as possible," he replied, and going out he left me to my toilet.

I dressed quickly, and dispatched with appreciation the plentiful if somewhat plain breakfast which a stolid constable brought in to me on a tray. It was while I was engaged in this latter occupation that the brilliant thought of writing to Lord Lammersfield suddenly occurred to me. I had been puzzling my brains all the time I was dressing as to what was the best course to pursue, and I think it must have been the Bow Street cocoa which inspired me with this happy idea.

I pushed aside the tray, and taking a sheet of the notepaper which the constable had brought in, I composed with some care the following letter:—

"Bow Street Police Station,
Thursday.

"Dear Lord Lammersfield,—The last time I had the pleasure of meeting you, at Sangatte's dance, you were good enough to say that I was to let you know if I ever found myself in prison. As you will see by my present address, this situation has arisen with unexpected abruptness. I don't know whether the interesting offence with which I am charged is now public property, but if so, I can assure you my present fame is quite unearned. If you could spare me half an hour of your time later in the day, I should be very grateful for your advice. In return, I can promise you a story which will help to relieve the regrettable monotony of the Home Office that you were complaining of last time we met.—Yours sincerely,

"Stuart Northcote."

From what I had seen of Lord Lammersfield, I felt

fairly confident that this letter would bring him to the station. The circumstances attending the charge against me were so extraordinary, and his own interests so closely tied up with mine, that his curiosity about the case, if he had been informed of it, must already be overwhelming.

I was just addressing the envelope when Inspector Neil came in again, accompanied by the barber.

"Here you are, Inspector," I said, handing it to him. "This is the only letter I want to send at present, but I should be much obliged if it could be delivered at once."

He read the address with a mingled expression of surprise and respect. Then, calling the constable into the room, presumably to assist the barber in case I made a sudden dash for the razor, he went out with the letter in his hand.

I felt rather sorry for that barber. I think he must have had some inkling as to my identity, for I could see that he was almost bursting with anxiety to break into conversation. The cold eye of the constable was on us, however, and the poor man had to pursue his task in silence. He had just finished, and was mournfully dabbing me with the towel, when Inspector Neil returned.

"Your friend of last night, Mr. Logan, is here," he said. "You can see him now if you want to."

"I shall be pleased to receive him," I replied, with dignity.

A minute later Billy was ushered into the room by the constable, who then withdrew, closing the door behind him.

Billy looked round with an expression of mild surprise.

"Hullo, my son!" he observed. "I expected to find you in a dungeon cell. What's the meaning of this magnificence?"

"'We try to make prisoners on remand as comfortable as possible,'" I quoted. "I'm sorry I can't offer you a whisky, but there's some excellent cocoa here, if that's any good."

Billy seated himself on the edge of the table and thrust his hands into his pockets. "Well," he said, "this is rather an unholy mix-up—eh?" Then he looked at the door. "I suppose we've got an audience," he added.

"I expect so," I said, "but it doesn't matter. I'm going to do the George Washington act in any case now. As Northcote's dead, I consider our bargain's at an end."

He nodded. "Of course it is. The only way is to make a clean breast of it. You'll have to have a lawyer or a counsel or whatever they call it over here to put the thing properly. I'd better see about getting one, hadn't I?"

"I've written to Lammersfield," I said, "and asked him to come and see me. I'll wait and hear what he's got to say before I take any further steps."

Billy slapped his leg. "By Jove!" he cried, "that was a sound notion. Nothing like having the Home Secretary behind you. Do you reckon he'll come?"

"I think so, Billy," I said complacently.

"Have you heard anything fresh about the facts?" he asked. "Who the devil put it across Prado, and how did the police get on to your track?"

"I think it must have been Da Costa," I answered, "but we shall know more about it before very long. I'm due to meet the magistrate at eleven."

Billy looked at his watch. "Eleven, is it?" he said. "I ought to be going, then. I've promised to call for your girl and take her to the court."

"Mercia!" I exclaimed. "Does she know?"

"Yes," said Billy. "I told her this morning when she rang up. Was that wrong?"

I shrugged my shoulders. "Lord, no," I said. "She'd have heard all about it by midday in any case. The papers will be shrieking themselves purple. The only thing is that I don't want her name dragged in if I can help it."

"Well, she'd have to come to court in any case," said Billy, "so I thought I might as well take her, and let her know the real truth right away. It'll save her a lot of worry."

I held out my hand. "Billy," I said, "you're a brick."

He gave me a vigorous grip, and jumped down off the table.

"Honour amongst thieves, my son," he said, with a laugh.

He walked to the door and tapped on it with his knuckles. It was opened by my friend the policeman with a promptness which was slightly suggestive, and waving his hand to me, Billy passed out into the passage.

For the next twenty minutes I occupied myself with straightening out in my head the exact date and sequence of each occurrence since my fateful meeting with Prado on the Embankment. I had determined to tell Lammersfield the entire truth, and I wanted to be able to present my story as briefly and crisply as possible.

I had just concluded this task to my own satisfaction when Inspector Neil returned.

"The magistrate has arrived," he said. "They are going to take your case first."

I got up from my chair. "I'm quite ready, Inspector," I said cheerfully.

Any doubts I may have had as to whether my arrest was known to the public were effectually settled the moment I entered the court. Despite the earliness of the hour, the place was packed with spectators. The only face I recognised, as I marched to a sort of wooden cattle-pen which the Inspector indicated, was that of Maurice, who, studiously avoiding my eye, was seated in the body of the court. The Press was there in force, and as I took my seat I could hear the quick buzz of whispered speculation going on all round me. This however, was almost immediately suppressed by a harsh observation of "Silence!" from a severe-faced gentleman whom I supposed to be the magistrate's clerk.

The magistrate himself I took rather a fancy to. He was not unlike Lord Lammersfield in appearance—a very pleasant, acute-looking man of about sixty, with sharp, twinkling eyes behind gold-rimmed pince-nez. I bowed to him politely, and he returned the compliment with a quick, penetrating glance that seemed to take in my entire personality.

The proceedings that followed were what the newspapers would designate as "Brief and formal."

First of all, Inspector Neil stepped into the witness-box, and described with commendable curtness the facts relating to my arrest. It appeared that another officer had already been dispatched to effect this at Woodford, and that my arrival at Park Lane in a motor had been a dramatically unexpected occurrence.

He was followed by Inspector Curtis, who at once requested the magistrate to grant a remand until the next day.

The latter looked at him rather quizzically over his glasses.

"As I did not grant the warrant for the arrest," he observed in a dry voice, "it would perhaps be as well to state your grounds."

I don't think the Inspector was pleased, but he was too old a hand to betray any sign of annoyance. In quick, short sentences he began a brief statement of the case for the police, to which I need hardly say I listened with the most intense interest.

To start with, he informed the magistrate that the body of the man found murdered in Baxter's Rents had been identified beyond all question as that of Stuart Northcote. Secondly, there was ample evidence to show that I had spent some time with the deceased at the Milan Hotel two days before the murder. On the night of the crime, I had attended Lord Sangatte's dance in the character of Stuart Northcote, and his lordship would bear witness that I had left early in a state of some agitation. I had not arrived home in Park Lane until the small hours of the morning, the clothes that I was wearing being subsequently found saturated with blood. The case still presented many mysterious features, but he maintained that this evidence was amply sufficient to justify a remand.

The magistrate heard him without interruption, and then turned to me.

"Do you wish to cross-examine the witness?" he asked.

I shook my head. "I shall be represented by counsel

when I appear again," I replied. "I shall have to pay him, so he may as well do the work."

A smile flickered across the magistrate's face.

"In-that case," he said, "I shall remand you until to-morrow. I presume the police are granting you the usual facilities for preparing your defence?"

"I have nothing to complain of," I answered, with an amiable glance at Inspector Neil.

The buzz of whispered conversation again broke out in the court, and looking round I caught sight for the first time of Mercia and Billy. They were sitting right at the back, but even at that distance Mercia's face stood out like some beautiful white flower. I made no sign of recognition, for I knew that the gentlemen of the Press were watching me with vulturean interest, and I was desperately anxious to avoid calling attention to her connection with the case.

I think my little tribute to the civility of the police had pleased Inspector Neil, for he conducted me back to my apartment in the most friendly fashion. Indeed, but for the fact that he was careful to turn the key in the lock when he left me, I might, from his manner, have been a private guest of his own instead of a suspected murderer. It struck me that perhaps he did not feel quite so certain as some of his colleagues as to the obviousness of my guilt.

I was not left very long to my reflections. A quarter of an hour could hardly have elapsed when my jailer returned, coming into the room with a slightly awestruck expression on his good-natured countenance.

"The Home Secretary is here," he said, with a befitting sense of gravity. "He will see you at once."

"Thank you, Inspector," I returned, in the same dignified key.

A minute later Lord Lammersfield was ushered into the room.

I got up at once, and as the Inspector withdrew, closing the door behind him, I bowed to my distinguished visitor.

"It is very good of you to have come so soon," I said.

For a moment Lord Lammersfield made no answer.

He was looking at me keenly—a half-puzzled, half-humorous expression on his handsome, cynical face. Then quite suddenly he held out his hand.

"Even a Cabinet Minister, Mr. Northcote," he said, "occasionally keeps his word."

I laughed, and we exchanged a grip.

"Lord Lammersfield," I said, "I asked you to come here so that I might tell you the truth." Then I paused and looked him straight in the face. "I am not Stuart Northcote," I added slowly. "That interesting gentleman is dead. It is apparently the only point on which the police are correctly informed."

Lord Lammersfield's expression remained unaltered. "Scotland Yard is making distinct progress," he observed. Then, placing his hat on the table, he pulled up a chair and seated himself.

For a moment I hesitated.

"I think it will be quickest," I said, "if I tell you my story straight through. I can at least promise you that you won't be bored."

His lordship bowed courteously. "I am never bored," he answered, "except by politics."

It is a little characteristic of mine to be able to talk better when I am on my feet. So while Lammersfield

sat on in his chair, motionless and without betraying
any sign of surprise, I paced up and down the room
and let him have the whole amazing narrative of my
adventures since the moment when I had met with
Northcote on the Embankment. I cut out one or two
private matters, dealing with Mercia and Lady Baradell;
but with these exceptions I told him the entire story, in
as brief and as straightforward a fashion as possible.

When I had quite finished, he sat up and looked at
me for a moment without speaking. Then he laughed
quietly, and taking off his glasses, polished them carefully with his handkerchief.

"I am much indebted to you, Mr. Burton," he said.
"I was under the impression that gentlemen of your
kind were extinct, except in novels. It is refreshing to
find that I was wrong."

"It is because I object to becoming extinct," I replied, "that I ventured to send you my message."

He replaced his glasses, and again examined me with
a kind of cynical amusement.

"Yes, I should imagine that life was eminently worth
living to anyone with your digestion and morals." Then
he paused. "I believe your story, Mr. Burton," he
added. "It is altogether too incredible to be doubted."

I bowed.

"Besides," he continued ironically, "it has the additional merit of explaining several facts over which our
good friend Inspector Curtis is at present straining his
intelligence."

"I suppose," I said, with some reluctance, "that I
shall have to tell the truth?"

Lord Lammersfield raised his hand protestingly.
"One should never consider the most desperate course
until the alternatives have been exhausted. I will send

17

George Gordon down to you this afternoon. He has a natural aversion to the truth that I have never seen equalled ; and if there is any feasible method of extract-ing you from your difficulties without resorting to accuracy, you may be sure that he will find it."

He had named the most famous young K.C. of the day—a brilliant criminal barrister, and the rising hope of the Conservative party.

I began to thank him, but he cut me short.

" I am looking at the question from a purely selfish point of view. Much as I admire the British Public, I have no wish that they should acquire an intimate knowledge of my private relations with the late Mr. Prado. I would rather you left that part of the story out when you are confiding in Gordon."

I nodded. " Of course I shall," I said; " but Prado is sure to have left some record of the business behind him, and if his cousin comes into everything—well, you know from my story what sort of a gentleman Master Maurice Furnivall is."

Lord Lammersfield shrugged his shoulders. " One attains a certain measure of philosophy in politics," he said. " At the worst, it will give me an additional breath-ing space; and I deserve to be worried if only for my stupidity in misreading our defunct friend the filibuster in the way I did. I made certain the fellow was after a title."

" I don't think we shall hear much more of ' The Amalgamated Goldfields of South America,' " I said, with a short laugh.

Lord Lammersfield got up from his chair. " A pity !" he said regretfully. " It was a good title, and I hate waste."

CHAPTER XXI

MR. GEORGE GORDON arrived at about half-past three. He was shown into my room by the Inspector, who announced his name almost as respectfully as that of the Home Secretary.

A tall, immaculately dressed young man, with a long chin, a tired white face, and sleek black hair carefully parted in the middle, he appeared more like a product of Ranelagh and the Gaiety than the most successful barrister-politician of the day.

As the warder withdrew we shook hands, Mr. Gordon looking at me from under his heavily-lidded eyes with a kind of fatigued curiosity.

"How do you do?" I said. "I'm very much obliged to you for coming to my rescue."

"If half of what Lammersfield told me is right," he answered, "I am glad to have had the chance."

It was only when he spoke that you got an idea of the real man. There was something in his voice that suggested the crack of a whip.

"Well," I said, "if Lammersfield has told you the story already, perhaps you'd rather ask me questions."

He sat down at the table and shook his head.

"No, Mr. Burton ; if you don't mind, I'd rather have your account of the matter. Lammersfield's ideas of accuracy are political rather than legal."

Remembering the latter's opinion of Mr. Gordon, I was unable to repress a smile.

"Right you are," I said; and without more ado I plunged straight into my narrative, telling it just as I had told it to Lord Lammersfield, with the exception of leaving out all references to that eminent statesman's private affairs.

My visitor listened, lounging forward on the table, one hand supporting his head, and with the other making occasional notes on a half-sheet of paper. Once or twice he interrupted with sharp, curt questions which showed with what acute attention he was following my story.

When I had finished, he lay back in his chair, crossed his legs, and stared reflectively at the ceiling. I was just beginning to wonder whether he thought the whole thing a colossal lie, when he suddenly sat up and pulled his notes towards him.

"I suppose you realise, Mr. Burton," he said slowly, "that by to-morrow you will be the most famous man in England?"

"One has to pay for one's amusements," I admitted regretfully.

"On the contrary," he replied, with a dry smile, "if you care to handle the newspapers in the proper way, I should think the exact opposite would be the case. Your 'reminiscences' will be worth a fortune. What I mean, however, is that after to-day every pressman in England will be on your track, and there will be precious little of what's happened to you in the last four months that they'll fail to rout out."

He was looking at me keenly while he spoke.

I shrugged my shoulders. "They'll find it devilish uninteresting," I said. "Up till last week my life here was a model of respectability."

He was silent for a moment. "If your facts are accurate," he said, "you are not in much danger, of course. To start with, the evidence of this man Logan constitutes a perfect alibi. On the other hand, it will be very difficult to avoid your being sent for trial. Your story is almost too incredible for a magistrate to swallow."

I made a wry face. "Well, if everything's got to come out," I said, "it's got to. That's all about it."

He nodded. "I will find out at once what evidence the police have, and go into the whole case. There will be no difficulty, of course, about the appearance of Miss Solano or your friend Mr. Logan?"

"None at all," I said. "Logan is staying at my house in Park Lane with a policeman in attendance. He is sure to be round here later. Miss Solano is at the Tregattocks', but I should like her name kept out of it as much as possible."

He took no notice of this last remark. "Send Logan round to my chambers as soon as he arrives," he said curtly. "The first thing I shall do will be to get a warrant for the arrest of Guarez and the others. Then we must find the butler, Milford—if he's still alive. That's the man who holds the threads of the case in his hands."

"You'll probably find him in the Thames," I said, "if you find him anywhere. My only hope is that he managed to kill Da Costa too."

Gordon got up from his chair. His languid manner had slipped off him like a cloak, and his dark eyes glowed with a quick intelligence and energy that fully explained his remarkable achievements.

"I will do what I can," he said. "The police are sure to ask for a further remand to-morrow, and they'd better be allowed to have it. By the next hearing we shall know where we stand, and we can then decide whether to fight or to let the case be sent for trial. By the way, can you give me some addresses of friends in the Argentine or elsewhere who can establish your identity ? "

I wrote him out the names of several of my more respectable acquaintances who knew about my journey to England, and he put the list away in his pocket.

"I will cable them this afternoon," he said. "Don't forget to send Logan round. I'll communicate with Miss Solano myself."

He went off, leaving me with the satisfactory feeling that, as far as professional assistance was concerned, I had certainly struck the right quarter. Indeed, the only thing that really worried me was the prospect of Mercia being dragged in to give evidence. I was determined that, whatever might happen to me, her true connection with the case should not be made public if I could prevent it. In France, of course, it wouldn't have mattered, for Frenchmen would have regarded her intention to assassinate Prado as the natural and laudable ambition which I myself considered it to be. But here in London—well, I could imagine what sort of an uproar such an admission would evoke from my smug fellow-countrymen. No, whatever happened, Mercia's real part in the affair must be discreetly cloaked.

I was curious to know what sort of a figure I was cutting in the Press. I realised, of course, that every sub-editor in Fleet Street would be straining himself in his efforts to do justice to such an opportunity, and it seemed a pity that I, of all people, should remain ignorant of the result. So when the constable brought

me in my lunch, I asked him whether it was against the
regulations to send out for some evening papers.

He looked a little doubtful.   " I'll inquire about it,"
he said.   " What papers do you want? "

" Oh, bring the lot," I replied spaciously.   " It isn't
every day that one's accused of murder."

Half an hour later he returned with a bundle of
evening journals under his arm.

I started on the *Star*, and my first glimpse showed me
that Gordon's prophecy as to my being the most famous
man in England was not far off the mark.

STUART NORTHCOTE STABBED TO DEATH.

MURDERED MILLIONAIRE'S DOUBLE AT BOW STREET.

WHO IS JOHN BURTON ?

AMAZING MYSTERY IN HIGH LIFE.

The staring headlines spread themselves all across the
front page, three columns of which were devoted to an
account of the morning's proceedings, followed by a
sensational description of Northcote's brief but dazzling
career in London society.

With regard to the murder itself, the paper seemed
to be almost as much in the dark as I was.   I gathered,
however, that the body of Stuart Northcote had been
found three days before in an East End lodging-house,
dressed in the commonest of seafaring clothes.   He
had been stabbed to death, apparently after a fierce
struggle, for a track of blood-stains down the stairs
marked where his murderer had escaped.

Beyond stating that the dead man had had a visitor
late on the previous night, the landlord of the house
had been apparently unable to throw any light on the

matter. He had heard no signs of fighting; and if he had, he declared that he would probably have taken no notice. Fights are not regarded very seriously in a Stepney lodging-house.

An examination of the murdered man's papers had, it seemed, led the police to the startling belief that he was none other than Stuart Northcote, the famous millionaire. They had conducted their investigations with the utmost secrecy and dispatch, and the result had been my sensational arrest, and what the *Star* described in its leading article as "a mystery of truly staggering dimensions."

"Truth," finished the editor in his summing-up, "is stranger than fiction, and even a Sherlock Holmes might at the moment be baffled to pronounce a judgment upon this amazing crime."

The penny papers, if slightly less dramatic, devoted an equal amount of space to the affair—in fact, as far as I could see, any other topic of discussion was temporarily shelved. In no paper did I find any suggestion as to the real identity of Stuart Northcote, while only one —the *Globe*—seemed aware of the fact that I had been staying with Maurice at Woodford in the guise of his murdered cousin. All were agreed, however, that it was an "astounding" and "mysterious" business, and one and all repeated the remark of the editor of the *Star* that "truth was stranger than fiction."

I began to wonder what Mercia's feelings must be. By now she knew from Billy the true part that I had played in the affair, and that it was only my intervention that had saved her father's murderer from the earlier vengeance of the League. I knew this would make no difference between us; for if her love for me had sprung into life when she believed that I was Prado, it would certainly survive any subsequent shock that Fate could deal out. I was more concerned as to the anxiety I feared she would be suffering. Billy, of course, would have tried to assure her that I was perfectly safe; but knowing what she did about the feelings cherished for me by Maurice and Sangatte, she would doubtless be nervous as to whether there was not some conspiracy on foot to connect me with the crime. I did not want to write to her, for I had a pretty confident notion that if I did my letter would be opened. In any case, it would certainly lead the police to subject her to all sorts of inconvenient questions.

I was just pondering over these problems when the constable entered and told me that Billy had again called, and that if I wished to see him no objection would be raised.

"I'm afraid I'm getting a bit of a nuisance, Constable," I said. "I shall have to present the Station with a new door-knocker when I get out."

He made no response beyond a non-committal smile, but retiring from the room, returned a minute later with Billy in attendance.

"Well, my son," said the latter, as soon as the door was shut, "been reading your Press notices?"

He waved his hands towards the pile of newspapers.

"I've looked at them, Billy," I said. "For a modest man, I seem to be making a bit of a splash."

Billy laughed grimly. "Oh, you're the real thing. You've got the sea-serpent done to a frazzle. The whole town's talking of you; and as for the newspaper men—well, they've lined up outside Park Lane thicker than fleas in a Spanish doss-house. I had to push 'em away with both hands when I came out just now."

"Tell me about Mercia, Billy," I said.

"She's all right. It takes a lot to upset the Solanos. I told her the whole story before we went to the court-house, and she never turned a hair. There's stuff in that girl, or else I'm a Dutchman."

"Did she send me any message?" I asked eagerly.

"Said she wasn't exactly tired of you," answered Billy, "or words to that effect; but we were too busy listening to your detective pal to bother much about love letters." He paused and chuckled. "It'll be a knock for Sherlock Holmes when he finds out the facts. He's reckoning that he's got you booked."

I shook my head. "He's none too certain about it," I said. "My sending for Lord Lammersfield gave 'em a bit of a shock; and when Gordon rolled up this after-noon and undertook my defence, I don't suppose it made him feel any more confident."

"Gordon!" repeated Billy. "What, the big Parliament guy?"

"That's the gentleman," I said. "Lammersfield sent him down to me, and he's going to run the show for us. By the way, he wants to see you at his chambers at once: I promised him I'd send you round."

"Where does he hang out?" demanded Billy.

"I don't know," I said, "but the Inspector will tell you." Then I sunk my voice. "Don't say anything to him about Lammersfield having borrowed money from Prado—I kept that dark; otherwise you can tell him the truth."

Billy nodded and jumped up from the bed.

"Right!" said he. "If I haven't forgotten the way, I will."

"And, Billy," I added, more anxiously, "keep an eye on Mercia. I'm not so much worried about Guarez and his lot—Gordon's on their track; it's that blackguard Sangatte I'm thinking of. Now he knows I'm tied by the leg, I shouldn't a bit wonder if he took the chance of trying some dirty trick."

"I don't quite see what he can do," said Billy. " Mercia's back with the Tregattocks now, and she ought to be quite safe there."

" l hope so," I returned ; " but I wouldn't trust Sangatte as far as I could kick him."

Billy laid a reassuring hand on my shoulder. " Neither would I, old son," he said, " but don't worry yourself about it. I'll ring her up on the telephone as soon as I've been to Gordon, and see that she's all right. As far as to-morrow goes, I'll call for her and bring her round to the court-house myself, same as I did to-day."

I reached up and gripped his hand. "Thanks, William," I said. " You're what the Bible calls a very present help in time of trouble."

He laughed, and walking to the door tapped on it for the constable to let him out.

" One gets a bit of practice," he answered, " knocking around with you."

I had no more visitors that evening ; indeed, nothing of any importance happened until next morning, when, about half an hour before I was due in court, Mr. George Gordon was ushered into my room. He was carrying a little black leather bag, but with this exception he looked more like a Bond Street loafer than ever.

" Well, it's good of you to come and relieve my harassed feelings," I said. " I was just wondering whether I should see you before the show started."

He put his bag down on the table and looked up at me out of his tired, expressionless eyes.

" Mr. Burton," he said, " I'm a busy man, even for a

K.C.; but there's no work of mine that won't go to the wall if necessary until this case is settled."

I laughed cheerfully. "That will suit me fine," I remarked. "But I don't quite see where you come in."

He opened his bag and took out several sheets of neatly written notes.

"I hope," he said dryly, "that I shall come in for the privilege of your better acquaintance. Your talents, Mr. Burton, are the sort for which a politician might find many excellent uses."

I shrugged my shoulders. "Well, I shall be wanting a job," I admitted, "now Prado's gone."

He pulled up the chair, and spread out his papers on the table.

"You've no special objection to my not opposing the remand this morning?" he asked, looking up at me sharply.

"It depends upon what you call a special objection," I said. "If you can get the magistrate to give me bail, or whatever you call it, I certainly shan't kick. With Guarez and his crowd still at large, I'd like to be outside, if only to look after Miss Solano."

"Miss Solano is already being looked after," he said curtly. "There's a private detective watching the Tregattocks' house night and day; and as far as Guarez and the others are concerned, I've got a warrant for the arrest of the whole gang. It's merely a matter of finding them now."

"It seems to me," I remarked admiringly, "that I can't do better than leave the whole thing in your hands."

He nodded. "I see no good in opposing the police this morning. Their evidence is too strong for the magistrate to dismiss the case. Sangatte and one of his servants are prepared to swear that you left the house at midnight, and we have only the testimony of Miss Solano and Mr. Logan to contradict them."

"What time was Prado murdered?" I asked.

"Some time between twelve-thirty and one. He seems to have had one visitor earlier in the evening, and then another, or else the same man back again, soon after midnight."

"How the devil did the police find out he was Northcote?" I interrupted.

"He had some papers on him, apparently—what they were I don't know, but enough to give them a hint of the truth. They wired for Maurice Furnivall, and he identified the body at once as that of his cousin. He told the police that he'd felt you were an impostor ever since you'd arrived at Ashton."

"There are the makings of a very fine liar about Maurice," I observed dispassionately. "How did they find out my name?"

"Partly by means of Northcote's papers, I fancy, and partly through your Chelsea landlady. She'd been to the police about your disappearance, and her description of you fitted in, of course, with that of the dead man."

"I never thought of that!" I exclaimed. "I ought to have sent the old lady a message to say I was coming back." Then I paused. "What's the plan of campaign now?" I added.

Gordon leaned forward, clasping his hands in front of him, and speaking in that queer voice of his which finished off each sentence with a kind of business-like snap.

"The police shall have their remand. I'm hoping that by to-morrow we shall have laid our hands on Guarez and his friends. They've bolted from the

Hollies, of course; but I've put Preston, one of our smartest men, on their track, and I expect to hear from him any minute. I'm also moving heaven and earth to find Milford. I've got the police with me there; so if he's above ground, he ought to turn up." He rose to his feet and paced slowly across the room. "You see, the truth is so wildly incredible that I daren't bring it forward until we have got every possible shred of evidence. The more the police find out about the case the better for us."

I was just about to express my agreement when the door opened and the constable came into the room.

"The magistrate has just arrived, Mr. Gordon," he said, in a manner that suggested it was rather impertinent of the magistrate to have done so before consulting Mr. Gordon's convenience.

"Very well," said my counsel, gathering up his papers. "I've still one or two points I want to discuss," he added, turning to me, "so I'll come back here as soon as the case is over."

Shyness is not one of my virtues, but I must acknowledge that I felt a trifle self-conscious as I marched into court for the second time under the wing of Inspector Neil. Apart from my recently acquired newspaper fame, which was embarrassing enough in itself, I was called on to face the eyes of practically every soul with whom I had been on speaking terms during the past ten days.

My first glance round the court showed me that the Ashton party was there *en bloc*. I caught sight of the white, startled face of poor Aunt Mary; the apoplectic countenance of Sir George Vane; and a few seats away the gracious and beautifully dressed figure of Lady Baradell, leaning forward, her eyes fixed on mine with a kind of passionate curiosity. Of Billy or Mercia I could see nothing.

As before, the loud buzz of excited conversation that broke out on my appearance was at once checked by the clerk. His call for order was endorsed by the magistrate, who, looking sharply round the building, observed with chilling disapproval, " If the public present are unable to behave themselves, I shall clear the court."

This threat had the desired effect. A complete and impressive silence at once descended upon everyone, broken only by the rising of a sombre-looking gentleman whom I took to be the counsel for the police.

" I am instructed to apply for a further remand, sir," he observed, addressing the magistrate. " The case for the police is still some way from complete."

The magistrate turned politely to my eminent counsellor.

" Have you anything to say in the matter, Mr. Gordon ? "

Mr. Gordon rose briskly to his feet, and a little shiver of excitement ran through the court.

" If the police ask for a remand in the interests of justice," he began, " we have no objection to offer. To remove any misunderstanding, however, I wish to state that my client has a complete answer to the altogether unfounded charge that has been brought against him. We are ready to assist the police in any inquiries they may be making."

Again the eager murmur of conversation broke out, and I caught a glimpse of Maurice's face, white and savage, staring up at the impassive Gordon.

" You don't wish to cross-examine the police ? " inquired the magistrate.

Gordon shook his head. "Not at present. If the case is persisted in after to-day——"

A sudden disturbance at the back of the building pulled him up abruptly in the middle of his sentence. The main entrance door had been flung open, and three men, evidently in a hurry, had stepped inside, to the indignant surprise of the policeman on duty, who was apparently attempting to bar their further progress.

The magistrate's voice rang out across the court with angry distinctness. "What's the meaning of all this noise? Who are these people?"

Like everyone else, I craned my head forward to get a better view of the intruders. One of them, I could see, was dressed as a priest; a second was a tall, clean-shaven man with grey hair. The face of the third was hidden by the shoulder of the constable, but as I looked that official moved hastily aside at the sound of the magistrate's voice.

I nearly jumped out of my skin. It was Milford! Milford himself standing there in the corridor, beyond any shadow of doubt. He looked pale and haggard, and his usually immaculate clothes were crumpled and untidy, but of his identity there could be no possible question.

I turned eagerly to Gordon, but before I could attract his attention the man who was dressed as a priest had pushed his way to the centre of the court and was addressing the magistrate.

"I must ask your pardon for bursting in on the proceedings like this, Mr. Cowden," he said in a clear voice, with the faintest possible touch of a brogue. "I am Father Merrill of Stepney, and I have brought you a very important witness."

The excitement of the spectators was naturally at

fever pitch, and despite the clerk's renewed demand for silence, the court buzzed with a low, eager whisper of speculation.

The magistrate inclined his head. "There is no need to apologise, Father Merrill. If you are in a position to throw any light on this case, you were quite right to attend. Who is your witness?"

"John Milford, the dead man's servant. He has a statement to make which will clear up this dreadful business—clear it up beyond question, I think. Doctor Robbins and myself are here to confirm his evidence."

There was a short pause. I saw the police counsel and Inspector Curtis exchanging some hasty remarks, while the magistrate bent down and engaged for a moment in consultation with his clerk. Gordon leaned across to me.

"Neither Logan nor Miss Solano are in court," he whispered quickly. "Do you know why?"

I shook my head. Even the extreme tension of the moment did not prevent a horrible feeling of anxiety from clutching at my heart.

Then the magistrate's voice broke in, sharp and decisive.

"I will hear what these witnesses have to say before granting the remand."

The counsel for the police rose as if to protest, but the magistrate waved him back and called on Milford to take his place in the witness-box.

Between my excitement at the unexpected interruption and my dread that something had happened to Mercia and Billy, it was a moment or so before I was able to wrench my mind back to its normal clearness. Then I realised that Milford was standing in the box, and that a great stillness had descended on the court.

18

The magistrate adjusted his glasses. "It will be best," he said quietly, "if you give us your evidence in your own way. Don't allow yourself to become hurried or confused. I shall ask you questions myself, but otherwise no one will interrupt you until you have finished."

With a slight bow, Milford stepped to the front of the box, and placed his hands on the ledge before him. Then, looking straight at the Bench, he began to speak in the quiet, respectful, unemotional voice of a well-trained butler. There was something delightfully incongruous between his own perfect self-possession and the feverish eagerness with which everyone else in court was hanging on his words.

CHAPTER XXII

"MY name, sir, is Milford — John Milford. Up till nine months ago I was a steward in the employment of the Blue Star Line. That was how I first came to meet Mr. Northcote. He was one of the passengers in the *Caledonia* last October coming from New York."

"Was he travelling by himself?" asked the magistrate.

"Yes, sir; he came on board at the last moment. He had one of the deck cabins, and it was my duty to look after him."

"How did he come to offer you the position of being his butler?"

Milford hesitated for a moment. "It was after he had saved my life, sir. I was washed overboard by a big sea on the third day out, and Mr. Northcote, who was on deck, jumped into the water and held me up until they were able to get a boat launched. I was naturally very grateful, sir; and I think it was that which first gave him the idea. Having saved my life, he felt that he could trust me with his."

A little flutter of excitement ran round the court.

"What do you mean?" asked the magistrate, leaning forward. "Did he think that his life was in danger?"

"He knew it, sir. Mr. Northcote was Ignace Prado, the President of San Luca."

Milford's statement, which he made quite quietly, did not arouse anything like the sensation which I expected. I suppose the fact was that very few people in court knew anything about San Luca except that it was in South America, in which case Prado's name would convey to them nothing of its evil significance.

The magistrate, however, appeared to be better informed.

"That's rather an amazing statement," he said, looking keenly at Milford. "I thought Prado was killed in the last revolution."

"Yes, sir. That was the general impression. As a matter of fact, he escaped in a boat the night the palace was blown up, and boarded a steamer in the harbour which brought him to New York. No one knew this at the time; indeed, there was never any suspicion that he was still alive until a couple of months ago."

"Did he tell you all this on the ship?"

Milford shook his head. "No, sir; I knew nothing about it until the other day. When Mr. Northcote engaged me, he merely told me that he intended to take a house in London, and that he wanted a butler whom he could trust. I accepted the post, sir. I was glad of the chance to serve him and to show that I was grateful to him. Mr. Northcote lived in a pretty big way in London at first, as I dare say you know, sir. We used to entertain a goodish bit, and I had an establishment of ten or twelve servants under me. Then one day, about a couple of months ago, something seemed to happen that changed the master entirely. He broke off nearly all his engagements, shut himself up in the house, and began to get rid of the servants until there were only three of us left. It was quite impossible for us to look after the house properly, but he didn't seem to mind that. He doubled our wages, without our asking, and told us to do the best we could. We all thought he was ill; indeed, he looked so bad that once I went so far as to ask him if he wouldn't see the doctor. But it was no use, sir, no use at all. He just laughed, and said that he was doctoring himself."

" He gave you no reason for this change in his way of living? "

"Nothing definite, sir; but I knew that he fancied himself in danger. He gave me special instructions to let no one into the house without bringing up their names to him first. Things went on like this for several weeks—in fact, up to eight days ago. That was the third, if you remember, sir. Mr. Northcote came to me on that day and told me to order him a taxi-cab, because he was going out at six o'clock. He had a motor of his own, but of course it was not my place to ask questions. I ordered him the cab, and he went off. I never saw him again until the night he was murdered."

He paused and took a sip from the glass of water which was standing at the side of the box.

" According to the evidence of the police," said the magistrate, " Mr. John Burton returned to Park Lane in his place."

"Yes, sir."

" And do you mean to tell us you didn't notice the change? "

"No, sir. Mr. Burton is the exact double of Mr. Northcote. Even his voice is the same. He was wearing Mr. Northcote's clothes, and he seemed perfectly at home, sir. There was nothing to make me doubt that he was the master."

Every eye in court was now turned on me. Under ordinary circumstances, I might have found such a sudden scrutiny a trifle embarrassing; but I was so interested in Milford's revelations that I scarcely noticed it. I was waiting to see how much of our mutual adventure he intended to make public.

"And when did you first begin to have suspicions about this amazing deception?" asked the magistrate.

Milford paused for a moment, as though to make quite certain of his facts.

"It was the night of Lord Sangatte's dance, sir—the night of the murder. Mr. Burton went off about half-past ten, and he hadn't been gone a matter of a quarter of an hour when a boy came round to the house with a note for me. It was in the master's writing, sir, and it told me to come down in a taxi to 7 Baxter's Rents, Stepney, as quickly as possible. I couldn't make it out at all, having, as I thought, just seen Mr. Northcote out of the house. Still, there it was; there couldn't be no doubt about the signature, and it wasn't my place to fail the master if he might be wanting me. So I looked out Baxter's Rents in the Directory, and then rung up a cab and told the man to take me down as far as the corner of East Street. It was a pretty rough neighbourhood, sir, just off the river, and seemingly fuller of foreigners than English people. Number seven turned out to be a sailors' lodging-house. I found the master there—he'd told me what name to ask for him under—but at first sight I shouldn't have known him. He'd always used to be most particular about his appearance, sir, but that night he was unshaved and dirty, and dressed in the roughest of clothes.

"Well, sir, he took me into the little room he'd got—like a pig-stye it was—and he shut the door tight and put the bed against it, as if he was afraid of something."

By this time the silence in court was so intense as to

be almost painful. From the magistrate to the police-man at the door every soul present was drinking in Milford's story with a fascinated attention. His strangely simple, unaffected method of telling it seemed to add to its effect.

"You no longer thought that he and Mr. Burton were the same person?" interrupted the magistrate.

Milford passed his hand across his forehead. "I don't know, sir; I was that mazed I can't rightly say what I did think. I just stood there and stared at the master without saying nothing. So far as I can remember, it seemed to me I was dreaming."

"What did he do, then?"

"He told me to sit down on the bed, sir. Then he started talking very slow and quiet. First of all, he told me that he was Prado. From what he said, it seems that he'd gone out from England when he was almost a boy, and that everyone in San Luca believed him to be a South American. He'd escaped from the palace just before they'd blown it up, and he thought at the time he'd got away without being seen. Of course, me being a steward in the Blue Star, sir, I'd heard all about the way he'd made himself President, and I didn't need to be told that there were plenty of people ready to shove a knife into him if they had half an idea he was still alive. Well, that was what the trouble was, sir. Somehow or other, it had come out that he hadn't been killed in the explosion, and the San Luca people had got on his track. He wasn't a coward, the master wasn't,—he couldn't have made himself President, or saved my life as he did, if he had been,—but he knew well enough that he was done for unless he could manage to get out of London. The people who'd come after him belonged to some secret society that he'd pretty near wiped out, and so long as they could get even with him they weren't the sort to mind much what happened after."

Milford paused, and again took a brief sip from the glass of water. I stole a quick glance at Maurice's face. He was staring at the witness-box with an expression of nervous apprehension that pleased me intensely. I was not the only person who felt anxious as to what Milford might bring out next.

"Go on," said the magistrate.

"It was then, sir, quite by chance, that he'd come across Mr. Burton. It was that night he went out in the taxi, sir. He'd gone to sign some papers at his lawyer's, and coming back along the Embankment he passed Mr. Burton standing on the pavement. He saw the likeness at once, sir, and it suddenly struck him that this might be a way of escape if he could work it properly. Anyhow, it seemed a chance, so he stopped the cab and got out and spoke to Mr. Burton."

With the re-introduction of my interesting personality into the story, I again became the centre of attraction. Everyone present leaned forward to stare at me, one or two of the ladies going so far as to produce miniature opera-glasses. It was a trying business, but I put my hands in my pockets and bore it as serenely as I could.

"He asked Mr. Burton to supper with him at the Milan, sir. According to what Mr. Northcote told me, they had a private room. I suppose the hotel management can say whether that's correct, sir."

The magistrate nodded. "Yes, yes. It has already been confirmed in yesterday's evidence."

It was at this point that the counsel for the police jumped to his feet and began to protest against what he described "respectfully" as the "utter irregularity of the proceedings."

The magistrate, who seemed to be a delightfully independent gentleman, cut his eloquence short.

"You will oblige me by sitting down, Mr. Gunn," he observed coldly. "I have no intention of granting a further remand until I have heard everything that these witnesses have to say. Go on, Mr. Milford."

"Well, sir, when the master saw what sort of a gentleman Mr. Burton was, he made him an offer straight out to change places. Mr. Burton was to put on his clothes, and go back to Park Lane, and pretend for three weeks that he was Mr. Northcote."

A kind of half-delighted, half-incredulous gasp ran round the court. Whether Milford's evidence was legally permissible or not, there could be no doubt that the public were intensely satisfied.

"Really, this is most interesting," observed the magistrate dryly. "And the accused apparently accepted Mr. Northcote's enterprising offer? Was he aware of the latter's reasons for wishing to disappear?"

"According to what the master told me, sir, Mr. Burton knew that he might be murdered, but that was about all, sir. He was paid well, and he was prepared to take the risk."

"And what do you call being paid well?"

Milford shook his head. "I don't know, sir. The master didn't say. He only told me that he gave Mr. Burton some hints about the house and about the people he was likely to meet, and that they dressed up in each other's clothes, and Mr. Burton went back to Park Lane."

"And what did Mr. Northcote do?"

"He put up at Bruce House for the night, sir. The

next morning he went down east, and bought some second-hand sailor's clothes. His idea was to get away quiet to Australia; but there wasn't any ship for four days, so he took the room in Baxter's Rents. He'd been lying up there ever since."

"What made him send for you?"

"Well, sir, there were several reasons. First of all, he wanted to know whether we'd noticed the difference between him and Mr. Burton, and whether Mr. Burton was playing the game like—doing what he'd agreed to. Then there was a paper he wanted me to sign and take to Mr. Horsfall, his lawyer."

"What was this paper?" inquired the magistrate sharply. "Have you got it?"

Milford put his hand in his inner pocket and pulled out a long blue envelope.

"This is it, sir. I don't know what's inside. I only wrote my name to say I'd seen the master sign it."

"Give it to me," said the magistrate. Then, raising his head and looking round, he added: "Is Mr. Horsfall in court?"

An elderly, clean-shaven man rose from his seat as the policeman handed up the envelope.

"I am Mr. Horsfall," he said, with a stiff little inclination of his head.

The magistrate put down the envelope beside his blotting-pad. "Very good," he replied. "I will ask you to look into this as soon as the evidence is completed." Then he turned to Milford. "Go on," he said: "what else did Mr. Northcote want you to do?"

"Please, sir, he wanted me to promise I'd write to him in Australia and let him know how things turned out. Also he wanted me to get him some more clothes, and to fix up about his ticket. It was too late to do

anything that night, sir, of course, but I told him I'd
find somewhere to sleep, and set about it first thing
in the morning. I was knocked all of a heap, as you
might say, sir, by what he'd told me."

"Why didn't you stay at Baxter's Rents?"

"The house was full, sir; there wasn't a bed to be
had, and I didn't fancy sitting up the rest of the night.
I hadn't been very well for a matter of a couple of
days."

"Where did you sleep?"

"There was a lodging-house just round the corner,
sir,—Number 10 Smith Street it was,—and I got a room
there. I asked the landlord to give me a knock-up in
the morning, for I was that tired I knew I'd sleep on
late if he didn't. Well, sir, he came to me at six
o'clock, and the very first thing he said to me was that
there'd been a murder in the night at Baxter's Rents.
'Done in a cove at number seven,' he says. 'The police
are round there now.' When I heard that, sir, my heart
seemed to go all queer like. I felt certain it was the
master, sir; and it come to me all of a sudden that
perhaps one of them foreigners had followed me down
and waited outside till I'd left him. I got up and
dressed, and then I went round to the house. There
was a big crowd outside, all pushing and shoving to
get a look, and an inspector standing on the doorstep."

He paused for a moment, as if to collect his thoughts.

"Did you go in?" inquired the magistrate.

"No, sir. As soon as I heard the people talking, I
knew it was Mr. Northcote. Some of them had seen
the body before the police came."

"But why didn't you go and tell your story to the
inspector?"

Milford made a kind of protesting gesture with his

hands. " How could I go to the police, sir, with a story
like that? They'd have thought I was mad. Besides,
I was that knocked over, I didn't rightly know what to
do for the time. I had a sort of feeling that if they
found out I'd been there the night before, they might
think I'd had a hand in it."

" What *did* you do? " inquired the magistrate gently.

" I went back to Smith Street, and I thought the whole
thing over. My first idea was to see Mr. Burton : then
I remembered that he was going down to Ashton, and
as likely as not he'd have started. There wasn't no
doubt in my mind as to who'd done the murder. I felt
as sure as anything it was one of the San Luca gang
the master had told me about. As like as not they'd
followed me down in a cab ; and it troubled me much,
sir, to think that maybe I'd brought his death on him
after he'd saved my life. In a way, as you might say,
sir, it made me feel I was responsible for finding the
man who'd done it."

Milford's voice shook, and he brushed the back of his
hand quietly across his eyes. That Prado, who had
proved himself to be one of the most callous ruffians
that even South America has produced, should have
been capable of inspiring such signs of affection was a
mystery which I will make no attempt to solve. It was
quite plain, however, that Milford's distress was genuine.

" Didn't it appear to you to be a pretty hopeless
business ? " inquired the magistrate.

Milford nodded. " I just had two things to go on,
sir. I knew it was a foreigner, and I guessed that he
couldn't be very far away. Mr. Northcote wasn't the
sort of gentleman who'd have let himself be killed easy,
and I'd heard the people outside the house talking about
the blood-stains down the stairs. So I reckoned it out

that he was probably lying low somewhere in the neighbourhood. There's many a house round that part would take a man in without asking no questions so long as he could pay what they wanted."

He paused to wipe away the perspiration which glistened on his forehead.

" Open another of the windows," said the magistrate irritably. " It's hot enough in here to make us all faint."

Milford waited a moment, while the policeman pulled down one of the long sashes at the back of the court.

" Well ? " asked the magistrate interrogatively.

Milford moistened his lips. " It was chance, sir, just pure chance, that put me on the right track. For three days I'd hunted round without finding out any more than the police had done. Then last night, just before eight o'clock it was, I was standing outside the Dock-yard Arms when a boy came by with some papers. I bought one, and the first thing I saw when I opened it was about the arrest of Mr. Burton. Finding it unex-pected like that, sir, gave me quite a turn. You see, sir, until I saw it in the paper, I didn't even know the police had discovered it was Mr. Northcote who'd been murdered. I felt that shaken, sir, I turned in to have a drop of brandy and to think it over quiet like. The Dockyard bar's divided into compartments — little wooden compartments—about as high as my shoulder. I was sitting there having my brandy and thinking over what I ought to do, when two men came in and sat down in the next division. They started talking, sir, not very loud, but enough for me to hear what they were saying. I listened for a bit without really taking in what they meant, and then all of a sudden it came to me, sir, like—like a blow in the face."

He paused.

" Yes," said the magistrate, " yes ? "

" One of them, sir, was telling the other about a lodger who was ill in his house, and who wanted to see a priest. The other man said something about Father Merrill, and the first man said, in a kind of queer way, ' Well, ye see he was stabbed in the street, and I don't want no fuss so long as he can pay the rent.' When I heard that, sir, I pretty near jumped out of my seat, for something told me it was the man I was looking for. I kept quiet, though, to try and hear some more; but after that they spoke so low I couldn't catch what they were saying. I sat on till they'd done their drink and got up to go, then I slipped out after them. They separated on the pavement, and my man—the one who'd spoken first—turned off down towards the river. He was pretty well gone in liquor, sir, and it was easy enough to follow him. He went all the way along to Shadwell, and turned in at a tumble-down, one-storey sort of place that looked as if it was part of an old warehouse alongside."

" What time was it then ? "

" It must have been pretty near half-past ten, sir. Anyhow, it was just striking eleven when I reached the church at the corner of East Street."

" You came straight back, then ? "

" Yes, sir. I thought it would be no use trying to get into the house on my own, even if the man was there. I wanted someone to help me—someone, too, who'd be the right sort of witness if there was any trouble. It seemed as like as not that I was the only person who rightly knew how things lay ; and now Mr. Burton had been arrested, it wouldn't do for me to make any mistake. Well, sir, I turned it all over in my mind, and I decided at last that I couldn't do any better than go to this Father Merrill that the man had spoken about in the Dockyard Arms. You see, I'd heard others speak of him too, sir, in the lodging-house at Smith Street."

"Everybody in the East End knows Father Merrill, I believe," interrupted the magistrate.

"I should say they did, sir, pretty near. Anyhow, even at that hour, 'twas easy enough finding out where the reverend gentleman lived. I went to his rooms, and late as it was,—getting on for midnight, to be correct,—he came down and opened the door himself. I'd fetched him out of bed, but he didn't seem to mind. He took me into his sitting-room,—I'd said 'twas a matter of life and death, sir,—and there I told him the whole story straight through from beginning to end. Of course, I'd got the master's letter to Mr. Horsfall, and some old letters of my own in my pocket to show him ; but even so, I was half afraid he wouldn't believe what I was telling him. But he did, sir. He just looked at me quiet, and asked me one or two questions, and he seemed to know I was speaking the truth. 'You stop here,' he said. 'I'll go and put on some things and come with you at once.' I waited for him, sir, maybe a matter of ten minutes, and then we set off together. We hadn't got half-way down the street before he stopped and knocked at one of the houses. 'We'll take Dr. Robbins with us,' he said to me. 'He's a big man, and he's used to murderers.'"

A sudden laugh ran round the strained court, in which the magistrate, Father Merrill, and the doctor himself joined.

"Stepney seems to be a most bracing neighbourhood," observed the first. "Go on, Mr Milford."

"Dr. Robbins was up and dressed as it happened,

sir. Directly the reverend gentleman told him what
was the matter, he came along at once, and we got down
to the warehouse just as the clocks were striking half-
past one. It's in a kind of little side street, sir, just off
the river, and at that hour it was quiet as the grave—
not a soul about nowhere. We went up to the house,
and the doctor he rapped on the door with his stick.
There was no answer, so he rapped again louder,
and after a bit we heard someone fumbling with the
latch. At last the door began to open slowly, and the
man I'd followed put his head out round the corner.
He seemed half-drunk still, sir, and the language he
used was something shocking. The doctor didn't take
much notice of him, though. He just shoved the door
wide open and took him by the shoulder. 'Look here,
my man,' he said to him, sharp-like, 'I'm a doctor, and
I've come to see your lodger. If you make any trouble
about it, we shall send straight away for the police.'
That did the trick all right, sir. Directly the fellow
heard the police mentioned, he crumpled up as if he'd
been shot. Then he began to whine out that he hadn't
done anything wrong, and that he knew nothing about
the man who was lodging there. 'No one's accusing
you,' said the doctor; 'all you've got to do is to take us
to him, and be quick about it.' Well, sir, he led us down
a passage into a most filthy-smelling sort of room. It
was quite dark at first, but the doctor he had one of
those little pocket-lamps, which he turned on, and there,
on a bundle of rags in the corner, was a man lying and
groaning something dreadful to listen to. The doctor
walked across and looked him over for a minute without
speaking. Then he pulled out a pocket-book and wrote
down something on one of the pages. 'Take this round
to my house,' he says to me, tearing it out, 'and come

back with the things as quickly as possible.   You'll find
my assistant there : he'll give you what I want.   Father
Merrill and I will wait here.' "

" What was the drunken man doing ? " asked the
magistrate.

" He was standing in the corner, sir, mumbling to
himself.   No one took any notice of him."

" And you went to the doctor's house and got the
things he needed ? "

" Yes, sir.   I was back at the warehouse in under the
hour.   Father Merrill let me in, and I found that he
and the doctor had lit some candles and got things a
bit straight generally.   The man on the bed had stopped
groaning, but he still seemed very bad.   The doctor
was bending over him, doing him up with bandages
and things : I could see he was cut about something
shocking."

" Was he conscious ? "

" Not rightly, I don't think, sir.   He was talking in a
kind of broken English, but it sounded to me all nonsense so far as I could hear.   More like singing than
talking, as you might say.   The doctor gave him some
medicine out of one of the bottles I'd brought, and that
seemed to quiet him, sir.   Anyway, he stopped the
noise he was making.   The doctor went on sponging
and strapping him up till he'd done what he could, and
then he comes across to Father Merrill and me.   ' He's
got it right enough,' he says.   ' He'll probably recover
consciousness before he goes off, though.' "

" What time was this ? " inquired the magistrate.

" About a quarter to three, sir, I should reckon.   Anyhow, I know it didn't begin to get light for some time
after.   There we stayed, all three of us, sitting on the
window-sill or on a bench there was against the wall

19

and watching the man. We didn't dare to leave the
room, for the doctor said he might wake up like any
minute, and if we wanted to ask him anything that
would be our only chance. While we waited, I told
the doctor the whole story the same as I'd told it to
Father Merrill."

"And where was the gentleman who owned the
house all this time?"

"He was in the next room, sir, asleep. They'd put
him in there while I was away. I think he was too
drunk to worry much about anything."

"He seems to have been of a philosophic nature all
through," said the magistrate. "Go on."

"Well, sir, it must have been just about nine o'clock
when the man on the bed gave a sudden sort of a groan
and opened his eyes. The doctor was at his side quick,
sir. He had some medicine all ready in a glass, and he
put his arm round him and lifted him up in bed, and
made him swallow it. It seemed to do him good almost
at once, sir, for he laid back and looked round quite quiet
and sensible like. 'Who are you?' he asks. The doctor
bends down and wipes his forehead for him.

"'I'm a doctor,' he says, 'and this is Father Merrill,
a priest. You wanted to see a priest, you know.'

"'Yes, yes,' says the man, and then a cunning,
frightened sort of look comes into his eyes.

"The Father comes up to the bed and speaks to him
very gentle and kind. He tells him that he is dying,
and asks him if there isn't something he wants to confess. The man reaches up to him, sir, and clutches hold
of his cloak. 'I *am* dying, I *am* dying,' he says, 'are
you sure?' Father Merrill bows his head, and the chap
drops back again on the bed. He lies there for a
minute, sir, without speaking, just breathing hard and

picking at the clothes.   Then Father Merrill bends over
him and takes both his hands.   ' Prado is dead,' he says,
very distinct, ' and an innocent man has been arrested
for killing him.'   That seemed, somehow, to do the business, sir.   The man on the bed gives a kind of gasp and
pulls himself up on the pillow.   ' No, no,' he whispers.
' I kill him.'   Then he takes a long breath.   ' Listen,'
he says, ' I tell you.'   We all three came round the
bed, sir, and the doctor pulls out a pocket-book and a
pencil and begins to write down what the man was
saying.   It was hard to follow, sir, for he spoke English
half-foreign like, and his voice was never better than a
whisper.   The doctor's got what he said wrote down—
he'll show it you, sir—but in a manner of speaking it
was just what I thought.   He was one of the San Luca
lot—Da Costa his name was, and he'd been watching
the house in Park Lane.   When I drove down in the
taxi he'd followed me, and he'd laid low outside
till I cleared off.   Then he'd sneaked in somehow without being seen, sir, and knocked at the door of the
master's room.   I suppose Mr. Northcote must have
thought it was me come back, for he unlocked it, sir, and
this Da Costa had got inside and stabbed him before he
could so much as call out.   But Mr. Northcote, sir, as
I said, he wasn't the sort of gentleman to go under easy.
He'd dropped to the floor, sir ; but it seems he was partly
shamming, for when Da Costa jumped on him to finish
him, he whipped out a knife and stabbed him in the
side.   How long they fought Da Costa didn't know, but
by the time he'd finished the master he was about done
in himself.   He'd crawled away, sir, hardly knowing
what he was up to, and got down somewhere by the
river.   Here he'd run across the man whose house he
was in now.   He told him he'd been stabbed in a street

row, and wanted some place where he could lie up. The man asked him if he had any money, and when Da Costa showed him a pound he took him to Shadwell, and there he'd been ever since. That was his whole story, sir, as he told it to us. You'll find it all written down proper in the doctor's book, with Da Costa's name signed at the end. He was just able to do that, sir, before he went off queer again."

"And you have come straight to the court from Shadwell?" asked the magistrate, as Milford stopped to finish the glass of water.

"Yes, sir. The doctor sent out and got a nurse to look after Da Costa, and then we came right up in a cab."

There was a short silence while the magistrate made one or two notes. When he had finished, he adjusted his glasses and looked up.

"Well, I congratulate you on the way you have given your evidence, Mr. Milford," he said slowly. "You appear, too, to have acted with courage and discretion all through these amazing experiences. I have no doubt the counsel for the police will want to ask you a few questions before we take the evidence of Dr. Robbins and Father Merrill; and meanwhile,"—here he turned to Mr. Horsfall,—"perhaps you, sir, will be good enough to examine these papers."

. . . .

Of the rest of the proceedings I could not, even if I wished to, give a very clear or detailed account. All the time Milford had been telling his story my attention had been so eagerly concentrated on his words that the reaction when he had finished left me curiously indifferent as to what the others might say. I only know I listened vaguely and in a restless fever of impatience. Milford's evidence had so plainly carried conviction to everyone in court that I knew my dismissal from the unpleasantly prominent part which I now occupied was only a matter of time. Even I could tell that the questions which the prosecuting counsel was putting were intended to clear up minor points rather than to cast any real doubt on the truth of Milford's narrative. Whatever the police might think about my conduct and character, they were obviously no longer under the delusion that I was a murderer.

It was another, and to me far more important, question than that of my immediate liberty which now occupied my thoughts. Ever since Gordon had leaned over and whispered to me that neither Billy nor Mercia was in court, a deep uneasiness had been lurking at the back of my mind. While Milford had been giving his evidence I had been too interested to think much of anything else; but now the tension was relaxed, all my previous anxiety about Mercia's safety returned with double intensity.

I looked slowly and carefully round the court to make certain that Gordon was right. Face after face that I knew stood out in turn before my eyes. I caught sight of the immaculately dressed figure of Lord Lammersfield leaning back in his seat, his arms folded—a cynical smile on his lips. A little farther on was the old gentleman who had unconsciously coached me for my first Company meeting. He was bending forward eagerly, his hand to his ear, as though unwilling to miss a single word of the case. York and his sister, my Chelsea landlady, Dr. Ritchie, the impassive head waiter from the Milan—it seemed that everybody who had played a part, however small, in Mr. Stuart

Northcote's highly successful comedy had gathered here to watch the last act unroll itself. Everybody, that is to say, with three exceptions. Not only were Billy and Mercia conspicuous by their absence, but with a curious and very unpleasant shock I suddenly realised that Lord Sangatte was also missing. Search as I would round the crowded court, I could find no trace of that heavy face and those hard blue eyes which I remembered and disliked with such peculiar distinctness.

It was this discovery which more than anything else filled me with a savage impatience to get the present proceedings over and done with. There was some mischief afoot,—something in which Mercia and Billy and Sangatte were all involved,—and here was I knowing nothing about it and powerless to help. I felt a wild impulse to jump up out of my seat and make a dash for the door; but fortunately my common sense was sufficiently strong to restrain me. I dug my hands deeper in my pockets, and with apparent calm listened first to the doctor and then to Father Merrill as, under the magistrate's skilful questions, they in turn confirmed Milford's story.

How long the inquiry went on I can't say. It seemed centuries to me, but I suppose as a matter of fact it was only about three-quarters of an hour from the time Milford had finished giving his evidence that the magistrate leaned over and addressed the prosecuting counsel.

" Do you still persist in pressing for a remand ? " he inquired.

There was a moment of tense excitement in court, while a certain amount of whispering went on between those responsible. At last the barrister in charge of the case rose to his feet.

"On behalf of the police, your worship," he replied, "I am prepared to withdraw the charge of murder against Mr. Burton."

"Bravo!" exclaimed a silvery voice at the back which I seemed to recognise, and instantly a general cheer went up all round the court. I presume it must have been the nervous strain of the moment which was responsible for this enthusiasm, for I can hardly believe that I cut a very heroic or sympathetic figure. Anyhow, the magistrate sat on the outburst with commendable severity.

"Will you be good enough to behave yourselves," he said sharply. "This is a police court—not a music hall."

Then he turned to the counsel.

"I shall hand this confession to the police," he said, "and I have no doubt Mr. Horsfall will be ready to lend his assistance to any further action that may be taken. Meanwhile, I do not think it necessary to prolong these proceedings."

Gordon was on his feet immediately.

"You dismiss the case, your worship?"

The magistrate bowed. "The charge is withdrawn, Mr. Gordon," he said.

CHAPTER XXIII

BEFORE the excitement had properly subsided, I was in the little room at the back of the court with Gordon and Inspector Neil. The latter closed the door, shutting out the confused murmur which we had left behind us.

"It's not my place to congratulate you, sir," he observed apologetically, "but I should like to do so if you will allow me."

"Why, of course, Inspector," I said, with a smile. " I don't wonder you suspected me on the evidence you had. It looked like a certainty."

He shook his head. " It's an amazing case, sir ; but to tell you the truth, I thought we'd made a mistake in the charge the minute I'd arrested you." He crossed the room to the door on the other side. " This room will be at your disposal, if you wish to talk things over. I must see what further steps our people propose to take."

"Let me add my congratulations," said Gordon, as soon as we found ourselves alone.

I gripped the hand he offered me. " Thanks," I said. "I'm very much obliged to you for all the trouble you've taken."

He smiled in his curious languid manner. "There is no reason to be grateful to me," he replied. " It was your amazing butler who took over the defence. I

have never had a case in which I've been quite so
superfluous."

As he spoke, my fears about Billy and Mercia, which
had momentarily lapsed in the excitement of my
acquittal, rushed back on me with redoubled force.

"Mr. Gordon," I said, "I may want your help more
than ever now. Something has happened to Miss
Solano. Billy was to have called for her and brought
her to the court, and neither of them has turned
up."

"I know," he answered quickly. "But don't be too
alarmed about it. I've had a very good man watching
the house since yesterday morning; and unless Preston's
quite wrong, Guarez and the others are lying up somewhere in the East End. They'd hardly dare——"

"It's not Guarez I'm afraid of," I interrupted: "it's
Sangatte."

"Lord Sangatte!" he echoed in surprise.

"Yes," I said. Then I remembered that, in telling him
my story, I had been rather sparing with my account of
the interview in Sangatte's study.

"He's in love with her," I added, "in his own way,
and I've good reasons for knowing that it's a pretty
poisonous one."

The words had hardly left my lips when there came
a sharp knock at the door, and a police serjeant entered
the room.

"There are two gentlemen, sir, who wish to see you
and Mr. Gordon immediately. Shall I show them in
here?"

"Yes, yes," I said. Then, turning to Gordon, I added
eagerly: "It's Billy and your man. It must be."

The serjeant stepped forward and held out a small
twisted note. "Very good, sir," he said. "And there's

this letter. I was asked to hand it to you by a lady who was in court."

I took the note. A glance showed me that it was addressed in Lady Baradell's writing, and I thrust it into my pocket without further consideration. I had no thoughts now for anyone but Mercia.

My first sight of Billy as he entered told me that there were grounds for my anxiety. His face was pale and his mouth set in that peculiar steel-trap fashion which in his case always heralds something in the nature of a tight corner. He was followed by a small, dark, sharp-featured man in a blue suit.

"Much wrong, Billy?" I asked quietly.

"Sangatte's got hold of Mercia," he said, speaking a little hoarsely. "We're after them in a motor now. I think we shall be in time."

Before I could get out a word, Gordon's voice broke in harsh and cold.

"What does this mean, Wilton?"

The dark man was just going to answer when Billy stepped forward and cut him short.

"Mr. Gordon," he said, "we've no time to explain now. You must let me take Wilton. Miss Solano has been carried off to Lord Sangatte's yacht at Burnham. I'm following them in a car which I've got outside, and I want a man with me who won't stick at trifles."

"And by God you shall have it!" I cried, with a savage laugh. Then, seeing his look of astonishment, I added quickly: "I'm free, Billy—the case is over. Milford turned up at the last minute with proofs that it was Da Costa."

With a low exclamation of surprise and satisfaction he gripped me by the arm.

"Is that right, Jack? Lord! but it's good news. Get

your hat, man, and come at once. I'll explain it all in
the car."

"Damn the hat!" I cried, snatching up a dusty-
looking cap from the table. "I'm ready, Billy."

"Go with them, Wilton," broke in Gordon sharply.
Then turning to me, he added in an encouraging tone:
"If it's a case of forcible abduction, you're justified in
anything short of murder."

"I'm glad to hear it," I said grimly.

"And don't worry about all this business," he went
on, jerking his head towards the court. "I'll look after
your interests here. Just send a wire to the House if
you're coming back to town to-night."

I nodded—I think my face showed my thanks—and
in another moment we had hurried down the corridor
and were outside the building.

In the roadway stood a powerful Rolls-Royce with an
embarrassed-looking chauffeur at the wheel. It was
already surrounded by a crowd of spectators, while the
stream of people coming out from the main entrance
was adding momentarily to the congestion.

Billy elbowed his way through with scant ceremony
and opened the door of the car.

"You come in with me, Jack," he said. "Wilton will
go in front."

The next minute we had glided down the street and
twisted noiselessly round the corner into the roar and
traffic of the Strand.

Billy didn't wait for me to question him. "It was
this way, Jack," he said quietly. "I went round this
morning to fetch Mercia at half-past ten as I'd arranged
yesterday. When I rang the bell and asked for her, the
servant said she'd gone out directly after breakfast.
Well, I didn't worry much: I thought that perhaps she'd

had some shopping or something to do first, and that she'd be coming back in a minute or two, so I said I'd call again in a quarter of an hour. I was just turning away when a taxi ran up alongside of me, and who should jump out but our friend Wilton here. I knew who he was—I'd met him at Gordon's yesterday—and I could see at once from his face that something was devilish wrong. The first thing he asked me was whether Mercia had come back. When I said no, he looked more worried than ever, and in about two minutes I'd made him choke up the whole story.

"It seems Mercia had come out of the house about half-past nine. Wilton, who'd been told by Gordon not to lose track of her on any account, followed her as far as Sangatte's house in Belgrave Square. She reached there at a quarter to ten, and he'd hung about outside for the best part of half an hour. Then suddenly Sangatte's motor rolled up to the door, and Sangatte himself came out with Mercia and got inside. Of course there wasn't a taxi handy, and before Wilton could find one the car was out of sight. It struck him as just possible that Sangatte might merely be seeing Mercia home, so he'd come along back to find out."

Billy paused for a moment as the Rolls-Royce, dexterously steered by its driver, wormed its way across the crowded Mansion House Corner. With my heart full of anxiety and torn with a murderous anger, I waited for him to continue.

"I guessed something of what had happened," he went on as the car turned off down Aldgate. "I knew Mercia had heard Sangatte mentioned in court as being one of the principal witnesses for the police, and it struck me at once that he'd probably used this fact to get her to come and see him. Nothing but the idea of helping you would have taken her to his house—I felt sure of that. The thing to find out, of course, was what particular dirty game he was trying to play. I chewed it over for a minute, and then it seemed to me that the best thing to do was to go to his house and see when he was expected back. Wilton agreed with me, so we jumped into the cab and ran down to Belgrave Square. His butler answered the door,—a white-faced, cunning-looking sort of skunk,—and when I asked for Sangatte, he said he was out of town. He wouldn't tell me any more at first—declared that he 'didn't know where his lordship was or which day he intended to return'; and when I pressed him a bit, he was half inclined to be cheeky. I saw the only way was to bribe him. He looked like the sort of man who'd sell his mother, so I told him straight out it would be worth a tenner to him if I could find Sangatte before the evening. With that he started to bargain. I suppose he guessed that it was Mercia I was after, and that I couldn't afford to break his neck—anyway, he stuck out for a pony, and of course I had to give it him. Then I got the truth—at least, I think so. Sangatte, he said, had gone off yachting for three or four days, and my only possible chance of catching him was at Burnham-on-Crouch, where his boat was lying."

"Billy!" I interrupted, rather desperately. "Do you mean that Mercia is alone on board with that brute?"

Billy laid his hand on my arm. "They're only two hours ahead of us, Jack," he said; "and it takes some time to get a boat of any size under way."

"But what does it all mean?" I broke out. "What devil's trick can he have played to get Mercia to Burnham? She knows——"

"It's my belief," interrupted Billy, "that she had no

idea the car was going there.   Suppose he got her round
to the house on the pretence of giving evidence about
you, and then offered to drive her down to the court.
It's only an idea, of course ; but it's in keeping with what
one knows about Sangatte, and it fits in with the facts.
Once in the car, it would be impossible for her to escape
until they got to Burnham ; and what could a girl do
then against two or three men?   No doubt Sangatte's
certain of his own crew."

With a bitter oath, I brought down my clenched fist
on the side of the car.

"If you're right, Billy," I said slowly, "I'll make
Sangatte sorry he was born."

There was a short silence, as the car swung on through
the dreary purlieus of Stratford at a pace which brought
belated shouts and curses from the carmen and hawkers
that we left behind.

"Go on, Billy," I said, staring out in front of us.
"Talk to me, for God's sake, or I shall go mad.   Tell
me how you got hold of the car."

"Hired it," said Billy.   "I saw at once that if this
butler skunk was speaking the truth, the only thing to
do was to make a run for Burnham.   I thought of your
car at first ; then it struck me there might be a bit of a
bother getting hold of it, so I drove straight down to
Garrett's in Bond Street and ordered a Rolls-Royce.
They took about ten minutes getting it ready, and
while they were messing about I sent Wilton round in
the taxi to make certain Mercia hadn't gone home.
Then we came right along to Bow Street to let you
know how things stood before we started for Burnham."

He paused and, bending down, lighted a cigarette.

"I never dreamed, of course, of the case being over,"
he added.   "Tell me something about it, old son : it's

better than sitting there thinking. We're doing all we can, you know, Jack."

I was glad of the chance he gave me. Anything was preferable to brooding over the thought of Mercia in the hands of Sangatte; so without waiting I plunged into the story of Milford's dramatic appearance in court and its amazing developments.

Through Romford and Brentwood the car sped on: the driver, who knew something of the extreme urgency of our journey, letting out the powerful engine to the full extent he dared. Outside the latter town, we turned off due east, and, free of the traffic, hurried on still faster through the miles of flat Essex corn-land that separated us from our goal.

I repeated to Billy the whole of Milford's story, as nearly as I could remember it. With his numerous questions and interruptions it took a long time—indeed, before I had finished we had already reached the straggling estuary of the Crouch, and the grey tower of Burnham Church was plainly visible in the distance. I shall never forget the fever of anger and impatience that seemed to scorch my heart as the driver turned to point it out.

Every minute of that last three miles the torture of suspense became worse. I could see Billy felt the strain almost as much as I did. His mouth set more grimly than ever, and we sat there side by side staring out silently towards our approaching goal.

At last we were in the village. Scarcely slackening our pace, we hurried up the long main street with its small, untidy-looking grey houses, and turning off sharp to the right swung round on to the quay. Regardless of his tyres, the driver pulled up with a jerk, and in a moment Billy and I were out of the car.

An old longshoreman in a blue jersey, who had been leaning over the railings staring down at the tossing collection of boats and yachts below, looked round with slow surprise at our abrupt appearance.

I walked towards him, followed by Billy.

"Can you tell me," I asked quietly, "whether the *Seagull* has sailed?"

He took out a small section of black clay pipe which he had been holding upside down in his mouth, and spat thoughtfully on the ground.

"The *Seagull*?" he repeated. "That'd be the schooner as came in last Tooseday—name o' Sangatte?"

I nodded.

He turned towards the broad estuary, and shading his eyes with his hand stared out to sea.

"There she be," he said at last, pointing down the river.

With a horrible sinking sensation at my heart, I followed the line of his finger. About a mile out a smart-looking vessel of perhaps a hundred and fifty tons was running swiftly seawards before the fresh westerly breeze.

"That's 'er right enough," said the old man. "Put out 'bout one o'clock, she did. The owner come down in a moty-car—same as you gentlemen."

"Was he alone?" I asked, still hoping faintly that we might be mistaken.

The old man shook his head. "'E 'ad a young lady with 'im—bit ill she seemed, too. I see'd 'im 'elping 'er to the boat."

I think I knew then what natives mean when they talk about "seeing red." Before I could crush back my fury sufficiently to speak, Billy broke in.

"Is there any faster boat in the harbour?" he cried.

"We've got an important letter for the owner, and money's no object if we can catch her before she gets to sea."

The man removed his cap and scratched his head with maddening deliberation.

"There ain't no sailing boat in Burnham as'll overtake her now," he observed slowly. "That's the only craft as could do it—that there petrol launch what come in this morning."

He pointed down to a rakish-looking little decked-in vessel which was bobbing about on the tide just below where we were standing.

"Who does it belong to?" I demanded sharply.

"Well, I don't know—not in a manner of speaking," drawled the old man. "A stout, youngish gen'leman 'e be. I did 'ear tell that 'e come from Woodford. If you're wanting to see him, as like as not you'll pick 'im up at the hotel." He turned to point to the building in question, and then gave a sudden exclamation. "Why, there be the gen'leman 'isself, sir, over by the lamp-post there."

I looked up, and my heart gave a sudden jump. In the square-shouldered, pleasant-faced man strolling slowly along the quay I recognised an old acquaintance. It was my friend Cumming the story-writer, the man whom I had met in the Bull Hotel when I was staying at Ashton.

Without stopping to explain to Billy, I strode quickly across the road to meet him. He recognised me at once, and raised his hand in greeting.

"How do you do?" he said, with a smile. "I hope you found Barham Bridge all right?"

I pulled up in front of him and looked him squarely in the eyes.

20

"Mr. Cumming," I said, "you did me a good turn that day. Will you do me another—a much more important one now?"

He paused for a moment, looking back at me as though to make certain I was serious. My expression must have shown him there could be no doubt about that.

"What is it?" he asked quietly.

I turned and pointed to the *Seagull*. "The woman I love is on board that boat," I said hoarsely. "She has been drugged and carried off by Lord Sangatte. There's just one chance of catching them—your petrol launch. If you could get us up alongside, we'd do the rest. I don't know how many men he has on board, but there are three of us, and——"

"I say," he broke in, with shining eyes, "are you pulling my leg?"

I shook my head with a rather wan smile.

"Oh, but this is delightful!" he said. Then, seeing my face, he added politely: "I didn't mean that, of course; but I've been spending years writing about abductions and murders and things of that sort, and this is the first real adventure I've ever been mixed up in."

"And you'll take us?" I cried.

"Take you!" he echoed. "Good Lord—rather! I wouldn't miss such a chance for the world."

Billy, who had come up in time to catch the last remark, clapped him unceremoniously on the shoulder.

"I don't know who you are, my son," he said, "but you're a man, and the breed's rare. Shake."

Cumming, who seemed to understand Billy at once, smilingly gripped hands, and the next minute we were all three hurrying towards the steps which led down to

the water. Leaving the car, Wilton and the chauffeur
came running along the quay to join us.

"Got room for me, guv'nor?" inquired the latter
anxiously.

"What about the car?" I asked, as Cumming, jumping into a dinghy, hastily pulled out the sculls from
under the seat.

He grinned cheerfully. "Car's all right, sir. I've
given the old boy five bob to look after her."

"Come on, then," I said; "the more the better." And
without wasting any more time, we all five scrambled
into the boat.

A few strokes brought us alongside the launch, to
which we rapidly transferred ourselves. Cumming at
once squatted down in front of the motor and began to
play with the levers and switches, while the rest of us
distributed our weight about the little craft in the most
even fashion possible.

"Shall I steer her out for you, sir?" asked the
chauffeur. "I've done a bit of this work over in
France."

Cumming nodded his consent, and as the man gripped
the tiller he started up the engine. The next moment
we were swiftly threshing our way through the crowd of
anchored vessels towards the centre of the estuary.

Directly we were fairly under way, and the engine
was running with proper smoothness, Cumming
scrambled to his feet and took over the charge of the
boat.

"She can do twenty easy," he observed, with a satisfied chuckle; "we shall be up to them before they're
past the sands." Then he paused. "What's the programme?" he added. "Hail them, or run up alongside
and jump?"

" Can you take her in as close as that ? " I asked.

" I could take her to hell," he replied cheerfully, " if there was enough water. The only thing is, can you chaps get on board ? "

Billy laughed grimly. " Some of us will," he said, " and the others can swim."

With a white curve of water foaming away from either bow, the little vessel ran on down the centre of the river. Far ahead of us, a beautiful picture in the cloudless afternoon sunshine, the *Seagull* swept forward on her way towards the sea. Crouched in the bows, I stared silently out over the long grey stretch of intervening water, which every minute was perceptibly lessening in distance.

Billy, who had been rummaging in the tool-chest, which Cumming had pointed out to him, crept forward and held out a heavy steel bar.

" Here you are, Jack," he said. " You freeze on to this. I've got a gun."

I took the short but deadly little weapon and thrust it into my side pocket. I felt somehow that my fists would be all that I should want.

" Billy," I said, " if we both get on board together, leave Sangatte to me."

He nodded. " That'll be all right," he replied. " There'll be quite enough fun for me with the rest of the crew ; you shall have his lordship all to yourself." Then he paused and looked out at the stern of the *Seagull*, now no more than half a mile distant. " Don't you think, Jack," he added, " that you'd better go down into the cabin, just in case Sangatte's on the watch ? If he spotted you, he'd guess we meant mischief at once, and we might find it a bit of a job to get on board. You can pop out as we run alongside."

Billy's suggestion was so obviously a sensible one that, although I was loth to quit the deck, I immediately adopted it. It would never do for Sangatte to see me in the boat, for the *Seagull* stood so much higher out of the water than our own little craft that our only chance of boarding her was to take the crew by surprise. So into the cabin I went, where I found the impassive Wilton, who seemed to consider the whole business as part of his ordinary day's work, stretched out peacefully on the bunk.

He sat up as I crawled in; but beyond exchanging a couple of remarks as to the quickness with which we were overtaking our quarry, we neither of us made any attempt at conversation. I was in too keen a state of suspense to talk; while Wilton, I should think, was a naturally taciturn person even for a detective. Anyhow, we sat there in silence, listening to the throbbing of the engine and the ceaseless swish of the water as it raced past the side of the boat.

How long our vigil lasted I can't say. It was broken at last by the appearance of Billy, who dropped down into the little well outside the cabin and thrust his head in through the door.

"We're just coming up alongside of 'em," he said, in a tone of quiet satisfaction. "There are three men on deck, but they don't seem to suspect anything."

"Sangatte?" I asked eagerly.

He shook his head. "No sign of him or Mercia; they must be down below."

I rose to my feet, followed by Wilton.

"We three are to make the first shot," went on Billy. "Cumming's going to run her alongside suddenly, and we must jump for the rails. One ought to be just able to do it from the cabin top."

"And then?" I asked; for I knew Billy would have planned the whole thing out.

He tapped his pistol pocket with a contented smile. "Then it will be up to me to keep order on deck while you and Wilton go below and rout out Mercia. The chauffeur's staying in the boat. He wanted to stick to us, but we must have someone to help Cumming."

He swung himself out of the well on to the narrow deck, and Wilton and I followed suit. We were running level with the *Seagull* at a distance of about thirty yards. The three men on her deck were not paying much attention to us. One of them was steering—the other two busy attending to the coiling of some loose rope. At the tiller of our own boat sat Cumming—a cigarette in his mouth, and his eyes fixed innocently on the water ahead.

Suddenly, and without shifting his gaze, he gave a quick, faint little whistle. Billy and I and Wilton leaped on to the cabin top, and at the same instant the launch swerved inwards towards the *Seagull* like a weasel darting on a rabbit. I heard a cry of dismay and surprise from the man who was steering as he shoved down his helm in a frantic effort to avoid a collision. At the very last moment, just when the crash seemed inevitable, Cumming again swerved, and as he did so we all three made one frantic jump for the *Seagull's* rails.

I missed with my left hand, and my other arm seemed to be almost wrenched from its socket with the shock. I clung on, though, and the next moment, soaked and half blinded with spray, I was scrambling over on to the deck. A swift glance round showed me that both Billy and Wilton had been equally successful.

Paralysed, apparently, at the suddenness of our onslaught, the two men who had been coiling the rope made no attempt to stop us until we were fairly on board. Then, as I leaped for the companion-way, they both dashed forward with a volley of questions and oaths. Only one of them reached me in time, and he got a smack in the jaw for his pains that sent him spinning against the rails. At the same moment Billy's voice, backed doubtless by his revolver, rang out in a harsh command, and the other stopped short and flung up his hands.

Without waiting for any further developments, I dropped down the companion, clearing the short ladder with one jump. There was a door in front of me—a white cabin door with brass fittings. I seized the handle and flung it savagely open, just as Wilton's figure appeared in the opening above.

Do you remember that hideous picture of " The Startled Robber " in Hogarth's " Two Apprentices "? It flashed into my mind then as, pale with amazement, terror, and rage, Sangatte started up at my entrance. He had evidently been sitting at the table smoking and drinking, for there was a bottle of brandy and a half-empty siphon in front of him, and the air was thick with the fumes of his cigar.

The same glance that revealed his glaring, terrified eyes also showed me Mercia. She was on the sofa at the farther end of the cabin, crouching against the wall like some beautiful, desperate animal at bay. At the sight of me her face lit up with a joy too wonderful for words, and she too sprang to her feet, crying out my name.

Then, silent as a wolf, I flung myself on Sangatte.

He seized the bottle of brandy by the neck, and struck at me wildly as I came in. I dashed it aside with my left arm, and the broken glass and liquor showered over us both. The next moment, locked in each other's arms, we swayed clear of the table and crashed heavily against the opposite wall of the cabin.

He was a powerful man, nearly as big as myself, and fighting with the fury of absolute terror; but his strength was as nothing against my own mad rage. Freeing my right arm with a desperate wrench, I drove my fist full in his face, and I felt the bone and cartilage yield under my knuckles as if they had been made of crisp wafer. He clutched me by the throat, but at that smashing blow his grip relaxed, and a horrible stifled cry burst from his lips. With a supreme effort, I lifted him clear off his feet and flung him full length on the cabin floor.

There came a long-drawn, gasping sigh from Mercia.

"A—ah!"

I looked up—my chest heaving, my face and clothes soaked in blood and brandy.

"Shall I kill him?" I asked quietly.

Mercia came forward—her dear face as white as death, but her eyes shining proudly and serenely.

"There is no need to kill him," she said softly. "You are always in time."

With a low, happy cry I caught her to my heart, and all blood-stained as I was, she put her arms round me and pressed her lips to mine.

CHAPTER XXIV

IT was the sudden stamping of feet and the sound of blows outside that abruptly terminated our embrace. Releasing Mercia, and snatching up the siphon from the table, I darted to the door, where I found the faithful Wilton, armed with heavy boat-spanner, vigorously opposing the attempted advance of two of Sangatte's crew.

At the sight of me—I must have been a horrible-looking object—their courage seemed to falter.

"Come on, Wilton," I yelled, and, swinging back my siphon, I leaped forward to the attack.

It was too much for the enemy. However strong their affection for Sangatte may have been, they evidently had no stomach for further fighting, and with a simultaneous motion they turned and bolted. As they disappeared down the corridor from which they had apparently emerged, I heard Billy's voice shouting my name from the deck.

I stepped back into the cabin.

"Time to go, Mercia," I said, holding out my hand.

She slipped her soft little fingers into mine, and as she did so, Sangatte, who had not moved since he had fallen, suddenly raised himself with an effort on to his elbow.

"Damn you!" he whispered thickly. "I'll be even

with you for this—damn you both!" Then, with a groan, he sank back again on to the floor.

If it gave him any small pleasure to swear at us, I did not grudge it him—under the circumstances.

Our departure from the *Seagull* was distinctly more ceremonious than our arrival. By aid of his persuasive revolver, Billy had apparently induced the crew of the vessel to strike sail; for when we reached the deck, it was to find ourselves rocking idly on the bosom of the tide, with Cumming's smart little motor bobbing alongside. The three defeated hands, one of whom was the skipper, were clustered in the bows, watching Billy with anything but an affectionate expression.

"Not hurried you, Jack, I hope?" he called out, as we emerged from the companion, with Wilton guarding the rear.

"No, thank you, Billy," I said. "I'd quite finished."

He stepped forward to shake hands with Mercia. "And how's our host?" he inquired.

"Our host," I replied, "when he's patched up, will probably be mistaken for Señor Guarez."

Billy nodded his head. "You were always a good hand at scattering keepsakes," he observed contentedly.

It was at this point that Cumming's face, appearing over the side of the yacht, inquired with some pathos what time we should want the cab.

"I suppose we must tear ourselves away," said Billy reluctantly. "It's a pity, though. I was just beginning to enjoy myself. Devilish smart crew Sangatte's got—when they're properly handled."

Despite this handsome compliment, the crew betrayed no particular signs of regret at our departure. They watched with sullen hostility while I lowered Mercia into the hands of Cumming and then jumped down

myself after her.   Then, pushing away the launch with
the boat-hook, we backed slowly astern, until there was
sufficient room to swing her round towards the shore.
A moment later we were racing back against the wind
and tide, while behind us the *Seagull* still drifted idly
down the centre of the stream.

A few hastily-exchanged explanations showed us that
Billy had been quite right in his surmises as to Mercia's
adventure.   By a cleverly-worded letter, hinting that
he was prepared to give evidence on my behalf,
Sangatte had induced her to come and visit him at
his house.   Here, after expressing himself as being
convinced of my innocence, he had offered to drive
her down to the court; and Mercia, suspecting nothing
of his purpose, had readily assented.   Once inside the
big, swiftly-moving limousine, it had been hopeless to
try and escape until Burnham was reached, and then,
just before the car drew up, Sangatte had thrust a
handkerchief soaked in chloroform over her face, which
had rendered her practically unconscious until she was
safely in the ship's boat.

That was the only actual violence she had suffered
from.   Once on board, Sangatte, who possessed an
abnormal opinion as to his own fascinations, had
adopted the rôle of the impassioned, half-repentant
lover whose emotions had run away with him.   I
suppose he had thought that his own charms, combined
with the hopelessly compromising position in which
Mercia was placed, would be a sufficiently strong
combination to effect his purpose.   Anyhow, he had
been giving this ingenious system a fair trial when
Fate and my right fist had so unexpectedly inter-
vened.

Such was Mercia's story, whispered out hurriedly as

we throbbed our way back up the grey waters of the Crouch.

In return, Billy and I told her as briefly as possible of the amazing sequence of events which had led up to our arrival on board. The astonished Cumming, who now for the first time realised our identity, listened with such spellbound attention that on two occasions he as nearly as possible ran us on to the shallows.

"Well, I'm blessed!" he gasped when I'd finished "Do you mean to say you're Burton—*the* Burton? Why, I was only reading your case while I was at lunch, and thinking how much I'd like to meet you."

"Well, you've done it all right," laughed Billy; "and devilish lucky for us, too."

"But, good Lord, what a yarn!" went on Cumming, looking with a kind of curious admiration first at me, and then back at Billy and Mercia. "It knocks spots off my woolliest efforts, and that's saying something. And to think of my being in at the death, too! It will make the Authors' Club blue with envy."

"Come up to town with us and see it through," I suggested. "They've turned me down as a murderer, it's true, but there are all sorts of pleasant possibilities still kicking about. I shall probably be arrested for stealing Northcote's ten thousand as soon as I get back."

"Anyhow," said Billy, smiling at Mercia, "we can at least promise you a wedding."

"And probably a funeral as well," I added, "if I happen to run across Maurice."

"I'd love to," said Cumming, steering us deftly in towards the quay through the crowd of anchored boats. "All the same, I think I'll run this little jigger round to Maldon first. It would be just as well to get her out of Burnham in case your pal, Lord Sangatte, puts back

here for plaster. I ought to go up to town to-morrow
in any case, so if you'll give me your address, I'll roll
round and 'pay my respects.'"

"Do!" I said heartily. "If I'm not in Bow Street,
you'll find me at Lammersfield House, Park Lane."

"You forget, my son," interrupted Billy. "It doesn't
belong to you now."

"Yes, it does," I said firmly. "I gave my promise to
Northcote, and I'm not going to shift out of it until the
three weeks are up."

"Good," said Billy. "We ought to have some fun
with the heir, whoever he is."

Cumming tied up his boat to the steps, and climbing
up on to the quay saw us safely into the car. I don't
know whether any of our operations on board the *Seagull* had been visible from Burnham, but, at all events,
our old longshore friend did not seem particularly interested in us. He just pocketed the five shillings I gave
him for looking after the car, and then promptly shuffled
off for the hotel tap without waiting to watch us depart.

"So long, then," said Cumming, as soon as we had
packed ourselves in and the driver was ready to start.
"I'll give your love to Sangatte as I pass him."

"Thanks," I said ; "and don't worry if he makes any
fuss. George Gordon says we were legally justified in
anything short of manslaughter."

"Skunk slaughter," said Cumming, "is what you want
an indemnity against."

We turned off round the corner of the quay, stopping
at the Post Office to send a wire to Gordon.

"Expedition successful," I wrote. "Will you meet us
Westminster Palace Hotel five-thirty."

"It's just opposite to the House of Commons," I

pointed out to Billy, "so he'll be able to run across even if he's busy. I'm dying to know what happened after we left."

"What I'm dying for is some food," remarked Billy, as we came out again to the car. "I expect Miss Solano agrees with me."

Mercia shook her head. "I am not very hungry," she said. "Let us wait till we get back to London."

"Just as you like," said Billy sadly. "I could do a chop, though—by Jove, I could!"

"Jump in, William," I said. "We'll all have the best dinner in London to-night—unless we're in jail."

Mile after mile, the big car carried us back swiftly through the flat lanes and roads which we had so lately traversed. I was too happy to talk: most of the time I just lay back in my seat holding Mercia's hand; while Billy, in the intervals of bemoaning his hunger, filled up the gaps which we had necessarily left in our somewhat hurried explanations in the boat. Any doubts that he may have originally felt about Mercia had plainly vanished. She was part of the firm now—"one of us," so to speak; and Billy's manner clearly signified that he approved of the change.

It was just a quarter-past five by Big Ben as we swung round the corner of Parliament Square and drew up outside the Westminster Palace Hotel.

We were all of us badly in need of a little tidying-up, so the extra fifteen minutes before our appointment with Gordon was a welcome interval. I know in my own case that, what with the dust from the road, and the still surviving traces of my argument with Sangatte, I found such a rare-looking ruffian gazing back at me from the bedroom mirror that I felt surprised the hotel people had consented to receive us.

However, a bath, a comb, and other toilet accessaries soon restored me to respectability, and sitting on the bed I waited for Billy, who was taking his turn at the looking-glass. It was then that, putting my hand in my pocket, I came across Lady Baradell's note. Although, to tell the truth, I had forgotten all about it in my somewhat strenuous employment since its arrival, I opened it now not without a certain pleasant curiosity as to what it might contain.

"I suppose I ought to be grateful to you, but I don't think I am. Now and always you have my good wishes.   A. B."

I read it through slowly, and the picture of a beautiful woman, her bronze hair streaming loose over her shoulders, her wonderful amber eyes fixed on mine, rose with extraordinary clearness before my mind. With a little sigh over Nature's well-intentioned, if ill-adjusted, efforts, I took out a match, and striking it on the end of the bed, set fire to the bottom corner of the note.

"What are you burning?" asked Billy, looking up from the depths of his towel.

"Only a little bit of the past," I said sadly.

He threw down the towel with his old mischievous chuckle. "If you're going to start that game, Jack," he said, "you'd better spend your honeymoon at Vesuvius. It'll save you ruining yourself in matches."

We went downstairs to the sitting-room I had engaged, where tea was already laid. A minute later Mercia joined us. Despite all she had been through, she looked radiantly lovely as she came half shyly into the room. Indeed, Billy was so overcome that he jumped from his chair with a little gasp of open admiration.

"By Jove, Mercia!" he said. "You ought to be abducted twice a day. It makes you better-looking than ever."

She laughed sweetly, and came across to where I was standing. "I am afraid I shall never be more beautiful, then," she said, "unless there are some very reckless men in the world."

I drew her arm tenderly through mine. "I don't want you to be any more beautiful, Mercia," I said; "it would frighten me if you were."

There was a knock at the door, and a waiter entering announced "Mistaire Gordon."

Sleek and debonair as ever, my gallant defender followed hard upon his heels.

"Don't trouble to explain anything," he said, shaking hands all round. "I've only got ten minutes, and I've already heard full details about the piracy, of which, by the way, I thoroughly approve. I met Wilton in the hall."

"I wondered what had happened to him," I remarked. "We were expecting him up here to tea."

Gordon shook his head. "You won't get him," he said. "Wilton has some intelligence as a private detective, but outside his business he's a miracle of shyness and stupidity." Then he smiled in his quiet, fatigued way. "He asked me to congratulate you, however."

"Congratulate me!" I echoed. "What about?"

Gordon accepted the cup of tea which Mercia offered him. "About fifty thousand, I believe," he drawled. "No doubt there's a good deal more somewhere, if we can find it."

We all stared at him in frank astonishment.

He looked round at us, smiling again from under his curious, heavily-lidded eyes.

"You remember the excellent advice given to us in the Gospels, Mr. Burton—to ' make friends out of the mammon of unrighteousness'? Well, you appear to have been doing it unawares—that's all. Those papers which the amazing Mr. Milford sprang on us in court —the ones addressed to Horsfall, I mean—were Northcote's confession, and incidentally his will. He has left you everything."

I jumped up from my chair. "Good Lord!" I cried. "Are you joking?"

Gordon shook his head. "I never joke outside the House of Commons."

"But why on earth——?" I began.

"As far as I can make out," he interrupted, "our deceased friend's mind worked in this way. It was rather more than possible, of course, that you would be killed before the three weeks were up, in which case all Prado's land property, which he had been unable to sell, would have gone to Maurice Furnivall, as the next of kin. This he was determined to prevent, for by then he seems to have quite made up his mind that it was Furnivall who'd given him away. He wrote out a full statement of how affairs really stood, and sent it to Horsfall with a note that it was only to be opened in the event of his death. As this statement claimed that he was still alive, and afforded pretty good proof of the fact, it would have been quite sufficient to hang up the settlement until he found it safe to re-appear, or, at all events, to communicate with the court."

"But the will," I broke in, "the will?"

"Ah!" said Gordon. "Like many robust scoundrels, I think that Mr. Prado was a bit of a fatalist. Although apparently he'd got off so neatly, I believe he had some

21

sort of feeling that his days were numbered. He practically hints as much in his will, which he tells Horsfall he had drawn up in case 'all his excellent precautions should prove useless.' It's quite a simple document. He leaves you everything, 'in the improbable event,' as he puts it, 'of your surviving him.' Failing that, the property goes to charity."

" And Maurice gets nothing ? "

" Not a bean," answered Gordon cheerfully. " If he finds himself hard up, the testator advises him to communicate with San Luca. I should think it was the only joke Prado ever made."

" But will it hold good in law ? " I asked.

Gordon shrugged his shoulders. " I think so," he said. " It's a little irregular, of course, but there's no one to fight it except Furnivall, and unless he's a fool, he'll lie devilish quiet. I've quite enough evidence to ask for his arrest for conspiring to murder you at Woodford. That reminds me, by the way. You're not likely to be troubled with your South American friends again for a little while—they got away on the *New York City* this morning. I can have them collared the other side, if we want them, of course; but, on the whole, I thought it best to let them go."

I nodded my approval. " We shall miss them," I said, " shan't we, Billy ? Still, the best of friends must part."

" They must," agreed Gordon, pulling out his watch. " I'm due to speak in the House at five forty-five, and it's ten to six now."

He hastily picked up his hat and gloves. " Goodbye," he added, shaking hands all round. " Come and see me at my chambers at ten-thirty to-morrow, and we'll straighten things out a little. Till then,"—his eyes twinkled,—"well, try and keep out of mischief as much as possible."

"Fifty thousand pounds!" exclaimed Billy, as the door closed behind him. "Good Lord! Give me some more tea; I feel quite giddy."

Mercia poured him out another cup, which he gulped down in silence.

"Fifty thousand pounds," I repeated slowly. "It's a sobering sum, isn't it?"

"*Sobering!*" gasped Billy. "It's—it's——" Words failed him completely.

"Well, come along," I said, jumping up from my chair. "Let's get back to Park Lane and see what's happening there. We've all sorts of things to do before dinner."

"All sorts of things to do?" echoed Billy reprovingly. "My dear Jack, you forget yourself: you are now one of the idle rich."

"Not quite, Billy," I said; "there's a lot of dust to sweep up yet. We'll start by paying for tea."

I rang the bell and settled my bill, giving the waiter a tip that made his hair curl. It pleased me to be able to pass on something of my own emotions.

We then went down into the hall, where a porter hurried off to inform our faithful driver, who by my instructions was refreshing himself somewhere in the hotel. A minute later, the Rolls-Royce drew up outside the door.

"Lammersfield House, Park Lane," I said.

Billy settled himself back luxuriously, facing me. "And to think," he murmured, "that ten days ago we were dining at Parelli's."

"To-night," I said, "we'll all three dine at Park Lane. What do you say, Mercia?"

Mercia nodded her head gravely. Ever since Gordon's revelations she had been curiously silent.

"That's to say, if there's anyone in the house," I went on. "It's more than likely that both the women have cleared out by now, and Heaven knows what's happened to Milford."

"Well, we shall soon see," remarked Billy consolingly. "In any case, you can ring up Harrod's and tell them to send some food along. That's the best of being a millionaire."

Mercia laid her hand on my sleeve. "I must let the Tregattocks know I am safe," she said. "They will be anxious about me. You see, I have been away ever since breakfast."

"Better send them a wire," I suggested, "saying that you'll be back by ten. We could ring them up, of course, only it's rather an impossible situation to explain over the telephone."

Gliding round the corner of Piccadilly and Park Lane, the big car swept forward for a hundred yards, and then drew up noiselessly outside Lammersfield House. By now, the fact that I was for the moment the most notorious person in England had gone clean out of my head. This lapse of memory nearly led to a regrettable incident, for as I jumped out to hold the door open for Mercia, a young man in a blue suit, who was standing on the pavement, made a sudden dash towards us. With a warning cry to Billy, I whipped back my fist ready to strike, and the stranger checked himself abruptly just out of distance.

"I say, I'm—I'm awfully sorry," he stammered. "I beg your pardon, Mr. Burton. The fact is "—here he began to feel in his pocket—"I'm representing the *Daily Wire*. 'Fraid I gave you a bit of a surprise."

"It was nothing," I said, "to the surprise I nearly gave you."

"If you could spare me a few minutes——" he began eagerly.

"Look here," I said, "I'm busy now—I've got some friends with me. Come back in half an hour, and we'll have a chat."

He looked at me sharply as though to see whether I were telling him the truth, and then, apparently satisfied with the honesty of my countenance, began to express his thanks.

"It's no business of mine," he added tentatively, "but I suppose you know Mr. Furnivall is in the house?"

"What!" I almost shouted.

"Yes," he said. "I was really sent to interview him, but he declines to see any pressmen."

"Does he!" I said. "Well, if you wait here a minute or so, perhaps I might persuade him to change his mind."

"This," broke in Billy, softly rubbing his hands together, "just completes our day."

I turned to Mercia. "Don't be afraid, dear," I said. "There's not going to be any more bloodshed."

She smiled faintly. "I am not afraid," she answered. "One does not fight with men of his sort. He is a coward and a traitor. He sold Prado to the League, and he would have killed you when you were at Ashton."

I nodded my head. "I know, Mercia," I said sadly. "It's on these very points we are going to remonstrate with him."

I led the way up the steps, and then with my hand on the bell I paused.

"By Jove, Billy!" I said. "I suppose Maurice still thinks he's come into all Prado's money."

"You bet he does," chuckled Billy.

I gave a joyous peal at the bell, and in a few moments the door opened, and I found myself face to face with the pretty housemaid.

She uttered a low exclamation of surprise and delight. "Oh, sir!" she cried, "you've come back, you've come back!"

"Of course I have," I said. "I told you I should, and I often speak the truth."

She stepped back to make room for us, and we passed through into the further hall.

"Where's Mr. Furnivall?" I asked.

She opened the inner door. "Mr. Furnivall——" she began, and then she stopped short; for there, at the foot of the staircase, stood Maurice himself, staring at me with an expression in which amazement, hatred, and fear were very evenly blended.

Some idea of bolting must have passed through his mind, for I saw him make a quick half-turn towards the banisters. Then I suppose the futility of the proceeding struck him, for with a big effort he regained his self-control, and advanced towards us with an ill-assumed air of dignity.

"I should have imagined," he said, "that this was the last place you would have had the impertinence to come to!"

I looked at him for a minute, with a slightly thoughtful smile.

"My dear Maurice," I said at last, "if you only had a little more courage, you'd be a really remarkable rascal. As it is——" I shrugged my shoulders and began to walk towards him.

He turned pale and stepped back.

"If you attempt to make any disturbance here——"
he began.

"Oh, shut up!" I said good-humouredly, and reaching
forward I caught him by the collar.

He squirmed furiously. "Send for the police," he
bellowed, "send for the police!"

"You can send for the whole British Army, if you
like," I observed, shaking him into something like silence.
"Now listen to me, Maurice. Your cousin may have
been a scoundrel, but, at all events, he trusted you, and
you sold him—sold him like the dirty little Judas
Iscariot you are. Besides that, you did your best to get
me murdered."

"It's not true," he gurgled.

"Yes, it is," I replied. "Don't contradict me, or I
shall get annoyed. Not only did you try to have me
murdered at Ashton, but you told the most unblushing
lies about me to the police." Here I lifted him up and
shook him again till his teeth rattled. "Now, Maurice,"
I added, "people who behave to me like that are asking
for trouble. Guarez has got it, Rojas has got it, and
I've just been squaring matters with our mutual friend
Sangatte."

"Look here," he gasped, "you're mistaken; on my
honour you are. It's no good being violent. If you
want money——"

He paused.

"Well?" I said grimly.

"I'll—I'll give you a cheque; and you can clear out
and start fresh."

"Billy," I said, "just open that hall door, will you?"

Then I jerked my prisoner round, so that I could see
his face.

"You appear to be under a slight misapprehension, Maurice," I said. "In the first place, you are not Prado's heir; and in the second, I don't happen to be in need of money."

Tightening my grip on his collar, I moved him slowly backwards across the hall towards the front door.

"What are you going to do?" he wailed.

"If I did my duty," I said pleasantly, "I should wring your neck. As I don't want to hurt your Aunt Mary's feelings, however, I'm merely going to throw you out of the house."

He writhed and twisted like a freshly landed eel, but step by step I shoved him inexorably backwards towards the door which Billy was holding open. In moments of great bodily stress the most carefully assumed refinement is apt to be dissipated, and I regret to say that Maurice's language would have disgraced a cow-puncher. I don't think Mercia minded in the least,—fortunately, she is not that sort,—but his confounded cheek at using it in front of her lent an additional stimulus to my efforts.

On the threshold we paused for a strenuous second or so, while I swung him round so that he could obtain a full view of his destination. Then with a mighty thrust, and one swift, accurately-planted kick, I sent him hurtling down the steps and out into the gutter.

"So perish all traitors," observed Billy's voice.

Maurice, who had fallen full length in the mud, slowly scrambled to his feet. The mixture of pain and fury in his face would have been funny if it had not been so repulsive. He was choking with emotion, but before he could recover himself sufficiently to get any of it out, he was suddenly accosted by the intensely interested representative of the *Daily Wire*, who had been watching his exit with a kind of paralysed fascination.

I suppose it is annoying to be asked for an interview under such circumstances ; still, no irritation could excuse the stream of blasphemy with which Maurice turned upon his interrogator. For a moment, the latter was too astounded to reply ; then, getting his chance, as Maurice paused for breath, he began to keep his end up with a vigour and resource that only the literary temperament can command.

Feeling that this dialogue was unsuitable both for Mercia and for my pretty housemaid, I was just stepping back to close the door when a voice that I had good reason for remembering suddenly cut into the uproar.

" If you don't stop using that language and clear out of here immediately, I shall call the police. You ought to be ashamed of yourselves, gentlemen, brawling like this in Park Lane ! "

It was Milford—the redoubtable Milford ! Even if I had not recognised the tone, I should have guessed who it was speaking from the sentiments.

At the sound of his rebuke, the exchange of compliments stopped abruptly. Maurice, who apparently realised that he had been making an ass of himself, looked round wildly to find some way of escape from the rapidly increasing fringe of spectators. There was a taxi on the farther side of the road, the driver of which had drawn up to watch the fun. Walking across, Maurice gave the man some directions, and then, without so much as a glance back at the house, jumped inside and slammed the door. The next moment he was bowling off up the street.

I looked round for Milford, but he was already disappearing down the area steps. Closing the front door,

I turned to the pretty housemaid, who had taken refuge behind the umbrella-stand.

"Ellen," I said, "Milford's coming in down below. You might send him straight up."

"Yes, sir," she gasped, and abandoning her hiding-place, she hurried off across the hall.

Billy took a deep breath. "I call this living," he remarked contentedly. "Fancy Milford turning up like that!"

"If ever a man had the dramatic instinct," I said, "Milford has."

The words had hardly passed when the door at the back of the hall opened and my incomparable retainer stood before us.

He looked all round, and then bowed gravely. "May I be permitted to welcome you back, sir? I regret I was not here to receive you."

I stepped forward, and held out my hand. "Milford," I said, "I'm not much good at thanking people, but"—then I paused—"well, I'm very grateful," I finished heartily.

He accepted my hand with a kind of apologetic movement. "Not at all, sir. Only too glad to have been of any assistance. May I say how pleased I am to learn that Mr. Northcote has made you his heir? I presume, sir, that explains Mr. Furnivall's——" He waved a significant hand towards the street.

"That," I said, "and a kick behind."

Milford nodded gravely.

"A bad lot, sir—a very bad lot. I always warned Mr. Northcote against him."

"Milford," I said, "I don't know how things are here, but do you think, if we rung up Harrod's or Gunter's or someone, that you could manage a little dinner for three at, say, eight o'clock? Miss Solano and Mr. Logan have been through the whole business with me, and we want to celebrate its success."

A smile of professional pride stole across Milford's face. "Certainly, sir," he replied, with a bow. "Everything shall be ready at eight o'clock; you may rely on that, sir."

"You're staying here, of course, Billy," I said, as Milford disappeared.

"Rather," said Billy. "You don't suppose I'm going to leave you now you've got fifty thousand? I'll just run down in a cab to my old digs, and fetch my traps before dinner."

"Right you are, Billy," I laughed. "And you might send the wire to Lady Tregattock at the same time."

.   .   .   .

We were standing in the very room where, ten days before, that midnight bullet had so nearly ended my adventures.

"Mercia," I said, "my own Mercia," and taking her hands, I drew them up on to my shoulders, and gazed down into her dear, upturned face.

I think she guessed what was in my mind, for she looked round at the curtain with a little shudder.

"Ah!" she whispered, "if I had killed you——"

"At least," I said, with a twinkle in my eyes, "it would have saved Sangatte's good looks." Then I bent forward and gently kissed those soft, sorrowful lips that I loved so well.

"Mercia," I said, "I know what you are thinking about this money of Prado's. I know that it was wrung and tortured out of your father's friends and followers, and that you would starve rather than benefit in any way by their sufferings."

"Yes, yes," she whispered; "I knew you would understand."

"Dearest," I said gently, "we will take it as a trust —you and I and Billy. God knows how much misery and suffering Prado caused, but over in Bolivia there's gold enough to undo even his work. It was Manuel Solano who saved San Luca: it shall be Solano's daughter who will save her again."

With a little cry of joy, Mercia seized my hand, and before I could stop her, raised it to her lips.

It took me at least five minutes to satisfy myself that this incorrect procedure had been properly atoned for.

Printed by MORRISON & GIBB LIMITED, Edinburgh

A Catalogue of Books

published by

Mills & Boon Ltd.

49 RUPERT STREET, LONDON, W.

(Close to Piccadilly Circus Tube Station.)

Telephone: 929 Regent.   Telegrams: "Millsator, Piccy, London."
Cablegrams: "Millsator, London."

THIS Catalogue is divided into two sections : the first (pages 1-10) contains the most recent books and announcements, and the second (pages 11-32) contains the books previously published, and Educational books.

Colonial Editions are issued of all Mills & Boon's Novels, and of most of their books of General Literature. In the case of forthcoming books the approximate prices at which they will be published are given. These may be altered before publication.

SPRING ANNOUNCEMENTS.

My Russian Year.

By ROTHAY REYNOLDS. With 28 Illustrations. Demy 8vo. Second Edition. 10s. 6d. net.

Times.—" Full of anecdote, sometimes indeed of gossip, but it is first-hand anecdote and the characteristic gossip which comes to the ears of a man who has lived in the country and understood its people. . . . Mr. Reynolds has succeeded in drawing a truthful and impartial picture of the ordinary Russian."

Daily News.—" The brightest book about Russia that has yet appeared in this country."

Truth.—" I have never read a book on Russia which gives such intimate and interesting, and at the same time vivid, pictures of social, domestic, political, and ecclesiastical life of Russia."

Nation.—"Mr. Reynolds writes with great simplicity, taking nothing for granted, and his knowledge is unusually intimate."

Punch.—" It is the best work of its kind I have seen for years."

Tatler.—"A book which everybody will find interesting. Quite one of the most vivid accounts of Russia of to-day."

What I Know : Reminiscences of Five Years' Personal Attendance upon His Late Majesty King Edward VII.

By C. W. STAMPER. With a Portrait of King Edward in Colour, never before published, by OLIVE SNELL. Demy 8vo. 10s. 6d. net.

An intimate picture of the private life of King Edward, including a faithful record or diary of the last five years of his late Majesty's life. Full of the echoes of conversations, the book is written throughout from the purely human point of view, dealing frankly with the life and ways of a gentleman who happened to be a king. Names of living men and women appear upon every page. Mr. Stamper has caught the smile upon the King's face. It is a unique book about a unique personality.

A Century of Famous Actresses (1750-1850).

By HAROLD SIMPSON, Author of "Yvette Guilbert," "A Century of Ballads," etc., and Mrs. CHARLES BRAUN. With 18 Illustrations. Demy 8vo. 10s. 6d. net.

The present volume aims at presenting vivid little pen-portraits of individualities through the medium of their art, and the position which they won for themselves in the world of acting. After a short account of the position of women as regards the stage from the earliest times, the author deals with those stars who were at their zenith in 1750, such as Mrs. Pritchard, Mrs. Cibber, Peg Woffington, George Anne Bellamy, and Kitty Clive. He next passes in review some of the stars who commenced to shine during the first half of the period (1750–1800 about), Mrs. Abington, Miss Farren (afterwards Countess of Derby), Dorothy Jordan, and others. Next follows the "Siddons Period," which includes, besides Mrs. Siddons, such names as Fanny Kemble, Mrs. Stirling, Helen Faucit, Madame Vestris, etc., and the volume concludes with a brief notice of "those who came after" (Mrs. Bancroft, Mrs. Kendall, Ellen Terry, etc.).

The Cruise of the "Snark."

By JACK LONDON. With 119 Illustrations. Demy 8vo. 8s. 6d. net.

"The Cruise of the *Snark*" is a record of Mr. Jack London's remarkable little boat, which he sailed for two years in remote parts of the world and never touched rock, reef or shoal. The voyage was the author's idea of a good time, and the book is dedicated to "Charmian," the only woman who did the trip. "The Cruise of the *Snark*" is a highly instructive and informative book, touching in a general way wanderings in Samoa, New Zealand, Tasmania, Australia, New Guinea, etc.

The Petticoat Commando ; or, Boer Women in Secret Service.

By JOHANNA BRANDT. With 13 Illustrations and a Map. Crown 8vo. 6s.

In this remarkable human document is described the perils and hardships connected with the Secret Service of the Boers and the heroism and resource displayed by the men. It throws a light on some little-known incidents of the South African War, and is an extremely dramatic picture of the hopes and fears, the devotion and bitterness, with which some Boer women in Pretoria watched and, so far as they could, took part in the war. The greater part of the narrative comes from a diary kept during the war with unusual fulness and vividness. No fictitious names have been employed, and the experiences of the diarist, as they were recorded from day to day, are correct in every detail.

The Wonderful Weald and the Quest of the Crock of Gold.

By ARTHUR BECKETT, Author of "The Spirit of the Downs." With 20 Illustrations in Colour and 43 Initials by ERNEST MARILLIER and a Map. Popular Edition. Large Crown 8vo. 6s.

Daily Telegraph.—" A charmingly discursive, gossipy volume."
Observer.—" This buoyant and charming book."

MILLS & BOON'S
SUMMER FICTION

Crown 8vo. 6s. each.

The Red Mirage.

By I. A. R. WYLIE, Author of " The Rajah's People,"
" The Daughter of Brahma," etc., etc.

In " The Red Mirage " Miss Wylie gives us once more
another, if different, Eastern setting for her story. The
scene is laid chiefly in Algiers, and concerns a phase of
military life there which, though full of dramatic possibilities, has been but rarely handled by the novelist.
The adventures of the chivalrous, hot-headed English
hero under the French flag, the strange chain of cir-
cumstance which links his fate with that of the other
characters, are vividly described, and the gradual
working-up of the climax holds the reader's attention
from chapter to chapter. No less fascinating is the
delineation of character and the brilliant touches of
Oriental colouring.

The Man from Nowhere.

By VICTOR BRIDGES.   [June 15 Novel.*

Mills & Boon have no hesitation in predicting that
" The Man from Nowhere " will be one of the most
successful novels of the year, and worthy to rank alongside the previous brilliant June 15 novels they have

** June 15. All fiction readers will remember with pleasure that
on this date in successive years Mills & Boon published notable
first novels of remarkable ability in " The Veil," by E. S. Stevens,
" The Rajah's People," by I. A. R. Wylie, " When the Red Gods
Call," by Beatrice Grimshaw, and the second novel by the author
of " The Rajah's People," viz. " The Daughter of Brahma."
Mills & Boon will publish " The Man from Nowhere " on June 16
(June 15, 1913, being Sunday).*

issued. "The Man from Nowhere" is a modern adventure story, the scene being laid chiefly in London, and it is told with a vim, a crispness, and a gay sense of humour that fascinate the reader from the opening paragraph. The hero is a creation of whom any author might be proud. He belongs to the "Legion that never was listed," one of those delightful, cheerful adventurers to whom all the world is home, and anything that promises excitement a profession for the time. His charming love-story, told with a rare blend of delicacy and naturalness, makes the whole narrative swing along with a grip and sparkle that place it very high among the notable novels of the last few years.

Wilsam. [Second Edition.

By S. C. NETHERSOLE, Author of "Mary up at Gaffries," "Ripe Corn."

Daily Mail.—"There is a leisured gentleness about the story, an unaffected delight in the scenery, a friendliness between the author and her characters, which things put the reader in a kindly mood. Some of the touches show insight and observation to a surprising degree. The pathos loses nothing for its restraint. The book is deft, tender, and well bred, three very admirable qualities and none too commonly found in novels."

Because of Jane. [Second Edition.

By J. E. BUCKROSE, Author of "Down our Street," "The Browns."

Morning Post.—"We can warmly congratulate the author on a book, quite rare in its sincerity and quite unique in its sympathy and humour."

Times.—"Full of the author's comprehending and humorous sympathy."

Hearth and Home.—"Congratulations to the author of a charming child character and a delightful story."

A Son of the Sun. [Third Edition.

By JACK LONDON, Author of "South Sea Tales," "When God Laughs."

Pall Mall Gazette.—"We lay this book down happily conscious of our familiarity with the South Seas, although we have never been within a thousand leagues of them."

Standard.—"Jack London justifies the claim to be considered the Kipling of America."

Penelope's Doors.

By SOPHIE COLE, Author of " In Search of Each Other."

The Friendly Enemy.

By T. P. CAMERON WILSON. (A New Mills & Boon Discovery.)

The Call of the Siren.   [Second Edition.

By HAROLD SPENDER, Author of " The Arena."

The Transformation of Timothy.

By THOMAS COBB, Author of " A Marriage of Inconvenience."

Mr. Sheringham and Others.

By MRS. ALFRED SIDGWICK, Author of " Cynthia's Way."

The Hidden Road.

By JOAN SUTHERLAND.

"The Hidden Road" is a novel dealing with the country of Tibet, and the arrival at Lhasa of a famous political Mission. The rescue of Ludar Stair by his cousin, the general in command, from the torture and darkness of a monastic cell, where he has been imprisoned by the Lamas, forms the main plot of the story. A strong love-interest centres round Ludar Stair, his rescuer, and the supposed daughter of the political head of the Mission, Sir Charles Wraythe.

In its action and drama the book is following on its predecessors, " Cavanagh of Kultaun " and " The Dawn."

Swift Nick of the York Road.

By GEORGE EDGAR, Author of " The Blue Bird's-Eye."

Middleground.

By The Author of " Mastering Flame " and " Ashes of Incense."

The Swashbuckler.

By MRS. BAILLIE REYNOLDS, Author of " The Silence Broken," " Nigel Ferrard."

The Gondola.
By ROTHAY REYNOLDS, Author of "My Russian Year."

The Brat.
By MRS. H. H. PENROSE, Author of "The House of Rennell."

Through the Window.
By MARY E. MANN, Author of "Bound Together," "Men and Dreams."

The Sphinx in the Labyrinth.
By MAUDE ANNESLEY, Author of "All Awry," "My Parisian Year."

Miss King's Profession.
By E. M. CHANNON, Author of "A Street Angel," "Cato's Daughter."

Lily Magic.
By MARY L. PENDERED, Author of "At Lavender Cottage," "An Englishman."

With Drums Unmuffled.
By L. A. BURGESS.

Margaret and the Doctor.
By MRS. RANYARD WEST.

Guppy Guyson.
By W. M. O'KANE, Author of "With Poison and Sword."

Attraction.
By LOUISE MACK, Author of "Romance of a Woman of Thirty," "Teens."

The Adolescence of Aubrey.
By HARRY JERMYN.

An Unknown Lover.
By MRS. G. DE HORNE VAIZEY, Author of "The Adventures of Billie Belshaw."

Outlaw's Luck.
By DOROTHEA MACKELLAR, Author of "Little Blue Devil."

Smoke Bellew.
By JACK LONDON, Author of "A Son of the Sun," "When God Laughs."

MILLS & BOON'S
SHILLING NOVELS.
New Volumes.

The Daughter of Brahma.   By I. A. R. WYLIE.
The Blue Bird's Eye.   By GEORGE EDGAR.
Pollyooly.   By EDGAR JEPSON.
The Bolster Book.   By HARRY GRAHAM.
Life.   By W. B. TRITES.
The Square Mile.   By HORACE W. C. NEWTE.
The Girl who Saved His Honour.
    (Entirely New.) By ARTHUR APPLIN.
The Frontier.
    By The Author of " Arsène Lupin " (M. Leblanc).
When God Laughs.   By JACK LONDON.
Sons of State.   By WINIFRED GRAHAM.
His First Offence.   By J. STORER CLOUSTON.

MILLS & BOON'S
SIXPENNY NOVELS.
With most attractive Picture Covers.

Calico Jack.   By HORACE W. C. NEWTE.
The Sins of the Children.   By HORACE W. C. NEWTE.
A Golden Straw.   By J. E. BUCKROSE.
The Pilgrimage of a Fool.   By J. E. BUCKROSE.
The Quaker Girl.   By HAROLD SIMPSON.
    (The Novel of the Play.)
Fame.   By B. M. CROKER.
The Silence Broken.   By MRS. BAILLIE REYNOLDS.
The Education of Jacqueline.   By CLAIRE DE PRATZ.
The End and the Beginning.   By COSMO HAMILTON.
The Adventures of Captain Jack.
    By MAX PEMBERTON.
Peter Pan (the Fairy Story of the Play).
    By G. D. DRENNAN.

BOOKS PREVIOUSLY PUBLISHED

GENERAL LITERATURE

These Books are arranged in order of price.

England *v.* Australia.

By P. F. WARNER. With 51 Illustrations. Autograph Edition, limited to 50 copies, on hand-made paper. Crown 4to. 21*s.* net. Popular Edition, demy 8vo, 7*s.* 6*d.* net.

Sporting and Dramatic News.—"We strongly recommend the volume."

Sporting Life.—"The book is one that every cricketer should possess."

The English Court in Exile : James II. at St. Germain.

By MARION and EDWIN SHARPE GREW. With 16 Illustrations. 15*s.* net.

Spectator.—"Should certainly be read by all students of the revolution; an exceedingly interesting and readable book."

Athenæum.—"Not a single uninteresting page. We had no idea so good a book could be written on such a story."

Truth.—"Excellent . . . picturesque and impartial."

The Court of William III.

By EDWIN and MARION SHARPE GREW. With 16 Illustrations. Demy 8vo. 15*s.* net.

Morning Post.—"Done with fairness and thoroughness. . . . The book has many conspicuous merits."

From Halifax to Vancouver.

By B. PULLEN-BURRY. With 40 Illustrations. Demy 8vo. 12*s.* 6*d.* net.

Daily Chronicle.—"Well written, well arranged, full and complete."

The Story of the British Navy.

By E. KEBLE CHATTERTON. With a Frontispiece in Colour and 50 Illustrations from Photographs. Demy 8vo. 10s. 6d. net.

Naval and Military Record.—" Contains practically everything which the average individual wishes to know."

Royal Love-Letters : A Batch of Human Documents.

Collected and Edited by E. KEBLE CHATTERTON. With 12 Illustrations. Demy 8vo. 10s. 6d. net.

Pall Mall Gazette.—" Full of interest and entertainment."

The Wonderful Weald and the Quest of the Crock of Gold.

By ARTHUR BECKETT, Author of " The Spirit of the Downs." With 20 Illustrations in Colour and 43 Initials by ERNEST MARILLIER. Demy 8vo. 10s. 6d. net. Popular Edition. Large Crown 8vo. 6s.

Daily Telegraph.—" A charmingly discursive, gossipy volume."
Observer.—" This buoyant and charming book."

Forty Years of a Sportsman's Life.

By SIR CLAUDE CHAMPION DE CRESPIGNY, Bart. With 18 Illustrations. Demy 8vo. 10s. 6d. net. Popular Edition. Large Crown 8vo. 6s.

Daily Mail.—" From cover to cover there is not a dull page."
Sporting Life.—" More enthralling than the most romantic novel."

Sixty-Eight Years on the Stage.

By Mrs. CHARLES CALVERT. With a Photogravure and 17 Illustrations. Demy 8vo. 10s. 6d. net. Popular Edition. Large Crown 8vo. 6s.

Morning Post.—" Agreeable and amusing."

Forty Years of Song.

By EMMA ALBANI. With a Frontispiece in Photogravure and 16 Illustrations. Demy 8vo. 10s. 6d. net.

Westminster Gazette.—" A very readable account of a very remarkable career."
Standard.—" Most interesting reading."

My Parisian Year.

By MAUDE ANNESLEY, Author of "All Awry," etc.
With 16 Illustrations from photographs and 1 in colour.
Demy 8vo. Second Edition. 10s. 6d. net.

Pall Mall Gazette.—"The 'joie de vivre' radiates from its
pages . . . never dull or commonplace."

Observer.—"Lots of wrinkles . . . a sprightly book."

Evening Standard.—"What Max O'Rell did for our country-
men Maude Annesley does for his."

Scotsman.—"Convincing as well as highly entertaining."

Country Life.—"This very happy book. . . . Always viva-
cious and amusing."

World.—"Entertaining, most quaintly illustrated, and most
informing."

Truth.—"It is a delightful book."

My Italian Year.

By RICHARD BAGOT. With 25 Illustrations. Demy
8vo. Second Edition. 10s. 6d. net.

The Observer.—"'My Italian Year' will tell the reader more
about the real present-day go-ahead Italy than any other book
that has come to our notice."

Daily Telegraph.—"A thoughtful, knowledgeful book."

Daily Mail.—"Absorbingly interesting."

My Sudan Year.

By E. S. STEVENS, Author of "The Veil," "The
Lure," etc. With 40 Illustrations. Demy 8vo. 10s. 6d. net.

British Weekly.—"Will take its place among the best of
Sudanese travel-books."

Dundee Advertiser.—"Really delightful. . . . Those who
remember Miss Stevens's Sudanese pictures in the second half
of 'The Lure' will know what to expect, and it is very high
praise to say they will not be disappointed."

Standard.—"Gives many delightful little pictures of the
people, their manners and customs, and much that is attractive."

Scotsman.—"An interesting and informative book."

Sphere.—"The pleasant easy style makes the book very
attractive."

My German Year.

By I. A. R. WYLIE, Author of "The Rajah's People."
With 2 Illustrations in Colour and 18 from Photographs.
Demy 8vo. Second Edition. 10s. 6d. net.

Evening Standard.—"Should be read by every household."

Westminster Gazette.—"A wise, well-informed, and very readable book."

My Irish Year.

By PADRAIC COLUM. With 12 full-page Illustrations. Demy 8vo. 10s. 6d. net.

Bystander.—" Intensely interesting."
Athenæum.—" Full of interest and charm."
Freeman's Journal.—" An epitome of Irish life, compounded of tears and laughter, despair and exaltation, with a strong leaven of hope running through it, to be re-read and digested by all who desire to know the real Ireland."
Sunday Times.—" A pure literary joy."

Turkey and the Turks.

By Z. D. FERRIMAN, Author of " Home Life in Hellas." With 16 Illustrations. Demy 8vo. 10s. 6d. net.

Pall Mall Gazette.—" This extremely fascinating and instructive volume is peculiarly welcome."

The Man Who Saved Austria:
The Life and Times of Baron Jellačić.

By M. HARTLEY, Author of " A Sereshan." With 18 Illustrations and a Map. Demy 8vo. 10s. 6d. net.

Bookman.—" A capital account of the life and times of Jellačić. Exceedingly readable."
Truth.—" Well written and interesting."
Daily News.—" Full of interesting matter, throws valuable light on the Croatian national revival."

A Mystic on the Prussian Throne:
Frederick-William II.

By GILBERT STANHOPE. With 12 Illustrations. Demy 8vo. 10s. 6d. net.

Morning Post.—" We congratulate Mr. Stanhope on a very genuine piece of work."

The Parson's Pleasance.

By P. H. DITCHFIELD, M.A., F.S.A., F.R.S.L., F.R.Hist.S., Author of " The Old-time Parson," etc. With 27 Illustrations. Demy 8vo. 10s. 6d. net.

Daily Telegraph.—" All lovers of the leisurely essay will here find a book after their own hearts."

Wagner at Home.

Fully translated from the French of Judith Gautier by EFFIE DUNREITH MASSIE. With 9 Illustrations. Demy 8vo. 10s. 6d. net.

Tatler.—" The whole book is very interesting indeed."

Yvette Guilbert : Struggles and Victories.

By YVETTE GUILBERT and HAROLD SIMPSON. Profusely illustrated with Caricatures, Portraits, Facsimiles of Letters, etc. Demy 8vo. 10s. 6d. net.

Daily Telegraph.—" The volume is a real delight all through."

A Century of Great Actors (1750—1850).

By CECIL FERARD ARMSTRONG, Author of "The Dramatic Author's Companion," etc. With 16 Illustrations. Demy 8vo. 10s. 6d. net.

Standard.—" An interesting series of pithy biographies—concise and entertaining."
World.—" An interesting and useful book."
Bookman.—" Very alert, very scholarly, and entirely readable."

A Century of Ballads (1810—1910), Their Composers and Singers.

By HAROLD SIMPSON. With 49 Illustrations. Demy 8vo. 10s. 6d. net. Popular Edition. Large Crown 8vo. 6s.

Daily Express.—" Deals brightly with a most fascinating subject."

Home Life in Hellas : Greece and the Greeks.

By Z. DUCKETT FERRIMAN. With 19 Illustrations. Demy 8vo. 8s. net.

Morning Post.—" Possesses the great merit of being written by an author who not only knows but also sympathises with the people whose life he describes."
British Weekly.—" Full of up-to-date information. It is good as a tourist's handbook, and still better for fireside reading."

Involution.

By LORD ERNEST HAMILTON. Demy 8vo. 7s. 6d. net.

Daily Graphic.—" Extremely interesting, an honest and lofty endeavour to seek the truth."

Twenty-four Years of Cricket.

By ARTHUR A. LILLEY. With a Portrait in Photogravure and 32 Illustrations. Demy 8vo. 7s. 6d. net. Popular Edition. 2s. net.

Tramps through Tyrol.

By F. W. STODDARD ("Dolomite"). With 20 Illustrations. Demy 8vo. Second Edition. 7s. 6d. net.

Standard.—"The outcome not of a mere holiday scamper, but of long residence. In his good company we explore the Dolomites, the Brenner Pass, cross the Fanes Alp, and make acquaintance with such delectable places as San Martino, Molveno, and Cortino—to say nothing of Innsbrück and Meran. He tells us a good deal about shooting and fishing and the delights of the swift ski. He takes us to beauty spots situated at an altitude of 4,000 or 5,000 feet, and beyond all this we learn about village life, the legends of the country, the costumes of the peasants, and much else that makes the picture attractive. Altogether 'Tramps Through Tyrol' is an alluring book. 'Try,' we say, therefore, 'Tyrol,' and take Mr. Stoddard's delightful 'Tramps' with you."

World.—"As interesting as it is comprehensive."

British Mountain Climbs.

By GEORGE D. ABRAHAM, Author of "The Complete Mountaineer." With 18 Illustrations and 21 Outline Drawings. Pocket size. Leather, 7s. 6d. net; Cloth, 5s. net.

Sportsman.—"Eminently a practical manual."

Swiss Mountain Climbs.

By GEORGE D. ABRAHAM. With 24 Illustrations and 22 Outline Drawings of the principal peaks and their routes. Pocket size. Leather, 7s. 6d. net; Cloth, 5s. net.

Country Life.—"As essential as good climbing boots."

A Queen's Knight: The Life of Count Axel de Fersen.

By MILDRED CARNEGY, Author of "Kings and Queens of France." With 12 Illustrations. Demy 8vo. 7s. 6d. net.

Liverpool Courier.—"Far greater than that of the ordinary novel is the interest in the story of his life as told in this book."

Daily Telegraph.—"Sympathetic and moving."

St. Clare and her Order : A Story of Seven Centuries.

By THE AUTHOR OF "THE ENCLOSED NUN." With 20 Illustrations. Demy 8vo. 7s. 6d. net.

Catholic Times.—" Fills a gap in our religious literature."

Home Life in Ireland.

By ROBERT LYND. With 18 Illustrations. Third and Popular Edition, with a New Preface. Crown 8vo. 6s.

Evening Standard.—"Briefly, then, Mr. Lynd's book can be most heartily recommended to those Englishmen who would gain some coherent idea of spiritual and material Ireland. No suggestion of a Blue Book ever intervenes to make the author's remarks stiff or formal. On the contrary, an optimistic Irishman gives us his views, as opinions are exchanged between men anxious to come to a friendly conclusion. He is a delightful companion, who knows his country considerably better than most of us know ours, and is intent on entertaining rather than educating us. All the same, he does educate us, and without tears."

Spectator.—" An entertaining and informing book, the work of a close and interested observer."

The Town of Morality : or, The Narrative of One who Lived Here for a Time.

By C. H. R. Second Edition. Crown 8vo. 6s.

Daily Graphic.—" In short C. H. R. has written a new ' Pilgrim's Progress,' a passionate, a profound and stirring satire on the self-satisfied morality of Church and of Chapel."

Liverpool Courier.—" One of the most thoughtful and best written books that has appeared in recent years."

Scotsman.—" An able book, both on its theological and literary sides."

The Romance of the Men of Devon.

By FRANCIS GRIBBLE, Author of "The Romance of the Oxford Colleges," etc. With a Photogravure Frontispiece and 16 Illustrations. Crown 8vo. 6s.

The Lady.—" A delightful volume."

Dundee Advertiser.—" Written with a charm and ease which are delightful."

The Romance of the Oxford Colleges.

By FRANCIS GRIBBLE. With a Photogravure and 16 full-page Illustrations. Second Edition. Crown 8vo. 6s. Popular Edition, with 12 Illustrations. 2s. 6d.

Westminster Gazette.—" Does not contain a dull page."

Out of the Ivory Palaces.

By P. H. DITCHFIELD, M.A., F.S.A., F.R.S.L., F.R.Hist.S., Author of " The Parson's Pleasance." With 12 Illustrations. Crown 8vo. 6s.

Globe.—" The author gives much curious and out-of-the-way information in these very readable pages."
Glasgow Herald.—" A most interesting book."

The Bolster Book. A Book for the Bedside.

By HARRY GRAHAM, Author of " Deportmental Ditties." With an illustrated cover by Lewis Baumer. Third Edition. Crown 8vo. 6s.

Sunday Times.—" Very amusing."
Daily Graphic.—" Most refreshingly and delightfully funny."
Tatler.—" What a vital want such volumes fill ! "
Observer.—" Most excellent jesting."
Manchester Courier.—" It is impossible to imagine anything more calculated to keep the reader wide awake, and even ' smiling audibly.' "

Letters of a Modern Golfer to his Grandfather.

Arranged by HENRY LEACH. Crown 8vo. 6s.

Outlook.—" A book in which the human interest is as marked as the practical instruction."

The Zoo Conversation Book (Hughie's First Visit).

By EDMUND SELOUS, Author of " Tommy Smith's Animals." With 12 Full-Page Illustrations by J. A. SHEPHERD. Crown 8vo. 5s. net. School Edition, 1s.

The animals dealt with are : the beaver, lion, tiger, Indian elephant, African rhinoceros, hippopotamus, giraffe, grizzly bear, polar bear, bison, crocodile and alligator, python, cobra, kangaroo, ostrich.

Country Life.—" A fascinating idea."
Scotsman.—" A happy idea."
Sheffield Telegraph.—" The kind of thing to go well as a Christmas present."
Morning Post.—"The genuine humour of Mr. Shepherd's drawings is all of a piece with the letterpress."

The Zoo Conversation Book (Hughie's Second Visit).

By EDMUND SELOUS, Author of "Tommy Smith's Animals." With 12 Full-page Illustrations by J. A. SHEPHERD. Crown 8vo. 5s. net.

The animals dealt with are : the wapiti, sloth bear, hyæna, puma, jaguar, wolf, pinniped, baby sea-elephant, emu, wild boar, springbuck, hunting dog, wolverine.

A companion volume to " The Zoo Conversation Book (Hughie's First Visit)."

Westminster Gazette.—" Hughie's second visit is even more crowded with fun and good entertainment than was the first."

The Motorist's Pocket Tip Book.

By GEOFFREY OSBORN. With 13 full-page Illustrations. Fcap. 8vo. Leather. 5s. net.

Scottish Field.—" Contains in the clearest, most condensed, and most practical form just the information one wants."

Stories from Italian History Re-told for Children.

By G. E. TROUTBECK, Author of " The Children's Story of Westminster Abbey." With 22 Illustrations from Photographs. Crown 8vo. 5s. net.

Tatler.—" These stories are so vivid and so interesting that they should be in every schoolroom."

The Children's Story of Westminster Abbey.

By G. E. TROUTBECK, Author of " Westminster Abbey " (Little Guides). With 4 Photogravure Plates, and 21 Illustrations from Photographs. Crown 8vo. 5s. net. Popular Edition, 1s. net. School Edition, 1s.

Egypt as We Knew It.

By E. L. BUTCHER, Author of " The Story of the Church of Egypt." With 16 Illustrations. Crown 8vo. 5s. net.
Spectator.—" Most entertaining and not a little instructive."

The German Spy System in France.

Translated from the French of PAUL LANOIR. Crown 8vo. 5s. net.
Standard.—" Ought to engage the serious attention of those responsible for the national security."

Canned Classics, and Other Verses.

By HARRY GRAHAM, Author of " Deportmental Ditties," " The Bolster Book," etc., etc. Profusely Illustrated by LEWIS BAUMER. Crown 4to, 3s. 6d. net. Also Fcap. 8vo, 3s. 6d. net.
Times.—" As fresh as ever."
Evening Standard.—" One long delight."

Deportmental Ditties.

By HARRY GRAHAM. Profusely Illustrated by LEWIS BAUMER. Fcap. 8vo. Third Edition. 3s. 6d. net.
Daily Graphic.—" Harry Graham certainly has the knack."
Daily Chronicle.—" All clever, generally flippant, invariably amusing."

Queery Leary Nonsense.

Being a Lear Nonsense Book, with a long Introduction and Notes by the EARL OF CROMER, and edited by LADY STRACHIE of Sutton Court. With about 50 Illustrations in colour and line. Crown 4to. 3s. 6d. net.
Daily Telegraph.—" A book full of fascinating absurdity, and the true spirit of the King of Nonsense."
Spectator.—" Lovers of true and sound nonsense owe a debt of gratitude to Lady Strachie and Lord Cromer for their respective shares in putting together a volume of hitherto unpublished matter (both letterpress and illustrations) from the pen and pencil of Edward Lear."
Observer.—" Adds a few more verses and a great many inimitable pictures to the treasure-heap of Lear's work."

Ships and Sealing Wax

By HANSARD WATT. With 40 Illustrations by L. R. BRIGHTWELL. Crown 4to. 3s. 6d. net.
Daily Mail.—" Very clever and amusing, the humour enhanced by quaint illustrations."

Nerves and the Nervous.

By EDWIN L. ASH, M.D. (Lond.). New Edition. Crown 8vo. Cloth, 3s. 6d. net.

Daily Express.—"One of the most refreshing books published for some time. Dr. Ash not only probes into exactly what one feels when one is nervous or worried, but the treatment is so free from fads that it does even an unnervy person good."

A Manual for Nurses.

By SYDNEY WELHAM, M.R.C.S. (late Resident Medical Officer, Charing Cross Hospital). With Diagrams. Crown 8vo. 3s. 6d. net.

British Medical Journal.—Answers to Correspondents, 22nd October 1910.—L. M. writes: "In answer to 'Lecturer' re up-to-date book on Medical Nursing, I have found that Mr. Welham's book 'A Manual for Nurses' a most excellent volume. It is very readable, quite up-to-date, and efficient."

Nursing Times.—"Clear and concise, with a good glossary and index."

British Medical Journal.—"A useful reference work for nurses both early and late in their career."

Child-Nurture.

By HONNOR MORTEN, Author of "The Nursery Nurse's Companion," "The Nurse's Dictionary." With a frontispiece in photogravure. Crown 8vo. 3s. 6d. net.

Athenæum.—"Deals clearly and sensibly with the upbringing of children."

Standard.—"Admirably practical . . . full of useful knowledge."

Yorkshire Post.—"Thoroughly sound."

Through the Loopholes of Retreat.

By HANSARD WATT. With a Portrait of COWPER in Photogravure. Fcap. 8vo. 3s. 6d. net.

Kings and Queens of France.

A Concise History of France.

By MILDRED CARNEGY. With a Preface by the BISHOP OF HEREFORD. With a Map and 4 full-page Illustrations. Crown 8vo. 3s. 6d.

Club Bridge.

By ARCHIBALD DUNN, Author of "Bridge and How to Play it." Crown 8vo. Popular Edition, 3s. net.

Evening Standard.—"This is, in fact, ' THE BOOK.' "

Manchester Guardian.—" A masterly and exhaustive treatise."

The Golfer's Pocket Tip Book.

By G. D. FOX, part-Author of "The Six Handicap Golfer's Companion." Fully Illustrated. Pott 8vo. Leather. New Edition. 2s. 6d. net.

Harry Vardon says:—"It is a very handy little book."

Morning Post.—"Concise, clear, crisp, brief, and business-like, worth as a teacher half-a-dozen ordinary books."

Peter Pan : The Fairy Story of the Play.

By G. D. DRENNAN. With a Photogravure of Miss PAULINE CHASE as Peter Pan. Fcap. 8vo. Leather, 2s. 6d. net. Popular Edition, Paper, 6d. School Reader Edition, with an introduction by A. R. PICKLES, M.A., Director of Education, Burnley, Cloth, 6d.

The Italians of To-day.

By RICHARD BAGOT, Author of "My Italian Year." Crown 8vo. Third Edition. 2s. 6d. net.

Scotsman.—"Shows the same intimate knowledge of Italian life and character as ' My Italian Year.' "

Mental Self-Help.

By EDWIN L. ASH, M.D. (Lond.), Assistant Physician Italian Hospital, London ; Physician for Nervous Diseases to the Kensington and Fulham General Hospital. Author of "Nerves and the Nervous." Crown 8vo. 2s. 6d. net.

Field.—" Full of interest and suggestions for keeping a sound mind in a sound body."

Athenæum.—"A lucid little book. His style is clear and convincing."

The Lear Coloured Bird Book for Children.

By EDWARD LEAR. With a Foreword by J. ST. LOE STRACHEY. 2s. 6d. net.

An Actor's Hamlet.

With full notes by LOUIS CALVERT. Crown 8vo. 2s. 6d. net.

Daily Chronicle.—Full of illuminating insight."

The Enclosed Nun.

Fcap. 8vo. New Edition. Cloth, 2s. 6d. net ; Paper, 1s. net.

Pall Mall Gazette.—" A remarkably beautiful piece of devotional writing."

A Little Girl's Cookery Book.

By C. F. BENTON and MARY F. HODGE. Crown 8vo. 2s. 6d. net. Paper, 1s. net.

Evening Standard.—" Well suited to all unextravagant cooks."

The Garden of Song.

Edited by HAROLD SIMPSON. Fcap. 8vo. 2s. 6d. net.

Scotsman.—" An excellent anthology of lyrics that have been set to music. They are, for the most part, songs that have enjoyed a wide popularity, and this collection of lyrical gems forms a very desirable little volume."

The Pocket Gladstone : Selections from the Writings and Speeches of William Ewart Gladstone.

Compiled by J. AUBREY REES, with an Introduction by the Rt. Hon. Sir ALGERNON WEST, P.C., G.C.B. Fcap. 8vo. Cloth, 2s. net. Paper, 1s. net.

Westminster Gazette.—" All admirers of the Grand Old Man will be glad to have a copy."

The Pocket Disraeli.

By J. B. LINDENBAUM, M.A. (Uniform with " The Pocket Gladstone.") Fcap. 8vo. Cloth, 2s. net ; Paper, 1s. net.

Spectator.—" From what other statesman's works could so entertaining an anthology be collected ? "

Santa-Claus : The Kinemacolour Fairy Play.

By HAROLD SIMPSON. With 34 Illustrations. Crown 4to. 1s. net.

The New Theology. (*Sixteenth Thousand.*)

By the REV. R. J. CAMPBELL, M.A. Fully revised and with a New Preface. Crown 8vo. 1s. net.

Votes for Women. A Play in Three Acts.

By ELIZABETH ROBINS. Crown 8vo. 1s.

MILLS & BOON'S
COMPANION SERIES

This series is written in simple and untechnical language by experts. Mills & Boon are confident that the volumes will appeal to that large class who want easily read and instructive books written by persons who thoroughly understand their subjects. Each book is crown 8vo.

THE DOG LOVER'S COMPANION.
By "AN EXPERT." With 16 Illustrations. 2s. net.

THE NURSERY NURSE'S COMPANION.
By HONNOR MORTEN. Cloth, 1s. 6d. net; paper, 1s. net.

THE FOOD REFORMER'S COMPANION.
By EUSTACE MILES, M.A. 2s. 6d. net.

THE MOTHER'S COMPANION.
By Mrs. M. A. CLOUDESLEY-BRERETON (Officier d'Académie). With an Introduction by Sir LAUDER BRUNTON, M.D., F.R.S. 2s. 6d. net.

THE CHAUFFEUR'S COMPANION.
By "A FOUR-INCH DRIVER." With 4 Plates and 5 Diagrams. Waterproof cloth. 2s. net.

THE LADY MOTORIST'S COMPANION.
By "A FOUR-INCH DRIVER." With 7 Plates and 4 Diagrams. 2s. 6d. net.

THE SIX HANDICAP GOLFER'S COMPANION.
By "TWO OF HIS KIND." With Chapters by H. S. COLT and HAROLD H. HILTON Illustrated with 15 Photographs of JACK WHITE Paper, 1s. net.; cloth, 2s. 6d. net.

THE RIFLEMAN'S COMPANION.
By L. R. TIPPINS. With 6 Illustrations. 2s. 6d. net.

THE AVIATOR'S COMPANION.
By D. and HENRY FARMAN and Others. With 21 Illustrations. 2s. 6d. net.

THE POULTRY-KEEPER'S COMPANION.
By ARTHUR TYSILIO JOHNSON. With 60 Illustrations. 2s. 6d. net.

THE GARDENER'S COMPANION.
By SELINA RANDOLPH. With an Introduction by LADY ALWYNE COMPTON. 2s. net.

THE FISHERMAN'S COMPANION.
By E. LE BRETON-MARTIN. With 17 Illustrations. 2s. 6d. net.

THE DRAMATIC AUTHOR'S COMPANION.
By CECIL F. ARMSTRONG. With an Introduction by ARTHUR BOURCHIER, M.A. 2s. 6d. net.

THE ACTOR'S COMPANION.
By CECIL F. ARMSTRONG. With an Introduction by ARTHUR BOURCHIER, M.A. 2s. 6d. net.

THE HOUSEHOLDER'S COMPANION.
By FRANCIS MINTON, M.A. 2s. 6d. net.

THE BEEKEEPER'S COMPANION.
By S. SHAPLAND ABBOTT. With 18 Illustrations. Paper, 1s. net. Cloth, 1s. 6d. net.

MILLS & BOON'S
FICTION LIST

Crown 8vo.   6s. each.

All Awry . . .	2nd Edition	Maude Annesley.
Nights and Days . . .		Maude Annesley.
The Sphinx in the Labyrinth . .		Maude Annesley.
Eve, Spinster . . .		Anon.
Some Experiences of a Political Agent		Anon.
Mastering Flame . .	4th Edition	Anon.
Ashes of Incense . .	2nd Edition	Author of " Mastering Flame."
Middleground		Author of " Mastering Flame."
Orpheus in Mayfair .	2nd Edition	Maurice Baring.
Two Men and Gwenda .		M. Barnes-Grundy.
The Palace of Logs .		Robert Barr.
Cardillac . . .	5th Edition	Robert Barr.
The Sword Maker . .	3rd Edition	Robert Barr.
The Story of Joan Greencroft . .		A. N. Bax.
Golden Vanity . .		Maisie Bennett.
The Room in the Tower .	2nd Edition	E. F. Benson.
The Glen . . .		Mary Stuart Boyd.
The Silver Medallion .		Percy J. Brebner.
The Man from Nowhere .		Victor Bridges.
Because of Jane .	2nd Edition	J. E. Buckrose.
The Browns . .	3rd Edition	J. E. Buckrose.
A Bachelor's Comedy .	3rd Edition	J. E. Buckrose.
A Golden Straw .	2nd Edition	J. E. Buckrose.
The Pilgrimage of a Fool .	2nd Edition	J. E. Buckrose.
Down Our Street .	6th Edition	J. E. Buckrose.
Love in a Little Town .	4th Edition	J. E. Buckrose.
With Drums Unmuffled .		L. A. Burgess.
Render unto Caesar .		Mrs. Vere Campbell.
The Bill-Toppers .		André Castaigne.
Miss King's Profession .		E. M. Channon.
Cato's Daughter .		E. M. Channon.
The Keeper of the Secret .		E. M. Channon.
His First Offence .	2nd Edition	J. Storer Clouston.
The Prodigal Father .	4th Edition	J. Storer Clouston.
The Transformation of Timothy .		Thomas Cobb.
The Voice of Bethia .		Thomas Cobb.
A Marriage of Inconvenience .		Thomas Cobb.
Enter Bridget . .	2nd Edition	Thomas Cobb.
The Anger of Olivia .	2nd Edition	Thomas Cobb.
Mr. Burnside's Responsibility .		Thomas Cobb.
Margaret Rutland . .		Thomas Cobb.

Phillida		Thomas Cobb.
The Choice of Theodora .		Thomas Cobb.
Penelope's Doors . .		Sophie Cole.
A Plain Woman's Portrait		Sophie Cole.
In Search of Each Other		Sophie Cole.
The Thornbush near the Door		Sophie Cole.
Blue Grey Magic .		Sophie Cole.
A Wardour Street Idyll		Sophie Cole.
Arrows from the Dark		Sophie Cole.
The Five of Spades .		Mrs. P. Ch. de Crespigny.
The Valley of Achor		Mrs. P. Ch. de Crespigny.
The Mark . . .		Mrs. P. Ch. de Crespigny.
Fame . . .	*3rd Edition*	B. M. Croker.
Rebecca Drew . .		Edith Dart.
Likeness . . .		Edith Dart.
The Education of Jacqueline	*3rd Edition*	Claire de Pratz.
Elisabeth Davenay . .	*3rd Edition*	Claire de Pratz.
Children of the Cloven Hoof		Albert Dorrington.
Our Lady of the Leopards		Albert Dorrington.
The Lady Calphurnia Royal		Dorrington & Stephens.
Swift Nick of the York Road		George Edgar.
The Blue Bird's-Eye .	*3rd Edition*	George Edgar.
The Battle .		Claude Farrère.
My Lady Wentworth		Allan Fea.
The Swimmer .		Louise Gerard.
A Tropical Tangle .	*2nd Edition*	Louise Gerard.
The Leech .		Mrs. Harold E. Gorst.
Sons of State .		Winifred Graham.
The Enemy of Woman .	*3rd Edition*	Winifred Graham.
Mary . . .	*4th Edition*	Winifred Graham.
The Needlewoman .		Winifred Graham.
The Love Story of a Mormon		Winifred Graham.
Guinea Gold . .	*2nd Edition*	Beatrice Grimshaw.
When the Red Gods Call	*3rd Edition*	Beatrice Grimshaw.
The End and the Beginning.	3s. 6d.	Cosmo Hamilton.
Brummell Again .		Cosmo Hamilton.
A Sereshan . .		M. Hartley.
By Force of Circumstances		Gordon Holmes.
Margot Munro . .		M. E. Hughes.
No. 19 . .	*2nd Edition*	Edgar Jepson.
Captain Sentimental .		Edgar Jepson.
Pollyooly . .	*2nd Edition*	Edgar Jepson.
Arsène Lupin . .		Jepson and Leblanc.
The Adolescence of Aubrey		Harry Jermyn.
Jehanne of the Golden Lips	*3rd Edition*	F. G. Knowles-Foster.
The Written Law		F. G. Knowles-Foster.
The Confessions of Arsène Lupin		Maurice Leblanc.
813 . . .	*2nd Edition*	Maurice Leblanc.
The Frontier .		Maurice Leblanc.
The Phantom of the Opera		Gaston Leroux.

South Sea Tales		Jack London.
Smoke Bellew		Jack London.
A Son of the Sun	*3rd Edition*	Jack London.
When God Laughs	*2nd Edition*	Jack London.
Attraction		Louise Mack.
Outlaw's Luck		Dorothea Mackellar.
Through the Window		Mary E. Mann.
Bound Together	*2nd Edition*	Mary E. Mann.
Men and Dreams	*2nd Edition*	Mary E. Mann.
The Last Lord Avanley		Gerald Maxwell.
The Yoke of Silence. 5s.		Amy McLaren.
The Prince		Thomas Metcalfe.
The Cost	*2nd Edition*	L. G. Moberly.
Wilsam	*2nd Edition*	S. C. Nethersole.
Mary up at Gaffries	*4th Edition*	S. C. Nethersole.
Ripe Corn	*2nd Edition*	S. C. Nethersole.
Calico Jack	*3rd Edition*	Horace W. C. Newte.
The Sins of the Children	*2nd Edition*	Horace W. C. Newte.
The Socialist Countess	*2nd Edition*	Horace W. C. Newte.
The Ealing Miracle		Horace W. C. Newte.
Guppy Guyson		W. M. O'Kane.
With Poison and Sword		W. M. O'Kane.
Draw in Your Stool		Oliver Onions.
Harm's Way		Lloyd Osbourne.
Stories without Tears	*2nd Edition*	Barry Pain.
The Adventures of Captain Jack, *3rd Edit.*		Max Pemberton.
The Summer Book		Max Pemberton.
Lily Magic		Mary L. Pendered.
Phyllida Flouts Me		Mary L. Pendered.
An Englishman		Mary L. Pendered.
At Lavender Cottage		Mary L. Pendered.
The Brat		Mrs. H. H Penrose.
The Stairway of Honour	*2nd Edition*	Maud Stepney Rawson.
The Year's Round		Maud Stepney Rawson.
The Swashbuckler		Mrs. Baillie Reynolds.
The Silence Broken	*2nd Edition*	Mrs. Baillie Reynolds.
The Queen's Hand	*2nd Edition*	Mrs. Baillie Reynolds
Nigel Ferrard	*2nd Edition*	Mrs. Baillie Reynolds
Force Majeure		Patrick Rushden.
The Sea-Lion	*2nd Edition*	Patrick Rushden.
Sport of Gods	*3rd Edition*	H. Vaughan-Sawyer.
Miss Pilsbury's Fortune		Christine R. Shand.
Mr. Sheringham and Others		Mrs. Alfred Sidgwick.
Odd Come Shorts	*2nd Edition*	Mrs. Alfred Sidgwick.
Isabel		Dorothy V. Horace Smith.
The Call of the Siren	*2nd Edition*	Harold Spender.
When Love Knocks		Gilbert Stanhope.
The Long Engagement	*3rd Edition*	E. S. Stevens.
The Veil	*7th Edition*	E. S. Stevens.

The Mountain of God .	*4th Edition*	E. S. Stevens.
The Lure . . .	*3rd Edition*	E. S. Stevens.
The Earthen Drum . .	*2nd Edition*	E. S. Stevens.
Tales of the Open Hazard	. . .	Halliwell Sutcliffe.
The Hidden Road . .	. .	Joan Sutherland.
Holborn Hill . . .	. .	Christian Tearle.
Written in the Rain . .	. .	John Trevena.
Stormlight . . .	. .	Lady Troubridge.
The Girl with the Blue Eyes	. .	Lady Troubridge.
The Woman who Forget .	. .	Lady Troubridge
The First Law . . .	*2nd Edition*	Lady Troubridge.
The Cheat . . .	. .	Lady Troubridge.
Body and Soul . . .	*2nd Edition*	Lady Troubridge.
A Creature of Circumstance	. .	Lady Troubridge.
The Fool of Faery . .	. .	M. Urquhart.
The Island of Souls .	. .	M. Urquhart.
Royal Lovers . . .	. .	Hélène Vacaresco.
The Adventures of Billie Belshaw	.	Mrs. G. de Horne Vaizey.
An Unknown Lover .	. .	Mrs. G. de Horne Vaizey.
Aliens near of Kin . .	. .	N. Vernon.
The Two Faces . .	. .	Marie van Vorst.
First Love . . .	. .	Marie van Vorst.
The Girl from His Town .	. .	Marie van Vorst.
Mr. Perrin and Mr. Traill .	*2nd Edition*	Hugh Walpole.
The Prelude to Adventure	*2nd Edition*	Hugh Walpole.
The Unknown Woman .	. .	Anne Warwick.
Toddie . . .	*3rd Edition*	Gilbert Watson.
Ifs and Ans . . .	. .	H. B. Marriott Watson.
The King's Highway .	. .	H. B. Marriott Watson.
The Captain's Daughter .	. .	Helen H. Watson.
Margaret and the Doctor	. .	Mrs. Ranyard West.
Tess of Ithaca . .	. .	Grace Miller White.
An Averted Marriage .	*2nd Edition*	Percy White.
The Wind among the Barley	*2nd Edition*	M. P. Willcocks.
Memoirs of a Buccaneer .	. .	Robert Williams.
The Friendly Enemy .	. .	T. P. Cameron Wilson.
The Prince and Betty .	. .	P. G. Wodehouse.
The Honourable Derek .	. .	R. A. Wood-Seys.
The Device of the Black Fox	. .	R. A. Wood-Seys.
The Court of the Gentiles	. .	Mrs. Stanley Wrench.
Ruth of the Rowldrich .	. .	Mrs. Stanley Wrench.
The Red Mirage . .	. .	I. A. R. Wylie.
The Daughter of Brahma	*5th Edition*	I. A. R. Wylie.
The Rajah's People . .	*. 8th Edition*	I. A. R. Wylie.
Dividing Waters . .	*. 4th Edition*	I. A. R. Wylie.
In Different Keys . .	. .	I. A. R. Wylie.
A Blot on the Scutcheon .	*2nd Edition*	May Wynne.
For Church and Chieftain .	. .	May Wynne.

MILLS & BOON'S
SHILLING NOVELS

Picture Covers. Crown 8vo. 1s. net.

* Novels of the Play.

EDUCATIONAL BOOKS

ENGLISH

As You Like It. Edited in accordance with the Board of Education's Suggestions (Circular 753) by C. R. Gilbert, M.A. With Notes and Illustrations. 1s.
Henry V. Uniform with the above. 1s. Plain text, 6d. net.
The Tempest. Uniform with the above. 1s. Plain text, 6d. net

FRENCH

Baron's Exercises in French Free Composition. 1s. 6d.
Barrère's Elementary French Course. 1s.
Barrère's Intermediate French Course. 2s.
Barrère's Précis of Comparative French Grammar. 3s. 6d.
Barrère's Récits Militaires. 3s.
Barrère's Short Passages for French Composition. 2s. 6d.
Bossut's French Word Book. 1s.
Bossut's French Phrase Book. 6d. net.
Delille's Beginner's Own French Book. 2s.
Shrive's First French Unseen Book. 6d. net.
Shrive's Second French Unseen Book. 1s. net.

DIRECT METHOD FRENCH TEXTS

Edited by R. R. N. BARON, M.A., Cheltenham Grammar School.
Claretie's Pierrille. 1s. 6d.
Daudet's La Belle Nivernaise. 1s. 6d.
Merimée's Tamango and José Maria le Brigand. 1s.

MODERN FRENCH AUTHORS

With Introductions, Notes, Exercises for Retranslation, Vocabularies, etc.
Balzac.—Ursule Mirouët. Without vocabulary, 2s.
Daudet.—La Belle Nivernaise. With vocabulary, 1s. 6d. Without, 1s.
Gréville.—Le Moulin Frappier. With vocabulary, 2s. Without, 1s. 6d.
Hugo.—Bug Jargal. Without vocabulary, 2s.
de Nerval.—La Main Enchantée. With vocabulary, 1s.
Toudouze.—Madame Lambelle. Without vocabulary, 2s.

GEOGRAPHY

Wetherill's New Preliminary Geography. 1s. 6d.
Bird's School Geography. 2s. 6d.

GERMAN GRAMMARS AND READERS

Advanced German Grammar. 3s. 6d.	By *FRANZ LANGE,*
Elementary German Course. 2s.	*Ph.D., late Professor of*
Advanced German Course. 1s. 6d.	*German at the Royal*
Elementary German Reader. 1s. 6d.	*Military Academy,*
Advanced German Reader. 3s.	*Woolwich.*

MODERN GERMAN AUTHORS

With Introductions, Notes, Vocabularies, Exercises for Retranslation, etc.

Auerbach.—Selections from Schwarzwälder Dorfgeschichten.
    With vocabulary, 2s. Without vocabulary, 1s. 6d.
Bechstein.—Ausgewählte Märchen.
    With vocabulary, 1s. 6d. Without vocabulary, 1s.
Benedix.—Doktor Wespe. With vocabulary, 2s. Without, 1s. 6d.
Ebers.—Eine Frage. Without vocabulary, 2s.
Freytag.—Die Journalisten. Without vocabulary, 2s.
Freytag.—Soll und Haben. Without vocabulary, 2s.
German Epic Tales. Without vocabulary, 2s.
Heyse.—Hans Lange. With vocabulary, 2s. Without vocab., 1s. 6d.
Hoffmann.—Meister Martin. Without vocabulary, 1s. 6d.
Hoffmann.—Schiller's Jugendjähre. Without vocabulary, 1s. 6d.
Moser.—Der Bibliothekar. With vocabulary, 2s. Without, 1s. 6d.
Scheffel's Selections from Ekkehard. Without vocabulary, 2s.
Wildenbruch.—Ein Opfer des Berufs and Mein Onkel aus
    Pommern. With vocabulary, 2s. Without vocabulary, 1s. 6d.

LATIN

Bell's Latin Extracts for Sight Translation. 1s.
Williamson's First Latin Unseen Book. 6d. net.
Williamson's Second Latin Unseen Book. 1s. net.

MATHEMATICS

Boon's Preparatory Arithmetic. 1s. Answers, with hints, 6d. net.
Boon's Arithmetic for Schools and Colleges. With answers, 4s.
    Without answers, 3s. 6d. Answers only, 6d. net.
Deakin's New School Geometry. Part I, 1s.; Part II, 1s. 6d.
Deakin's Rural Arithmetic. With answers, 1s. 6d. Without ans., 1s.
Deakin's Household Accounts. 6d. net.
Harrison's Practical Mathematics. With answers, 1s. 6d. Without, 1s. 3d.
Stainer's Graphs in Arithmetic, Algebra, and Trigonometry. 2s. 6d.
Walker's Examples and Test Papers in Algebra.

READERS

Peter Pan : The Fairy Story of the Play. Illustrated. 6d.
Selous' The Zoo Conversation Book. Illustrated. 1s.
Troutbeck's Story of Westminster Abbey. Illustrated. 1s.

SCIENCE

Hood's Problems in Practical Chemistry. With 22 Illustrations. 5s.
Oldham's First School Chemistry. With 71 Illustrations. 2s. 6d.
Oldham's Elementary Quantitative Analysis. With 11 diagrams. 1s. 6d.
Bucknell's Practical Course in First Year Physics. 1s.
Norris' Experimental Mechanics and Physics. Illustrated. 1s. 6d.

Hazell, Watson & Viney, Ld., London and Aylesbury—12/645.

Ingram Content Group UK Ltd.
Milton Keynes UK
UKHW020636050623
422889UK00008B/1161